A Sparrow's Flight

Series Editor:
Anne McManus Scriven

A Sparrow's Flight
A Novel of a Future

Margaret Elphinstone

with an introduction by
Alison Phipps

Kennedy & Boyd

Kennedy & Boyd
an imprint of
Zeticula
57 St Vincent Crescent
Glasgow
G3 8NQ
Scotland

http://www.kennedyandboyd.co.uk
admin@kennedyandboyd.co.uk

Copyright © Margaret Elphinstone 1989, 2007
Introduction © Alison Phipps 2007
Cover photograph © John McGill 2007

ISBN-13 978 1 904999 52 2
ISBN-10   1 904999 52 2

First published in 1989 by Polygon, Edinburgh, ISBN 0 7486 6025 9

In memory of Sabra, who enjoyed the walk.

Introduction

'Those are the names of the mountains. There are many more, which you don't see from here.'

Naomi looked at them again, turning in a slow circle of her own. 'And this one? What is the name of this one?'

'The place where you stand now,' said Thomas, smiling at her so that she was suddenly and irrelevantly aware that she loved him, 'is called Glaramara.'

'Glaramara,' repeated Naomi. 'It should be the name of a tune.'

- A Sparrow's Flight.

Margaret Elphinstone.

Born in Kent in 1948 and educated at Queen's College London and at the University of Durham, Margaret Elphinstone is now Professor of Writing at the University of Strathclyde, Glasgow. Her formal education may have been through academic interest in Scottish women writers, historical novels and the literature of islands, but she has also learned greatly from the land and the sea, through walking the hills, living on small islands and working as a gardener. Her novels include *The Incomer* (1987), *A Sparrow's Flight* (1989) and *The Sea Road* (2000), a collection of short stories, *An Apple From a Tree* (1991), books on organic gardening, as well as a volume of poetry, *Outside Eden* (1990). Her fifth novel, *Hy Brasil* (2002), and her seventh novel *Light* (2006) are both set on islands with *Voyageurs* (2003) set amongst the Quakers in North America in the 1800s.

Her second novel, *A Sparrow's Flight,* (1989) continues the story of Naomi, a travelling fiddler, begun in her first novel *The Incomer.* It is set in the hills which run through the debateable border country between England and Scotland and it is set in the movement of a journey through the past, present and future hopes in the lives of Naomi and her travelling companion and friend, the troubled magician and shepherd, Thomas.

A Novel of a Future.

In 1989 the world changed, borders fell and the way things are became the way things used to be. The novel is subtitled: *A novel of a future.* Although not addressing the seismic changes which political revolutions bring in their wake, saving this as the back drop for her later novel *Hy Brasil*, the future world *of A Sparrow's Flight* is one in which the present of the novel bears a resemblance to our past. As with her later historical novels, Elphinstone's early science fantasy writing tilts the world, helping us to view the contemporary through a different lens, that of the past. What *is*, for us today, is judged in the subjunctive mood, *as if* it had already been.

In her novel following the fall of the Berlin Wall the former East German writer Christa Wolf asks 'Was bleibt?' 'what remains?'[1] What is left when the world changes, beyond all former recognition? What is left when there is no more mass literacy, no work in factories, no tarmac roads, no steel, no cities, nothing but the work of life on the land and the sea, some merchant trade in oxen and cloth and wool and grain from the rich lands of the south? What happens when a few are travellers, following the arts of music and magic to bring life to festivals and inns? Who are such people in such different times? What does their familiarity, garnered from the pages and literatures of history do to illuminate our present? What remains when the protagonists of a novel unweave the Enlightenment spell and have learned to live in ways which judge us from their vantage point in this novel of a future? What remains when our present is judged in this way as poisonous, deep in evil, leading to death? What might it mean to live with this as knowledge, to contemplate the ruins of our present existence four hundred years later in what is left of a great industrial city?

To help think of a future where these questions have been answered in new patterns of living, *A Sparrow's Flight* works with evocations of the past. Elphinstone's own study of the Anglo-Saxon period and of early English in the very place where so much of its drama is recorded and unfolded, Durham and Northumbria, is in evidence here. The world of the future also bears uncanny resemblance to descriptions found in particular in Bede's *The Ecclesiastical History of the English People* (c. 731). The title, for example, is taken from Bede's famous poetic description:

> This is how the present life of man on earth, King, appears to me in comparison with that time which is unknown to us. You are sitting feasting with your ealdormen and thegns in winter time; the fire is burning on the hearth in the middle of

the hall and all inside is warm, while outside the wintry storms of rain and snow are raging; and a sparrow flies swiftly though the hall. It enters in one door and quickly flies out through the other. For the few moments it is inside, the storm and wintry tempest cannot touch it, but after the briefest moment of calm, it flits from your sight, out of the wintry storm and into it again.[2]

The land through which our protagonists journey in search of promises fulfilled and with the healing of past wounds an ever present reality, is one which is rich in the ways Bede describes his own present. 'Britain is an island', says Bede '[…] rich in crops and trees and has good pasturage for cattle and beasts of burden. It also produces vines in certain districts, and has plenty of both land and waterfowl of various kinds. It is remarkable too for its rivers which abound in fish, particularly salmon and eels, and for copious springs.'[3] *A Sparrow's Flight* has its life in such a land, a familiar north Pennine and Cumbrian landscape to many readers, but with the tempest and storm of Bede's sparrow being part of the 'cliffs of fall' and the fragile tissue of minds wounded by grief and loss. For all its resemblance to Bede's world, however, there are some important changes. The people of this world speak often of when 'the world changed' and the dreadful deeds of executions, of the terrible building of cities where metal may still be found in the ruins that will never rust. As they journey together Thomas and Naomi ponder the familiarity of their roads of grass and stone and contrast these to strange occurrences where old roads may be found which cut sinister shapes through the grain of the land, and where traces of a strange, evil looking dread black substance can be found that is not natural, or right:

> "I've heard stories of course [...] The story I heard was that these lands were cursed by the power of sorcery. That in the past there were men who were so arrogant in the pursuit of power that they change the very substance of life to poison. And so those who thought they would rule life were destroyed by it, and in their fall they brought the whole land down with them."[4]

The changing of the world has caused different patterns of morality, of understanding and social life to emerge, which have learned with the past, but which never seem to quite tell the whole story or get at uncomfortable truths about human existence.

Promises and Contracts.

Thomas and Naomi enter into a contract. They make a promise to each other and this promise is kept. The extent to which the social world of human life is maintained through the keeping of promises is a structuring thread which holds the warp and weft of the plot. Without Naomi's promise to journey with him Thomas knows he is too weak, too alone, to make the journey back to the home of his exile at all. Without the promise kept by a people exiled from their own land by the poisonous living of the past, that eventually empties itself out into the land, destroying the birds, the plants and the children, born dead and deformed to generations, there will be no return. There will be no knowledge of home, of the names of the hills, the patterns of life, the way the world needs to be. Without the promise of music Naomi's exile and own loss is unlivable, there is no way forward for her that will not consume her in unmourned grief. Without the promise of the Island home from which they both journey and to which both return, there is no haven for the study of new things, the learning and lengthening of the reach of beauty and wisdom. Without the promise of hospitality – an inn, a kind word, a tune, a warm embrace – there is no hope for the life of the world, there is only cold ground and a path which is dreary, perfunctory, which survives, but, as Naomi says, does not know how to live.

The philosopher J.L. Austin in *How to do Things with Words* (1975), introduced such acts of speech, these promises and contacts, as invisible bonds, binding human life together.[5] Rowan Williams in *Lost Icons: Reflections on Cultural Bereavement* [6] names such bonds as the 'social miracle' of neighbourliness, which may, or may not blossom into friendship, into trust, but without which there is no hope of stories going on between us, of hunger being sated, of a warm bed, clean sheets, a fire and the hope – always the hope – of music.

Thomas, long absent from his home which is a place of untold and unimaginable grief and common suffering, journeys through the novel to the very edges of his mind. Naomi, a travelling musician with immense talent and the ability to take peoples' hearts dancing, learns to open out the solitude she has learned to love, and to trust others. Both find each other, by chance, in an inn, near the tidal Island which for both is home, and out of the music, mutual irritation and conversation which ensues, as conversations must, in inns, when the night falls and the space between us is very little, the promise is made. This pact is the contract which sees them beginning a journey, as interwoven and complex as the Celtic knot work of the illuminated manuscripts from whose margins they seem to spring and whose patterns they trace.

A Sparrow's Flight is a novel about friendship, about the 'quick' of human relationship and what happens to it when it is tested into new ways of living and understanding. It is friendship imagined anew, out of different social possibilities, which can only come when the world of gender relations has changed.

Music, Memory and Notation.

What happens when the world has changed in such a way to mean that we forget how to read and write music on a traditional score? What was music in Bede's day? What happens when the music we learn and know how to play is folk music, passed on orally between the fingers and mouths of musicians? What happens when the world forgets how to write, save for a few, who dwell on artistic islands and who have the work of learning and illuminating and writing to do? What does the world look like for ordinary folk when suddenly, hidden away in an attic in the empty lands is the sheet music of Bach's Partitas. What is this music and how might a skillful, musician, called by her talent and passion into her trade, how might she, a daughter of the dance and a maker of music find her way into the secret of the score? Learning, when Naomi encounters the score, becomes the hard, intellectual work of decoding. Through the descriptions in the novel we are given a glimpse of the work of those who laboured to understand hieroglyphs, and of the wonder of artifacts like the *Rosetta Stone,* which open new worlds up for our understanding. The anthropologist Tim Ingold in *Lines: A Brief History,* describes some of the odd ways in which the post-Enlightenment, literate world has changed fundamentally the ways in which music, memory and notation are related one to another through speech and writing.[7] Elphinstone demonstrates through her fiction what Ingold shows with his scholarship; that notation works to aid and change the way memory works. She gives us as sense of what it might mean to begin with a score of music and not to know what it was, other than that is magical symbols – 'magicians marks' as she calls them – might be to the unfamiliar eye. 'Tadpoles', Naomi calls them, swimming along five lines, with tails and different flags:

> She found the page with the minuet again, and stared at it for a long time. Slowly she began to separate details in her mind. A long curly symbol with a little box beside it, then three, four. Three tadpoles in a row, with a line piercing their hearts. A line, more tadpoles moving up, right over the top of the five lines.[8]

Tadpoles that mean a music which may go far beyond the normal length and pattern of the memorized folk tune. These 'tadpoles' – musical notation and score – take Naomi to the borders of her musical knowledge and fill her with desire for a different music. 'She pressed her hands to her head, and thought furiously. It was those straight lines. Music did not happen in straight lines.'[9]

What may seem true for music we also find is true for journeys, history and the patterning of memory. It does not happen in straight lines. The line taken in *A Sparrow's Flight* shows that the inner journeys of learning, friendship and love and outer journeys across the landscape trouble the perceptions which have been long won and cherished about the way life is. The novel works with the malleable textures of perception, troubling the protagonists, troubling the lie of the land, troubling the settled perceptions of past and present so that, with time, effort and daring, the patterns which defy may make some sense.

Borderlands.

The lands in north west England, what today we know as Cumbria, are known in this book as the 'empty lands'. They were long empty, emptied of life by the desire of former people – of our people perhaps - to bind the very atoms of life and use to give us unimaginable power. The geography in Bede tells of a verdant land, a land dripping with greenness and with birds of the air and fish in the waters. *Debateable Lands* is the name given to a suite of music by the contemporary Northumbrian piper, Kathyrn Tickell,[10] it evokes the contested borders of the north west, places of vagabondage and danger, as well as isolation and the harmony that comes when the crops grow and the harvest does not fail. The 'empty lands' of *A Sparrow's Flight*, are debatable lands. There, history is shrouded in the mystery of the tragedy that changed the world. It is hidden in the ruins of the city, the strange things of the past which Naomi finds in the room of the past, in the shelter of the village in the heart of the 'empty lands', in objects which are discernable to us through their description, but which Elphinstone, like an ethnographer of the past and the future at one and the same time is able to render both strange and familiar:

There was an object like a dresser, that had a kind of shelf half way up, with a close-fitting lid. Naomi lifted the lid carefully, and nearly dropped it again. There were teeth underneath. A row of yellowed teeth, interspersed with strange black patterns as if someone had written out a secret spell.[11]

In the 'empty lands' there is both the possibility of understanding life and the clinging on to the tragedy which makes rituals both powerful and empty. In an age of borders and contest, at a time when the world was changing geo-politically, Elphinstone brings her world of border life into being and shows what it is to live in the ritual eye of the storm where death and life merge with guilt and hope.

What happens when lines are crossed, borders transgressed, rituals are broken? What happens when the heart of the promises kept alive over centuries by a people, what happens when they break? 'If you break a ritual, you break everything', says the anthropologist Victor Turner.[12] Everything. Thomas's journey is into the heart of a ritual dance in which the shadowy figures of the tarot cards come alive and tell of the fool, the moon, of death, of the hanged man. The dance is sacred because it seems to hold together all the fragile strands of the life of the past and the hopes for prosperity and safety into the future - such as the hope against hope that the first born will survive that there will be sons for the women and men for the daughters and that the ewes will lamb on the high fells.

Binding the power unleashed when the ritual breaks and the collective power of love and death and fear and longing surge into the mind of a single individual; that is the heart of tragic action. When Lear is no longer of sound mind, on the high moor with his fool and the moon shines we are in the heart of rituals broken power – a liminal time, a time for consolidating, for unmaking the past. For Thomas and Naomi, the high moor of the dancing ground is the site of a similar encounter between the moon, and the fool and the very edges of endurance where the past must be named, unmade and remade, in new patterns.

At the heart of Elphinstone's writing is a concern for human life and its place in the integrity of the created order. Folklore and romance are present in the pages but not sentimentalized, rather they dare into the wounded brokenness that is carried in self and in community and without which there is no integrity to be found. Elphinstone works to make the image of Bede's sparrow into a story of the 'present life of man [and woman] on earth'. The reader experiences the 'wintry tempest' of the world outside Bede's warm feasting hall, and is also given 'the briefest moment of calm' when the storm is done and for a time, all is right with the world. For the duration of its narrative *A Sparrow's Flight* tilts and opens the world, making narrative and story do the unexpected through the expected, telling the old tales so that they are new, fresh and stark in their clarity. "The greatest stories are those that resonate our beginnings and intuit our endings, our mysterious origins and our numinous destinies, and dissolve them both into one." says the magical realist Ben Okri.[13] In *A Sparrow's Flight* there is realism to this magic.

Alison Phipps

1   See: Wolf, C. (1990) *Was bleibt?* Berlin: Luchterhand.
2   Bede. (c.731 rpt., 1999) *The Ecclesiastical History of the English People.* Oxford: Oxford University Press. (Book II) p.95
3   Ibid., p.9
4   Elphinstone, M. (1989 rpt., 2007) *A Sparrow's Flight: A novel of a future.* Glasgow: Kennedy and Boyd. p.93
5   See: Austin, J.L. (1975) *How to do Things with Words.* Harvard: Harvard University Press.
6   See: Williams, R. (2000) *Lost Icons: Reflections on Cultural Bereavement.* London and New York: T&T Clark.
7   See: Ingold, T. (2007) *Lines: A Brief History.* London: Routledge.
8   Elphinstone, M. (1989 rpt., 2007) p. 165.
9   Ibid., p.166
10 See: Tickell, K. (1999) *Debateable Lands.* Oxford: Park Records.
11 Elphinstone, M. (1989 rpt., 2007) p.160.
12 See:Turner, V. (1995) *The Ritual Process: Structure and Anti-Structure.* New York: de Gruyter.
13 Okri, B. (1997) *A Way of Being Free.* London: Phoenix House. p.114

First Day

The tide was going out fast. A long stretch of sand was appearing, still gleaming with seawater, dividing the long arm of dunes from the rim of wavelets that marked the edge of the sea. The whole bay was emptying, leaving a waste of empty sand that belonged neither to earth nor water.

The island was growing larger. The marks of the sea were imprinted right up to the edges of the marram grass that held down the dunes: patterns of ripples caught and held immobile, like the ghost of the vanished sea. But now the shore was expanding, so that the island was no longer self-contained and separate but merely an excrescence on a flat plain, a lump of rock and sand strangely embellished with plants and fields and buildings.

Something new was happening. Where there had been an island there was now only a promontory, a scrap of earth that had broken loose from the land to which it belonged but was not quite detached. A long cord still held it: a thread of sand in the shape of a road connecting land to land. The place was not an island after all. It was part of the country on the opposite side of the bay, a long coastline fringed with sandy beaches that merged into a forest, shadowy now in the descending twilight.

There was not very much time between the falling of the tide and the descent of night. Enough time for a traveller to walk across as soon as the road was open and reach the far side before the darkness closed in upon it like the shadow of the sea.

The man who was crossing the causeway this evening had almost left it too late. He hurried along the wet road, sidestepping long puddles of water while the night thickened round him. He carried a pack on his back, but that didn't seem to slow him down. Sometimes he glanced up at the distant hills ahead where a pale glow still illuminated the western sky. He never looked behind. He had left it until the last moment to leave the island, and now it seemed he dare not look back in case the parting should prove too painful, and he couldn't trust himself not to retreat, letting the next tide cut him off from whatever faced him on the mainland.

By the time he reached the mainland shore and was treading through tussocks of grass and thrift, the island had disappeared. There was only darkness behind him, and the faint sound of the sea. There was just enough light left for him to make out the path. Luckily the leaves were still too thin and patchy to shut out the meagre light; only the birch trees along the shore were in full leaf, the oak and ash within were bare. He hurried uphill, treading over treacherous spreading roots, well worn by passing feet. Luckily he hadn't far to go, less than three miles. He had no lantern with him, and there would be no moon tonight.

*

She had no lantern with her, and there would be no moon tonight.

She stood with her back to the doorway of the mill and frowned into the gathering dusk, biting her lip. It was infuriating to have come so far in one day, knowing that the tide was right, and still to be defeated by the night. She'd realised a couple of hours ago that she probably wouldn't make it, but had pushed on stubbornly as though through sheer determination she could make the night wait for her. It seemed desperately important that she should get across tonight, and she was genuinely upset, even while she recognised that her disappointment was out of all proportion. After all, no one was expecting her, and it would be perfectly convenient to cross first thing in the morning. The miller was an old acquaintance who would be quite willing to let her stay the night. A wild idea crossed her mind of borrowing a lantern and finding her way over tonight. She toyed with the thought, then dismissed it. The sky was ominously cloudy, and no stars showed. She didn't know what state the road was in. It was still early in the year, and might well not have been made good after the winter storms. She didn't want anyone to imagine she was anxious. Because she wasn't. She turned round with sudden decision, and knocked smartly on the door of the mill.

The mill was not such a bad place to wait, if one must wait. Being so near the road, they kept a room for guests. It was bare and plain, but they lit a fire for her, and after the long road and the forest the place seemed rich with polished wood and firelight. It was furnished only with a table and bench, and a thin mattress piled with blankets in one corner. The floor was innocent of rugs or cushions, but the glowing logs in the hearth awoke luxurious colours in the surrounding wood, so that, sitting crosslegged on the bare boards by the hearth, she was lapped in the glimmer of red and gold.

It was raining outside now. There were no curtains at the window, and the drops on the pane were quite audible in the quiet room. Occasionally there was the hiss of water on fire as the wind blew the rain down the chimney. Beyond that, there was the regular sound of running water flowing only a few feet outside the walls. The fire seemed static, bright embers fading imperceptibly to ash. She turned and threw on more logs. Sparks danced in the chimney, and small flames crackled. Ash floated in the air above the hearth, then slowly settled again in a fine dust, invisible in the dim light.

The woman absently stirred the fire with the poker. She seemed wrapped in thought, quite unconscious of her surroundings. But she fitted them well enough, reflecting back all the colours of the fire itself. Her hair was the colour of the rekindled embers, touched by flamelight, standing up in curls all round her head. She wore a red shirt and pink trousers tied at the waist with an orange sash. Her clothes were patched and mended, and the colours had faded to a curious harmony, striking, but not unpleasing to the eye. Her skin was pale in contrast, faintly freckled. Though her dress was fantastic, her face was serious, even formidable in profile, with strong, slightly irregular features. Just now her expression was unguarded, her green eyes dark and thoughtful, but her movements were quick and forceful, her hands never still. There was a suggestion of toughness about her body at variance with her brightly patched clothes. Her arms, where her sleeves were rolled back, were strong and muscular, though her hands were not those of a worker, being smooth and pale. Her feet were bare, though clearly she hadn't been travelling barefoot, for they too were white and clean. There was a suppleness about her that implied youth, as did her bright hair, untouched by grey. But her face lacked the roundness of a young woman's, and in the privacy of solitude, persistent thought had etched lines upon her face, revealing itself as the habit of long years.

*

He had avoided the mainland shore for a long time. The island was a safe place, being much the same for him as for anyone else. To him, that meant sanctuary. When he had looked across to the long shore opposite he had been aware that the wooded slopes concealed something that still lapped at the shores of his dreams, but it could not break into the island itself. He hadn't thought much about returning, but the time had drawn steadily nearer, and was now upon him. He tried to resist the tide of images that flooded in, but he could not. He was alone now, for no one had accompanied him across the strand. Even if any of them had, they would not have arrived in the same place.

The past is a nightmare. Don't think of it. This is merely a wood, he assured himself, a wood of small birch and oak, with scrub just quickening into green. There is nothing else here at all.

Yet the place was thronged with possibilities. When he stared into the falling dusk there was not only an absence of light, but images: questions hovering at the borderland between sense and imagination. For a moment the wood was clear again, tangible and empty, greening trees fading into twilight, and a soft rain. Then again there was no wood, only a charred plain stretching up from the sea like a swollen black beach. The plain was featureless and dead. The setting sun, visible again without the blanketing trees, dropped red and angry in a dirty sky. The trees swam slowly back into focus, and he could smell damp earth. But perhaps it was not a proper wood after all, only a ragged cluster of bent trees clinging to some shreds of soil. Surrounding him was a desert, bones of rock ribbing the sand, and, pressed in among the trees, the humped shapes of huts, and a red glow. He dared not look again, in case it were not a habitation after all, or only of the dead. He shuddered and stepped back into a young birch that swiped his face with thin branches as he stumbled against it.

He recovered himself, and stood still. The trees settled into place around him. Absently he still clung to a birch branch and found it solid in his hand. There are various possibilities, he told himself. The past is a nightmare, but there are still many possibilities. Or is it I who have many choices? As far as this world is concerned, only one thing has happened. I have only two miles further to go, and I can do that.

There were sounds outside. A door opened and shut. She heard voices, one low and almost inaudible, which she recognised as that of the miller, the other high-pitched and quick, oddly familiar. She laid down the poker and turned to face the door. Abstraction vanished. She was alert now, perhaps a little wary. There were footsteps in the passage. The door opened, bringing in a draught of cold air and the smell of rain. Someone entered; she couldn't see clearly, her eyes still dazzled by firelight, but the voice was clear and familiar.

'Naomi! It is you!'

Naomi stood up, and received a damp embrace from someone much smaller than she was. Naomi hugged the newcomer, then stood back, blinking until she could see properly again. The woman who held her hands was small and dark, and was smiling at her with frank delight.

'Jenny,' said Naomi, smiling slowly back, still half dazed. 'How did you know I was here?'

'I didn't, of course. They told me. You look just the same. What brought you? Why didn't you come before? Oh Naomi, it's good to see you again!'

'It's good to see you. I meant to cross tonight, but it got too dark.'

'So you're on your way to the island?'

'Where else?'

'To stay?'

Naomi glanced down at her hands, still held in her friend's. 'You know I never stay. But I've come for a bit.'

*

It was quite dark by the time he reached the mill, and raining hard. Luckily there was a good road for the last half mile so he could guess his way by the smoothness of bare earth underfoot. The going was slow. He felt his way uphill, sometimes tripping over ruts in the track. He felt as if he had been walking for ever. The dark offered no sense of time or place. There was nothing to hold on to but the sureness of earth under his feet. That was not enough, for every image possible included that. In itself, it gave no hope or reassurance. He hadn't forgotten what was real, but he had a long and dangerous journey ahead of him, and already he was aware of danger.

If it's like this after only three miles, I can't do it.

At that moment the lighted window of the mill came into view above him. He hurried forward, and promptly tripped again. He swore, and steadied himself. He could feel his heart thumping. At first sight the window spelt safety, and renewed hope. But that was illusory. No one there was going to help him, because they belonged to this place. They had no idea what it was to be outcast, wandering on the boundaries of other people's lives, having nothing to hold them anywhere. His journey would be incomprehensible to them, his fears even more so. They were comfortably rooted in what they thought was real, and he knew that he dared not even show them that he was discomposed.

And if I can't do it alone?

*

'So that's all my news really,' said Jenny. 'But what about you? Four years, you say? I can't believe it's that long.'

'It is.'

'So where have you been, and what have you been doing?'

Naomi tried to assemble her thoughts. Jenny hadn't changed at all. Always very affectionate and very practical, with no sense whatever of anyone else's state of mind. 'I thought you said you had to go?' suggested Naomi tentatively. 'If you've got someone to visit tonight, then my story will keep.'

'I ought to go soon. But there's so much to catch up on. How far did you come today?'

'About fifteen miles.'

'As far as that? Is someone chasing you?'

Naomi grinned. 'Hardly. I wanted to get back, that's all. No, I've just been playing music. What else would I do?'

'I never doubted that. Have you brought us anything new?'

'New?' Naomi considered the question. 'New tunes, certainly, if you mean that. But the music isn't new. At least, I didn't find anything new. Not this time.'

'It's always new when you come back. Anyway, it's been a quiet winter. We've had a few travellers passing, but nothing very exciting.'

'What do you want to be exciting?'

Jenny shrugged. 'I know it's foolish. I've lived here fifteen years and I'd like to call myself a musician. The fact is, I'm more useful in the kitchen. I resent that, and yet I can't blame anybody. I'm free to make what I like of it, and no one has ever deterred me, but I know. On the island, I see genius. Francis is there, and Kathleen, and I see how they work, and I think I can do no better than think about how to feed them. And now you. Where I get politeness, you can expect acknowledgement. But I shouldn't throw all this at you just when you're coming home. I'm sorry.'

'So Francis is here, is he?' Naomi was aware that Jenny's speech required a better answer, but she hadn't expected this. 'Has he been back a long time?'

'He's been here all winter. He's been across the sea again. He came back with a lot of poetry, only it was in another language. He's been translating it, trying to put it back into songs. I suppose it's difficult, trying to remember it all in two languages at once. To be honest, I find it hard to be sympathetic. He gets in a state about it, but it's not real life, is it? It seems to matter to him, and he does his best to make us all suffer with him.'

'No wonder you came visiting.'

'It annoys me,' explained Jenny unnecessarily. 'Maybe you can help him. No one else seems to be able to.'

Naomi smiled into the fire with sudden amusement. 'Maybe I can. I've worked with him before.'

Jenny glanced up, suddenly embarrassed. 'Oh, Naomi! I'm sorry, I forgot. How could I forget about that? Only . . .' She hesitated. "I should warn you, he tends to live in the present. So it's easy to forget about the past.'

'I should hope he does. What else should any of us do? I haven't come back for love of Francis, and I don't expect to find him pining away for me. Only it will be nice to see him again, I think,' she added, and smiled into the fire.

*

He didn't know the people at the mill. He hadn't once left the island since he arrived, and there was no reason for anyone from here to cross the strand. But he had often heard this place spoken of. It was the nearest house to the island path, standing a little apart from the village beyond it, and over the years it had become a habitual meeting place for those waiting to cross to and fro. The man knocked at the door, and, receiving no answer, stepped into the porch out of the rain, and knocked on the inner door.

There was a lamp burning on a chest in the hallway. It was difficult to concentrate, to take in clearly what this place was. All he could see was a whitewashed passageway with a flagged floor, and the chest with the lamp upon it, and a doorway at the far end. It could have belonged anywhere. Things might be as they were in the place he had just left, or his brief journey might have traversed something greater. There was no surety about it. He leaned back against the wall, exhausted. He knew that he had to call out, to draw attention to his presence, but he was inexplicably afraid. If only someone would come, a person with no illusions about anything, who would put the reeling world back firmly in its place. For a moment the hallway seemed to dissolve again, whitewashed walls blurring into the night. A heap of stones, a broken gable end, and the rain beating on empty earth. No other eyes to see it, no human voice in all that ruined world.

'Good evening. Can I help you?'

He pulled himself together. A man had entered the hall, a plump man with round anxious eyes that saw nothing. He found himself hating him for his complacency, for what he didn't see. At the same time he could have fallen on his neck with tears of gratitude, that he should be responsible for this place existing, for the whitewash and the ugly chest and the lamp. I am safe, he thought, so long as these people with no imagination exist. But having none, they cannot accompany me, so even that safety is an illusion. I am in two countries, and they are too far away even to see that there is a border.

'I've come from the island,' he said, and was relieved to hear that the words sounded completely normal. 'I was hoping you could give me shelter until morning.'

'Oh yes,' was the reply. 'Then there's a friend of yours here already.'

'I don't think so,' he answered blankly.

'I've two from the island here already. You'll want to join them. Supper and a place to sleep, is that it?'

'That's it,' he said, and let his mind come to rest among small things.

*

'When you get back,' said Jenny, 'we must have a feast. It'll make a change from fish and potatoes. You know what it's like at planting time. Do you want more bread?'

'Please.'

Jenny broke a piece of bread in two and handed half to Naomi, across the remains of their supper. 'We haven't left much,' she remarked. 'And you look as though you could do with feeding up.'

'Thanks,' said Naomi, helping herself to cheese.

She was aware that she wanted Jenny to go on whatever errand had brought her across, and felt ashamed of herself. This was an old friend, a woman who genuinely cared about her, who had looked forward to her return all this time. Naomi hadn't thought about Jenny much at all, but then she had seldom thought about anyone on the island, until the last few days while she had been coming nearer. After all, the people on the island were not her family. They hadn't made her who she was, and so had no enduring part to play in her solitary life. She had been away a long time. The years stretched behind her, forming no recognisable pattern. But then how could they, thought Naomi, when the circle was not complete?

'I do want to see you all,' she said aloud, inconsequentially. 'I've been on my own a long time.'

'Do you get lonely?' asked Jenny with quick compassion.

I don't want sympathy, thought Naomi, and felt a pang of guilt. 'No, I don't get lonely. But perhaps I get less kind.'

'Never!' retorted Jenny, indignant and uncomprehending.

There were voices outside in the passage, and the sound of a door shutting. Then their own door was pushed open so that it swung right back on its hinges, letting in a gust of cold air. A man came in, balancing a mug, and a plate piled high with food, in one hand, and a flickering lamp in the other. He kicked the door shut behind him, and peered into the gloom.

'Hello Thomas,' said Jenny, obviously surprised.

'Jenny? I didn't know you were here. Why are you sitting in the dark?'

'We're not. Why have you come off the island?'

He set the lamp down in the middle of the table and laid out his meal. Then he pulled up the bench and sat down before answering. 'I just got over before dark,' he said, which was not an answer, thought Naomi, watching him silently. He unsheathed a knife from his belt, and hesitated. 'Excuse me if I eat,' he said. 'Do you want some?'

'We've eaten,' said Jenny. She seemed uncertain how to react. Clearly she had been startled to see him here, but she could hardly question him in front of a stranger. She should introduce us, thought Naomi, though there might not be much point. He's not interested in anyone but himself. The lamp from the table illuminated him dramatically, though he seemed unconscious of it. Naomi leaned back against the wall on the further side of the hearth, quiet as the shadows that hid her, and studied him.

He ate singlemindedly and rather too fast. Not hungrily, but more as if hunger were a possibility, if he were not vigilant. His hair was dark, and clipped very short. If he let it grow, thought Naomi, his face would look softer. He was plainly dressed, in woven grey jacket and trousers, but under the jacket she caught a glimpse of blue. He was frowning, in concentration over his food perhaps, or perhaps because his business on the mainland preyed upon his mind. There was a look of strain about him, the lines on his face deeply scored, the brown eyes exhausted. But it was not naturally a solemn face; his mouth was too wide for that, and his nose turned up too much. He doesn't see me, thought Naomi, because he's living in a world where chance strangers are insubstantial as ghosts. So what is real for him, if we are not? There was no peace in the room now. The man's distraction had broken into the web of renewed friendship woven by the two women, without even knowing that it had existed.

'I didn't know you were leaving the island,' said Jenny at last.

He looked at her vaguely. 'The island?' he repeated. 'Yes. A man cannot live in sanctuary for ever.'

'It seems very sudden.'

'No.' There was a pause, and he added, 'It's not sudden. Only I don't want to go on, and I've ignored it for as long as possible.'

I was wrong, thought Naomi. He's not conceited, nor insensitive. He is appallingly unhappy. She turned her face away from him, and looked into the fire instead, stretching out her legs to warm her bare feet. The night chill was beginning to seep into the room in small draughts. I would like to go to bed soon, thought Naomi, and now I suppose I shall have his company until morning. Damn.

'Will you be coming back?' Jenny was asking.

'Within the month, I hope.'

'Oh well, that's not so bad, then.'

'No.'

To Naomi, Jenny's curiosity was palpable, but perhaps the man was unaware of it. He didn't seem to know her very well. But to ask more questions would be discourteous, and Jenny was never rude. When necessary, she used subtler methods to find out what she wanted. Naomi was fairly sure Jenny was now considering who on the island could throw more light on this potential mystery. She watched Jenny's face, and wasn't at all surprised when she announced, 'I really ought to be going now. They'll have been expecting me hours ago, but it's so good seeing you again, Naomi. But I'm going back first thing in the morning. I'll see you then, won't I?'

'I'll be crossing as early as I can.' Naomi stood up.

'I can't believe it,' reiterated Jenny, hugging her again. 'I'll see you tomorrow. Goodnight. Goodnight, Thomas,' she said over her shoulder.

Thomas jumped. 'Goodnight,' he managed to say before the door closed again.

There was a long silence after Jenny had left. Thomas finished his meal and wiped his plate with his bread. It was getting colder, and Jenny's friend was standing right in front of the fire. He glanced at her. She was looking down into the flames, her hair shining like the flames themselves. His eyes widened a little in surprise. He thought of asking her to move aside a bit, but that might mean starting a conversation. Presumably she was staying the night. They might have told him, when they offered him their guest room. Thomas frowned more deeply, and pushed the bench away from the table, so he could lean back against the wall.

Unhappy he might be, but his rudeness was unforgivable. To walk in and take possession of a room that she was already in, and to completely ignore her, was about as uncivil as anyone could be. There was no question of tolerating it, but she could hardly confront him in a house in which she was also a guest. If he behaves like that, thought Naomi, then as far as I am concerned he need not exist. I shall do exactly what I was going to do if I had been left alone.

He felt a welcome touch of warmth on his face, and looked up to find the hearth empty. Gratefully he moved over to the fire and laid on more logs. Then he began to unlace his boots. There was a small click from the shadows, like someone opening a case. Thomas jumped. He could just see her now, standing by the window. Well, if she had nothing to say to him, he could only be grateful, in his present mood. He set his damp boots by the fire, took an apple out of his pocket, and began to peel it with his knife.

There was an eerie wail from just inside the window. He jumped again, and the knife slipped. The peel dropped to the floor. It came again, a horrible creaking sound, that wavered between two notes unpleasantly, and stopped. Thomas recognised the sound for what it was, closed his eyes, and took a deep breath. It would be laughable, if it were not so uncivil. He shrugged, and threw the end of apple peel on to the fire. He watched it shrivel up, and tried to avoid listening while she went on tuning her fiddle.

It badly needed tuning, after a day's travelling. Naomi took her time. Soon she had quite honestly forgotten all about him. She began to play the first tune that came into her head, an old lullaby that came from this coast long ago, before the world changed. There were words to it that meant something to her, because the first songs that had been sung to her were also about the sea. She let them surface in her mind as she played, so that the notes took on a silent meaning. No reason to play it now particularly, just old memories. Naomi brought the tune round to its beginning again, and let it blend into a melancholy air that belonged to her real home. Not so melancholy, either. She picked up the same notes and turned them into a dance, and then let that slip into another, a whole web of sound woven out of a few strands. Then the first theme resurfaced, the lullaby like a single fine thread fading away into the dark. Naomi lowered her fiddle, and realised that she was frozen. She looked towards the hearth, and saw the man still sitting there.

The atmosphere in the room was electric.

It struck her like a physical shock. She stood quite still, jerked into attention. The fire had died right down, and the dark had infiltrated, a hazy film separating her from the still figure by the hearth. But he was alert; she could sense it. His tension pierced her like a current of cold air. Naomi laid the hand holding her bow flat across her fiddle, as if to protect it from a blow, and with her other hand she made a sign of protection, slightly despising herself as she did so. He was not evil, she was sure of that. It was a hunger in him, or a fear. Only she wanted no share in it.

When he spoke it was with an effort, as though he were trying to translate something desperately important into words that were not strong enough to contain it. 'You are a musician, then.'

'Yes,' said Naomi, and waited.

'I have been seeking a musician for many years.' It was a statement, not a request.

'A musician is not so hard to find.'

'It depends what one is looking for.'

'I'm only a travelling fiddle player. If that's what you want, you could find a dozen in this land alone.'

'But not one of them could do what I require. The reward would be beyond their understanding. I haven't sought out any travelling players. No ordinary musician could take what I have to offer.'

'I am not an ordinary musician.' She realised as soon as she had spoken that he had trapped her into that deliberately. So he was astute enough to tell that she did want acknowledgement. Take care, she told herself, he sees too much.

'Do you think I failed to recognise that?'

'What do you want?' she said sharply.

'I told you. I want a musician of imagination, of genius, if you like. I have a gift for such a one, if they are fit to take it.'

'And that is?'

'I don't know. I am not a musician myself, you understand. To me, there is only a locked door. But you have the key. I knew that when I heard you play.'

It was too dark to see his face, but his voice was urgent and excited. Naomi frowned. Perhaps he was out of his mind, in which case the most sensible thing to do would be to leave at once. But it would be hard to live with herself afterwards, if she left this matter unresolved. She hesitated for a moment, then laid her fiddle on the table and bent to retrim the lamp. The flame flared up again, revealing the room in soft light. Naomi poked the fire into life again, and fed it with fresh wood. Then she sat down opposite him, on the other side of the hearth, and looked him over critically.

He did not look unhinged. His expression was no longer harsh, but eager and animated, the brown eyes alight with interest. It could be a different man, she thought. He'd make a good actor, all expression and nothing constant. She found herself beginning to smile at him, and instantly he smiled back, a crooked grin that reminded her of a friendly dog. His teeth were bad, and there were gaps between them. There was a comic quality about him, but she had been right about the unhappiness, she was sure of that. Naomi looked away from him, to stop herself grinning back, and said, 'I understand why you talk in riddles. I do it myself sometimes, when I'm trying to get an audience. But if this is important, I'd rather you told me straight.'

'Oh come,' said Thomas. 'You know better than that.'

'Meaning?'

'Tell me straight, then,' said Thomas. 'What made you play the way you played just now?'

'What I played? I don't understand. What do you want me to say?'

'Precisely,' said Thomas.

'No, not precisely at all!' said Naomi crossly. 'I don't have to listen to you. But if I have the courtesy to do so, do you have to be deliberately obscure?'

'Yes,' said Thomas simply.

'Oh, for goodness sake!' Naomi jumped up and began to pack away her fiddle. 'It's late. I'd like to get some sleep.'

'Partly,' went on Thomas as if she hadn't spoken, 'because that's my art, as the music is yours, and partly because I don't know how to explain the matter anyway. The whole thing is very complicated, but when I was listening to you, it all became quite simple, just in a moment, and I saw how everything could be connected together, and all be solved at once. If you dared to do it, that is. Matters that have lain for many years could be resolved, a burden would be lifted from me, and the reward for you would be greater perhaps than I am able to imagine. But it would need courage, of course,' he added on a note of despair.

Naomi was not to be tricked twice. 'That's a pity,' she remarked sympathetically.

Their eyes met, and this time she could not repress a chuckle.

'I'm sorry,' said Thomas, smiling at her. 'I could have sworn you had your pride. In fact I think you have, but no matter. Your trade is after all not so very different from mine.'

'Which is?'

'Like yours. To entertain.'

'But you're not a musician. A storyteller?'

'You name it,' said Thomas. 'I'm not proud. How can a travelling entertainer be proud?'

'I am what I am because it's entirely pointless, That was why I chose it. I don't work for my living and neither do you — no, don't interrupt — work is important. Food must be grown and people must eat, and the world is full of business. All I have to offer is quite useless, and that is why people want me all the time.'

'And you think music isn't work?'

'Would life be easier without it?'

'I never had a life without it, so I can hardly tell you that. I can't imagine what I'd think about, anyway.'

'And are you happy?'

'I think that's a very silly question.'

'The more I talk to you,' said Thomas, 'the more sure I am that you're the musician I have sought for seven years.'

'You still haven't told me why.'

'Don't you think I am telling you?'

'No. I think you're trying to lead me round in increasingly smaller circles.'

'Nothing is increasingly smaller.'

'Decreasingly, then.'

'No, don't change it. It was a very profound statement as it was.'

'I'm going to bed,' said Naomi, losing all patience. 'You can talk nonsense all night if you like, but don't disturb me.'

'As you wish,' said Thomas pleasantly. 'You're very welcome to the mattress.'

'What mattress? Oh I see, there's only one. I'll draw lots for it if you like.'

'So you do accept chance? That settles it.'

'Oh shut up,' snapped Naomi. 'I can't stand much more. What are you, a professional fool?'

'That's right.'

'Too bad. So I don't have to believe a word you've said so far. Is that it?'

'As you wish,' repeated Thomas. 'I'm offering you a fool's errand, which only a fool could refuse. Listen.'

Naomi knelt on the mattress and turned to him reluctantly. 'Yes?'

'I am talking now about music,' said Thomas, suddenly quite serious, emphasising his words with vivid movements of his hands. 'There are two kinds of music, you know that. There is music which has been handed down through all the generations of this world, passed on from one musician to another. The tunes have been remembered faithfully, but also changed, as you changed the music you played just now, and made it your own. But there is another kind of music, that belongs to the time before the world changed. It is not a part of history, only perhaps fragments beyond living memory have made us what we are. But there are places in this world where it abides, if we know how to find it, and when it is played again it comes fresh as a voice just spoken, unaltered by anything that may lie between. You know something of that kind of music?'

'Yes.'

'I thought so. I'm returning to the place where I belong,' said Thomas, with apparent inconsequence. 'Not willingly, but because I must. There is a dance, you see, in which I have a part, and I cannot fail them. It would be very fitting if I brought a fiddle player back with me.'

'To play for your dance?'

'To play for our dance. You would be paid well for it, because your presence would bring good fortune upon us all. It's not a rich country, but we would reward you as much as you ask.'

'I have everything I need. I'm on my way to the island.'

'I understand that. But I'm not offering you coins or goods in return for playing for my people. I'm offering you music.'

'The music of the dance?'

'I told you, there are two kinds of music. The dance has been danced through all the centuries since the world changed. The music out of the past has been hidden away in quiet corners of the earth all that time, and through all the years of suffering it has never been heard in any daylight world. There are some who have caught echoes of it, and seized upon fragments. Some have sought it all their lives, wandering through all the lands and never hearing so much as one note of it again, and there are a few to whom it has been passed on. It has been safeguarded, so that it has never passed out of the world altogether, but for it to live forever, it must be played. There are not many who can bring it back to life again, but I think that you are such a one. Do you think I'm right?' he asked her suddenly. 'Do you follow me at all?'

Her fiddle was still lying in its case on the table. She sat still, but she had nearly reached out for it, and she knew that he had seen that she had. 'Possibly,' said Naomi coolly, and there was only the faintest tremor in her voice to show that he had moved her at all. 'But I am nearly home, after many years, and I've no desire to make another journey.'

'They have some music of the kind on the island,' said Thomas. 'I've heard it played. I also know the story: how it was brought back from over the sea by a woman who travelled to the land from which it came. She taught it to the people on the island, and left it with them for safekeeping, to be passed on to whoever should ask for it, so that what had been lost for many centuries could be brought to life in this world again.'

'I've heard something about that,' admitted Naomi. 'So where is she now? Why don't you ask her?'

'I would if I could,' said Thomas humbly. 'But what power have I over fate, to bring such a one as she into my company?'

'I dread to think,' said Naomi flippantly.

'That being so, I must make do with what I can get. I thought you played quite tolerably.'

'I'm not a complete idiot,' said Naomi, and stood up. 'I've listened to you. Now you can listen to me.'

This time she did pick up her fiddle. She knew that was exactly what he had intended, but she didn't care. She was going back to the island tomorrow, but his words had moved her, and he was not evil. He deserved a response. He was sitting quite still, his face expressionless, not even watching her. But he was listening. He was simmering with excitement, and she could feel it.

She had rarely played this music to so receptive an audience. She seldom played it on the road, because most people had no use for it at all. When she did play to those who cared about such things, she was aware of interest, incomprehension, excitement, busy minds fitting what she presented to them into a framework they had already made, working out implications, trying to remember, always reacting in one way or another. This man didn't seem to react at all. He was listening, however; more than listening: he was wide open to the music. It was like being able to pour wine freely into an empty vessel, not being confronted by thoughts, ideas, different images. Even on the island they hadn't been like that, because they knew too much what they wanted to expect. He had no expectations. Naomi played for him as if he were the only person left in the world, and when at last she stopped, she felt that she had never played better.

There was a silence. Naomi sat down again, and waited for him to speak.

'Please,' said Thomas unexpectedly, at last. 'I know I'm right. Trust me. I have been seeking you for many years, but you have also been seeking me.'

'It was made by someone who lived before the world changed,' said Naomi. 'You can tell. It requires a different kind of imagination.'

'I don't know about that. There have been many worlds. In each one people thought they knew what was real, and what was not, and so they each brought about their own end. What you played had nothing to do with that. It expressed the things that are the same.'

'But in a different way.'

'May I ask you your name?'

'My name? Naomi. And I heard yours. Thomas.'

'And I know what you are. I'll tell you what I am, if you like.'

'I thought you had told me.'

'You made one or two suggestions,' replied Thomas. 'Do you have a handkerchief?'

'In my pack.'

'Bring it.'

Naomi glanced at him, and slightly shook her head. Then she fetched a battered pack from the window seat, rummaged in it, and pulled out a green spotted handkerchief. 'It's clean,' she said, and handed it to Thomas.

Thomas shook it out, and examined it on both sides. 'There's nothing in it, is there?'

'No.'

'I'm going to fold it in half. Watch carefully.' Thomas brought the lamp nearer. 'Can you see? All right. I shall fold it in half again. You saw me do it? Now take it, it's all yours.'

Naomi took it. 'Now what? What's it got in it?'

'Undo it.'

'It's an egg! What am I supposed to do with an egg?'

'You don't want it?'

'Not until breakfast, anyway.'

'Very well. Fold it up again. In half. And again. Give it to me.' Thomas took the handkerchief with the egg wrapped up in it, and shook it out, holding it in his finger and thumb by one corner. Naomi blinked. 'There you are. Tell me if you want it back for breakfast, only it might be raw. I don't know.'

'Are you a magician?'

'That's right,' agreed Thomas. 'Do you want your handkerchief?'

'And that's how you entertain people?'

'I hope you feel entertained,' said Thomas with irritating humility. 'Have you been away from the island a long time?'

'Four years.'

'And a month more, perhaps. What difference will it make?'

'I've not said I'll do anything.'

'And if you let it go, will you sleep well tomorrow?'

'Explain to me about the dance.'

'I have done.' The laughter left his face abruptly. 'There is a dance, and I have a part in it. If I bring in a fiddler, it will change many things. In the old days they would always seek out a musician if they could, and make them play for the dance.'

'For how long?'

'Only a night. Every seven years.'

'And how would I know the music for the dance?'

'You can learn it. And as I told you the reward is the thing you have been seeking all the time.'

'I'm tired,' remarked Naomi. 'It's been a long winter, and I kept on travelling, which isn't my usual habit. I'm on my way to the island, and I've been looking forward to it for a long time.' She pushed her hands through her hair so that it was all sticking up on end. 'Just tell me,' she begged, 'in words that I can understand. How far, and how long?'

'Within the month,' he replied promptly, 'and the journey can be done in a few days, in this weather.'

'Journey to where?' He seemed reluctant to answer. 'To where, exactly?' demanded Naomi.

'I come from the empty lands.'

'What? That's not a few days' journey! That's right the other side of the country!'

'There is a path to it. We can be there within six days.'

'I have travelled in the west,' said Naomi, 'and I know. There is no road west from here for a hundred miles, either to north or south, only the mountains.'

'There is a road.'

'Oh yes,' agreed Naomi sarcastically. 'And there was an egg in my handkerchief. I've seen those mountains, from both sides. I've travelled to the very edges of the empty lands. And I saw that there was no road.'

'Excuse me,' said Thomas. 'There was an egg.'

'I can't fly.'

'Don't limit yourself. But on this occasion you won't have to.'

'Do you truly come from the empty lands?'

'They're not empty now, you know. People have inhabited them for more than two generations.'

'And they have lived?'

'Am I living?'

'I heard that the lands lay empty because they were poisoned, in the years of bitterness before the world was changed. "And nothing will dwell there again, until the earth is healed, and the people have learned once again to know themselves",' quoted Naomi.

'I don't know about knowing myself. But I lived there all my life, and we flourished. The poison decays, so first the birds return, then the fish and the small animals, and last of all, the people. There is no danger there now. The mountains of the empty lands are the most beautiful piece of land ever created in this world.'

'That was the way it was, to destroy the things which were most beautiful.'

'But now they're healed.'

'You're sure of that?' said Naomi quickly.

'Are you afraid?'

'For myself, no. It's a sickness that threatens the young, and I'm not young. I shall have no more children.'

He regarded her thoughtfully. Naomi realised that once again she had given away too much, and was annoyed at herself. 'I'd heard that people lived there once again,' she said, to distract him. 'But I never met any before.'

'We stay in our own valleys. There was never any reason to leave them.'

'You left.'

'Yes,' said Thomas, and looked into the fire. 'If we're to travel tomorrow, perhaps we should sleep. I came today because the weather was right. We can't afford any delay.'

'I haven't said I'll come.'

'You will never let such music fade out of the world,' said Thomas with certainty, 'but you don't have to decide now. It's very late. Did you make up your mind about the mattress?'

'We draw lots.'

'I could cheat that way. You'd never see how I did it either.'

'But you won't.'

'No.'

'Which hand?'

'The left.'

Naomi turned up her empty palm. 'You'd better take most of the blankets then,' she said.

Second Day

The road was wide enough at first for the two of them to walk side by side. It took a straight line inland up a steep hill. About a mile beyond the mill they could look back over the trees on the slopes below and see the island. It was half hidden in bright haze where the rising sun burned up the sea mist. Naomi turned to watch while Thomas shifted his pack on his back, and looked at Naomi.

'Within the month, I promise,' he said.

'I love that place,' said Naomi. Then she turned her back on it, and trudged on. Today was the first day this year that might be called hot, and she had agreed to spend it tramping uphill through yet more forests, walking away from the place where she most wanted to be, with far too many things on her back so that she felt loaded down like a donkey at harvest. 'I'd like to take my boots off and paddle in the sea,' announced Naomi, and wiped her forehead with her sleeve.

'It's hot, certainly,' said Thomas. 'I like it, Don't you?'

'Until it makes me sneeze, but that shouldn't happen until haytime. It won't stay like this long, anyway.' She turned and faced the sea again. 'See that bank of cloud? It's the mist coming in.'

Thomas looked eastward to the sea beyond the island. 'I don't think it'll reach to where we're going. I hope not, anyway.'

He knew the heat was deceptive. It might be like summer down here, but ahead lay the possibility of winter, and danger. Thomas told himself that he was hardly responsible for the weather turning out to be so persuasive. That was merely a trick of fate which had played into his hands. He hadn't deceived her. At least, he had played with words and woven them around her, dazzled her with ideas and vague promises. But the promise is true, he insisted to himself. She is as clever with words as I am, almost, and if she allowed me to persuade her, it was because she wished to be persuaded. I have told no lies.

Even so, it wasn't easy to be with her. She was accustomed to travelling alone, and was not afraid. Perhaps that was courage; perhaps it was merely that she inhabited only half a world. They were walking along a straight hard road that unfalteringly traversed marshland and hillside, finding a smooth path through rocky places, and clear space where the undergrowth grew thick and impassable about them. Such a road in itself posed a question. It had not always been empty, nor had it always led nowhere. Thomas thought he knew the power of roads, and yet this one seemed to be unavoidable, for his purpose. Did she truly believe it had no power over her?

When they reached the crest of the hill, the sea vanished behind the forest, which seemed to press closer, enclosing them all around. Grass and scrub had encroached upon the road, and saplings had pushed their way through the ancient stone. In places they had to pick their way through young brambles. It was not a way Naomi would normally have chosen to come. The thickness of the forest and the overgrown state of the path didn't suggest much of an audience at the other end. Naomi's wanderings had taken her into the wilds before, but she never reckoned to stay there long, simply because she never carried more than she needed for a day and a night. Until now. Naomi stuck her hands into the straps of her pack to ease the load on her shoulders. It must be a strange road where there was neither food nor shelter. She could see nothing ahead but more ridges of wooded hills disappearing into a haze where the mountains lay to the west.

'Thomas?'

'Yes?'

'This road goes nowhere. I can tell.'

'It goes to the mountains.'

'Where there is no road.'

'There is a fine road,' replied Thomas. 'If you know how to see it.'

'I don't, but it seems that I must follow it.'

'Of your own will,' pointed out Thomas.

'Oh yes,' answered Naomi, with a hint of irony.

Presently they came to a group of scattered cottages. A couple of dogs barked, and some children put their heads over the wall, staring. 'Hello,' said Naomi, and the heads vanished. Someone whistled, and the dogs ran back behind the houses.

'They don't see many people passing,' remarked Thomas.

'Everywhere is different. In some places that would make it hard not to stay for a week.'

After the hamlet the path grew narrower. They walked in single file, Naomi following Thomas. The path was soft underfoot, the stone blanketed by years of moss and leaf mould. The sun was lost in the haze. The forest seemed subdued; the calls of hidden birds were the only sound from the thicket surrounding them. They were going downhill now, deeper into the trees. It was difficult to hold on to any sense of direction: no horizon, no sun, no sky. Only the trees, and the mist that wreathed over them.

Naomi sneezed. She felt hot and sticky. It was far too hot for spring. That was supposed to mean a bad summer. She sneezed again, and a cuckoo called across the valley, like an echo. She stopped and listened, until she heard it again.

'That's the first.'

No answer. Thomas was striding ahead, almost out of sight. She sneezed again, and hurried after him.

'We get to the river soon,' he said when she caught up. 'There's a settlement there. That's where the road stops.'

'I could do with some water.'

'There's a ford. It gets a bit marshy after that.'

'I might have known it,' said Naomi, sneezing.

On the island the sea mist would have rolled in by now. It would be cold like the sea itself, clean and salty. The mainland would have disappeared under cloud. The tide would be rising again; she could have crossed by now, and be unreachable. Jenny would be wondering where she was. She would tell everyone how near Naomi had been, and they would be thinking about her. Last night, Naomi had been quite certain that she would cross over today. There hadn't been time to think. She must have been more tired than she knew, for as soon as she lay down she had slid into sleep, so that waking up had been like being dragged back from drowning. She couldn't remember dreaming, only the morning had been like a dream, cool and misty with the promise of summer in it. She had found Thomas outside eating porridge, evidently waiting for her to wake up. It had begun so brightly, this morning, like the beginning of a quest. She felt deceived by it. She had hardly been properly awake, and the sun had shone so clearly. And the man had been different again, neither anxious nor whimsical, but briskly cheerful, obviously keen to be off. Maybe it was all put on for her, but she'd let it affect her. The offer of the music haunted her. It had woven its way into her apparently dreamless sleep, so that when she woke the idea had taken possession of her, and it seemed impossible to refuse. She stared resentfully at Thomas's back. But he could hardly have bewitched her in the night; she had been too deeply unconscious for that. No, it wasn't his doing. It was her own, and the promise of the music. Because he was right. If he was telling the truth it was indeed what she was seeking, and had never ceased to seek through all the years of wandering.

'There's the village,' said Thomas, stopping. 'The ford is just beyond.'

There were only three houses, along with barns and sheds, among the tumbledown shells of abandoned buildings. The land had been cleared for some distance around, and the open fields were already tinged with the green of young barley, and new rows of peas and beans. The river flowed below, where cattle grazed among the kingcups.

'So where's the ford?'

'Round the bend in the river. There's a bridge, but there's not much left of it. They use the ford for cattle. If we skirt the field, we shouldn't meet anyone. They're not used to strangers.'

They did as Thomas suggested, and after negotiating the bridge, squelched through the water meadows opposite. The forest loomed ahead with no noticeable break in the undergrowth.

'There's a path, but I have to think where it is. I hope it's not too overgrown.'

Naomi waited patiently while he scanned the trees ahead. 'Over that way.' Thomas turned and glanced at the sky. 'Mist's coming in. I reckon we've got about three hours' daylight. We may need every bit of it.'

'You don't have a lantern?'

'No.'

'And you can't produce one out of the air?'

'There are ways of creating fire, but not for that.'

'Not for what?"

'Not for prosaic purposes.'

Naomi shuddered and crossed her fingers. She hesitated, then said, 'At home they talk about wildfire. Sometimes you see it in the mountains, but there's no heat in it, and to follow it is perilous. We shouldn't be flippant about it.'

'I'm not,' said Thomas soberly, his eyes on the forest.

Naomi considered him. 'This magic,' she said presently. 'Did you learn it when you were a child?'

'It would have been easier if I had. Children sometimes have clearer minds for it. They don't necessarily think in straight lines.'

'Have you taught a child, then?'

'No. He taught himself — Julius, my nephew. At the time I thought nothing of it, but later, I remembered, and it served me well.'

'And he worked it out for himself, you mean?'

'I see it,' said Thomas. 'We have come the right way.' They crossed the last patch of bog, and indeed there was a break in the scrub, an overgrown path thick with briars. 'I hope it doesn't get any worse.'

'So do I,' said Naomi with feeling. 'I'm fond of these trousers. Did Julius work it out for himself?'

'I forget,' said Thomas brusquely, and plunged into the forest, so she had to scramble painfully through the briars to keep up with him. So what pain lies behind that? thought Naomi. I wasn't curious; he brought it up himself, so he can't be insulted. He never meant to say so much. I can understand that: I've done the same. So I must forget it, as I would expect him to do for me.

The way was barely visible. Only the fact that they were able to press forward at all was evidence that people had made a path here, for to left and right of them the undergrowth was too dense to penetrate. Naomi felt sweat trickling down her back. Brambles caught at her clothes, and she kept stopping to disentangle herself. Thomas forged ahead, indifferent to the trailing stems that caught at his ancient jacket and trousers. When he turned to wait for her, he looked hot and dishevelled, with bits of twig clinging to him, but he seemed to have recovered his equanimity, and waited patiently.

'I take longer,' explained Naomi, as they stopped for breath in a place where the path sloped steeply upward, 'because I like my clothes. Don't you care about yours?'

'I knew I was coming. I wore clothes that didn't matter to me.'

'So you don't usually go around in grey?'

'Would it tell you something if I said no?'

'Yes, it would.'

'No,' said Thomas.

'I'm relieved to hear it.'

'It should get easier soon. The further up we go, the thinner the forest gets. If we get above the treeline tonight, you'll see my road.'

They said nothing more, as the way got worse. Forest trees gave way to scrub, but that was of no help to them. Birch and juniper slapped their faces as they passed. Mist wreathed across the slopes above. They could be anywhere, adrift in a sea of trees.

'Can we rest a minute?'

For answer, Thomas lowered his pack and stripped off his jacket. Underneath he wore a bright blue shirt, streaked with sweat. He rolled up his jacket and tied it to the top of his pack. 'I should have done that hours ago.'

Naomi uncorked a bottle of water and lifted it to her lips. Then she stopped and asked, 'How soon do we get to water again?'

'There's one more stream to cross. An hour maybe.'

He watched her while she drank, realising that he was glad of her company. It was impossible now to imagine what this place would have been like without her. When he planned his journey he hadn't dwelt on this part, that took them through the lowland forest. Once they reached his own road, and were in the hills, he knew himself safe. The hills presented no conflict, because they were as they had always been. It was down here, among lands which had once been different, that he had to cope with two worlds. There was something in this land that refused to resolve itself, like two pictures of the same place that would not blend into one image. The place where they stood was dank and oppressive, the air today heavy with undischarged thunder. He knew where they were: it had a name, given to him once by a man from the settlement they had passed. The event that had occurred here was inconceivable to him, yet it hovered at the edges of his mind, and would not be ignored. An image of violence. He wondered if she even knew the word, and almost despised her, so that when she did speak he was astonished, and ashamed.

'I don't like this place,' she told him. 'It frightens me.'

'You can tell? They say there was a battle here, in the time before the world changed. You know what that is?'

'I know what I've been told. Between men and men, a kind of ritualised killing, for making settlements about land. Is that it?'

'Or money,' added Thomas. 'So they say. All we have is poetry. In these lands there were always such killings, between the men of the north and the men of the south. I think many of them died round about here.'

He stopped, proud of the indifference with which he managed to say it. The trees were very still. Swarms of flies droned beneath them, where blood had once soaked into this ground. The smell of death, or the memory of it, did not seem so far away. Naomi stood there, frowning, as if trying to grasp a concept beyond her comprehension. She comes to the borders of the world, thought Thomas, but refuses to frighten herself. So she hears only music, and so people listen only to poetry. No wonder she clings to it so passionately.

'But poetry is about love, or magic,' stated Naomi, interrupting his thoughts.

'Not necessarily.'

'You don't think so? Well,' said Naomi, too exhausted to consider the matter further, 'you should know. You're a magician.'

'So you told me.'

Naomi stood up. 'I can't have that sort of conversation now,' she said firmly. 'It's getting late, and this land is full of ghosts. I'd like to spend the night away from here, so we'd better go.'

'All the lands are full of ghosts.'

'But these are the ghosts of men, and have nothing to do with me.'

'Then it is I who should be afraid.'

'And are you?' asked Naomi, facing him.

'Those days are beyond imagining,' said Thomas. 'If I had anything to do with such a killing, then it would be me that you should fear.'

'I'm sorry,' said Naomi at once. 'The past is no more yours than mine, and I know that you're one of my own people. Shall we go on?'

'I don't want to sleep in the forest either,' said Thomas, and swung his pack on to his back again. 'I don't think it'll be much further.'

By the time they reached the stream the sun had almost set. The valley was dank and marshy, and alive with midges. There was no bridge, but there were stepping stones, slightly awry after long neglect. The water was high with winter rain. Naomi sighed, and began to unlace her boots.

'We can fill the water bottles,' said Thomas. 'There's no water on the road tomorrow.'

'No water?' Naomi stared at him, her boot in her hand. 'What kind of road is this, Thomas, where there is no shelter and no water? I never heard of such a way, not in this world.'

'Not in your world.'

'So what kind of a world is yours?' She wasn't afraid of him, she was sure about that. After a day in his company, she was beginning to think she liked him, but he was unaccountable, and he had said himself he was leading her on a fool's errand. There is a border between one kind of land and another, thought Naomi, which is to easy to define. The forest is disorientating. But I live in the waking world, and I won't be part of any man's dream.

'No stranger than yours,' replied Thomas. 'Only different. I said you could trust me. I come from a country that you don't know at all, but it seems quite ordinary to me. I'm not playing any tricks. The road is only what you see.'

'All I see is the mountains, where there are no roads.'

'I was born among mountains.'

'Very well,' said Naomi, starting on her other boot. 'Either it's magic or it's to do with the way you know your land. I reserve judgement, and I'll carry water, if you tell me there is none.'

'Thank you,' said Thomas, picking up his boots. 'I think tomorrow you'll understand.'

It was a relief to get away from the water and leave the midges behind. The hill rose almost sheer above them, and soon the scrub gave way to grassland.

'That's it,' said Thomas, waiting for her again. 'It's a straight path now right across.'

'Only it's dark, just about.'

'There was a bit of shelter, further up.'

He was right. Presently they came upon a semicircle of tumbledown stones that might have been a sheep shelter, when flocks grazed on these remote hills. No creature had lain here for a long time, so grass and nettles had grown tall in the shelter of the broken wall. They trampled down a patch of lush vegetation, and spread their blankets over the top.

'We shouldn't feel the nettles through that.'

'Wonderful,' said Naomi. 'I hope someone sneezing doesn't keep you awake.'

'I'm sorry. Would anything help?'

'A bath,' said Naomi, 'and a particular kind of tea. In fact it won't be a problem. It's too cold and damp up here. I wouldn't mind some supper.'

'We could make a fire. There's plenty of kindling in the scrub down there.'

It didn't take long. They were both used to making themselves comfortable in whatever shelter the roads might offer. He had chosen her for her music, but, thought Thomas, it was just as well she was the right kind of person for this journey. Not necessarily easy to be with, she was too critical for that, but she knew exactly what needed to be done. Not long-suffering, decided Thomas, and smiled a little as he built up a little pyramid of dried grass and twigs inside a ring of stones. But at least she only complains, and then gets on with it.

'Is it dry enough?' Naomi was standing over him, and a bundle of twigs was dumped at his feet.

'I think so. The grass is dry, anyway.'

Naomi squatted down, and took a little metal box out of her pocket. 'Shall I light it?'

'If you like.' She was quick, and very efficient. Thomas watched her thoughtfully, and when she had a good blaze going, and had set a pan of water on to boil, he remarked, 'I suppose a musician who follows the road doesn't always live a life of complete luxury.'

'No,' said Naomi. 'I can look after myself, if that's what you're asking. But I prefer complete luxury, when it's around. Do you want some tea?'

'Thank you. Shall we have bread and cheese with it?'

'Or an egg?'

'It's hardboiled, if you must know everything. And I might be needing it again.'

'Fair enough. Give me the bread, and I'll make toast.'

When they had eaten they banked up the fire with moss, took off their boots and buttoned up their jackets, and rolled themselves in their blankets right under the shelter of the wall. It could be worse, thought Naomi. The ground was hard and cold under her hip and shoulder. She rolled on to her front, and before the cold had time to seep up from the earth, she was asleep.

She woke abruptly about four hours later. It was quite dark. The fire had shrunk to a small red glow. She was very cold, her legs cramped from being curled inside the blanket. The air was raw and damp. There was no sound from Thomas, but she knew that she had been woken.

As soon as the sound came again she knew what it was. She sat up, eyes wide against the dark. 'Thomas?'

'Yes?' He was awake too, not lying down either, invisible on the other side of the fire.

'You heard that?'

'Dogs.'

'Wild dogs,' repeated Naomi. 'Well, that just about puts the lid on it.'

There was another howl, this time from the slope just below them. She shuddered, torn between fear and anger. 'It's probably a whole bloody pack out there! I should have known it, in a place like this.'

'I'll make the fire up.' She heard him moving in the darkness.

'There's nothing to make it with. It'll only bring them closer.'

'They've been moving this way anyway.'

'You've been listening to them?'

'You sleep very soundly.'

Naomi knelt on the ground in the dark, and realised she was shaking, either with cold or fright, probably both. She was furious. It was always a danger in the wild, but this was his road, and she had trusted him. There was nothing they could do if the pack came this way. Thomas sounded quite unmoved. He must know the danger. Or perhaps there was no danger for him, merely another illusion. But dogs on the hills were real. One howl answered another, and Naomi felt a tingle of fear down her back, and shuddered again. They could tear her to pieces, and there was no one in the world to know. Or it was truly the stuff of nightmare, and he had known it all the time. A magician, a shape-shifter, one whose world was utterly alien to her. There was no telling what he knew, that she did not.

'Thomas.'

'Yes.'

'What do we do?'

'There's nothing we can do. Wait.'

She must have sounded frightened, but there was no fear in the voice that answered her. A dog howled, very close. She jumped, expecting to hear the pad of feet, snuffling in the undergrowth, to see eyes glowing in the firelight, shapes within the shelter of the wall. And there was a movement, a rustling in the grass, a thicker blackness suggesting a figure right beside the fire. Naomi got to her feet, and unsheathed her knife. There was an answering chink of metal, and silence.

'Is that you?'

'It's me,' whispered Thomas. 'Where are you?'

'Here. What are you doing?'

'Waiting.' Then: 'I'm sorry, Naomi.'

His voice was as mild as ever, gentle, even. Unreal. She knew nothing of him, had asked nobody. A fool's errand. Her heart thumped: she could hear it, or feel it. He was invisible. It was so dark, darker than it should be. He could be anything, unknowable in the darkness, waiting beside the dying fire, a naked knife in his hand, and the howling of wild dogs behind him. The border between one country and another. There would be no waking up from this. There was the cry of a dog again, right behind her. Naomi leapt round, and there was sudden movement in the shadows behind her. She swung back and faced him, where she thought he was, her knife poised.

'Thomas?'

'They're all around,' he said. 'Come closer, Naomi.'

She stood still, her knife ready, trying to understand. His voice was the same, and the words might mean what she chose. She tried to picture the man, but there was no substance to him; always equable, yet too changeable. She couldn't grasp him, couldn't imagine him as he was, or as he had seemed to her to be. The dogs howled, and she sensed him raise his head.

'Thomas!'

'Come closer!' There was urgency in his voice at last.

'Give me your hand,' demanded Naomi,

No answer. She reached out and fumbled in the air, towards where the voice had been. For a second she panicked, clutching at empty air. Then her hand met his. It was a warm hand, entirely human, clasping hers firmly, but not constraining her at all. It was the hand of Thomas, who had become familiar to her during a day's journey through a land she recognised.

'Thank you,' said Naomi, letting out a long breath. 'That's very reassuring.'

'Please,' said Thomas. 'Come nearer. I can't see a thing.'

She stepped round the fire. 'I don't know what we can do if they come,' said Thomas, almost in her ear. 'But at least there's two of us. They may back off if we just make a noise.'

'You never know your luck.' Naomi turned round so she had her back to him, and stared into the night.

He stood with his back to hers. She was aware of the tension running through him as he listened. There was a long silence, only a faint breeze stirring on the hill around them. When the next howl came they both jumped, but it was farther away. It was answered from the distant valley.

Naomi heard Thomas's indrawn breath. 'I think that's it,' he said, and turned round. 'You keep very cool, don't you?' he remarked. 'Does nothing frighten you?'

'Me? But you never said a thing!'

'What was there to say?'

'What do you think you could have done?' asked Naomi.

'I know,' said Thomas. 'I brought you into danger, and there's not much I could have done at all. I'm sorry.'

'I see.'

'I don't think they'll come back. There's no moon. I'd have expected it to be quiet.'

Naomi put her knife away. 'Then we can go back to sleep?'

'I hope so.'

But she never heard him lie down. Naomi wrapped herself up again, and pulled the blanket right over her head. She firmly banished her surroundings from her mind, and began to reconstruct another place from her memory, a place where she hadn't felt alone at all, where someone had held her in their arms, whom she had loved. Sleep began to catch at her, and the image dissolved in her mind. She tried to cling to it, as to a last shred of comfort, but she was too tired, she was falling back into the darkness, this time into a dreamless sleep.

Third Day

Thomas sat by the fire in the cool of the morning, watching small bubbles rise in the pan of water he had set to heat. One bottle of water nearly gone, two to go. And the dangerous places lay behind them. He realised the irony of that thought. His road was perilous, and he might well expect Naomi to be daunted. But to him the road led to an unbroken world, where all messages were the same, none contradictory or displaced. A man might not sustain life there for long, but while he could stay, he would be whole.

In spite of everything, they had come as far yesterday as he had hoped. She could travel as fast as he could; she only held things up when her priorities diverged from his. But there could be no distractions today.

He regarded her thoughtfully. She still slept, but in the warmth of day she had rolled over on her back, and stretched out so that the blanket barely covered her. She seemed very vulnerable like that, her jacket all twisted up round her, and her hair spread out in a tangle. Her mouth had fallen open slightly, and she was snoring, not very loud. This was the second morning he had been able to observe her as she slept. She seemed to abandon herself to sleep almost fiercely, her eyes tightly closed, as if she needed to sleep with the same energy she applied to her waking life. She was certainly almost impossible to wake. He found that endearing. Awake, she was so sure of herself, alert to every situation, and very self-contained. She may be suspicious when she's conscious, thought Thomas, but she sleeps with the trust of a baby. Yet she's survived. She's strong, and certainly courageous, and uncompromising, which may be difficult. I dare not be anything but honest with her, but I'm not sure how much I want to give away. Not the easiest companion I could have chosen for what I want done, but more likely to succeed than anyone else I've met.

The water was boiling. Thomas added some tea and let it draw by the fire. Then he poured it into two mugs.

'Naomi?'

No answer. He looked down at her uncertainly, and gently shook her by the shoulder. She rolled away from him, frowning in concentrated sleep. Thomas sighed, and shook her harder.

'Naomi!'

'Now what?' She stared up at him with puzzled eyes, trying to focus.

'I've made you some tea. It's a nice morning.'

Naomi sat up suddenly, and rubbed her eyes. 'One thing about having a terrible night,' she said thickly, 'is that the morning seems like a miracle. If any of this is real, I hope it's this bit.'

'Have some tea,' said Thomas consolingly.

'Thank you.' She unravelled herself from the blanket, took the mug, and considered Thomas over the top of it. 'I wonder if you had the same nightmare as I did,' she remarked presently.

'It was real.'

'All of it?'

'I don't know. The part which was the same for you as it was for me.'

'So that part which was different for each of us was a dream? That's a curious view of the world,' said Naomi, sipping tea. She looked round. 'At least the mist has gone. Can we see your road?'

'All round us. We can start as soon as you're ready.'

The country he led her into this time was completely different. It was hard work at first, struggling up a steep slope, so that she had no chance to look about her. Her pack seemed heavier this morning, and the hill seemed endless. Naomi kept her eyes on Thomas's feet, just in front and above her, and ploughed doggedly after. This was his country, not hers, and her legs were less used to climbing. She said nothing, though it was hard to get her breath and keep going, until at last he stopped and lowered his pack. 'Now look,' said Thomas. 'This is the beginning of the Road.'

It was more like the sea. A long swell of hills, their curves smooth as a whale's back, birds circling over them, the cry of curlews desolate as the calling of gulls over open water. It seemed one could follow those long undulations, slide down into the troughs with the smoothness of a narrow boat, then rise up slowly, carried by the moving swell of the land. Only this was not water, but earth, stripped to its bones and carved to deceptive smoothness through ages of ice and wind. It was land, but land limitless as the sea, an open road above the tree-choked lowlands that encircled it.

'You see why we must go on while it's fine. If the weather turns on you up here, there's no shelter.'

There was indeed no shelter. That too was like the sea. To be caught out was the ever present danger, to be benighted might be a matter not of sleep but death. Already the mist was banked up to the east, rolling in slowly from the coast. This was not a road, but a voyage, with all the risks that implied. In spite of herself, her heart soared.

'I'm used to that,' she said to Thomas. 'Where I come from, they used to make many voyages. It's the only place in the world where they still have sailing directions for the lands to the west. I know about the weather.'

'There's snow lying up there. It's still winter here. The road hasn't been open long.'

'I'm used to that too. As long as you bring me back before September.'

'May,' said Thomas. 'I promised you, within a month.'

The ridge was not entirely bare. The grass grew long and tussocky, interspersed with bog myrtle and juniper that scratched their boots as they passed. The ground was soaking, perhaps still wet with vanished snow, or perhaps only with the cloud that had recently rested here. In the hollows the bare peat was moist and squashy, so that brown water filled the deep footprints they left behind. Slowly the water seeped into Naomi's boots, cold at first, then soggily warm inside her socks. She stopped bothering to leap from tussock to tussock, but marched doggedly on, squelching as she went. The upward slopes were easier, the ground hard and unyielding. It was much colder up here, with a breeze from the east bringing the smell of rain, chilly and slightly threatening.

Thomas strode ahead like a man in his own element at last. He seemed to know exactly where he was going, although there was no vestige of a path. He made the way seem easy, following the ridge. But in fact, Naomi noticed as they went on, further ridges loomed all round them, featureless as an ocean, and as easy to get lost. Automatically she noted the lie of the land, the great bulk of mountain appearing to the east, hiding the ominous cloud behind it, and the lower ridges stretching to south and west. They seemed to be travelling a little west of south. It was hard to tell; the sun was nowhere to be seen. She looked back. There were faint gleams of light over the forest, where the clouds broke beyond the hills.

Presently Thomas stopped and waited for her to catch up. 'All right?'

'All right,' she assured him 'This is your kind of country then?'

'No. My own is more specific than this. You'll see.'

'Specific?'

He seemed to search for words. 'It has more shape to it.'

'But the empty lands are mountains too. I've seen them in the distance from the western road.'

'Mountains, yes. These aren't mountains.'

'Then what are they?'

'Hills,' said Thomas, and turned to go on.

'But you said before . . .' began Naomi, and saw that he was out of earshot. She tugged at the straps of her pack to ease her back, and followed him.

But there was a shape looming ahead, where a touch of cloud drifted across the hill; straight shapes like people against a horizon of shifting grey. The mist dropped lower, and it was gone again. 'What's that?' called Naomi, pointing.

'That's our next summit. I wish the mist would hold off. It'll grow thicker yet.'

As if in response, the cloud gathered itself together, and withdrew. The hilltop swam back into view, revealing a toothed edge of rock, black and forbidding. Naomi thought she felt a hint of rain on her cheek. The air was greyer, and cold as the sea. A gust of wind caught her, and she was in daylight again, and there was a faint warmth from the hidden sun.

The slope was steeper than it looked. Thomas quickened his pace, determined to keep ahead of the weather. Naomi hastened after him, stumbling over rocks half hidden by grass. The cold was piercing. It wasn't long since this place had been deep in snow, and the shadow of it still seemed to lie upon the land. She had been cold all night, and frightened and disturbed. Everything was grey around her. She felt curiously lightheaded. Her breath was beginning to come in gasps. There was no keeping up with him: he was almost fifty yards ahead. Naomi stopped, and realised to her astonishment that she felt faint. You never faint, she told herself sternly, and breathed hard. Her stomach churned. It's because you haven't had any breakfast, thought Naomi, and began to climb again, much more slowly. The toothed rocks towered above her. There was no sign of Thomas. Well, she had never agreed to keep up with him. Naomi climbed steadily, her eyes on the ground, picking out the way.

The rocks took her by surprise, rectangular shapes crowning the hill, with dirty snow caught in their eastern crevices. Thomas was sitting sprawled at the foot of them, his pack at his feet. 'It's sheltered here,' he said as she reached him. 'Do you want a rest?'

'I want to eat something.'

'Bread?'

'That'll do.'

They divided a loaf and ate in silence, while the cold gradually pierced their clothes, and small draughts eddied round the rock at their backs.

'How long did you live on the island?' asked Thomas presently, with his mouth full.

'A year. Then I went over the sea. Then I came back for two years. But I've been away a long time now.'

'I've heard the music that was given to the island about that time.'

'You have?'

'Yes. I'm surprised the woman who brought it didn't stay on the island. She would have had recognition and respect, and could have lived in relatively complete luxury.'

'I like being on my own.'

'But you wanted to get back to the island yesterday.'

'And so I do today. You offered me something you knew I wouldn't refuse.'

'Yes.' There was a pause. 'I'm not going away by choice,' said Thomas abruptly.

'Of course you are. There is always choice.'

'Not for me.'

'So who pushed you off the island?'

'I don't understand.'

'You crossed the strand,' said Naomi patiently. 'You came through the forest, and now you are returning over the hills by the way you came. On your own legs, of your own will. That's choice.'

'But not the one I wished to make,' said Thomas, speaking so low she hardly caught the words.

'Well, that's another thing: choosing and wishing. There's a world of difference. I'm cold. Are we going on?'

Once they set off, conversation languished. Naomi felt much better. There was food inside her, a pale glimmer of sun above her, and she had got her second wind. There was water not so far below, a small beck that fell in a series of waterfalls, but it would have been a long climb down to it. They skirted the corrie through which it flowed. At the top the wind greeted them again, heavy with dissipating cloud.

'That's the other thing about the mist,' said Naomi, following her own train of thought. 'It won't do the fiddle any good either.'

'The other thing?' Thomas didn't wait for an answer. 'We'll keep ahead of it today. There's no wind. It makes things easier.'

'And how far do we go on like this?'

'There's a bit of shelter, and water, in about twenty miles.'

'What!' said Naomi. 'Are you joking?'

'Have a toffee,' said Thomas consolingly.

'Thanks for offering,' said Naomi, after waiting expectantly.

'It's in your pocket. No, the other one. That's it.'

'Thanks. I'll have strawberries in the other one in half an hour, please. Which way now?'

'West,' said Thomas, pointing.

Naomi frowned. 'I don't expect straight lines, but this is getting ridiculous.'

'I forgot you were a traveller. But we have to follow the ridge. There's no confusion really.'

'We're not going round in a circle?'

'Not on this journey.'

'It's hard to imagine,' said Naomi, as they walked on, 'to relate one side of the country to the other, when there has never been any point of connection. But the way I see it in my mind, I think we should be travelling west, maybe south of west.'

'There are points of connection, and you're right.'

'You mean the mountains?'

'They make landmarks, but that's all in the eye,' said Thomas. 'That's why we want to keep ahead of the mist. The ground tells a little, but not so easily.'

'It does here,' remarked Naomi. 'There are going to be flowers. What are they?'

Thomas glanced down. 'Cloudberries. If it was summer, I'd give you your wish, more or less.'

'What wish?'

'If it were summer, I'd fill your pockets with cloudberries. It would be dry enough to play your fiddle to the stars, and I'd fill your pockets again and again until you had no wishes left in the world.'

'Oh you would, would you?' said Naomi, as her feet sank into a sudden bog, filling her boots with icy brown water.

The cairn at the top of the next hill was the most distinctive landmark they had seen in miles. They sat down in the shelter of it to eat their dinner.

'Do you ever have fantasies about food?' enquired Naomi, slicing off a piece of dry cheese.

'Food?' asked Thomas absentmindedly, laying his cheese on his bread in neat slices. 'No, not about food. Do you?'

'Yes. Particularly when travelling.'

'Such as?'

'Trout,' said Naomi dreamily, through a mouthful of stale bread. 'Roast trout. Fresh peas. Blackcurrants and cream.'

'If you like,' said Thomas, resigned, 'you can eat the hardboiled egg. I can always get another.'

'You're very kind. We could share it.'

'It's all yours.' Thomas produced it from nowhere particular, and tossed it into her lap. 'It's better not to think about food like that at this time of year.'

'I know. Porridge and potatoes.' Naomi cracked the egg against a stone, and began to peel off the shell.

'We do nothing to earn it, you and I,' said Thomas. 'All we produce is dreams.'

'Speak for yourself.'

'I do. We eat what we're given, not what we grow. There's no labour in that.'

'I've worked the land. And a poor sort of land it was, too.'

'You didn't like it?'

'I didn't think about it. It's just the way the world was. I never knew it could be different.'

'It can't be different. Not really. The land must be worked and the people must eat. All the rest is illusion. We can play with it, you and I, but that's a privilege. We have to remember we're only playing, however much we make them all think it's real.'

'So you've worked the land, Thomas?'

'I never wanted anything else. Where I grew up — but you'll see it, in a few days. Land there is a gift, left by the mountains, enough for the people to live among them. We made a farm out of soil that was never more than a few inches deep, and we flourished. We made it from land at the edge of the hills that hadn't been worked for hundreds of years, and we made it good. That's a better thing to be proud of than being able to deceive you with the evidence of your own eyes, and dazzle you into believing that's magic.'

'But if magic is your trade, you must be proud of it!'

'It's no trade.'

'Then what?'

'What you said. Fantasies. My work all came to nothing. Reality is unbearable in the end. I deal in illusion because I'm a coward. You shouldn't trust me, Naomi.'

'I never said I trusted you! Not for one moment!' She almost threw the egg at him, but let it fall unheeded. 'I don't! You can speak for yourself, if you like. But not for me! What do you know about the music? Do you think it's a conjuring trick, something I produce for you like a rabbit out of a hat? You tell me it's not real. Well, then, I tell you: you have no right to hear it, nor ever shall do, for I'll never play for you again, if you won't believe in what I do!'

'Please,' said Thomas, dusting the soil off the egg. 'I didn't mean to make you angry. All right. I only speak for myself. I'm a fool, I know, Naomi.'

Naomi stared at him, frustrated. 'I'm not interested in apologies,' she said at last. 'They don't mean anything. You said what you thought, and I don't agree. You called the music a deception. But you hear it. You hear it very well. Do you think I couldn't tell, when I played to you? So how dare you deny it? You're deceiving yourself, Thomas. That makes me angry. I wouldn't care if you didn't understand.'

'Of course I'm not honest,' said Thomas patiently. 'You must have realised that much. If I were honest, I wouldn't know what you had in your pockets, would I?'

'And do you?' asked Naomi, diverted.

'I know that your music hasn't made you rich, anyway,' said Thomas, smiling at her. 'Are you still angry, or would you like this egg?'

Naomi accepted it again. 'I'm as rich as I want to be, and there's nothing you can take from me,' she said. 'Do you want me to believe that you're a thief?'

'I'm tired of making anyone believe anything. Listen, Naomi, I hope you didn't mean what you said.'

'What did I say?'

'That you wouldn't play for me again. I don't think I deserve that.'

'I probably didn't mean it.'

After they left the cairn, the hills enclosed them completely. Whatever landmarks Naomi tried to fix in her mind seemed fluid even as they walked, hills changing shape, revealing new aspects, fading into the distance unremarkably.

I doubt if I could find the way back without him. Naomi stopped, frowning down into an empty corrie that had come into view on the left this time, confusingly. It can't stay as mild as this, was her next thought, not in April. She began to see the implications of what she had done. There was a road all right, he had told her the truth about that, but it wasn't a reliable road, not for her. And the man couldn't be relied upon, for he was merely a man. She felt a chill in her stomach, and shivered, pushing the idea away. There's no danger in it, she told herself. The worst thing that could happen is that I find myself stuck on the wrong side of the mountains, and it takes me weeks to get back again to the same side of the country as the island. Months probably, because I should certainly be distracted along the way, taking so long a journey. But I would be in my own world; I would need no guide, and I would know my own way back to the island. I've given him no power over me.

Thomas was aware that she was having a hard time keeping up, but he guessed that encouragement would only earn him a few sharp words. But I like her, he thought, and surprised himself. And as her defences become clearer to me I can respect her, in spite of them. If she uses music to keep herself from the emptiness of being cast out of the world, then who am I to blame her? Music is better than ignorance or complacency, and it's infinitely better than madness. And perhaps in itself it's also something more. She deceives herself, but she is right about her music. Why try to take it from her, if all I have to offer instead is my despair?

He waited for her on the next hilltop. 'Not far,' he said. 'One more mile, one more hill. You can see into the west now, look.'

Naomi looked. More hills, disappearing into twilight. She was in the heart of it now, a vast country traversed by this road of his she couldn't even see. It was like a place in a dream. All she wanted now was to sleep, and for the dream to stay with her. She had no more words, so she merely nodded, and let him lead on.

There was a fold in the hills below them, not quite a valley, but a grassy platform half lost in the twilight. They stumbled down the slope in the half dark. Long grass brushed their knees, soaking them with heavy dew. There was a new sound, like an echo from a far remoter past than yesterday: the noise of running water. They crossed a patch of bog buried in rushes, and jumped the stream at the bottom. They were standing on a flat ledge in the lee of a little cliff. The hint of ice in the air had vanished. It was cool and wet, but no longer threatening. Naomi realised she was swaying a little on her feet, mesmerised by the sound of water. She lowered her pack, crouched by the beck, and drank. Then she stripped off her soaking boots and socks, put on three pairs of dry socks, rolled herself in her blanket and closed her eyes. There was only the sound of water, and welcoming sleep.

Fourth Day

When Naomi awoke, it was to find another body curled tightly against her own. The ground was freezing and there were cramps in her legs. She stretched out painfully and kicked something solid. Thomas groaned and rolled over.

'Oh, it's you, is it?' said Naomi.

'I'm sorry,' mumbled Thomas. 'It seemed preferable to freezing to death. I hope you don't mind.'

'Not at all,' said Naomi politely, wriggling her toes to see if they were still there. She opened her eyes cautiously, to see grass frozen into white spikes just in front of her nose. 'I must have been mad,' she added, and sat up.

'I'd have asked, but of course you didn't wake. It's just as well you snore, or I'd have thought you were dead.'

'I don't snore,' stated Naomi. 'Can you strike fire from frost, or is that beyond you?'

'You shall have a cup of tea tonight, if we do as well as we did yesterday.'

Naomi stood up. 'Where do you expect to be tonight?'

'At the end of this road. There's an inn in a valley. I think we should make it.'

They set off quickly, chewing hunks of bread as they went. It was far too cold to linger, and the only way to get warm was to go on. In daylight Naomi saw that the place was hardly even a valley, just a sheltered hollow dominated by the rushing water. Someone had taken advantage of it before. There had once been an enclosure on the level land above the stream.

'That was made before the world changed,' she remarked.

'Or even before that. Those people never built in the mountains. This was made before, like the great wall.'

'What wall?'

'It does what we do, only further south. It crosses the whole land, from one side to another.'

'No,' said Naomi, considering. 'It can't do. What for?'

'To divide one country from another.'

'But why? The mountains do that. Land makes divisions, then people make connections between them. A wall like that would be going the wrong way.'

'You can't say that.'

'Why not?'

'Because it exists,' said Thomas patiently. 'If the evidence of the past is all around you, you have to accept it, even if it doesn't fit in with your calculations.'

'But it has to add up to the present!'

'Why?'

'Stop playing with words, Thomas! Because what we have now is what has happened. You can't deny that!'

'I do deny it.' He spoke so quietly she wasn't sure if she'd heard him right.

Naomi bit her lip. It was impossible to talk to this man sometimes. All he seemed to do was lead her into meaningless traps, created out of words that said nothing at all. It made her want to argue with him, but she resisted, because the journey was urgent, and it seemed that further words would lead them nowhere.

When they reached the ridge the wind met them. They pulled their hats down and turned up their collars, but it was relentless. It found its way inside their jackets and stung their faces until their eyes watered. Naomi tucked her trousers into her socks to stop the draughts, and clenched her fists inside her gloves. The ground was white with frost, and crunched under their boots.

'North-east,' called Thomas cheerfully. 'Right behind us. Perfect.'

'Quite,' said Naomi, and turned her back to the wind. It immediately shoved her forward, sending cold fingers up the inside of her shirt as it did so.

Today she took less notice of their route. It was impossible to raise her eyes anyway, because the wind blinded her. They walked fast. It was a relief to stretch her cramped limbs after lying all night on cold ground. Naomi kept her eyes on Thomas's feet, just in front of her, and trod where he trod. Soon she felt the familiar icy wetness seeping through her socks, as they tramped through more peat bogs. She realised now that the place was dangerous. The road was open, but only just. There was a long day's fight with wind and land between her and anything human, and if she were to fail, this land would offer her no mercy. Strangely, the thought excited her. She was warm again now, and strong. Her legs were tired, but that was all. It was a test, this journey, like learning the music of the past had been: struggling with something at the edge of her comprehension, feeling her imagination stretched to its limits, and exulting in the possibilities.

They didn't talk; any words would have been whipped away at once by the wind. Thomas kept his attention on the route. There was the same endless procession of hills as yesterday, harder to make out because of the wind that confused his vision. There were landmarks for one who had eyes to see them, all carefully hoarded in his memory; so long as he concentrated, and kept his directions in the right order, he could identify them one by one, and so pick out a path across the empty hills ahead. One mistake, and they were done for. He hadn't expected this drop in temperature. He'd been more worried about mist. He should have guessed the fog was only along the coast. It was still winter up here. When it froze so hard last night he'd been apprehensive, but neither of them seemed any the worse for it, as long as she kept up today. I was a fool to bring her, thought Thomas, a less seasoned traveller would have killed both of us, but luck shines on fools, sometimes.

On the island, thought Naomi, it may be a beautiful spring day. They may be sitting outside in the sun, on the benches outside the hall. The cattle will be out again, and new crops beginning to appear along the rigs. There will be a smell of sweet new grass, and the sound of the waves breaking on the shore. Francis will be there, turning poetry from one language to another. What better thing could a man be doing? This man Thomas is confused and fearful, although not difficult to be with, and sometimes amusing. Francis is always difficult to be with, and knows exactly what he is doing. As I do. Most of the time life has to be solitary, if it's to have any purpose at all, but it's delightful when it isn't. I made Francis my lover, and I was right. I realised that as soon as I'd done it. I might so easily not have bothered. I was thinking all the time about the music, and how to pass it on. But when I talked to him in the hall that night, sitting among all the empty tables after everyone else had gone to bed, talking about . . . what were we talking about? I can't remember now, but I remember that I made up my mind, and said his name so he looked right round at me, then I leant across the table and kissed him. Passionately. Naomi chuckled out loud, and jumped across a peat hag with more energy than she knew she had. And then we slept together that night, and many more. I do want to see Francis again, she decided, though it's not what I was going back for, and it doesn't matter if I don't.

It was too cold to stop for a break that morning, and the hilltops had no cairns to shelter them. They might have been the only people who had ever passed this way, for they were now so far beyond any human habitation that the land seemed quite untouched by the presence of people. An empty valley began to appear to their left, with a gleam of still water shrouded by trees. Thomas turned and raised his voice across the wind. 'We have to cross between the valleys, at the watershed. There's scrub, but it shouldn't be too thick.'

Naomi looked down at barren slopes, and the thin trickle of water where they converged at the bottom. A patch of brownish rock shifted on the other side of the valley, and began to move slowly across the slope. She tugged Thomas's sleeve and pointed. 'What's that?'

Thomas narrowed his eyes against the wind and looked. 'Deer,' he answered. 'They'd be up here, if it were summer.'

She watched, fascinated. Now that she could see them at all, she saw that they were everywhere. They were red deer, seldom seen in the inhabited lands that she was used to, and then only in small groups, foraging in winter. This was a bigger herd than she had ever dreamed of, crowded together in the shelter of the valley. So this was their land then, and when it was habitable up here they would come to claim it. No wonder the place felt so foreign to her. I never even knew there was a country between the lowlands before, thought Naomi, only that the mountains lay between. And there are many countries, and many inhabitants, stranger than any human dream. There are so many stories about such lands, and I thought they were part of fairytale, of enchanted forests and animals that speak. But perhaps that is only because I know nothing. The wind whistled round her ears, and the deer below moved like dream figures against a silent background. For them, she thought, I don't exist. And perhaps in a way I don't, for all I have of that world down there is eyes to see into it, which touch nothing. There is no way to touch, no communication at all. Perhaps even the music can only express the sorrow of it, and touches nothing. She shivered, and felt a touch on her arm.

'All right?' asked Thomas. 'Can we go on?'

'Have you ever been down there?'

Thomas looked down at the slowly moving herds, drifting against withered grass on both sides of a ribbon of water. 'No. It's not on the way to anywhere. There's nothing there.'

She realised she'd been standing still too long, and was beginning to shiver. She turned and followed him.

Soon they came to a break in the hills, and looked down on a wide gap where two valleys had met and broken a way through the ridge. Thomas and Naomi began to descend cautiously, for the ground was still slippery with melting frost. Soon they were back among thickets of bog myrtle. The wind fell away behind them, and with the resulting warmth came sounds, ordinary sounds of birds, of their own bodies pushing through scrub, of distant running water. Small birch trees began to appear, new leaves stirred by a gentler wind than on the mountains. A snipe flew up from almost under Thomas's feet, protesting.

'We could stop and eat down here,' said Thomas.

'And then we go up the other side?'

'Up there. This isn't a valley, just the watershed. There's nothing here. You'd think there were never people here since the world began, if it wasn't for the road.'

'Your road?'

'No, no. You'll see.' He said nothing more until they reached a rough clearing carpeted with smooth grass, much harder than the peaty land surrounding it, and only colonised by a few saplings. 'Look,' said Thomas. 'The road.'

Naomi looked round, puzzled. It was only a long clearing, made by a slope of rock just below the surface. It was almost warm, and a few flies hovered over mossy puddles. She didn't like it. It was nothing like any road, or if it were, it was a way made by creatures quite alien to her, perhaps malevolent. 'Whose road?' she asked, although that was perhaps not the right question.

'Out of the past,' said Thomas. 'Look.' He bent down and broke something away from a clump of mosses. 'You know what that is?'

She recognised it at once. It was a lump of tarry stuff, which one often found along old roads, part of the way they built them before the world changed. Nothing alarming about that. 'But here? This place has nothing to do with people! How can there be such a road here?'

Thomas shrugged. 'Who knows what ways they came, before the world changed?'

'But what about the deer?'

'How do I know? I told you, this isn't my country. There are things that can't be explained, everywhere. They leave their marks, but they don't necessarily leave the connections.'

'But their mark is not upon this land.' Somehow it seemed important to prove that. This country belonged to no human world. The idea that it should have been invaded seemed intolerable to her, though she could hardly understand why.

'Does it matter?' he asked with a casualness that did not ring quite true.

She looked at him, unable to find words for impressions so nebulous. 'It matters,' she said eventually. 'But perhaps not much. The land has been reclaimed, if it were ever so. That matters to me. I only know that some places must not be violated, if the world is to remain in balance. It doesn't all belong to the people, and if we take too much, the unknown will be stripped bare and all our dreams cast down.'

'And if they have been cast down already?' He spoke more harshly than he intended, and saw her jump. 'It worries you that they came as far into the wilderness as this? Why? What are you afraid of?'

'I don't know. It's irrational, I know. The past is over.'

'And that comforts you? You think that death will wipe things out, or that it has no power over you? You think you can say the past is dead, and dismiss it?'

She stared at him with startled eyes, and remembered her uncertainty when the dogs had howled. She had never met anyone so changeable. Easy to be with, amusing sometimes, and friendly, then suddenly this outburst of what seemed to be despair. There is a tension in him, thought Naomi, that doesn't show until something touches him, and then he would make me afraid, if I allowed myself to be affected by it. 'But I see how things have turned out,' she protested. 'So what have I to be afraid of?'

'Do you believe everything that you see?' He sounded jeering.

'I don't understand.'

'How do you know,' said Thomas, spelling out the words emphatically as though he found her stupid, 'that what you think you see is what has happened?'

'You confuse me.' She was annoyed to find herself alarmed by him 'Why, what do you see?'

'These people,' replied Thomas. 'These people, you have seen as many of them as I have. You go from place to place and play your music. There are places that you must avoid, as we all do, and places where you find what you believe to be your own kind. There are many empty buildings in this land. Have you ever noticed how the rats scavenge among the ruins?'

'I keep away from rats. I don't like them.'

'You make it sound very simple,' said Thomas ironically.

'I wish I could say the same of you.'

They stared at each other in frustration. She didn't understand him at all, but she could see the pain in his eyes, and that she recognised too well. Thomas watched her, and saw beyond the doubt in her expression, a touch of understanding. He smiled at her suddenly, and she blinked in surprise.

'It doesn't matter,' said Thomas. 'It's only a road. You see something more than that, and so do I. Perhaps you don't realise that most people wouldn't. I think you have been cast loose from your own place in the world, as I have, and that's never very safe. Shall we go on?'

They stopped about half a mile above the road, in a hollow sheltered by juniper. Standing up, they could look north into the next valley, over a new expanse of forest fading into a far horizon of low hills. The wind still came straight at them out of the north, but when they sat down the hollow was quiet and dry, and the wind was only a stirring in the juniper overhead.

Naomi shut her eyes, and jumped when Thomas nudged her sharply in the ribs.

'Don't go to sleep here! Have something to eat. We've a long way to go yet.'

'I wouldn't dream of it.'

A moment later he nudged her again. 'You'd better talk to me. I daren't let you go to sleep. What are you thinking about?'

'I was thinking about the island,' said Naomi sleepily.

A shadow seemed to cross his face. 'I know,' he said. 'I find myself thinking about it too. And I took you away again. I'm sorry.'

'No, you're not. You wanted me to come, and so far you think you were right.'

He looked at her sharply. She was lying with her eyes shut, not looking at all telepathic. Thomas smiled, and admitted, 'That's true, as far as it goes. If I had to come, I'm very glad I brought you.'

'One can't stay on the island for ever.'

'I would choose to. It's not possible.'

'You didn't find that you lacked solitude?'

'If I ever had any desire for solitude, it was met long ago. To me, it's important to have somebody to love.'

'A friend, do you mean, or a lover?'

'Both, perhaps. And having found someone to love, it isn't easy to let it go again.'

'What else can happen? People can't hold on to one another till one of them dies, can they? You have to go on living, and you can't expect two people to do that simultaneously, so there have to be partings. Does that trouble you?'

'I find it hard. There was someone I loved on the island, and I hope I shall return, but I'm afraid of what I go to.'

'There is someone I love on the island too,' said Naomi dreamily. 'I chose to come with you because you mentioned something that matters more. I wasn't going back because of him, but I realised today that I want to see him.'

'And he's there now?'

'Yes, you must know him. He's called Francis, and he's a poet.'

There was a long silence.

'I do know him,' said Thomas eventually, staring hard at the clouds. 'Very well. He's my lover, as a matter of fact.'

There was a longer silence.

'Well, it's interesting to find things in common,' said Naomi conversationally, not opening her eyes.

'I hope it's not the only thing we have in common.'

She hadn't heard him sound nervous before. Naomi opened her eyes, and sat up. 'Oh, I don't think so,' she said reassuringly. 'It would be a bit of a conversation-stopper if it was, wouldn't it?'

*

It was becoming a real effort to plod on after Thomas. The wind seemed to have more bite to it, piercing Naomi right through, though she was too tired even to start shivering. She knew she was strong, but she wasn't used to coming so near her limits. It scared her a little. Her will seldom failed her, but it couldn't drive her body on indefinitely. But there would be shelter tonight. Naomi visualised a bed, with sheets and a quilt and thick dry blankets. She wasn't even hungry now; she just wanted to sleep. That meant she must keep walking. The magic seemed to have faded from the hills. They were merely land, bare of life, sour with peat hags, offering nothing.

After all, she knew by now that life promised nothing but what the moment offered. There had been times that offered richness: she had taken it, and let it go again, keeping only memories. She knew very well there was nothing else to expect, except for the music, which endured for ever. A dry room, and a dry bed. It would be safe to unpack the fiddle, which was tucked up in its case, insulated from the weather by her clean shirt. The reason she was tired and edgy was that there had been no music, not for two days. If she set her mind to it, she could accomplish any journey a person could do, in any weather. Thomas had offered her something that mattered far more than comfort, and so far he had proved honest. There was everything to hope for, and tonight she would be allowed to stop and sleep.

Thomas kept his mind firmly on the route. It was difficult on this featureless plateau, marked only by treacherous pools of peat. It would be too easy to lose the ridge without noticing, and find oneself descending into barren marshes. If she hadn't missed the daylight that night, he would have passed her on the causeway, and neither of them would have known anything. When he had persuaded her to come, it was honest, he had genuinely not known. He knew that, but would anyone believe it? And afterwards, if they were able to return, would they go back together? And then? She could never take this route unless he brought her, even now. The advantage was his. But if he did that, he would no longer be innocent. He had kept her away from the island, but in innocence. If he were she now, he might not believe that. And not believing, what would he do then? Thomas stopped, scanning the horizon. The next summit should have a cairn upon it. What did she expect, after so many years? Surely she hadn't spent all that time alone? He realised he was tired, and not thinking too clearly. He must think about the way, or they would be lost, and there were no reserves for that.

The hours were stripped of meaning. If time passed, there was no sign of it. They had walked like this for ever, and there was no end to the circle. Naomi trod in Thomas's footsteps and asked no questions. It no longer mattered where he was taking her, or whether there were any truth in his promise. The promise was already fulfilled, and the road was everything. But she was too weary. It seemed she might go on for ever, but that would only be a dream, for her body would fail her. It seemed irrelevant, merely the passing of a tune from one world into another. Naomi tripped over a heather root and fell to her knees. It was an effort to get up again. Thomas heard nothing because of the wind. This would not do. A day's journey, he had said, and there must be an ending. She was cold, and very tired. Naomi brushed her hand across her eyes, and forced herself on.

Once or twice Thomas glanced round to make sure she was still following. She must be exhausted. He was a little lightheaded himself; he had hardly slept the last two nights, and it was bitterly cold. If she found it too hard, there was not very much he'd be able to do about it. But she never complained, and never lagged behind, although she was a stranger to the mountains. The road had never been so precarious before. There was no margin for error, none at all. Thomas studied the land vigilantly, and did not allow his mind to wander.

They passed a group of standing stones, the only landmark in all that desolate moorland. Naomi noted them in passing. Earlier she would have been interested. She had no energy for that now, only something deeper than interest, a recognition of something fitting, a gaunt tribute to the same dream.

On the next summit Thomas touched her arm. Naomi looked up, and saw a valley following the course of a little river that must feed into a larger one, because to the south of them stretched a long level plain between the diminishing hills. They were cut off from the hills to the north, standing on the last outcrop of the long ridge they had followed.

'Look,' said Thomas. His voice sounded harsh and unused. Neither of them had spoken for hours.

Naomi followed the line of his outstretched arm, shielding her eyes from the wind with her hand. There were mountains in the distance, blue and remote, half hidden in the distant sky. Between solid land and the mountains there was a gleam of water, and she realised she was looking at the Western Sea.

'That's the empty lands?'

'That's my country,' said Thomas, and turned his face to the wind again.

*

Once they had left the ridge there were streams to cross, and steep slopes to negotiate. Soon there was a bulk of hill looming behind them, then they found themselves back among waist-high scrub. There was a river below. Naomi raised her eyes to look and saw white specks among the grassland. Sheep. There was a wall, a dry stone dyke straddling the valley, and trees planted, a shelter belt of spruce above the pasture. The hills were high, blocking the horizon, and the sky had retreated far above her. She knew what lay up there now. She was right, and had always been right: there was no road, only the mountains. Thomas was right too, because there was a road, for those who knew the key to it.

They came down to just above the dyke.

There were buildings down there, small rectangles of grey, with slate roofs. Smoke, caught by the wind into a tail of grey that streamed down the valley. Brown fields enclosed by stone walls, scarred by the plough. It looked foreign, small and jumbled, out of place among the sweeping contours of the land.

He had expected her to say something. Tentatively, Thomas took her hand. She regarded him with the same half woken look she had when he tried to rouse her from sleep. He found himself staring back at her, quite forgetting to be guarded, letting her see both admiration in him, and affection. She had come by this road, and not only had she not complained, but she had understood. He knew they had only just made it, and naturally he was relieved. He realised confusedly that he was also sorry.

*

Rain and fire. Rain drumming on the low roof over her, and fire roaring in the round stove next to her. The rushing of air, air consumed by flames in the chimney, wind in the trees outside, rain driven by wind, and cold water turning to steam above the stove. Freezing outside, and in here a heat that made her sweat, melting away the stiffness of her body. Naomi stretched out on her back. It was like being restored to life, her body no longer cold and separate, only heat flowing through her, taking her back to herself, or to something else that had been forgotten.

She opened her eyes, and it made no difference at all. There was only darkness, full of heat. Slowly images began to form in front of her: rough planks overhead, full of knotholes, a red glow from the bottom of the stove, a curved arch of walls around her. No movement to be seen, yet there was movement everywhere, rain and wind and fire, and herself in the centre of it, untouched.

And other noises, small and specific, from the other side of the stove. Someone getting up from the bench opposite, the stove door opening with a clink, a rush of red light and heat into the hut. Naomi turned her head.

'I'm just putting more wood on,' said Thomas.

She didn't bother to answer, but watched drowsily. Thomas naked, with skin flushed in the firelight, was, she decided, good to look at. It was hard to tell what a man was like when he was wearing several layers of shapeless grey clothing, and was only to be observed tramping through peat bogs in a high wind. Thomas without his clothes was not all shapeless. He was slightly built but muscular, smooth-skinned, not particularly hairy, with sunburned neck and forearms, but otherwise surprisingly pale for one so dark. His back was half turned to her as he bent over the fire. It looked vulnerable like that, in a way that was not unattractive. Not very broad, but strong, and indisputably male. I can see what Francis sees in him, thought Naomi. I wonder . . . No, she said to herself, and turned to face the ceiling again, shutting her eyes.

'Shall I pour more water on?' asked Thomas.

'If you like.'

He dipped a jug into a pail of water, and poured a little water over the stove. It leapt and spluttered in sudden drops, then hissed into thick steam. Thomas dipped the jug again, and splashed more water. He couldn't quite stand upright under the sloping roof, so that the curve of his body was magnified behind him into a fantastic shadow, doubly rounded by the slope of the roof. The firelight caught his features, relaxed and unaware of anyone's eyes upon him. There was a grace about the way he moved quite out of proportion to the simple action, as if he were performing an important ceremony. He's forgotten his act, thought Naomi, but perhaps the magic is real, after all. She realised she was looking at him again, and once again she turned away.

Thomas moved away, and a wave of steaming air caressed her, slightly stinging her skin on the side nearest the fire. She wriggled her toes. It was almost too hot, only she had thought that nothing could ever be too hot again, after that night on the hill. It couldn't be too hot. Oh yes it can, thought Naomi practically. It'll be too hot for you before it's too hot for him, and if you start feeling dizzy you'll have to move.

'That's enough,' she said. 'For me, anyway.'

'All right,' said Thomas. 'It is quite hot.'

'I'll have to go out in a minute.'

'And jump in the river?'

'Don't. Not if I think about it first.'

'In this light,' remarked Thomas. 'You look as if you're on fire. All red and red.'

'What? Like a boiled lobster?'

'No, much more dramatic than that. Sort of fire-coloured, but quite pale at the same time.'

'How interesting for you,' said Naomi, at her most polite, and sat up.

'I didn't mean to make you move.'

'Very well,' she said, lying down again and shutting her eyes.

'Have I annoyed you?' asked Thomas.

'Why should you have done that?'

'I'm not sure,' replied Thomas, and went on slowly, 'I'm not sure how well I know you. Three days isn't very long, but the journey was long, or seemed to be. We're strangers, yet perhaps we know each other well.'

'Or we know each other now. For this journey. There's an intimacy in that which may not apply anywhere else. It doesn't need to.'

'As a travelling companion I couldn't wish for better,' answered Thomas readily. 'I want you to know that. It doesn't mean I expect anything more. Is that what you mean?'

'I suppose so. As a travelling companion I would be loyal to you, and expect the same. But only on this journey.'

'I doubt if we shall ever be travelling companions again,' said Thomas. 'And I think I shall be sorry.'

'One is always sorry, if a good thing ends.'

'I didn't think of this journey as good. It's painful for me, and it was hard to make it.'

'And I too have reason to look forward to the ending. Does that mean that this may not be good?'

Thomas lay on his front, his arm dangling over the edge of the bench, and closed his eyes. It was a relief to hear some of her real thoughts at last, but it was a little frightening too. He was very hot. He could feel sweat trickling off his back down his sides. It would be easier to withdraw, and soon he'd have to go out into the cold anyway. It was different in here. He had thought her aloof, very self-contained and tough. But then there was the music, which suggested something different. How she lived her life he had no idea. In a way it would be easier not to know. It wasn't what his journey was about, and he must concentrate on that. Up to now it had been very cold, and lonely. In here it was hot, and the temptation was not to be lonely.

'No,' he said eventually. 'Perhaps it is good. It's not the object of the journey, but it helps, I suppose. I find you easy to be with, though I'm not sure I would if I knew you better.'

'I find you easy to be with, for a man.'

'Meaning?'

'Don't sound defensive. I only mean that expectations can become more complicated. I suppose that makes me wary, but perhaps I needn't be. I wouldn't be, if you were a woman.'

Thomas wiped the sweat off his nose. If this conversation went on, he would find himself speaking to her as if she were a friend. It might be safer not, but it would be more desolate. 'I don't know whether you need or not,' he answered eventually. 'You're speaking as a woman who falls in love with men, I think. There's always a tension about being with a person you might fall in love with. I've felt it just as much as you. Only I don't fall in love with women, so I suppose you won't feel that tension coming from me.'

Naomi stared at the ceiling. She thought of Thomas standing in front of the stove, slight and vulnerable, his skin tingled with firelight.

Quite deliberately, she filed it away in her mind as a moment of beauty, something worth remembering. Then she said casually, 'I wouldn't know. You seem to have thought it out more than I have. It's true that the people I fall in love with are most often men, but I don't see why that should make me a more complicated companion now.'

'Nor do I. As I say, I don't know you. I think, though, that the reason I've found you easy is because you like yourself.'

'How do you work that out?' she asked, intrigued, turning her head so she could see him.

He looked up and met her eyes, grinning. 'I knew as soon as I saw your clothes.'

Naomi chuckled. 'I'm glad you noticed.'

'But quite apart from that,' Thomas was suddenly serious again. 'You said it's easier if there's no expectation of falling in love.'

'Did I say that?'

'About two minutes ago. I'm sure you're right.'

'I'm not, even if I did say that.'

'Less exciting perhaps,' said Thomas, 'but easier. It's only people who don't like themselves who find the opposite, don't you think?'

'Explain,' demanded Naomi.

'They need to have people falling in love with them. For proof, I suppose. If they don't get a passionate response they can turn quite nasty.'

'I'm not sure I know these people. I've nothing against passion when it's around. But it usually isn't, and I've nothing against that either.'

'That's what I mean.'

'Is it? I'm not sure I know what you mean.' Naomi sat up slowly. 'I'll have to go out. It's too hot.'

'Are you going to jump in the river?'

'Shut up,' said Naomi crossly, and left the hut.

Thomas sat up and checked the fire again. He could hear rain still drumming on the roof, and the wind beating on the walls. They had only just got off the hill in time. He shivered. There was a loud splash outside. Typical, he thought, and smiled crookedly. She didn't even scream. He got up and followed her out into the dark.

Naomi returned before he did, and stood dripping in front of the stove. She opened the fire door and stared into the flames, where

Thomas had put on fresh logs. Then she shut it again, and sat down crosslegged on her bench, looking thoughtfully into the shadows. Drops of water rolled down her and dried in the heat. She wasn't even cold, just awake. Outside it was all water, the river full with floodwater, and the rain dissolving into it in the darkness. The air in her lungs felt cold and clear, welcome as the touch of water. If one were never cold, thought Naomi, it would be a very sensual world. To lie on wet grass, dripping from the river, and let the rain fall all over me — it would be wonderful to live like that, if only I could stay hot enough.

The door opened, letting in a blast of chill air, and Thomas came in. 'That's better,' he said, brushing water out of his hair.

Naomi watched him lie down again.

'This matter of the journey,' said Thomas, lying on his back with his eyes closed.

'Yes?'

'You're a traveller. You speak about it as one who knows. There must have been many journeys in your life.'

'Nothing else.'

'I was thinking about what you said: that what belongs to one journey can't be taken out of it. If you leave something behind, you can't take it with you, and you can't return to it either, because neither you nor it will be the same, not after a journey. Isn't that so?'

'That is definitely so.'

'You've been away from the island a long time.'

'Yes.'

'So you knew that you were different, and that the island would also be different.'

'Yes. And I knew when I came with you that that would make us all different again.'

'I've been travelling too,' said Thomas. 'For seven years. But I never saw it like that. It's all been clouded by the pain of partings, which are sometimes unbearable.'

'No. If they were unbearable, you wouldn't be here now, in your right mind.'

'You think I'm in my right mind?' He sounded amused.

'Why, don't you?'

'At the moment. It may not always have been so.'

'People change. I'm not sure that's a very useful way of measuring it.'

There was a pause. A log cracked in the stove, and Naomi jumped. Thomas took no notice, and presently he spoke again. 'I suppose you have your music, and that keeps you from feeling lonely.'

'You must be joking.'

Thomas opened his eyes and looked at her. 'I'm sorry,' he said, startled. 'I'm wrong, then?'

'Since you ask so many questions, I'll try to make it clear to you,' said Naomi coldly. 'I am in my right mind, and I have my music, and so I choose to make journeys. If I have a companion, I'm glad of it, because I'm human too. But to go the way I want to go, I must usually go alone. And so must you, if you're a traveller. I know as well as you do that the end of anything is pain as well as pleasure. I knew from the moment I decided to come that this journey would change everything for me, as it will for you. How could it not? If you should come to matter to me, it will bring me happiness and it will cause pain. That's true of everyone I ever loved, and it must be true of everyone you have ever loved as well. How could it not be? Now do you begin to understand?'

'I don't know. I know that it would be easier not to know you too well, but I'd be sorry now if I didn't.'

'Why?' demanded Naomi.

'I'd know I'd have missed something important. I like you. When you know you must always move on, do you try not to love people too much?'

'No. I couldn't live like that. But I don't love anyone casually. I remember the moments which are important, and I hope I don't try to turn them into something else. Time is only short if you want to use a person. Otherwise there is the present, which is all the time in the world. Isn't it?'

'I don't know. Can I ask a question?'

'You've asked me dozens!'

'Well, this one is embarrassing. Let me explain. I travelled until I came to a place where I felt at home. But I didn't stop there because of that. It would in itself have been quite enough reason to move on. I stopped because I loved someone there, and I didn't want to leave even when I had to. Not only as a friend, I mean, but as a lover. I changed my life because of him. But from what you say, you wouldn't do that. You'd see it as a compromise, a false direction. And you don't love anyone casually. So I wanted to ask, does that mean you're celibate?'

'What?' exclaimed Naomi, astonished. 'No! But certainly,' she added more mildly, 'there are times when I might as well be.'

'You don't mind?'

'Oh yes, I mind. Sometimes I consider myself, and think what a terrible waste it is,' said Naomi cheerfully. 'But I'd rather be myself, and have my music, and choose my own journeys. Speaking of which, how far are you hoping to travel tomorrow?'

'To the end of this valley. About twenty miles, I suppose.' Naomi groaned. 'But it's all flat. We just have to follow the river. Then the track meets a road, the main road from north to south. There's the plain to cross, east of the sea, then we reach the mountains of the empty lands. We should get there the third day from now.'

'I know that road, and I know the plain you're speaking of. Near where it meets the sea there are the ruins of a city. Am I right?'

'You are. That's why the road keeps near the coast, I suppose, to avoid them. But you've never been in this valley before?'

'I'll tell you that in daylight. But, Thomas . . .'

'What?'

'I'm not planning to get up early. Not at all early. I don't want to be woken. Is that clear?'

'Very clear. How long are you capable of sleeping?'

'You'll find out,' said Naomi, standing up. 'I'm going out once more, and then I'm going to bed.'

'So am I,' said Thomas.

*

Sleep that night was warm and comforting, being able to let go at last. Sleep on the hills had been a painful necessity, a need to be fought for and held on to grimly; an uneasy hovering between levels of consciousness, between the longing to sink into sleep and the demands of cold and cramp and danger. Her dreams had been troubled, half waking, too full of the world outside her, and the world within being held away, which in the small hours of the night was almost unbearable. I need to dream, thought Naomi, lying sprawled face down, her face buried in clean linen. At the moment, nothing in the world seemed more important.

The place itself was like a dream, or perhaps only a fantasy come true. It was only a small inn, serving plain food and offering a room for them to sleep in, with beds. Proper clean soft beds. It felt like a miracle. And the sauna had been something extra, unexpected in such an isolated place as this. To be clean and warm and comfortable, and allowed to dream. Naomi stretched herself right out until her hands and feet met cold air. She tucked the quilt more firmly round her, and slept.

The mountains of the empty lands greeted her, silent and desolate. She stood on a lifeless summit, and looked down into a crater, lost in blue shadow. The light had no warmth in it: cold and lunar, the shadows frozen, unmoving. She knew this place too well, but could not place it. A landscape in cold light, and the shadow crossing it, until every night more empty land sank into oblivion. Then she recognised it, and her terror grew. This was not her earth, and with its waning she too would be lost. There were white mountain ridges stretching behind her, and when she looked again they were gone, and there was only empty space, and the shadow obliterating the white land. A shadow reaching to her very feet, swallowing up the land into endless night. She would have stepped back, but there was only the round valley; the way down was impassable. The shadow touched the edges of the valley, and she screamed.

She had not screamed. She was in bed, in an inn, and she had been asleep. Thomas was here, sleeping undisturbed in the same room. Her fiddle was quite safe, on the chair. Her heart was still thumping, although there was nothing in the world to be afraid of. Naomi stared into the darkness for a while longer, then turned over, and closed her eyes again.

Fifth Day

'So you'll be on your way to the fair?'
Naomi looked at the woman in surprise. 'What fair?'

She received a look that could have been suspicious. The woman set down the tray on which she brought them food, and said questioningly, 'Surely you must know of it? Whatever road you came by, folk will have been on their way. And you carrying a fiddle with you. Don't tell me you didn't know.'

'No,' answered Naomi steadily. 'I didn't. We came by a little-used way from the other side of the country, and just walked down the valley this morning. It's early in the year for a fair, surely?'

'For the cloth,' replied the woman slowly. 'They sell the weaving after the winter. It's not such a great event to an outsider, but whichever of these valleys you came down by, you must have heard of it, on any road. I never met a musician who would avoid a fair.' Her eyes rested on Naomi's pack as if she suspected something far more sinister within than a fiddle.

'I'll not avoid it now I know, certainly. Where is it?'

'At the end of this road, surely, where the two valleys meet. You're heading straight for it. You must have come that way to be in this valley at all. There's no other road.'

Naomi didn't answer that. 'You don't go yourself then?'

'My sister has gone from this household. But you won't find any folk in this village today. There'll be plenty of entertainment there tonight. Here's your friend.'

Thomas appeared at the door, his shoulders damp from the drizzle outside. 'Thanks,' he said, his eyes on the tray of food. 'That's very welcome.'

As soon as the woman had left them, Naomi turned to him. 'There's a fair at the end of the valley,' she said. 'Did you know of it?'

He looked puzzled, then remembered. 'For the weaving?' he said. 'Yes, it would be about now. Too far from my country, so I've never been, but I've heard of it. It's happening now?'

'Yes. She couldn't understand how I didn't know, so I stopped asking questions. Thomas, how far is it?'

He shrugged. 'Eight miles. Maybe more.'

Naomi sighed. 'I'm stiff all over. But so be it.'

'You want to get there? Today? We've come further than that already, and it's getting late.'

'Don't say it.'

'What?'

'I could have got up earlier. But I could do with something, Thomas. And you — your trade isn't so different from mine. Don't you want to go too?'

He shrugged, and stirred his soup. 'Yes. No. I could easily be distracted. I suppose I'd avoid it if I were alone.'

'And I would not. It's in such places I should be, not alone on a mountain top with only the birds to hear me.'

'I'm not a bird.'

'You think you're all the audience I need? You'd have to be more than one man for that.'

'I heard you playing this morning, and I never asked you to hurry, because I wanted to hear. I'm probably as good an audience as you'll get, although there's only one of me.'

Naomi leaned back, cradling her soup bowl. 'That could be true,' she admitted. 'I didn't even know you were listening. Why does it matter to you?'

Thomas shrugged again. 'Unworthy reasons, I suppose. It's my journey. I've a reason for wanting you and something to give you. Meanwhile, I suppose I don't want to share. Though it's not easy to admit to it.'

'You're more honest than you lead me to believe,' said Naomi, smiling at him. 'I like that in you. But the fact is, I'm not yours, not even for one journey. I've other business, which won't harm your plans. So I'll go to the fair, but I'll keep my contract with you, as I promised.'

'I've no right to ask more. In which case, we should push on. Have you eaten?'

'Nearly.'

'I'll give her something for it. No,' said Thomas, as Naomi was about to speak. 'I will. It's my journey, and all the currency you have is music, which I don't want to take the time for. Do you mind?'

'No. That's fair. I'll come in a minute.'

The woman who had given them the meal was right. As they went further it became obvious that they were on their way to an event. There were others on the road: people leading ponies, people driving carts, people with packs on their backs, and people with nothing to carry, dressed in their holiday clothes in spite of the persistent drizzle that hid the hills on both sides of the valley. The valley itself was opening out, and the river flowing alongside the road was growing gradually wider, meandering through lush meadows. There were many more settlements here, both hamlets and solitary farms, and only thin stretches of woodland between each cultivated clearing. The road was wide and deeply rutted, so that passers-by had trodden down the verges in an attempt to keep out of the dirt. Thomas and Naomi picked their way after them, occasionally overtaking slow processions of laden beasts and people.

At last the road diverged from the river, cutting across the foothills to the west. Naomi was really tired now. Her boots felt damp and tight, but she ignored her aching legs and led the way. Thomas trudged behind her, apparently inexhaustible.

There was another river below, with a humped bridge over it, and a small market town beyond. The field above the river was a mass of colour, a jumble of tents and animals and people. The noise that rose from it was like a hive of bees about to swarm in summer. Through the hum of people there were faint strains of music. Naomi held on to the straps of her pack to steady it, and began to run. Thomas stood and watched her go, looking a little bewildered. Then he walked slowly down to the bridge, and was caught up in a crowd of people going the same way. He hesitated at the bridge, as if debating whether to go on, but there were more people pushing from behind. He allowed himself to be swept along with the crowd, and the fair engulfed him.

*

He heard Naomi again before he saw her. It was already growing dark, and the place was lit with fires and torches. With the darkness the atmosphere changed, for no serious business could be done without daylight by which to see that everything was done fairly. The merchants' stalls were empty, and the seed sellers and drovers were gone. Instead, other tents and stalls had come to life, advertising gambling or fortune telling or various marvels within. There was music everywhere, mostly indifferent, all adding up to a dramatic confusion of sound, with a steady beat underneath coming from the centre of a crowd that had gathered round a huge fire on the far side of the field. The people who thronged the muddy alleyways between the tents were on holiday now. As Thomas wandered through the fair, children shoved past him and ran away, laughing, and couples drifted away towards the darker perimeter. Thomas ignored them all, only once stepping into the shadows to avoid a group of drunken men. He had left his pack in a safe place, and only carried a red cloth bag with a gold pentacle embroidered on it.

As he drew nearer to the fire the crowd got thicker. Thomas slipped through it like a shadow, and few were even aware of his passing. He could hear the music now, not just the drum, but pipes and stringed instruments as well. And a fiddle. Thomas emerged at the front of the crowd, ducking under a fat man's elbow, and blinked in the sudden light.

He looked round, then without hesitation detached himself from the audience and went to sit right at the feet of the band, crosslegged on the ground with his bag beside him. From this vantage point he could watch the musicians without seeming to do so, although it was hardly the best place to hear the music. Thomas had other objects in view.

He didn't think Naomi had seen him. He wondered if she had known any of these people before. She seemed quite at home now. Earlier in the day he had realised that she was more tired than she was going to admit, and had slackened his pace accordingly. She hadn't appeared to notice. But there was not a trace of weariness about her now. Whereas he had spent the last two hours eating a large meal and drinking more beer than he usually did, he was fairly certain she had been playing from the moment she got here. This wasn't the sort of music she played when she was alone. This was fast and exciting, sets of reels and jigs slipping into one another, music for crowds and for dancing. People were dancing; a space had been cleared on the other side of the fire. The ground was slippery with mud, not all the dancers sober, but the pace was wild, and growing wilder. Someone nudged him, and he jumped. It was the flute player, handing him down a leather flask that was being passed around the band. So he was accepted. Thomas took it with a word of thanks, and raised it to his lips. It wasn't wine, it was potato brandy that caught his throat like liquid fire.

Thomas choked, passed the flask back again, and took a bottle of water from his bag. There was a break in the music, and shouts for more. The dancers dispersed, and the crowd surged forward. Bottles were handed across to the band and passed around. He saw Naomi shake her head, and sit down to retune her fiddle.

There were more players now, another fiddle player among them. The flute player stepped down and disappeared into the crowd. The musicians consulted together, then took their places again. The crowd moved back a little, leaving a clear space between Thomas and the fire. He waited to hear the beat, then as they launched into another set he stood up, and opened his bag.

There was a murmur from the crowd when they saw him, and the circle formed round him, another part of the act. The drummer whistled at him from the stage, and the music swept on. Naomi glanced at him, and saw, not Thomas, but the juggler, dressed in yellow and gold, firelight catching at the braid on his jacket, coloured balls tossing in time to the music, yellow and red and orange. Naomi watched him as she began to play, as if he were giving her the beat, not the other way round. She hardly saw his hands move, but the balls were everywhere, all round him, like sparks of firelight round his head. The tune changed: the juggling moved to a different pattern, too fast to follow, with Thomas spinning round in the middle, turning apparently all ways at once, the crowd seeming to hold its breath. The set ended with a flourish, and he seemed to catch all the balls at once, so they vanished. There was a burst of clapping, and yells from the crowd. Thomas took off his hat and bowed to them.

The other fiddler called a tune across to Naomi. She nodded, and stepped forward. She found herself opposite a thin dark woman with heavy features which were faintly familiar to her. Something nagged at the edge of her memory, but she couldn't place it, and the woman was counting the time. Naomi concentrated on the music, and forgot.

When she glanced at Thomas again there was only fire: points of flame swirling with the music. She kept her attention, recovering herself, and glanced again. It was fire. Not coloured balls this time, but flaming torches, moving as fast as her music, making patterns in the air with the fiery tails they left behind them, circles and spirals, flames orbiting round him, the shadow of Thomas in the middle, a face caught in sudden flamelight, concentrated, then lost again in a whirl of light. The tune was growing faster, the whole band behind her, the drumbeat still with her, and the other fiddler who was good, but not as good as she, the music growing wilder and the flames leaping higher in front of her, following her lead, circling faster as she played them faster, and a blur of faces beyond, a crowd transfixed like the painted backcloth to a play.

The music stopped. There was sudden darkness. Then there was only Thomas, bowing again, taking another torch from his bag, a long thin taper, which he held over his head, exhibiting to the people. Naomi lowered her fiddle, and stared. Only the drummer went on playing, when he saw what was happening, a frantic beating, culminating in a roll of thunder. Thomas lit his taper at the fire, and held it aloft. His face shone with sweat. Naomi held her breath. Thomas threw his head back, opened his mouth wide, and the flames descended and vanished down his throat. There was a crash on the drums behind her. Then Thomas was swirling the taper round his head again, undoused, acknowledging the cheering of the crowd.

Naomi let out her breath and raised her fiddle. This time she chose her tune, without asking anybody, and played alone. She could sense the uncertainty in their response, but she didn't care. This wasn't dance music; this was a lament, remote and poignant, solitary high notes full of longing unfulfilled. Then there was a response, the same tune played back to her by a single mandolin, notes echoing hers like clear drops of water. Naomi looked, and it was the dark woman again, her fiddle exchanged for a mandolin. Again, there was that tug of recognition, but it was lost in the music. The rest were silent, except for the faint crackling of the fire. Naomi played on, and the other woman played with her, following her lead and never taking her eyes off her. When they stopped there was a moment's quiet, then applause like a hailstorm. Naomi put down her fiddle, and brushed her sleeve across her eyes. Silly to play that tune here. She was too caught up in it all. Must be hungry, she told herself. You've eaten nothing since midday. You can't cry here, that's for sure.

They were passing round the drink again, but she refused. She was about to turn away when someone spoke just next to her. 'Naomi?'

It was the woman who played the mandolin. So there was something. 'Do I know you?' asked Naomi uncertainly.

'I don't suppose you remember. But I'd like to talk to you, when you've finished playing.'

Naomi looked round. There was temporary confusion on the stage. The musicians and the crowd were mingling, and nothing else would happen for a while. 'I have finished for the moment. I need to eat. Do you want to come with me?'

'Is that all right? They do a good meal in that tent over there.'

They had hardly stepped out of the firelight when they were overtaken. 'Naomi?' said Thomas. 'Are you going?'

To his astonishment she turned round and hugged him. 'Thomas,' she said. 'You're an artist. Not a fool — a magician. Would you like some supper?'

'You too,' said Thomas, smiling in the darkness. 'Not a fiddler, a magician.'

'Or a fool. I said, have you eaten?'

'Twice. But I'll come with you, if it's not private.'

'No. At least,' Naomi turned to her new companion. 'It's not private, is it?'

'Not to me.'

'Then come. I don't think I've got any secrets.'

There were only a few people in the tent, which was dimly lit by two or three lanterns set out on the tables. There was still hot stew being served from a big pot on a brazier by the door. Naomi took a large helping, along with a hunk of bread.

'Can I have a drink of water?'

'We have beer.'

'No, water please.'

'We'll have beer,' said Thomas cheerfully. 'Won't you ... I don't know your name.'

'Helen. Thank you. I will.'

'I still don't have any money,' remarked Naomi.

'They're passing round the hats now. You mustn't go without claiming your share.'

'I'm not bothered. I get my expenses paid, this trip,' said Naomi, and the other woman looked at her questioningly, but said nothing. They sat down in a corner, and Thomas fetched one of the lanterns over to their table.

'So tell me,' began Naomi, with her mouth full. 'How do I know you?'

Helen hesitated, as if wondering where to begin. Then she said, 'I'm sure you don't remember. It was all of ten years ago, in your own country. There was a festival at harvest, and we were playing. But there were a lot of musicians, and you were much better than me. I wouldn't bother to remind you, only I have a message.'

'But of course you should remind me! You're from my own country? You don't sound like it.'

'No, I was travelling, as you are now. Who I am isn't important. I'm a travelling player too, but not as good as you.'

She paused. 'But that's not the point. There was a party at that festival. There were a group of us, talking. You spoke about the man who first taught you, in your own village. You gave his name, and the name of the village on the west coast. You weren't speaking to me directly, I knew that, but all the same, I remembered.'

Thomas sipped beer, apparently abstracted, but he was listening intently. He sensed Naomi stiffen, suddenly on her guard. 'And so?' He was beginning to know that casual tone.

'I remembered. The years went by, and eventually I found myself travelling in that country. I began to ask about this fiddle player that I had heard of, who knew many tunes that were virtually lost to the outside world. I was moving slowly northwards into a wild and rocky country, where the living was very poor, and the villages few and far between. But I carried on, and in the end I met someone who'd heard about him.'

She waited, but Naomi said nothing.

'Well, to cut a long story short, in the end I came to the village, and I found him. He made me welcome. I stayed a while, and learned a great deal of music from him.'

'He would do,' said Naomi softly. 'He would make anyone welcome.'

'I appreciated it. I knew my limitations, and so did he, but he was patient. Naturally, he also asked me how I came to hear of him.'

'Yes,' said Naomi shortly. 'And you said?'

'I told him. And he said, would I ever see you again? I said I doubted it. I didn't think that you knew I existed, and the world is wide, and all roads long. It would be a rare chance that brought us together. He said, but if it happened that such a chance should come, he wanted me to give you a message.'

Naomi had stopped eating, and was sitting very still, her head propped on her arm so her face was shielded from the light. Helen waited for her to respond, then carried on with her story. 'He said, tell her this if you ever find her again: "You did the right thing Naomi, and no one is hurt by what you chose".'

'Oh,' said Naomi, so softly that only Thomas heard her.

'I stayed over a month in that village,' offered Helen presently.

Naomi raised her head. 'Tell me about the village,' she said imperiously.

Helen searched for words. 'It wasn't my sort of country. I suppose it hasn't changed much. It lies at the head of an inlet, and at the entrance there are great grey cliffs, and all the time you can hear the Western Sea beating against the rocks, and the cry of the seabirds that nest outside the bay. The sea is everywhere. When you lick your own skin you taste the salt on it. All the trees are withered by it, and the smell of it gets into everything. The sea provides a living for the people, for there is little richness in the land. I can understand why anyone should leave such a place, for life must be hard, especially in winter.'

'I don't think so.' Naomi's voice was cold, and Helen looked up quickly, as if she had expected a different answer. 'And Gavin — the musician — tell me more about him.'

Helen spread her hands helplessly. 'I don't know what to tell that you don't know. You believe me, I hope. He's a big man, taller than you. His hair is grey and curly, and he has a beard. He belongs to his sister's household, which is at the top of the village, next to the field gate. And he goes fishing. What do you expect me to say?'

'I believe you,' said Naomi. 'You must excuse me if I'm not gracious. How old are you?'

'Me?' asked Helen, nonplussed. 'Thirty. Why?'

'It's what happens,' said Naomi. 'The people who bring us into this world are not the same as those who see us out of it. My roots are in a time and place which no one in my present can perceive, and my end is hidden in the future. I stand half way, if you like, and when you speak to me about my past, you speak to me of ghosts. My beginning matters — it's who I am, but it's only in my head now, like a dream. You're like a messenger out of a dream, and I don't know how to receive you.'

'I don't think I understand,' said Helen.

'I understand,' said Thomas simultaneously, and Naomi glanced at him. He looked down. He had never seen her look so vulnerable, and he thought she would rather he didn't see it now.

'You don't have to,' said Naomi. She sounded cold and arrogant, and the other woman stiffened with annoyance. 'Tell me more about the village.'

'I don't know what to tell.' Helen sounded almost sulky.

'Did you meet anyone else?'

Thomas watched them both, and was aware that he was afraid for Naomi. Helen was perhaps offended, not surprisingly. Thomas suspected that she had been hoping by her news to claim an equality that she was far from feeling. Naomi wouldn't have noticed that, because such feelings were quite foreign to her. But if Helen were hurt, she might use what she knew to hurt back. Naomi might be strong, but she had no defences, not in this situation. Thomas listened, and waited.

'I met a lot of people. One in particular I wanted to tell you about, if you're willing to hear.'

Helen turned her mug round and round on the table, and stared down into the dregs. 'I was down at the jetty one day. I forgot to tell you it was late summer. There were people working on a boat on the beach below me. I was sitting on the wall, enjoying the sun. It was usually pretty cold, with the wind off the sea, so the sun was something special.

'Someone came up behind me and said my name. I was quite startled. It was a boy.'

Naomi leaned her head on her hand again, so her face was hidden. 'Go on,' she said.

'A boy about ten years old. He asked me if I wanted to come out fishing. I was doubtful. I asked if he had a boat, and if he were allowed out on his own, because I didn't know anything about the sea.

'He said, "I know this sea. I've had a boat since I was five. My uncle made it for me, after they caught me trying to sail out of the bay in a fish box. I can take you. You'll be safe with me." '

'"You like boats, then?" I asked him. He said "yes," and showed me his. It was just a tiny rowing boat, but there was room for two of us. He was very efficient. He rowed me right out to the mouth of the bay. I was scared. I said, "Surely we shouldn't go out into the open sea?" "Tide's right," he said, "and the saithe are out there. You're safe with me." He took me out a little way beyond the entrance, right under the cliffs where the sea had hollowed out great arches and caves. It was a calm day, and the tide was high over the rocks. The cliffs were sheer, overhanging us so the sound of the waves echoed back from the rock above us. I couldn't help asking again if we were safe. He just grinned at me, and said, "You should see it in winter." I asked him about that. He started telling me about the ocean, and about the sailing directions to unknown countries away to the west. He knew all about those. He said there were sailing directions remembered in the village, accounts of islands and strange countries that were forgotten by all the rest of the world. He wouldn't tell me them though. He said that was secret. And he wouldn't show me the signs on the hills that marked out the fishing grounds, though he told me they were there. Then he showed me how to fish with a handline. "It's easy," he said. "You just jig it up and down. Like this. And when you feel a tug, a kind of movement, pull in hard. You try." So I tried, and when I caught a fish he watched me bring it in, very critically. Then he said, "Can you take it off the hook, or are you squeamish?" I got the message, and I took it off, though I didn't fancy it much. He watched me do it, then he suddenly said to me, "Tell me about the woman who told you where to come".'

Helen stopped for breath, and glanced at Naomi, but Naomi didn't look up. 'Go on,' said Thomas sharply.

'I tried to describe you,' said Helen to Naomi. 'I told him what you looked like, and about the festival where I met you. I told him you were one of the best musicians in the west. He just nodded, and went on fishing. Then he asked me what you'd said about the village. "Nothing," I said. "She was speaking about the fiddler here. That was all." "I see," he said, and soon after that he suggested that we go back again. I agreed to it. I was getting pretty cold. That was all.'

This time Naomi did speak. 'There was no message?' she said hoarsely, without looking up.

'No message. I don't think it would have occurred to him. He was very young.'

'What was he like?' asked Naomi, as though the words were dragged out of her.

'To look at, do you mean?' Receiving no answer, Helen went on, 'Quite striking, I suppose. Red hair, very thick. And greenish eyes. Hazel, perhaps.' She glanced at Naomi, but Naomi's eyes were hidden. 'Not very big, but sturdy, and very handy with his boat.'

'What else?'

Helen was at a loss. 'I don't know what else. I'm not used to children. What is there to say, really, about a boy? I liked him.'

'Did he tell you anything about himself?'

'He told me his name.'

'Colin,' said Naomi harshly. 'Was that his name?'

'That was his name.'

Naomi stood up abruptly. 'Thank you. Thank you for the message. Perhaps I'll see you again. Perhaps not. Farewell.' She looked down at Thomas without seeming to see him, turned and picked up her fiddle, and left the tent.

Helen looked after her uncertainly. Then she turned to Thomas, as if afraid of his reaction. 'Perhaps I shouldn't have told her just like that,' she said, 'but she seemed so sure of herself, it made me angry. And all this happened six years ago. I forgot to tell her that.'

'I think she can work that out for herself.'

'Yes. She'd hardly forget how old he was.'

'No.'

'It can't be easy for her really,' went on Helen, fidgeting nervously with her mug. 'But I suppose you know all about it.'

'I know nothing.'

'But you're her friend!'

'I don't know,' said Thomas.

'I'm sorry. I've got myself into deep water. I don't know what this is all about. I could have been more sympathetic. Not being in exile myself, I could go home whenever I liked. It must make a difference.'

'It does.'

'So you do know?'

'I know nothing about Naomi. But I can't think of anything a woman could do to deserve being exiled from her own child.'

'You knew he was her child then? So she does talk about it?'

'I told you, I know nothing except what I heard you say.'

'Anyway,' continued Helen. 'She wasn't exiled. It was her own choice.'

'You said she was in exile.'

'By choice. She went away before I could tell her, but I went to her own household. I met her sisters, and her brother. They talked to me. They assumed I was her friend, I suppose,' said Helen, with a touch of bitterness. 'It would have seemed rude to disillusion them. So they talked to me.'

'I see.'

'Yes,' said Helen, apparently oblivious to his tone. 'It's not as if they didn't care about her. The way they saw it, she was young at the time, and confused. She knew all the time it was the music that mattered most, but because she loved the fiddle player, she chose to have a child. Having made the other choice already, you understand. And then she realised that if you take one thing, you lose another. She would never have become what she is if she'd stayed there, but her child belonged to her mother's household, and to be a mother to him herself, that was where she would have to stay. In my village, I think they'd have made her abide by the consequences. If she was old enough to have him, she was old enough to stand by him, you'd think. But she didn't, and they supported her. Only they made her agree that if she went away, she must stay away, so the choice didn't become confused again. Everyone could see, they said, that it was impossible to keep your heart in two places at once. Everyone except Naomi. Because she loved him — they kept telling me that. That was why she stayed till he was weaned, though it made it more difficult. Then she left. Her agreement with them was not to go back. And she hasn't.'

Thomas was silent.

Helen began to wonder if she had said too much. 'But you can understand it,' she said in a more conciliatory tone. 'There was the music. She knew what it could offer her. She knew what she might become. You can understand why she chose to leave her child. He's sixteen now, I suppose. Much too late to decide anything different.'

'No!' said Thomas suddenly, so passionately that she recoiled. 'No, I can't understand! I can't understand that at all!'

'I don't follow,' said Helen quickly. 'I thought you supported her. I thought you believed she'd done right.'

Thomas thumped his hand down on the table so that all the crockery clattered. 'I tell you, I know nothing! I know nothing at all. Why throw her private life at me like this? Why should I agree with you? I don't! I don't want to hear about it at all!'

'What do you mean?' Helen was angry now too. 'You both treat me like dirt, and all I've done is answer your questions. I'd have thought I'd get some thanks! What's it to you, anyway? You don't have to make any choice. You're nobody's mother! What right have you to judge?'

Thomas leaned on the table, all the fight gone out of him. 'Please,' he said. 'Leave me alone. And her. What's a mother? Do you suppose no man ever loved a child?'

She stared at him, bewildered, but he didn't look at her or speak to her again. She watched him pick up his bag with the pentacle, and sling it over his shoulder. He kept his face turned away from her, not in anger, she suddenly realised, but because he was crying. She watched him in horror, not knowing how to react, as he walked away, ducking under the tent flap, out into the night.

Sixth Day

The cloth sellers began their trade early, less than an hour after dawn. It was a cold clear morning with a heavy dew, but it wasn't raining, so they could lay out their rolls of cloth in the open, spread on groundsheets. They were from villages in the hills. Some brought only the weaving from their own households, while others represented whole villages. The buyers strolled around the fair, examining wares, and having whispered discussions among themselves. They were mostly people from the south, and in exchange for cloth they brought corn, just at the hungry time of year, when the new crops were hardly sown in the north. At the bottom of the field their wagons were drawn up, the shafts empty, full of last year's wheat and barley from rich southern farmlands. The prices were high after the winter, and it was worth the long trek north.

The atmosphere was already brisk, though still a little subdued by the chill of the night. The fire of the evening before was a heap of smouldering ash, and the grass where the crowd had stood was churned to mud, slippery with skid marks where the dancing had been. The platform on which the musicians had played was revealed as the base of an old wagon, its paint peeling off. There was a steady trade in breakfast at the tent opposite, this morning's customers being sober business people wrapped up against the cold in thick jackets of undyed wool. There was no telling the revellers of the night before, though some had deep shadows under their eyes.

Thomas passed unremarked in the crowd; even those who had watched the juggler failed to give a second glance to the tired-looking countryman clad in grey. He looked sharply at each small group, then ignored them, walking slowly round the temporary alleys. He came once again to the food tent, lifted the flap, and looked inside. Then he let it drop again, and wandered on, down to the bottom of the field where the wagons were. There was nobody there but a couple of men whose job it was to guard the corn. They bade him good morning and he nodded to them, then walked on down to the river. The little town huddled close to the shore ahead. He began to walk towards the houses.

Just at the curve in the river he saw someone else walking up from the shore in the opposite direction, a solitary figure still wearing the colours of fire like a muted echo of last night. He nearly called out, but hurried on instead, so his track would cross hers just before they reached the houses.

Naomi didn't see him until they were almost facing each other. Then she halted. Thomas came up to her, and stopped a few feet away. A gust of wind off the river caught them, and in the town a couple of dogs barked, but they took no notice. Each stood quite still, unable to think any further, and waited for the other to say something.

Thomas realised she was trembling a little. She looked exhausted, and the brightness of her hair made her skin quite white in contrast. He had thought of her as youthful, though he knew she wasn't, but this morning she looked older, her face drawn and remote. She was waiting for him to do something, not because she didn't know what to do herself, but because she didn't care. He knew then that while he had been dreading emotion, he was quite unprepared for indifference.

Poor Thomas. The thought struck her quite unexpectedly. She had been looking for him because she must. His quest was a matter of indifference to her at the moment, but she had promised him. She would do what she was obliged to do, and keep her emotions out of it. She hadn't expected to be so nakedly confronted with his. He looked distraught, his face pale and strained, as though he had received some grievous hurt. She didn't understand that. It was her hurt, she'd thought, merely his inconvenience, and she had no intention of burdening him with it further. But he had clearly felt it: he looked as if he'd been through everything that she had suffered in the last six hours. But why? Her brain felt too tired to struggle with it. Thomas's feelings were nothing to do with her.

'Good morning,' said Naomi coldly.

'Are you all right?' He sounded anxious.

'Of course. I'm sorry I left you so abruptly last night, and that you had to look for me.'

It was like a slap in the face. Do we know each other no better than this, thought Thomas, bitterly hurt. To have struggled so hard to understand, and to have come back, and be given credit for nothing, is this what I deserve? He was too proud to say that, so he replied, 'Not at all. I hope you found somewhere to stay the night.'

Naomi shrugged.

'Are you ready to go on?' asked Thomas.

'It's your journey. I'm ready when you are.'

He stared at her helplessly, furious and upset. But he couldn't say so. If she was too proud, then so was he. 'Now?'

'Certainly. I have to get my pack though.'

'So do I. Can we meet by the bridge?'

'Very well.' She turned away from him, back towards the houses. So that's where she must have ended up. After how long? Thomas watched her go, frowning, then ran back to the fair.

*

It was a huge effort of will to set out again, to be civil to Thomas, to keep walking, although her whole body ached with weariness, and her legs were stiff after so much unaccustomed travelling. The road followed the river, a broader river than yesterday's, flowing down into a fertile plain that offered no difficulties to a walker, and no distractions either. Naomi plodded on, too tired to think.

Luckily Thomas was silent. They walked side by side, because the road was broad enough here for a wagon, each keeping to a verge, with brown puddles dividing them. The sound of the river slowly permeated her thoughts, offering a suggestion of something temporarily forgotten, a world where all was as it should be, moving yet unchanging. There was a pattern to things, the river implied, which she could not have altered. The road was the same; through all her exhaustion it demanded her attention, taking her out of the past and into an unknown future. They were coming out of the hill country now. It was warmer here, and lusher. The way was lined with hawthorn, emerald leaves unfurled already, and leafless hazel decked with catkins. Outside the town the banks were thick with daffodils. The sky had cleared to a delicate blue, and sunlight dappled the river as it flowed.

Her thoughts drifted, but less painfully now. Despair belonged to the night. Everything that was lost or damaged in her life had seemed intolerable in the slow hours before the dawn, but now there was warmth in the sun, and a pair of thrushes singing among the hawthorn. It was possible to live with what was done, and to go on, though there was an emptiness in her heart that was not curable, not in this world. But I knew that before, thought Naomi. Would I rather she had never told me? A radical thought struck her: I'm not sure that she was kind to me. I think that she was not. Naomi pushed her hair off her forehead, and considered that possibility. It was irrelevant, perhaps. She had been left with a picture in her mind, like a glimpse of the sun through fog. It hurt, because it showed her what she would never have in waking life, and what she had foregone. But I wouldn't be without it, she realised, even while it's still hurting, I know that. To say she was kind or not kind is meaningless. She has given me a gift beyond price, and I shall never forget it, not the smallest detail. I would have had her tell me more, tell me everything, even if it destroyed me. But she had no more words, I could see that, no imagination. But the value of a gift isn't determined by the worth of the giver. I deserved it, both the pain and the delight. I deserved something, out of all this time. Naomi felt the tears rising again, and wiped her nose fiercely on her sleeve. That was for the night, and privacy. She made herself look up, and take note of the place where she was.

There was another noise behind them, just audible in the distance, cartwheels grating on a rough road, and hooves clopping over stone. Naomi stopped. There was the creak of harness and the sound of voices, not so very far away. 'Thomas?'

He looked up, startled. Since she obviously didn't want to talk, he had allowed his own thoughts to fill his mind, and they were not pleasant. Now that he was suddenly bereft of cheerful company, he realised how important it had been to him. This was like walking in a nightmare, his feet weighted down by stickiness, knowing he dare not stop, or he would fail. It had meant more than he knew to have someone with him who was not involved in his private pain, but she had betrayed him, though he could hardly hold her responsible. She had flung him right back to the centre of everything he wished to forget, and she had not a single thought to spare for him, now that she had done it.

'What?' asked Thomas dully.

'Do you hear that cart?'

'What of it?'

'How far do we follow the road? Does it bring us to the great road south?'

'In less than three miles, I reckon.'

'I know that road. It crosses the plain, skirting the ruins of the city. Am I right?'

'Yes,' said Thomas, trying to attend. 'I assumed you'd be on familiar ground, now we're off the hills. It's the only road going from south to north, west of the mountains.'

'And we follow it. How far?'

Thomas shrugged. 'Twenty miles. More, maybe.'

The cart was in sight, coming round a bend in the road, following the curve of the river.

'I can't walk that far today,' said Naomi flatly. 'I must have walked a hundred miles in the time I'd usually walk thirty, and I've had no sleep. But I can still get myself there, if you'll let me speak to them.' She nodded towards the cart. It had a round canvas roof, like the carts the merchants had used to bring the corn, and was pulled by two enormous horses.

Thomas frowned. 'It's probably the best thing to do. You should have said if you were tired.'

'It would hardly have helped. Wait here, if you like.'

Thomas shook his head, and followed her back to the cart. Naomi waved, and the driver reined in his horses.

'Are you going far today?'

'As far as I can get.'

'Have you room for two?'

The man frowned. 'I'm not sure about that. I've a load in the back. But wait a minute . . . haven't I seen you before? You're the fiddler, aren't you, that was playing last night?'

'That's me.'

'Then you're welcome. You can give us a tune or two along the way. But you'll need to hop in the back, you and your friend, for there's two of us already, as you see.'

'Thanks, said Naomi. 'And I will play later. But first I'll sleep.'

'You'll be lucky. You'll be seasick more likely.'

She shook her head at him, laughing. 'Not me. Too tough. Thanks a lot.'

'Give us a shout when you're in. You can move the cloth over a bit. Make yourselves comfortable.'

It would have been hard to sleep in the back of the wagon if she hadn't been utterly exhausted. Naomi wriggled herself among the rolls of cloth until she was wedged securely, and fell almost immediately into an uneasy doze. It was such a relief to lie down. She hadn't realised how hard she had been struggling until she had to struggle no longer. The wagon creaked and jolted, its solid wheels grinding through the potholes. Sometimes it jarred against the rock beneath, and there was a harsh scraping of iron on stone that made her shiver. Occasionally low boughs brushed against the canvas above her, like giant fingernails drawn across cloth. There was a murmur of voices from in front, like the ceaseless buzzing of flies on a foggy day. Naomi realised her nerves were all to pieces. She tugged her jacket off and bunched it up for a pillow, pulling the sleeves tightly round her ears to shut everything out.

A white beach, a perfect curve of pure shell sand, whose end was lost in a grey blending of rock and water. Sea lapping at the shore, clear as air, green over white sand, blue over the depths beyond. A low mist hanging, muting the sun and the sound of the sea, still white air, and a trail of seaweed at the far end of the shore. Walking through water, paddling slowly at the sea's edge, stirring up a trail of soft water, bare feet sinking into yielding sand. A child in a blue shirt and ragged salt-stained trousers trailing through sea that swished round its ankles and obliterated its faint tracks in the sand. A thin freckled child with bright red hair, on an empty beach curving to an unknown end.

The wagon jolting, the strong sour smell of fresh wool against her nose, a shout and the sudden crack of a whip, the steady plodding of hooves through water. Running water under her through a thin partition of wood and cloth, water over stones, a sharp jerk, and the wagon tilting up, slithering, swaying back again, hooves clipping over stone.

Running water under her, the swell tilting her, creaking of oars in rowlocks, lap of water under the keel. Water rising and falling against rock, a sucking and the muffled crashing of the sea in unseen caves, swirling against hollowed cliffs, seals slithering off rocks, riding the waves watching, snorting like old men woken from their midday sleep. The boat breasting the wave, descending into the trough as if it would fall for ever, then the slow rise again. To know your boat like your own body, bare feet taut against damp boards, the feel of the sea through the oars, riding the swell and never missing, not for a moment. Because although you are tough you are small and skinny, with no strength against the sea, only a perfect balance, and a knowledge of the rhythm that you have made your own.

A harsh-voiced woman in a tent, gibbering mindlessly, mouthing platitudes which hang in the air when she has spoken them, turning into shining images, sacred unmentionable things which are the very source of all there is, without which the music could not exist. A tent with a brazier in the corner, lanterns on the tables, the place smelling of stew, shifting in and out of focus, and the dream hanging in the air, intangible, mocking at the people sitting in the dark, inside a tent where you cannot even hear the sea.

The cart still straining, as if there could never be any rest in the world again. Bereft of stillness so there can be no sleep, with a creeping cold that touches like a ghost, drawing cold fingers across your body, engulfing your feet so that the blood flows thinly through. If there were warmth and stillness, the dream might still be recaptured, if there were a dream.

Hills extending for ever, rising and falling like the long waves that gather in the open sea, vanishing into a horizon where the sun turns the mist so bright you cannot see. Riding the hills like the flocks of birds that gather on the ocean, letting the waves take you, the slow swell to the summit, and the long dip. To move without effort or weariness, having the measure of the land. Hills rising to mountains, you gliding faster, taking off so the ground is only an image down below, skimming the ridges as they rise to meet you, more and more of them, always rising towards a horizon that has no end. Time curving onwards, just touching the highest hills as it passes, never waiting, never turning. The child following behind, gliding expertly on steady feet, rising up and sliding down, always following, blue shirt flapping in the wind, red hair streaming. But there is no waiting now, and the end is in sight at last, the dark point on the horizon where the way no longer follows the curve of the land but breaks off into the night, and the child falling further behind, still perfectly balanced, but too slow. For the darkness rushes upwards, and the flying is too fast, rising too high, falling too far, and the earth growing fainter, further and further below. And the child, boy or girl, whoever it is, vanishing into the distance, left alone, but always confident in that vast land.

Creaking and cracking, and the smell of wool heavy inside her nose, gasping for breath, eyes streaming. Grasping at the shreds of a dissolving landscape, finding only rigid shapes, solidness, roughness of a jacket against her cheek, hardness against her aching back, and the endless creeping cold, Voices, sharp and high, and a sudden standstill. Silence flooding over her, and broken again, so the dream was shattered into fragments. Voices saying things she could understand, but didn't want to comprehend.

'She's asleep then, your friend?'

'Seems like it.'

'I was hoping she might give us a tune. Anyway, there's hot soup, if you want it. In the haybox there. Do you want to wake her?'

'I'll keep it for her.'

There was a movement beside her, a slight jolting, and a thump.

'That's it. Here you are.'

'Cheers.'

'Come far, have you?'

'Never stop. And you?'

'Across the plain. Should be home tomorrow. Travel together, do you?'

'Only this journey.'

'Now I know you!' exclaimed a third voice. 'You're the juggler, aren't you? The fire-eater?'

'So you are. I'd never have known you. Now that was something, that was.'

'Thank you.'

'Take you long to learn?'

'No. Just born that way.'

General laughter. Naomi pulled the jacket over her head and tried to breathe through her mouth. If she couldn't bear the wool, she'd have to wake up. She'd bear the wool.

This time it was only the darkness, unconsciousness wrapping her tenderly so that when she woke again it was to daylight, like resurfacing from the sea on a summer's day.

'This wool stinks,' said Naomi clearly. She sat up abruptly, and sneezed.

'You've been asleep for hours,' said Thomas. 'Do you want some soup?'

'In the haybox,' said Naomi vaguely. There was a blanket over her which hadn't been there before. She struggled out of its folds.

'So you were awake then?'

'No.' Naomi sneezed again, and shivered.

'Here,' said Thomas, handing her a bowl. 'It's still quite hot.' The cart lurched. Naomi grabbed the bowl, and licked spilt soup off her fingers.

'Where are we?'

'In the forest,' said Thomas. 'Look.'

Naomi slithered over the rolls of cloth and sat beside him on the tailboard, bracing herself against the wooden frame that held up the canvas. It was bright and sunny outside. They were on a bigger road than before. The trees had been cut back about twenty yards on each side of the road, and the space between was colonised by catkinned thickets of willow and hazel, and gorse just coming into bloom. Where the road dipped into hollows it had spread itself right into the scrub, as passing carts and travellers had tried to avoid the soft mud in the middle. Beyond, the trees grew closer together, forming a solid curtain tinged with green. Whatever lay in the depths was silent, and invisible.

'I know this road,' said Naomi. 'Are we anywhere near the ferry?'

'Not far off. We've passed some of the ruins, right up close to the road.' He watched her closely as he spoke, trying to gauge her reaction.

'Then I know exactly where we are. It's a desolate place to walk alone, I can tell you, especially in winter.'

'Do you think I don't know? Thomas didn't intend her to see what it meant to him, so he remarked casually, 'The land's good, if anyone were to make clearings.'

'They never would, not so close to the ruins. No one would dare.'

He wasn't sure of her. Anyone in this land might say the same, and all they might mean was that they had heard the stories that everyone knew: ancient legends and taboos that meant nothing now, except a cold feeling down the spine when such things were mentioned. He had never yet met anyone who had made the connections that he found so obvious. He didn't try to tell her what the last hour had been like for him, but merely said, 'Would you dare?'

'Me?' said Naomi, swallowing soup. 'I'm no woodcutter. I've come to terms with the forest the way it is.'

'From the outside,' corrected Thomas. 'You wouldn't choose to go in amongst those trees. Do you think the ghosts of that time rest so easily?'

'Ghosts? I don't know. People speak about the ruins, and cross their fingers, and stay at home after dark. But you're talking about people, Thomas, who lived their lives like we do. There wasn't one of them who had nothing to love, or no memories to leave behind. Where they have left fragments of their world it's not all bad. You know that.'

'I hope not. Those fragments are all that we are.'

'No, that's not right. We are ourselves.'

'You speak as if that were something new. What we are is all that's left. You can call it good or bad, if you like. It doesn't mean you don't belong to them, or have nothing to do with them. We're just the remnant that happened to survive. Nothing new, or better.'

'Of course it's new. It's new with every generation!'

'I don't think so. Bless you! Have you caught a cold?'

'No,' said Naomi, sneezing again. 'I think it's the wool, this time. I had my nose right down in it. And I'm cold.'

'Here. This might make you feel better.'

He delved in his pack and produced a small wooden box, roughly carved. He removed the lid and offered it to Naomi.

'What's that?'

'To cheer you up. A box of dreams.'

'A box of dried mushrooms,' said Naomi, looking. 'I have enough dreams already, thank you.'

'You're very abstemious, aren't you?'

'No. But I don't need that, thanks all the same. Did you pick them last summer?'

'I bought these at the fair, but I do pick them in season. One may have enough dreams, but too often they're the wrong sort. Why suffer, if you can pick comfort off the hillsides?'

'It's a nice box,' said Naomi, instead of answering. 'Did you carve it?'

He hesitated, and handed it to her. It was carved of oak, with an oak leaf and an acorn in relief on the lid. It wasn't done very expertly, but harmoniously, as though the design had been something more than an inexperienced hand could accomplish. Naomi turned it over, and saw the carver's mark, a circle with two lines joining inside it, like two rivers meeting in a valley. 'No,' said Thomas, watching her examination. 'I was given it.'

Naomi handed it back. 'It deserves something more than magic mushrooms,' she said lightly.

'Such as?'

She shrugged. 'Nothing perhaps. Then you could produce white rabbits out of it.'

Thomas opened the box, then apparently changed his mind, and shut it again. The cart lurched through a sudden pothole, and he was flung against Naomi.

'Sorry,' he said, and moved so that for a moment he had his back to her. 'My nephew made it.' She just caught the words. 'Jonathan.'

'He's talented, then.'

Thomas sat down again on the tailboard, holding on to the wooden frame, and swaying in rhythm with the wagon. He didn't say anything for a while, then changed the subject abruptly. 'I was thinking while you were asleep. I'm sorry about last night. I did nothing to improve matters.'

She stared at him in surprise. 'You? But it was nothing to do with you. You don't have to be sorry.'

'But I am. I was no friend to you, doing nothing.'

'If you'd done anything at all, I'd have been furious,' said Naomi roundly. 'You can't rescue me from my life, and I don't want to deal with you feeling guilty about it now.'

'There's no question of guilt. I don't like to see my friends treated unfairly. And you were. That's all. I might have said something.'

'You owe me nothing. I'd prefer not to talk about it.'

'About your own life, never. I respect your privacy, just as you respect mine. That's why I might have stopped it, as soon as I realised what was happening. I had no more right to hear than she to speak, if I counted myself your friend.'

'Do you count yourself that?' asked Naomi, puzzled.

'I can choose to, I suppose. Or do you think I should ask your permission?'

'Of course not. Who am I, to give you permission about anything you are? So having listened, you think you have the advantage of me?'

'I shall make it equal, but not easily, if you'll give me time.'

'Any amount. I have plenty. So,' said Naomi, considering, 'you reckon she had no right?'

'Don't you?'

'I'm confused. I wondered if she'd behaved well towards me, afterwards.'

'You can't mean it!'

She turned quickly to face him. 'You don't agree?'

'Oh, I agree. I'm just overcome by your perception.'

'Meaning?'

'It didn't occur to you, I suppose,' said Thomas, choosing his words carefully, 'that she was eaten up by envy, and behaved accordingly?'

'Envy?' Naomi narrowed her eyes, thinking it out. 'Of me, do you mean? Is that why . . .? But why?'

He glanced at her sharply, and realised she was quite genuine. 'Yes,' he said kindly. 'I do mean of you. I wouldn't worry about it.'

'There's the river,' said Naomi suddenly. 'We must be nearly at the ferry.'

The river was wide and smooth, with sandy banks blending into marshland. The road ran parallel on a rough embankment which had subsided in places, making the cart tip alarmingly. There was no cleared land here; tangled bushes grew so close to the track that they scratched the cartwheels as they passed. Thomas sniffed. 'You can tell we're near the sea. Smell the salt?'

'I wish I could.'

Presently the cart halted. There was a shout from the driver. 'Hey there! Ferry!', followed by an answering call, presumably from the far side of the river.

'Shall we get down?'

There was almost nothing in the place, only the road running down to a jetty, and another jetty opposite, with a low building beside it. A rowing boat was pulled up on the shore, and its twin lay on the shore opposite. They could see a couple of figures moving on the other shore, and presently part of the jetty seemed to detach itself and reform in the shape of a raft, poled by two people, pulling hard upstream to counteract the current.

'We could leave the carters here, and use the rowing boats,' suggested Thomas. 'This is going to take some time.'

'How much further do we follow the road?'

'Six, seven miles, maybe.'

'I'd rather stay put. And I offered them some music.'

As it happened, the carters were glad of their help. The horses had to be led out of the shafts, and the wagon manoeuvred on to the ferry. It was a tricky job, for the raft was not much larger than the base of the cart, and even with the drag on the wheels there were moments when the whole thing threatened to spin out of control, sending them all flying into the river as it went. When at last the wagon was embarked, the ferry looked alarmingly low in the water.

'You've a heavy load there.'

'And a valuable one.'

'Then keep your fingers crossed.'

The carter shrugged. Naomi caught sight of the second carter, who had her back to them. She had taken a coin out of her pocket, and stood facing the river. Naomi didn't hear what she said, but she saw the coin spin out over the water, catching the sunlight as it went, to be swallowed up by the hungry current.

'Right then, better get going while we've got the light.'

They dumped the harness on board.

'Ready then?'

It took four of them, with long poles, to keep the top-heavy craft steady. Luckily there was no wind, but as soon as they had left the shore, the current tugged at them, sending the whole raft spinning. There was a sudden jerk. The rope to the far side surfaced and tautened, waterdrops flying out of it as it took the strain. The raft swung back again. They faced forward, taking the weight on their poles. The cart creaked, and they kept an anxious watch on the wedges holding it in place. The ferryman shouted orders, while they began to pole across. There was a splashing in the river behind them, as the two carters urged the reluctant horses into the water. Naomi saw the horses hesitate, then pick their way down. Then they launched forward, swimming steadily, their riders wet to the thighs.

The poling was heavy work. They headed steadily into the current, so the boat kept on a parallel course. Just as it seemed impossible to strain against the river any longer, there was a grating noise as they touched the further jetty. The ferryman's mate leapt ashore, hauling in the last of the rope.

By the time they had hauled the cart on to the jetty, and harnessed the horses again, the sun was sinking fast.

'Just in time,' said the carter, looking at the sky. 'Thanks for the help. We'd been twice as long, without.'

'Quite a load that,' remarked the ferryman. 'Should've taken the cart separate, if I'd known. Then you'd have to wait till tomorrow, for it wouldn't have been done by dark.'

'Tough crew,' said the other one. 'Just as well.' She winked at Naomi. 'Want a job?'

'No,' said Naomi. 'Never again. I'd have left you to it, only my fiddle was on board.'

'Here,' interrupted the carter. 'Let's settle up, and be off.' He turned to Naomi. 'Want to sit up front now, and give us a tune?'

They reached the next village just as the stars were pricking out.

The wagon was lantern lit, one on the shaft, one hanging from the roof, the lights swaying in time to the horses' steady feet. They came in with music, a slow halting march fit for the end of a long day, played by a solitary fiddle and the carter's tin whistle. The scene changed from dense hedgerows picked out in yellow light, the blank dark beyond, to lamplit windows, rough stone walls, and faces peering from behind doors and shutters to see where the music was coming from. They drew up in the inn yard. A door opened, spilling light out on to the cobbles. The tune came to an end. The horses whickered and shook their heads so that the harness jingled, impatient at the promise of a night's release. There was a short flurry of activity in the yard, a pattern of moving lanterns, doors opening and closing. Then silence, only the cart standing with empty shafts, and the new moon rising over an empty street.

Seventh Day

'This is the border of my country,' said Thomas. He flung out his arm to embrace yet more bare hills, announcing it as though all the islands of the west lay before her, where there is neither death nor winter, only eternal summer and the springs of immortality. She couldn't see what he saw, but she could understand. She moved to windward of a rotting sheep that was lying in a hollow just below the summit, and politely followed Thomas's eager gaze.

To Naomi, it just looked like more mountains, not so very different to the ones they had crossed before. When she had seen them towering above her that morning, and realised that their way led straight through them, her heart had momentarily quailed. She didn't say anything, but followed Thomas, and after the first couple of miles she found that she was used to it again. At least he had promised her a roof over her head tonight.

It was a little alarming, walking deliberately into the empty lands. She had seen the outline of these hills before, and heard them spoken of as a place apart, a country which had been cast out of time, cursed by an evil wrought in the distant past, dangerous and impenetrable.

She wasn't sure what she had expected. She had never troubled to think about what was fact and what was legend; such a distinction had never concerned her. There was no point worrying about it now, she decided. She could only keep her eyes open and her wits about her, and accept what came.

So far nothing had occurred at all. The only living creatures she had seen were the birds, to whom all roads were open, and sheep, which might or might not indicate the presence of people. In any case, she had to concentrate most of her energy on keeping up with Thomas. The return home seemed to have endowed him with renewed strength and fleetness, and his excitement was palpable.

'If we climb down to the beck, we can stop and eat where there's water.'

They sat down on a patch of bilberry plants, prickly but relatively dry, on a little outcrop just above the beck. There was fresh bread to eat, a different kind of cheese, and unlimited drink. One could almost imagine that the sun held some heat in it.

'It's just a question of how you choose to look at it,' said Naomi aloud.

'What?'

'Nothing. I was just trying to be cheerful company for you. In case you thought I complained too much.'

Thomas grinned, and blushed slightly.

'I thought so,' said Naomi. 'Well, you never stopped to ask what kind of companion I would be.'

'I think you're an excellent companion,' said Thomas at once, and was suddenly silent, the smile wiped from his face, as though struck by a thought too full of pain.

'I'm glad,' said Naomi, giving him a puzzled glance.

Thomas absentmindedly uprooted a tuft of moss, and began to pull it to pieces. 'I brought you for an honest purpose,' he said sombrely, his eyes on the ground. 'But to tell you the truth, I've become very glad of your company. It's too full of different feelings, coming home. You stand outside the situation, and that helps.'

'I'm glad,' repeated Naomi. 'As far as I can understand.'

'It won't affect the music, that I promise you.' Thomas began to replant the moss, pressing it down with his forefinger. 'But there are reasons why I find it hard to come back.'

'To your own home?' Naomi searched her mind for a possible reason. 'Did they ask you to remain in exile? I can understand your temptation, if it was that, but if there was a bargain, ought it not to be kept?'

'No,' said Thomas slowly, 'it's not that.'

'You chose to leave them, and yet you're afraid to return to them?' She wasn't being impertinent; she sensed that he wanted to tell her, and needed help to do it.

'Not of them,' said Thomas with an effort. 'Afraid of myself.'

'How?'

'Of my own mind.' Thomas pulled out the moss again, and began to dissect it, shredding the scraps and dropping them one by one on to the turf. 'It's not so much what I have to face, as that I may not be able to face it.'

'It seems to me that you've made a choice,' said Naomi thoughtfully, 'and that it was a brave one. Am I right?'

'I don't know.' Thomas shivered suddenly, and jumped up. 'It's too cold to stop,' he said briskly. 'Are you ready to go on?'

'Of course,' said Naomi at once, and got up.

'What are you laughing at?'

'Do you know what a chameleon is?'

'No.'

'It's a kind of dragon. Whenever it moves, it changes colour, like a rainbow, all the time.'

'Disconcerting.'

'Not at all. It isn't very big.' Naomi swung her pack on to her back, and waited for him to lead the way.

This time he didn't stride ahead, but fell into step beside her. They crossed the beck, and began to climb again.

'I'm always hearing about dragons,' said Thomas conversationally, 'usually in the next country but one. Don't you find that?'

'I've always heard that they live in the empty lands.'

'Yes, I've heard that one too. It's common enough — if you don't know the truth, you invent dragons. Very convenient.'

'People have to find explanations,' countered Naomi. 'They want to make sense of things. It's hard to make sense of the lands being empty, isn't it?'

'No,' said Thomas, frowning. 'Not hard at all. It means facing the past, and no one does that unless they have to. The difference between my people and yours is that mine have had to.'

'And you think we haven't?'

Thomas stopped and regarded her, and Naomi stood beside him, panting. It was hard work to climb and talk simultaneously, but Thomas didn't even look hot, only troubled. 'You chose to have a child once,' he said, quite unexpectedly. 'Were you afraid?'

'What? No. Afraid of what?'

'Precisely,' said Thomas drily.

'I don't understand.'

'There are no dragons here,' said Thomas. 'There are other things to fear. Danger isn't usually so dramatic. It's more often sordid. You don't know?'

'As long as you speak to me in riddles, I've no chance of knowing,' said Naomi tartly.

'There's no riddle. You have to face the past, that's all. Do you know what happened here?'

'I've heard stories, of course. That's all. What else could I know? The story I heard was that these lands were cursed by the power of sorcery. That in the past there were men who were so arrogant in the pursuit of power that they changed the very substance of life to poison. And so those who thought they would rule life were destroyed by it, and in their fall they brought the whole land down with them. So their curse has lain upon it through uncounted generations, until your people were able to return at last.'

Thomas was silent for a moment, apparently thinking this over. Then he shrugged. 'Well, it makes a very pretty story. That's what art does for you, I suppose.'

'Don't sneer at me! You asked me to tell you what I knew. If I'm wrong, then tell me the truth, if you know it.'

'The truth?' repeated Thomas, glancing at her sideways. 'You ask a lot, don't you? But I can tell you another story. Sit down.'

Naomi sat down beside him, barely containing her impatience. She didn't look at him, but gazed down at the green slopes opposite. But she was listening intently, he could tell. Thomas squatted beside her, and told his story, without taking his eyes from her averted face.

'Before the world changed,' began Thomas quietly, 'these lands were among the most beautiful on earth, and many people prospered here. But in the days of the old world, it was as you say. There were men in this country who pursued power, with no regard for life, or for what was fitting for this world. The secret of what they did is lost, and had far better remain so. For although that particular danger has departed from the world, evil has not. If people have the opportunity to hurt, be sure that sooner or later they will take it. You may think our world better then theirs, but the people are no better. We only have less power to harm, that's all.'

'I don't agree.'

'Are you willing to listen?'

There was a short pause. 'Go on,' said Naomi unwillingly.

'They built a fortress on the coast, on the far side of the empty lands, and within it they pursued a kind of sorcery. It was a way of taking power from the earth — that's how I've heard it described. You know that there is power which is freely given — the powers of earth and water, fire and air, which were gifts given to people at the beginning. This power was not a gift. It could only be taken by destroying those elements which are the source of life. And so it was clearly evil. But at that time, just before the world changed, people were no longer concerned about life.'

'That's impossible.'

'Not impossible. Only unbearable, which is why you refuse to believe it.' She shook her head impatiently, and Thomas put his hand on her knee. 'Naomi, I know. I didn't want to believe it either. People are capable of too much evil, and we daren't face it, because although the world has changed, we know too well that we have not. We are quite capable of destroying a land, if we had the means to do it.'

'No! It's nonsense, Thomas. People want to survive, if nothing else. No one ever meant to destroy their own land. But they tried to take too much, and earned what they got.'

'Do you want to hear or not?'

'I'm listening,' said Naomi reluctantly. 'But I can't accept everything you say.'

'They took more from the earth than they were ever intended to have. The land suffered, and gradually became sick through exploitation and neglect. But the people ignored it, and within their fortress they couldn't see what was happening. All they could see was naked power, forged out of the elements which were supposed to give life. They became mad with power, and forgot that they belonged to this world, and that they had needs, like every living creature. They pursued no other end but sorcery, and within their fortress fires blazed day and night, forging a new element out of the old, which withered every living thing that it touched.'

She frowned in confusion. 'You mean like alchemy? Gold?'

'No, no, you don't understand. Not a metal, an element. It was alive, but not with life like ours. It was dangerous, because it fed upon the elements of which life is made.'

Naomi sighed. 'I'm not a magician, Thomas. And if it's sorcery, I'm not sure I even want to understand. But I want to know what happened.'

'It happened as it couldn't fail to happen. No one controls the elements, although people may make use of them. They thought they had the power over life, but it is life that has power, not us. They brought something into being which couldn't be controlled. They ignored the danger, and the end was inevitable. The thing escaped them, and broke loose.'

'Like a dragon.'

'No, no. You're thinking in the wrong images. It's not a story, at least, not of the kind you're used to.'

'Well, if you don't like the way I think, can you suggest how I do it differently?'

'Naomi, don't be offended, please. It's as hard for me as it is for you. I think the problem is, that when the world changed, the language of these matters was lost. We can't describe it in our terms, so, when we try to understand, we find ourselves groping among forgotten symbols that don't belong in our world. The only way to think differently is to try to look directly at the past. Have you ever entered the ruins of a city?'

She looked at him, genuinely shocked. 'The ruins? No, of course not! And nor have you, Thomas. There is evil in the world, as you say, but no one would deliberately seek it out!'

His eyes dropped, and he was silent for a moment. 'Never mind. No one could get near the ruins of the fortress, anyhow, for the place is still too dangerous to approach. But I think, if it ever becomes possible to reach it, we might begin to understand their secret.'

'But you said it was better forgotten.'

'Perhaps. But perhaps it's better to understand.'

Naomi tried to imagine the ruins of a fortress, lying in a poisoned land by a deserted sea, and wondered what they could possibly reveal. She felt thoroughly confused. Thomas seemed to think in a different way from anyone else she had known. Some of his conclusions were outrageous, but she began to see his train of thought. He was clever, decided Naomi, and had clearly thought about it deeply. Perhaps too much. Was it possible to think too much? She eyed him doubtfully, and waited for him to continue.

'There was a great explosion,' said Thomas. 'And the walls which had contained the thing were blown apart. It broke loose, and the poison of it spread throughout our land. When my people began to realise what had happened, they fled. But the land was devastated, and the people could not escape fast enough. Many of us became sick, and quickly died. But an element that feeds on life can't be easily eradicated. The people fled, but they took the poison with them, and it lived on in their bodies. Which is why we were afraid to have children. You understand that?'

'No.'

'An element that destroys elements,' repeated Thomas patiently. 'Life that feeds on life. It lived on in us, and fed upon our own unborn children. So that when the children were born, they were not human.'

She looked at him blankly. 'I don't understand that. I only heard that the land was poisoned, and a danger to children still unborn.'

'They were not human,' said Thomas again, as if she hadn't spoken. 'They were the children of a different element, but also part of what we were. Neither the one nor the other. A deformity. And so we had to destroy our own children, because they were not ours, not made of the stuff that we are made of. And so we became untouchable, and so you still regard us.'

'Me?'

'You're not one of my people. It's true. What did you ever hear about the people of the empty lands?'

She didn't speak for a moment. 'I can't help what I've heard. I don't have to believe it.'

'So you have heard about us?'

'Not the truth,' said Naomi.

'Even those of us who seemed to be as you are, who were like enough you to be allowed to live,' went on Thomas, 'we've been touched by something that you want nothing to do with. There is an element in me that should not be part of any human being, and so we're not the same. That's true, isn't it, Naomi?'

'I don't know,' she said, embarrassed. 'I'm confused.'

'But you wouldn't want a man from my country to father a child of yours?'

Naomi stared at the hill opposite. She felt obscurely guilty, and also that he had trapped her into reaching some conclusion she didn't want. His tale was horrifying, but it had nothing to do with her. And yet he insisted on bringing her into it, as though the people of the empty lands had ever been part of her life. 'No,' said Naomi at last. 'If what you say is true, I suppose not. But it's not a thing I've ever thought about, and it's not something I've been thinking about you.'

'Of course not. Why should you think about it? It's our problem, not yours.'

She didn't miss the irony of his tone, but she didn't know what to make of it either. 'But the land itself?' she asked, changing the subject. 'The land is no longer dangerous?'

'Are you afraid?'

'I told you at the beginning. I've had my child, and so I've nothing to lose.'

'I hope not,' said Thomas soberly. 'As I told you at the beginning, you have something to gain.'

'Yes.' She looked round at him again. 'Thank you for trying to explain to me, Thomas. It's difficult, because it's unlike any story I ever heard before, but if it means I'll know this place a little better, then it will help me.'

'I'm glad you want to know. Shall we go on?'

Naomi got up, and waited for him to take the lead. They followed the line of the beck up to the watershed, and came down by another, between two great masses of mountain, higher than anything she had seen so far south before. They towered over her like giant sentinels defending the hidden land that lay within. As they descended, a new country came into view, a flat plain surrounded by hills, across which she could see an expanse of water which was not the sea. Between them and the water the lowlands were green and rich, and they could see clearings among the trees: open fields and pasture, with a track winding between.

'It's like being a hawk,' remarked Naomi. 'Being able to look down from above. It gives you a different picture in your head.'

'Does it? It's always been like that for me, being able to look down over my lands. I can't imagine how you picture it, if you never think of it like that.'

'From the inside, I suppose. Are there no other ways into your country except over the hills?'

'Who would make them? No one comes, except the people of these lands, and all our ways are through the mountains.'

Naomi stared down at the clearings, and thought fleetingly of the stories she had heard. 'Is it so different in this country, then, from the places we have just left?'

'Of course it's different.' He looked at her, and perhaps caught something of her thoughts. 'I know what they say,' he said, 'but we're only people, like any people. There won't be an inn, because we're not used to strangers, but whatever door you knocked on in my country, you would be honoured as a welcome guest. Tonight we'll stay at the settlement down there,' — he pointed at one of the clearings — 'then tomorrow I shall take you on a hidden path into the very heart of this land. I think you'll find it beautiful, and not dangerous. Not dangerous for you. There's nothing you need to be afraid of.'

'I don't believe that,' said Naomi, 'not of any place on earth. But I'll take your word for it, as I gave you mine.'

'Thank you,' said Thomas, and led the way down.

Eighth Day

The path above the lake was narrow, but trodden down to the rock beneath. Young bracken grew thickly on the surrounding slopes, small coiled fronds like a miniature forest. Flies swarmed over it, hovering in clouds around the heads of the travellers. The lake below was flat and still, the shapes of the mountains seeming to plunge to its depths, as though this world were the illusion, and only the image in the lake were real.

As they walked the mountains crowded closer. At the head of the lake they drew together so that there appeared to be no way through, only a green barrier of wooded crags. It was very quiet. Sky and water were still, both adorned with the same suspended drifts of cloud. If there had been no path the land would have seemed entirely empty. The blanket of trees on the far side of the lake was dense and unbroken right up to the line of precipice above. There was no sign of any clearing ahead, no smoke rising above the treetops. The path wound up and down the ferny hillside, avoiding dense thickets on the one hand, and tumbled scree upon the other.

They reached the head of the lake and looked down on an indeterminate shore backed by marshlands. There were soft sounds from the multitude of inhabitants, low throaty calls, and stirring among the rushes. The bog was thick with swans, massed together so they looked like a carpet of grey and white feathers strewn over turf. They covered the waters of the little bay below. Here and there one lowered its head and dived, or rose up in the water, wings flapping.

Naomi stopped and looked down. 'Is this your village? Something seems to have happened to them.'

'No, these are visitors. Off north, for the fishing.'

'There's so many.'

'They fly far, so they can afford to gather thick.'

'That's not why. We could fly, if we had wings. We couldn't live in multitudes, whatever we had.'

'Why not?'

'It's against nature. There's enough emotions between people just in one village. Imagine if there were thousands.'

'Well, it couldn't happen, because we'd starve,' said Thomas prosaically. 'Shall we go on?'

'Yes. Though the farther we go, the less I can see where we're going.' Naomi looked at the hills surrounding them. 'You said we'd be there by dinner time, and we're heading into the heart of the mountain, if I didn't know you, I'd be more than suspicious.'

'And knowing me?'

'I'll believe anything,' said Naomi lightly. 'Lead on.'

Their path skirted the valley, but didn't descend. There were trees lining the slopes right up to the path. Soon they were deep among them. They were all oaks, with twisted roots that gripped the hill like ancient fingers. Their new leaves were delicately green, almost shutting out the sky. Naomi looked up to see if she could still see the hills, and tripped over a root. A jay rose from the tree above her, squawking jeeringly.

'Who uses this path?' demanded Naomi.

'A few. Why?'

'It doesn't feel like there's a village at the end of it. I saw the head of the valley, and the precipice. I don't see where we're going.'

'No, you can't see it.'

Naomi brushed the dead leaves off her trousers. 'Very well. I may be your guide one day, and then I'll get my own back.'

'You can take me home again. Listen. Can you hear anything?'

Naomi stopped again, and listened. 'Water.'

'It's the beck. Come on.'

There was a new urgency about him. He quickened his pace, and Naomi scrambled after him. The sound of the beck was suddenly louder. The oak trees parted. They stood on top of a huge boulder, rolled into the heart of the valley by an unimaginable power, and saw a clear pool below them, with white shingle beaches. A rowan hung over the far bank, decked in blossom. The water was cloud-coloured, slow circling patterns of white and dark borne inexorably downstream.

Thomas gazed down at it. Then he tore off his pack, slithered down the rock and stood at the edge of the pool. Naomi watched him crouch down and fill his cupped hands with water. She couldn't hear what he was saying, but she caught the rhythm of it, and understood. Thomas poured out water on water, like a libation, and filled his hands again, letting the stream flow over his cupped palms. Then he raised them to his lips and drank. He stood on the shore for a long time. The clouds parted, and the rowan blossom was bright with sunlight. Naomi sat on the rock and waited. When he climbed up again she saw that his face was wet with tears. He made no attempt to hide them, but merely picked up his pack again, and turned to follow the path. Presently he waited for her to negotiate another rock after him, and remarked as she did so, 'This is the boundary of my own valley.'

'I thought so,' said Naomi, in the same casual tone.

Having brought them to the beck, the path was in no hurry to leave it. They followed it through the heart of the valley, though the way was rough. It twined among rocks like a thin thread, slipping almost invisibly between the trunks of the oaks. Sometimes they were high above the river, treading cautiously along the edge of jutting cliffs; sometimes they were right down on the shingle, and the water lapped their boots. Sometimes they were taken away into the trees out of sight of the water, but never out of earshot. Thomas moved fast, flitting between the trees like a grey shadow cast by the moving clouds, never searching for a foothold, with a skill that might have seemed uncanny, but Naomi recognised it as born of lifelong knowledge.

She was a stranger, however, and had to clamber after him, slithering noisily over the rocks, trying as hard as she could to keep up. Up till now, she had steadfastly stuck to her own pace, but she knew what was driving him now, and the hunger within him found an echo in her. When he turned to check that she was still with him she saw that he was still weeping without even noticing. He wasn't thinking about himself now, or his fear, or his homesickness. He was swallowed up in the place, in a silent passionate reunion with the only spot on earth where he belonged.

The ground was growing smoother. The path widened, so that they could walk side by side through a grove of oak trees, the river flowing evenly beside them between banks of white boulders. Now and then a fish jumped and fell back with a smack, its ripple instantly obliterated by the sweep of the river. Then without warning the oak trees ended. There was a stile in front of them set over a stone wall, and sunlight on grass beyond. Thomas sprang on to the wall and jumped down, and almost ran ahead. Naomi climbed over neatly, and stepped into the meadow.

*

It must be the strangest place that people ever lived in.

Naomi stood quite still, staring round her. It was a valley, but quite unlike any other valley she had seen. The hills encircled it, and were it not for the indisputable fact of the flowing beck, it would seem that there was no way in or out. The path by which they had come was entirely hidden, a secret entrance to which without Thomas she would never have found the key. If one wished to hide, thought Naomi, this would be the safest place in the world.

The floor of the valley was quite flat, like a huge dancing floor. Level green fields were dissected by straight stone walls, as if some giant geometric pattern were laid out, only comprehensible to a hawk hovering above. It was impossible to see right across, but the mountains rising sheer on all sides suggested that it was roughly circular. A ring of oakwood divided the fields from the hills, enclosing the valley inside a living barrier. It was uncanny to find so perfect a valley where there had appeared to be only hills, so completely hidden from the world. It seemed magic, sealed off from time and the ordinary world, obeying different laws. It was too flat, too circular, too hidden. And they were in the very heart of the empty lands, about which people knew nothing. A place that denied all her expectations of place, perhaps it would also make nonsense of time? Naomi crossed her fingers, and wondered at herself. She was content to live in a world of half belief, but unlike most people, she recognised the fact, and still accepted it. Thomas had put his finger on it when he had said . . . what? She couldn't remember. But the world was full of unknown things, always in the next country but one.

Stories crowded into her mind. The hidden land, the musician who played for a night and was lost to the world for a hundred years, the land of the ever-young, where it was always springtime — well, thought Naomi, common sense reasserting itself, it's spring anyway, so I can't prove it. And Thomas is a mortal man. I've had seven days to check that out. And the clouds are moving, just, so it's still the same sky. I may have come closer to the boundary of my world than usual, but I can still look after myself, I reckon.

She looked round, wondering what to do now, and caught sight of Thomas waiting for her at the next stone wall. She followed slowly, along the curve of the beck. The beck seemed like an old friend now. It reasserted two facts: one, that there was a way out of the valley, although it was invisible, and two, that time was the same here as outside, or else the water could not flow from one country to the other. Thanks a lot, said Naomi out loud, addressing the beck, and laughed at herself a little wryly.

Thomas no longer seemed impatient. Instead he was pale and subdued, all his enthusiasm extinguished. He nodded to her, but seemed to have nothing to say, and opened the gate on which he had been leaning. It was a good gate, Naomi noticed, stout and new, and the wall was in similarly good repair. There was a track beaten through lush meadowland, wide enough for a small cart. The next field had young stirks in it, which lowered their heads and stared at them as they passed. They were small but sturdy, and obviously well fed.

They reached another gate, and another square of pasture, empty. The next field contained ewes and lambs. The grass was grazed right down, but there were signs that hay had recently been scattered, and the sheep looked as healthy as the cattle. The field after that was ploughed, and already long rows of turnips were appearing. The path did not deviate from the river, but followed every curve meticulously. There was no sign of any human being at all.

'Naomi?'

She jumped, as if she had forgotten that he could speak. 'Yes?'

'Perhaps I should have explained more to you.' He sounded unhappy, rather than nervous. Naomi waited for him to go on. 'It wasn't easy to find words.' Thomas hesitated again, then continued. 'It was always thought to be lucky, you understand, to welcome a musician to the valley, a stranger who would play for the dance. It's not that we don't have our own music. But they say that in the early times one of us would go out and seek such a one, and bring them back to play for us that one night. So when one came by chance, it was thought to be lucky. I thought that it was lucky.'

'In which case you could hardly have passed me by,' said Naomi ironically. 'But it's not what you promised me before.'

'It's both. I can't explain,' said Thomas, on a note of despair. 'Truly I've tried, and it's too hard. Naomi, I made no false promise. Can you trust me?'

'I never trust anybody,' said Naomi flatly.

Thomas wiped his forehead with his sleeve. 'We're nearly there,' he said. 'You will understand, I promise you. It's true that I have a gift out of the past for you. At least, I firmly believe that it is. And it's also true that I needed you to come.'

'What for?' He didn't answer. 'I respect your privacy, as you know,' said Naomi stiffly, 'but I think you owe it to me to explain that.'

Thomas stared at his boots. 'To lay a ghost,' he muttered.

'Then it's not a musician you want. It's a sorcerer.'

'Please,' said Thomas. 'I knew what I was doing. And you shall see. Tomorrow I'll give you a gift beyond price. I think you'll find it so. And as to the rest, all we shall ask of you is your music. It's our fate we're dealing with, not yours.'

'Look at me,' said Naomi severely.

He met her eyes unwillingly.

'Was that supposed to be the explanation?' she demanded.

'It's all that I can give. I'm sorry. I wish that you could trust me.'

'I wish that I could fly. But words will clearly get us nowhere. Shall we go on?'

He bent his head in acknowledgement, and turned to lead the way.

Presently they crossed the beck by a stone bridge, and almost immediately a cluster of buildings came into view ahead.

'Is that where we're going?'

'No. Our household is beyond. We have to cross the other beck. There's two rivers flowing off the hills, and they meet in the middle of the valley.'

Jonathan. The name slid into her brain unsummoned. And the other one — Julius? Thomas had told her something after all. There were clues, but there was no thread to hold them together. Perhaps Thomas had done his best. All she could do was wait, and keep her eyes open.

The path led them right through a farmyard. Chickens scattered as they tramped by, and a cat regarded them from an open barn door. There were no dogs, so someone must be out. Smoke rose from the chimney in a vertical stream, and as they passed the kitchen door Naomi caught a whiff of new bread. There was nobody to be seen.

They passed an area of rough humpy ground covered with nettles and willow herb. Ruins, just like anywhere else. The track forked, and Thomas turned left. They crossed the beck, over another stone bridge.

Naomi glanced down at it, acknowledging a friend. There were oak trees in front of them, then the steep sides of the valley. But before that, there was a house.

It was much bigger than most houses which had been restored from the past. It stood at the top of a grassy mound where tethered goats grazed. There was a flower garden at the top, protected from animals by a raised dyke, the top of which was thick with wallflowers in rich browns. A track bordered by daffodils led up to the front door. The house itself was extraordinary. It was only two storeys high, like most houses, but the row of windows on each floor was so tall and symmetrical that it looked much higher. The main part of it had a peculiar regularity to it, almost as though someone had designed it from a pattern drawn with a ruler. The outbuildings were more normal, being long and low, and running higgledy-piggledy off to the side away from the track. Naomi could see walled gardens and fruit trees over the top of a higher wall beyond.

She stared at the house, trying to relate it to the world she knew. Her overwhelming impression was of glass, the windows being so huge. They were criss-crossed with wooden frames, for obviously no glazier could produce a pane of such immoderate size. It must be very light inside, and the view must take in the whole valley, thought Naomi. How would it be to sit at a window like that, and look over one's land, safely hidden from the whole world? Perhaps the people there will expect strangers to do what they want. Naomi scowled at the thought. Perhaps they won't understand about respect. But I belong to a different world, and they won't move me.

She fell a pace or two behind Thomas, and followed him silently up to a large oak door. Thomas lifted the latch, and walked in.

It wasn't like being indoors at all. They were standing in a rectangular room with doors opening off in all directions. The floor was tiled black and white like a chessboard. Naomi wondered if it was intended as a joke. There were windows, one by the door, and one at the far end which extended right up to the ceiling, filling the place with daylight. There was a stair going up under the far window, very wide and shallow, with some ornate carved banisters, and stout pieces of wood fixed across the gaps. In the middle of the chessboard there was a round table, and in the middle of the table was a bowl of hyacinths. So it is a joke, thought Naomi. A game with a circle in the middle, and four blue hyacinths to mark the centre. I was never in any building like this before. No wonder Thomas took to magic.

'We'll leave our packs here,' said Thomas. He led the way across the chessboard and opened a door in the far wall. There was a passage beyond, cold and high-ceilinged, then more doors.

Thomas chose the last one on the left, holding it open for Naomi. 'Welcome,' he said.

She found herself standing in the largest kitchen she had ever seen. The floor was red, and the ceiling seemed to tower out of sight behind a great rack full of washing. There was a long scrubbed table down the length of the room, and in the middle of the table was a bowl of white hyacinths. Naomi stared at them unbelievingly. There was nothing else on the table. The rest of the furnishings were quite normal, if over large. There was a dresser laden with unpainted earthenware, and big copper pans on the shelf beneath. A rocking chair stood in one corner, complete with a large ginger cat, and a rag rug lay in front of the immense cast-iron stove. The fire was lit, and three kettles steamed gently on the hob. There was nobody there.

'Why?' began Naomi, and tried to formulate a question out of all these unfamiliar things. 'Why are there flowers growing inside the house?'

'Why not?'

'Well, aren't there plenty outside?'

'Look.'

She obediently looked at the windowsill at which he was pointing, and gasped. There were flowers there, too, but quite unlike any in the country round. There were lots of little pots full of leaves like primroses, but the ones that had flowers weren't primroses at all. Instead they were bell-shaped, in pink and red and blue. There were curious spreading leaves in large pots of a kind she had never seen, and huge shiny dark leaves like giant rhododendrons. For the first time in the journey Naomi felt she had lost her bearings completely. She thought of men with asses' heads, lions with the heads of women. She had seen no human being in this valley at all, and now there were primroses sprouting the flowers of fantasy, and outlandish plants bearing no relation to anything in the world outside.

'I don't understand,' she whispered. 'Where do they come from?'

'My mother collects them,' said Thomas. 'I'm glad to see them. It means my mother is here, and well. Unless Linnet did it.'

Naomi recovered herself, and said with some asperity, 'Are all your relations invisible?'

'Not when I last looked. Someone's about. The fire's not shut down.'

As if in answer to this remark, there was a thin wail that appeared to come from directly above their heads. Naomi clutched Thomas involuntarily, and felt him jump. He was as startled as she was. The wailing rose higher, then stopped. She drew in her breath. It came again, and she recognised it. A baby crying. Naomi let go of Thomas, and giggled. 'The baby's awake,' she said, a little hysterically.

'What baby?'

She stared at him. 'It's your house!'

'But. . .'

There was a sound of footsteps overhead. They stopped somewhere about the middle of the ceiling. The wailing ceased. 'That's Linnet's room,' said Thomas, sounding completely dazed.

More footsteps overhead, a door banging, and silence.

'Who is Linnet?'

'Didn't I tell you? She's . . .'

The kitchen door swung open, and a young woman came in with a baby on her arm. She saw them and stopped abruptly. For a long moment they were all three frozen to the spot, staring at each other open-mouthed. Naomi was the first to recover, as the recipient of the smallest shock. The only odd thing about Linnet and her baby, she thought, was that they seemed quite normal. Linnet was slight and sunburned, with short dark hair and a decided chin. The baby was only a few months old, with tear-stained red cheeks, and a film of darkening hair on the top of its head. Naomi looked from Linnet to Thomas. They were still staring at each other as if turned to stone. Naomi looked at the baby. It regarded her with interest, and dribbled.

'Thomas?' said Linnet hoarsely.

He responded with a stifled sound that might have been a question. Then Linnet rushed across the room, baby and all, and hugged him passionately in a one-armed embrace. 'Thomas!'

'Linnet,' said Thomas in a choked voice, and hugged her fiercely. The baby whimpered in protest. Naomi waited politely.

'Linnet,' said Thomas again. 'Who is this?'

'She's called Joanna,' said Linnet standing back and regarding the baby with the satisfaction of a gardener exhibiting a prize marrow. 'She's all right, isn't she?'

'I didn't know you'd had a baby,' said Thomas, still dazed.

'Well, of course not. How could you possibly?' Linnet looked at him again. Now that her first reaction was over, Naomi thought she looked rather critical. 'Who's this?' demanded Linnet, turning to Naomi.

'Naomi,' said Thomas, recollecting himself. 'This is Linnet, my sister. Linnet, this is Naomi.'

'You are welcome to our house,' said Linnet, sounding doubtful. The baby looked at Naomi and gurgled, and another glob of dribble ran down its chin. Linnet turned back to Thomas. 'I knew you'd come. They were all for taking a replacement, but I said you'd come, and I forbade it. I was expecting you really, but not yet. You still have a week.'

'I had a long way to come, so I left plenty of time. As it was, the journey went very smoothly. Linnet — your baby . . .'

'What about her?'

'I can't quite believe it. Will she come to me?'

'Give her a minute. Are you hungry? How far did you come today?'

'Only up the valley. I'm not hungry,' said Thomas. 'It's too much, coming back.' He sat down in the rocking chair. 'But our guest might be.'

'Are you hungry?' demanded Linnet.

'Yes,' said Naomi.

'Would you like bread and cheese for now? It's not long till dinner time. I was just coming down to cook.'

'Where is everyone?' asked Thomas.

Linnet stared at him. 'And you a farmer!' she said. 'It's the middle of lambing, and planting time as well. I hope you're staying a while. There's plenty to do.'

'Only for the dance,' said Thomas, looking at the fire. 'As I promised.'

'Well, that gives us a week.' Linnet began to lay the table with one hand, the baby balanced on her hip. She set food in front of Naomi. 'And what about you?' she asked. 'Are you a plant collector?'

'A plant collector?' repeated Naomi. 'No. Should I be?'

'They come looking for my mother,' explained Linnet. 'They hear stories about her, you see, and they hope she'll be interested in what they've got. She usually isn't. Personally, I think they should get a prize for finding their way at all.'

'Oh,' said Naomi, trying to work all this out.

'Is she here?' interrupted Thomas.

'No, she's gone down to the coast. She was expecting a shipment. Something about delphiniums, whatever that may be. And she's left us with all the pricking out. I wouldn't mind, but what with the lambs and the vegetables, I can't sit down all day to a job that no one can eat at the end of it. And she doesn't trust the others. Me or Peter, she said. Well, that means me. Are you any use at pricking out?' she asked Naomi suddenly. 'Can I give Jo a bit of your bread? She's seen it.'

Naomi handed over a crust. 'I can try,' she answered. 'I've done it before. I'm not a gardener though. I'm a musician.'

There was a horrified silence. Linnet stared at her. As if I'd got the plague, thought Naomi, startled, and waited. Linnet faced Thomas accusingly, but whatever she was about to say, she thought better of it. Instead she turned back to Naomi, and said in a voice that utterly failed to be conversational, 'I see. And what do you play?'

'A fiddle,' said Naomi, hoping that was the right answer.

Linnet went quite white, and clutched her baby. 'How nice,' she said in a hollow voice. 'So do I.'

'Linnet,' said Thomas.

'What?'

'I was going to tell you later, but I can explain it.' He sat with his elbows on his knees, his head propped on his hands, and began to speak slowly, thinking out the words carefully. 'I met her by chance, when my journey had begun. So I asked her to come, to play the fiddle for us at the dance. That was seven days ago. We have travelled together all that time, and I can tell you now I know I did right. I know it. Linnet, can you understand why?'

Linnet looked at Naomi, and at Thomas, and then at Naomi again. 'I'll support you,' she said suddenly. 'I think I understand.' She spoke to Naomi. 'Listen, fiddle player.' Naomi stiffened, and turned pink. 'I'm sorry I was surprised. I'm glad you've come, and in my mother's absence I welcome you to this house. What did you say your name was?'

'I didn't. It's Naomi.'

'Naomi. I'm sorry. It was a shock, that's all. I hope you'll feel at home among us.' Naomi thought that unlikely, but she nodded in acknowledgement.

'Thank you, Linnet,' said Thomas.

'Not at all.' His sister's expression suddenly softened, as it had when she first saw him. 'I think you're very brave,' she said, and kissed the back of his neck. Thomas took her hand and gripped it hard.

Naomi frowned at the white hyacinths. It had been a good journey. He had been good company, and it had been an adventure belonging to the two of them. It was over, and nothing would be the same again. She sighed, and retreated into her customary solitude. She was vaguely aware of Linnet recounting exhaustive details about the farm, and of the baby, now ensconced on Thomas's knee, trying to put her fingers in his mouth. The hyacinths gave out a heavy fragrance. The waxy petals shone as though bedewed with water drops. She reached out and touched one gently with her forefinger. I have grown fond of him, Naomi admitted to herself, but he belongs to this household. He is not mine.

Ninth Day

Thomas stopped on the river bank, realising that Naomi hadn't seen him. She had her back to him, uncharacteristically clad in a large jersey of faded green. She was crouched on the stones at the water's edge with a wooden bucket beside her.

She was too busy to notice him, and the sound of the beck drowned out his footsteps. She was busy pounding wet washing against the stones. Her feet were bare, the patched green trousers she wore were rolled up almost to her knees. The stones around her were all splashed with water, and her face was unusually pink with exertion. Thomas watched her heap a pile of soaking washing on to the stones, and begin to wring it out item by item, scarlet and orange and purple. Thomas moved nearer until his shadow fell across her, and she glanced up.

'Hello,' said Naomi, picking up a wet shirt.

'How are you?' said Thomas. 'I'm sorry I wasn't there this morning. They needed help with the lambing. There's not that many of us. Did they look after you?'

'I don't take a lot of looking after.' Naomi chucked the shirt in the bucket, and extricated a few socks.

'I thought you'd sleep in,' he explained apologetically.

'I did. Then your cousin Peter gave me breakfast. Then I practised. Then another cousin showed me where I could do my washing, which is what I've most looked forward to for several days, and he lent me some clothes. So now you can stop feeling guilty.'

'Thank you,' said Thomas humbly. He watched her throw a selection of multi-coloured socks into the bucket, and added inconsequentially, 'You look very beautiful in green, you know.'

He received a withering stare in reply, and grinned cheerfully. 'There's a mangle,' he said. 'Did Peter tell you?'

'It wasn't Peter. Yes, I'm going there now. I'm glad you're feeling so happy,' added Naomi sardonically.

'I like lambing. Shall I carry the bucket?'

'I'm not entirely incapable. Wait while I put my shoes on.'

They walked slowly back to the house together. Already it had begun to look quite normal to Naomi. Partly, she supposed, because there were signs of life today: windows wide open, nappies hanging on a line beyond the orchard, a couple of dogs sprawled on the front doorstep.

'Would you mind if I went back on the hill this afternoon?' asked Thomas, breaking into her thoughts.

'Of course not. Why?'

'There's a lot of ground to cover, to check them every day. I said I'd take a young cousin of mine. Show him how.'

'You go in for males in your family, don't you? I thought that at supper last night.'

'This generation,' assented Thomas. 'It's a problem. My mother had two sisters, but Linnet is the only young woman in this household.'

'And now she has a daughter,' replied Naomi consolingly. 'You'll need more women, or this household will get too big, and there'll be no one to make another.'

'True,' said Thomas, and changed the subject abruptly. 'My sister plays the fiddle. I think she's good, or used to be. Talk to her.'

'If she lets me, I will.'

The wash house was situated round the back of the vegetable garden, being one among a row of outbuildings. It was hot and steamy inside after Naomi's washing, and in front of the copper a big pail of sheets had been set to soak. Naomi dumped her bucket by the mangle.

'Shall I turn for you?'

'Don't you want to get back to your sheep?'

'Not till I've had my dinner. Carry on.'

For a while there was no sound except the turn and thump of the mangle as Thomas kept the handle spinning, and the splashing of water into the basin below. Naomi fed her clothes through, then tossed them into a basket. 'I used to do this at home, when I was little,' she remarked presently. 'I used to find it very satisfying.'

'So did I. Only once I tried to dry my sister's hair with it, and then I was banned, I think. I don't remember.'

'The worst thing I ever did,' said Naomi reflectively, 'at least, the thing I most remember being punished for, which of course is not the same, was putting sand in the bread.'

'Why?' asked Thomas, intrigued.

'Why did you put her hair through the mangle?'

'It was wet.'

'Ah. This was more complicated. My mother was making bread, and I was standing on the bench at the table watching her. I had a little bucket of sand off the beach. I think it was the flour being the same colour that made me think it was a good idea. She was adding flour, you see, so I just chucked in a bit of sand.'

'Fair enough. Was she cross?'

'Furious. That's why I remember, because it was so unfair. I did a lot of bad things, but that one was innocently meant. Truly,' added Naomi, as if he might doubt it.

'I believe you,' said Thomas, and stopped the handle. 'Are you done?'

'Thanks. Now I need clothes pegs.'

'Behind the door. At least, they were seven years ago.'

'Still are,' said Naomi, looking. 'Are you going to escort me to the washing line as well?'

He led her through the orchard. Some of the apple trees were pink with blossom, and the ground was strewn with petals like late flakes of snow. Hens wandered through the grass between the trees amongst clumps of withered snowdrops. Naomi stopped, her basket on her hip, and surveyed the scene. 'It's very pretty, this country, isn't it? I'd miss the trees now, after so long, I think.'

'Miss the trees?' queried Thomas. 'But there's trees everywhere.'

'Where I come from there are none.'

He stared at her. 'I don't understand.'

'It's quite simple. Where's the washing line?'

'Over here.'

Naomi ducked under the trees after him. They passed another ancient fruit tree, gnarled and grey, but covered with white blossom. Two bluetits flew in and out of it, evidently with young to feed. 'That's a pear tree,' said Thomas, pointing. 'But they don't usually ripen, not to eat fresh, anyway.'

Naomi studied the tree. 'I've eaten pears,' she said. 'I once played at a naming, and the day after, the baby's uncle, I think it was, brought me ripe pears for breakfast in bed. That was about as far south as I've ever been. I liked it.'

'You fascinate me,' said Thomas. 'I'm surprised you ever came north again after that.'

'I surprise myself all the time.'

They left the orchard by a green gate in the wall. The drying green was on the slope between the oak wood and the vegetable garden. One line was already hung with nappies.

'Do the mountains have names?' asked Naomi presently, through two pegs in her mouth.

'Of course.'

'Will you tell me them,?'

She had her back to him, so she didn't see his face light up, but when he spoke she realised that he was smiling. 'It would be a great pleasure. But I'd rather do it properly. Tomorrow.'

'How do you mean, properly?' asked Naomi, facing him while she shook out her pink trousers.

'I'll show you.'

'I'm not walking very far.'

'No, not far.' Thomas took the empty basket. 'I'm glad you came, Naomi. And the other matter, that I brought you for. I've not forgotten that, either.'

'I never supposed you had. I assumed you had a time for it.'

'Trust me,' replied Thomas promptly

She shook her head at him, half laughing. 'No, but I believe you this time, Thomas.' She slung the peg bag over her shoulder, and swiftly kissed his cheek. 'That's for showing me the pear tree. Thank you.'

He stared after her in bewilderment, then ducked under the line and followed her back with the basket.

*

Linnet sat at the kitchen table pricking out lettuces. She worked fast, and every now and then pushed a completed tray down to the end of the table. Naomi sat opposite her, darning a large hole in her red jersey with brown wool. They had not found much to say to each other, but the silence between them was not unfriendly. It was hot in the kitchen; the smell of suet pudding hung in the air, although all the dinner dishes had been cleared away. Rain beat against the grey expanse of window, and over the stove damp washing added its distinctive scent to the atmosphere.

'Weather's changed,' remarked Linnet. 'It'll be wet out on the hill.'

'Yes,' said Naomi. 'You don't work with the sheep, then?'

'Of course I do. It's feeding Jo. It was all right in the winter, but now there's so much to do outside, it's like trying to be in two places at once all the time. You've no idea.'

'No.' Naomi carefully finished her darn, and bit off the end of the wool.

'But having Thomas back, that makes all the difference.'

'He can take your place, then?'

'More than that.' Linnet paused while she carefully extricated another infant seedling. 'Thomas is the best shepherd in this valley, or any another, come to that. He's wasted doing anything else.'

'Is that so? Have you got any button thread?'

'At the bottom of the box somewhere. Do you want a button?'

'No, I found it, thanks.' Naomi got up, and pulled a heavily patched shirt off the rack.

'Looks like you could do with making a new shirt.'

'I'm fond of this one. A friend gave it to me, in a place where I once stayed the winter.'

'I'm not sentimental,' observed Linnet dispassionately, firming down the lettuce with her thumb and forefinger.

'Is that so?' said Naomi again.

There was another silence. A log cracked in the stove, and sparks flew out from the open door on to the rug. Linnet got up and stamped them down. 'Do you want a cup of tea?' she asked. 'I'll put the kettle on again.'

'Please. It'll keep me awake.'

'I get like that in the afternoons,' agreed Linnet. 'Especially when it's raining. Jo still wakes up twice every night. Sometimes I just sleep in the day when she does.'

'Do you?' replied Naomi politely.

Neither of them spoke again for a while. The kettle began to sizzle on the hob. Linnet finished another tray of lettuces, and fetched a teapot and two mugs. 'What sort of tea?'

'I'm not bothered.'

'I'll make a mixture. I've had to stop using mint. I don't think it agrees with Jo.'

'Oh.'

'I don't suppose you know much about hill farming?'

'No, I'm afraid I don't.'

'It was Thomas who established these flocks,' said Linnet. 'Having so little ploughland where he was, it was the obvious thing to do.'

'Where he was?'

Linnet cocked her head on one side, listening to something else. 'That's Jo. I'll be back in a minute. Can you pour the tea?'

Naomi laid down her shirt. She heard Linnet's footsteps thumping up the boards of the staircase until she was out of earshot. Naomi contemplated the kettle until it began to boil in earnest, and made tea, still deep in thought.

Linnet reappeared breathlessly, the baby held against her shoulder, tightly wrapped in a red shawl. 'Oh well done,' she said to Naomi. 'There's a crock of biscuits in that cupboard. I'll just change her.'

She pushed the lettuces to one side, laid the baby on the table, and unwrapped her. Jo grizzled a little, trying to rub her eyes with small clumsy fists. Her hair was soft and downy, sticking to her head on the side where she had been laid, and her cheeks were flushed with sleep. She wriggled as Linnet stripped off her clothes with the same thoroughness that she applied to the lettuces.

She was a healthy looking baby. Her skin was faintly brown, almost honey-coloured. She had lost the red fledgling look of the very young, and had grown clear-skinned and compact, with a rounded tummy, and strong arms and legs. There was nothing fragile about her, although she was so small. Linnet left her for a moment while she pulled a clean nappy off the clothes rack. Jo stopped fidgeting and stared at the rack from upside down, where it was left swinging above her head, her blue eyes suddenly wide and concentrated. Linnet folded the nappy and slid it under her. Jo squirmed, and screwed up her face to wail.

Naomi returned her attention to tea and biscuits.

'All right, all right,' said Linnet. 'It's coming.'

'Are you ready for your tea?'

'Yes thanks.'

They sat down again, Linnet in the rocking chair and Naomi on the bench nearest the fire. Linnet propped her elbow on the arm of her chair, settled the baby in the crook of her arm, and pulled up her shirt. Jo latched on to her breast at once, her crying abruptly extinguished, to be replaced by the inimitable sound of steady sucking.

'Where do you want this?'

'On the edge of the stove there. That'll do.'

'Biscuit?'

'Thanks.'

'Where was Thomas?' asked Naomi, sitting down. 'When he started the flock of sheep?'

'On the other side of the valley,' said Linnet. 'Have you always been a musician?'

'What?' Naomi hadn't expected the conversation to come round to her, certainly not quite so suddenly. 'Yes. No. I started to learn when I was quite small.'

'I'm looking forward to playing with you. Thomas says you're going to play for the dance. There are six of us. I'm the fiddler. I'll need to show you what the tunes are.'

'Can you tell me something about the dance?'

'I'll try. Can I have another biscuit? Thanks. I don't know how to describe it really. There are eleven dancers, and the dance is in two parts. They each start off as one thing, and they become something else.'

'How?'

'They wear masks. The second is like the opposite of the first. And each dancer follows from the last. Like a journey.'

'A journey to where?'

'I'm not sure. I don't suppose it matters. Through life, I suppose. Something like that.' Linnet spoke abstractedly, her eyes on her baby. Presently she sat Jo up, and rubbed her back. Jo belched, and dribbled. Linnet offered her the other breast, settled back in her chair and reached for her tea.

Naomi decided to try a different approach. 'What is it like watching the dance?'

Linnet considered. 'Well, I have to play the music. I don't know, really. Every adult in the valley is either a dancer or a musician. Only the children just watch.'

'So once you just watched?'

'That's true.'

'And what did you see?'

Linnet sipped tea, and frowned down at her child, as if seeking inspiration. 'Thomas took me,' she said eventually. 'It was dark. We went over the hill to the dancing ground. It was lit with a circle of fire. We stood by the tarn. Thomas told me to stay still, and hold my cousin's hand. Thomas was in the dance, you see. When he put his mask on I was scared, though I knew it was only Thomas. Thomas is the first dancer, the Fool. I watched, and I was scared, but excited too. I knew really it was only Thomas, and everybody else, but it would have been easy to forget.'

'You must have been quite small.'

'Five, six, maybe. I don't remember.'

Naomi dipped her biscuit into her tea, then sucked it thoughtfully. 'How much older is Thomas than you?' she asked.

'Thirteen years. I was nineteen when he went away. I'm the baby,' said Linnet, smiling. 'Why?'

'Just a thought. Do you want more tea?'

'No thanks. She'll probably stay awake for a bit now.'

'What do you do with her?' asked Naomi.

'How do you mean?'

'When she's awake and not actually eating.'

'Carry her on my back, usually, so I can get on, but it's too wet today. Stay in here, I suppose, and keep her amused. Aren't you used to babies?'

'You could play her the fiddle,' suggested Naomi. 'And I should like to hear you too.'

'Play the fiddle to her?' repeated Linnet. 'I don't think she'd make much of that.'

'She might. I've known it work on wet days when there's not much for a baby to look at.'

Linnet gave her a doubtful look. 'I'll get my fiddle if you like, as it's a job we've got to do anyway. I can sort out the onions later.' She wiped Jo's mouth with the corner of a clean nappy. 'Just hold her a moment, will you, and I'll fetch it.' She dumped Jo in Naomi's arms.

'Will you get mine too? I left it on my bed.'

'All right.' Linnet left the room at speed, and Naomi heard her thump up the stairs again.

Jo considered crying, but evidently thought better of it. Naomi carried her to the window, and they watched the patterns of rain slowly gliding down the panes. Before any had dropped from top to bottom, Linnet burst into the room again, clutching two fiddles and two bows.

Linnet put Jo securely in the corner of the rocking chair, and set it rocking just a little. It took her some time to tune up. She seemed nervous, and at the same time impatient, as if there were a hundred things she might more profitably be doing. Entertaining guests, or even babies, was clearly not high on her list of priorities. 'Play to me,' demanded Naomi, ignoring this, as soon as Linnet was ready.

Linnet raised her bow and obediently played a march that Naomi recognised at once. She had never heard it sound so matter-of-fact before, rather as if it were being used to summon the family in to dinner. Suet pudding, thought Naomi, with an inward smile. Aloud she said, 'Go on.'

Linnet launched into a hornpipe, and in spite of herself, it began to flicker into life. Naomi glanced at her sharply, and picked up her own fiddle.

'Go on,' Linnet went on, frowning in concentration, trying not to be put off by the second fiddle.

'Do you know this?' asked Naomi, when they had finished, and played a few notes.

'Of course I do. It belongs to this country.'

'I thought so. Count time then.'

Jo sat in the corner of the rocking chair with a circle of interesting objects round her: a spoon, an eggcup, and a string of painted beads. She ignored them all, gazing wide-eyed at the musicians who were so unexpectedly supplying her with a concert of her own. They had forgotten to keep her chair rocking, but she never noticed. She picked up the spoon and waved it vaguely, as if keeping time for them. They ignored that too. Music poured over her in a shower of sound, filling her whole body, so that her toes wriggled with pleasure inside her stripy socks. If her mother had forgotten all about her, she never noticed, or never minded. Oddly enough, it was the other one who sometimes glanced in her direction, and smiled at her. Jo stared back, and the music swept on.

When they stopped at last, Linnet firmly laid her fiddle down. 'That's enough. I've the onions to do. Do you want another cup of tea?'

'It'll go straight through me at this rate,' said Naomi. She watched Linnet refill the kettle from one of the buckets by the sink, and said abruptly. 'I suppose you know you're good?'

Linnet frowned. 'I don't know. Paul taught me. And I have a lover who says so. But he'd say anything. I ignore him, mostly.'

'The poor man,' said Naomi flippantly. 'But he's right, as it happens. When you stop thinking about onions, or whatever it is, and think about the music, you play very well.'

'Someone has to think about onions,' said Linnet defensively.

'Of course. And someone has to play music.'

'You can't eat music,' stated Linnet.

'You can't live without it.'

'Oh come on, you'd survive.'

'I didn't say survive. I said live.'

'We seem to have finished the biscuits,' said Linnet, peering into the tin. 'Oh, don't you start as well,' as the baby let out a wail, realising that the entertainment was over. 'Here, have this.' She hastily peeled an apple, and offered Jo a quarter. Jo dropped it on the floor, and wailed again.

Naomi made no further attempt at conversation until order was restored. Jo sat at the table in a too-large high chair, wedged between cushions, and bashed at pieces of apple with her spoon. Linnet returned to her pricking out, while Naomi cleared away Linnet's sewing box.

'Who is Paul?' asked Naomi.

Linnet frowned. 'Hadn't you better ask my brother?'

'Thomas? Why? You said Paul taught you the fiddle.'

'Oh that,' said Linnet, evidently relieved. 'I thought you wanted me to tell you about Thomas's lovers. I can't do that. Paul lives in the next valley. He farms sheep, and he plays the fiddle wherever he's asked, for feasts and namings in the valleys. When I was growing up he used to be over here a lot, and he gave me lessons. Of course it's hard for him to come here now. He'll have heard Thomas is back, because someone went over today to see about some hens. I don't know if he'll come. You'd be better playing with him than me, I reckon.'

'I doubt that,' said Naomi, trying to assimilate all this.

'We have to have a fiddler,' said Linnet practically. 'For our own feasts. We can't call in a stranger every time. It's just something that needs to be done.'

'I don't think you believe that. It's a hard thing, when you know you'll learn no more by staying in the place where you are.'

'No,' argued Linnet. 'It's not hard, it's just a fact. I'll play as well as I can for my own valley, and they don't need anything else. I've plenty of other things to worry about.'

'Such as?'

'I'm a farmer. I have a child. I'll probably have more. It's good, the music. I like it. And useful, especially for the dance, but I'm not going to eat my heart out about it. What would be the point of that?'

Naomi regarded her helplessly, lost for an answer. 'I don't know,' she said at last. 'I'm sure I don't know at all.'

Tenth Day

Even in the middle of the dream, Naomi recognised it for what it was, and tried to push it out of her consciousness back to wherever it arose from. She was walking along the beach. It was night: there was a half moon shining fitfully through drifting clouds, briefly illuminating the sea so she could see currents rising and meeting, white water foaming out of the turmoil, a line of broken sea beginning to form between her and the island opposite.

The island itself was merely an outline, a black shadow across the sea, but she knew it. At first it was the island where she should be now, her haven after so many years of travel. Then it was no longer that land, but another place, where grey cliffs were forever scoured down by an insatiable sea. She knew that coast. From here she could sense where the entrance lay, a narrow inlet between high cliffs, within which the breakers were channelled by the westerly winds until they broke like thunder on a crescent beach.

The sea was not dangerous yet. Tide and wind were rising, but there was still time to cross. Even in the dark, she might still cross, if only there were a boat. There should be a boat, lying upturned on this beach, a boat to take her back, crossing this tide and all the uncounted tides before it, if only she could find it. She stumbled over seaweed and boulders. The smell of salt was sharp in her nostrils. Only there was no boat. And she was burdened. There was a baby to carry, a baby that grew heavier, dragging on her arm, that must also be taken across in the boat. Linnet's baby, or some other baby, she wasn't sure. Only there was no boat.. .

'Naomi?'

No boat. She was lying face down, arms outflung, like a body thrown up on the shore by an incoming tide. Naomi turned her head, fighting to be free, and awake.

'Naomi? It's not pears, I'm afraid, but I've brought you some breakfast.'

Naomi rolled over. 'Thomas?'

'I'm sorry to wake you.' Thomas laid a tray down on the bed beside her. 'Only it's fine this morning and the rain won't hold off all day. You wanted me to show you the names of the mountains.'

'Oh,' said Naomi vaguely, and sat up. 'Is it late?'

'Not for you. I brought you some tea. I won't talk to you until you've had some. I'll go away if you like.'

'No, don't.' Naomi looked at him more clearly, and began to button up her shirt which was all twisted round her. 'Thank you. I'm sorry, I was dreaming.'

'You shouldn't be sorry for that. It's porridge. Not very exotic, I'm afraid.'

She watched him draw back the curtains, and began to eat her porridge. 'Sit down,' she commanded. Thomas meekly sat down at the end of her bed. 'Did you know,' asked Naomi between mouthfuls, 'that your sister is an excellent musician?'

'Do you think so? I didn't think she had enough imagination.'

'Everyone has imagination. Most people prefer to forget it.'

'I don't blame them,' said Thomas feelingly.

She looked up at him. 'Are you all right, Thomas?'

'Of course. How do you mean?'

'I'm sorry if I seem inquisitive,' said Naomi evenly, 'but I find that I begin to care.'

'I've never found you inquisitive.'

'You were afraid to come.' She looked away from him after she had said it, to give him a chance to answer as he pleased.

'I'm still afraid,' said Thomas eventually, 'but also happy. What I fear most, I also love most. Can you understand that?'

'Yes.'

'I belong here. I know about the sheep, and I know the hills. I'm at home, and so of course content. But there's a shadow, and it comes closer. Since we arrived, I haven't looked at it, but it's there. Do you understand?'

'I think so.'

'Soon I shall give you what I promised anyway, even if my mother's not back. I hope you've not felt impatient?'

'No, I'm not impatient.'

'No,' agreed Thomas, looking at her affectionately. 'You're not.'

'There are things I don't understand, but they're becoming clearer. I appreciate that you would have told me, if you could.'

He gave her another quick look. 'That's true. It's not that I don't trust you —'

'You have no reason to trust me.'

'—because I do. But I didn't bring you here to bother about me or mine, and I won't trouble you with it now you've come. I spoke to Linnet about what I want to offer you. She wasn't interested, or she pretended not to be. My mother is very wise, and will agree. I intended to speak to her first, but if she's not back tomorrow, I'll show you anyway.'

*

It was quite like old times, following Thomas into the mountains, but better, because it was sunny, and they had nothing to carry, being already warm and dry and well fed.

He led her down a track that followed the beck southwards, up the valley. Soon they left the beck behind, and crossed more flat fields, skirting the young crops: oats, barley and potatoes. Gradually the valley opened out, until Naomi saw that it was not circular at all, but diverged into two long arms that pointed into the hills. Between the two, a mass of mountain dominated the head of the valley, buttressed by impassable precipices. Thomas pointed at the crags above them. 'Eagle!' Naomi looked, and saw a dark shape soaring upwards, its wings spread wider than any hawk she had ever seen.

'They always nest there, since before the world changed. The crag bears their name. We have to watch them with the lambs. There was a man climbed up there once, and killed one of the birds, and smashed the eggs. But he's dead long ago, and the eagles are still there.'

'Naturally.'

There was only a thin fringe of oaks between the fields and the foot of the mountain. They crossed a tributary of the beck, then followed it uphill. There was a faint path made by sheep, or shepherds. It took them along the exposed edge of the ridge, where it had been worn down to meet the valley floor. On both sides of them the ground fell away steeply. To their left lay the bulk of the hill, hiding the crag where the eagles nested. To the right, they could see down into the right arm of the valley, where a long fertile strip was now revealed, divided into squares of ploughland and pasture by straight stone walls. There was another farm down there, but more normal than Thomas's home, with the usual huddle of slate roofs, comprising dwellings and outbuildings indistinguishably.

Naomi paused and looked back. Already the valley was spread out below, a flat circle of green amid its hedge of oakwood. There was a break in the hills to the west which hadn't been visible before, and a clearing among the oak trees where a few buildings stood right at the edge of the hill. 'Is that a pass?' asked Naomi.

'Yes. Into the next valley. Wait until we get further up.'

She went on obediently, and didn't look back until they were considerably higher. She was rewarded when she did turn round. The valley had diminished into an irregular chessboard, dissected by two lines which were the rivers, meeting in the middle, flowing down towards the narrow exit lost in the trees. Beyond, she could see the lake again, its two islands like distant ships in full sail, and beyond that the mountains to the north through which they had come. To east and west new peaks were appearing, mountains upon mountains, blue in the distance and merging with the sky.

'It's a good clear day,' said Thomas. 'I hoped it would be.'

The path grew rougher as they ascended. These hills were quite different from the rounded ridges of their journey. These were mountains, worn by the weather to rough peaks and crags. There was nothing uniform about them; they were as sharply individual as any place on earth. However disguised by dreams or memories, they would always be recognised again by one who knew them.

Thomas stopped again once, on the summit of a small crag overlooking the long arm of the valley. Naomi sat down to get her breath, and studied the ground below her like a map. It was all falling into place in her mind, She could see the last two days of their journey spread out at her feet, and it was quite clear now why the valley seemed so well hidden. It was divided from the lake by a strong fortress of living rock, and only the river indicated a way through the forest that hid all paths. She began to study the fells that encircled the valley, now that she could see their upper slopes.

'Are you ready?'

Naomi got up slowly, and followed.

The last part of the climb was a stiff scramble over rock. Naomi clambered on uncomplainingly. Indeed, there was no one to complain to, for Thomas had vanished out of sight. She found him standing at the summit cairn, gazing south. Breathlessly she climbed up beside him, and looked round.

She looked south, and drew in her breath sharply. There were great ranges of mountains, all sharp and blue under the spring sky. It looked as if there were no land beyond them, only the place where earth met sky at last, and the world ended. The other mountains had been like the sea, but this was like looking out of the world. No wonder they were called the empty lands. She had thought it referred to a human deed, but there was nothing human in this emptiness. It was like being a child and imagining countries in the shifting clouds, and seeing paths across them. The first step was taken, and the place was real. The man who had created such an alchemy stood regarding her, looking rather pleased with the success of his efforts.

Naomi went on looking, as if she were trying to learn it all by heart. 'And these are the empty lands?' she asked him at last.

'That's so. These are the lands where the sky meets the earth, which is how the earth is healed. You know that?'

'But you told me they were called the empty lands because they were laid waste, and poisoned. I never thought of anything like that.'

'That's so too,' agreed Thomas. He sat down on the cairn, picking up two or three pebbles, and began to juggle them absentmindedly. 'It's true my people were forced to flee, and the land wasn't safe to live in for generations. But they were farmers and shepherds, as we are. They knew the land, and no other place was home to them. They spent many years in exile, and they did not forget.'

'So they came back.'

'When they could. When they saw that the birds and animals had returned, and that the plants were growing as they did before, they dared to go back. They knew what they would find. Not one of them had seen this place with their own eyes, but the knowledge of it was handed on, and had never been forgotten. As I say, we were farmers, and this was our own land. We would not forget.'

'So you have that knowledge still?'

'The names of the mountains,' said Thomas, standing up. 'They were made by shepherds like myself many centuries before the land was abused, and before the world was changed. The names were remembered in all the years of exile, and so I know them now.'

'And I'm a stranger. You're willing to tell me?'

'Come here,' said Thomas.

She went over to him, and he took her by the shoulders and turned her round, so she had her back to him, facing east. 'These are the names of the mountains as they were named by my people, and have been remembered ever since, through all the generations of exile, and as I inherited them.'

'To the east,' — he pointed over her shoulder, so she could follow the direction of his arm — 'in the far distance: *High Street, Doup Crag, Red Screes,* and in front of them, *High Raise,* beyond it, *Pavey Ark,* and the two outcrops, *Harrison Stickle, Pike o' Stickle.*'

He turned her slowly southwards. '*Wetherlam, Pike o' Blisco, Swirl How, Old Man of Coniston, Grey Friar, Crinkle Crags, Bow Fell, Esk Pike, Alan's Crag, Ill Crag, Great End.*' The bulk of their own summit was in front of them now, a long plateau stretching from south to west. '*Ling Mell,*' recited Thomas, turning her to face the west, '*Middle Fell, Yowe's Barrow,* the one below it, *Seat Alan, Grey Gavel, Red Pike, Green Gavel, Scoat Fell, Pillar, Brandreth, High Crags, High Stile, Blake's Fell, Carling Knott, Mellbreak, Fleetwith Pike, Low Fell.* ' They were turning now from west to north. '*Grass Moor, Wandope, Eel Crag, Sail, Grisedale Pike, Lord's Seat, Maiden Moor, Cat Bells.* And the line in front of those: *Robinson's Fell, Dale Head, High Spy.*'

Thomas let out a long breath, and faced her due north. '*Long Side, Carl Side, Skiddaw, Skiddaw's Little Man, Lonscale Fell, High Pike, Blencathra, Souther Fell, Clough Head, Great Dodd, Stybarrow Dodd, Raise, White Side, Helvellyn, Nethermost Pike, Dollywaggon Pike, Fair Field, Hart Crag.* In front of them: *Blaeberry Fell, High Seat, Ullscarf.* And just below us: *Eagle Crag.*'

'Those are the names of the mountains. There are many more, which you don't see from here.'

Naomi looked at them again, turning in a slow circle of her own. 'And this one? What is the name of this one?'

'The place where you stand now,' said Thomas, smiling at her so that she was suddenly and irrelevantly aware that she loved him, 'is called *Glaramara.*'

'*Glaramara,*' repeated Naomi. 'It should be the name of a tune.'

'Make it one,' said Thomas lazily, sitting down and leaning back against the cairn, his face turned towards the sun.

Naomi shook her head. 'The tunes are made already. Thomas, what water is that, just above where your house must be?'

He sat up and saw where she was pointing. 'Speak of music,' he said, 'and you're magic. You're looking at the dancing place.'

'Up there? At night?'

'There's a path. Have a toffee.'

'In which pocket?'

'Mine. Come and get it.'

Naomi sat down beside him. 'I tried to ask Linnet about the dance,' she said casually.

'And what did she tell you?'

'A great deal.' Thomas looked faintly surprised. 'Much more than she thought. But I didn't ask her about the music.'

'No, don't ask her about that. That's something else. Peppermint or nut?'

'Yes please,' said Naomi absently, still looking down at the thin gleam of water cut off by an outcrop of hill. 'Thomas, tell me if you can, why is the dance important?'

'Here, it's peppermint. The dance was made in exile, so that the generations might be counted, and the number of years of our exile not be forgotten. When we returned, we brought the dance with us, and made a home for it in every valley. That tarn is ours. We do it every seven years, and never fail, and so we keep count of our history.'

'I see. And the dance itself?'

'Is the journey. I can't explain it well, but you will see. You could see it as the path through the generations, or the parts that people may play, or the living of one's life. It's all the same, I suppose. What happens each time we do it is important, for it gives us a guideline for the seven years to follow. We use it.'

'And who traces the guideline?'

'The people. It's what happens to us when we dance.'

'But no one sees the dance but the children.'

'Who but the children need to see it? There's no other future.'

'Well,' said Naomi, giving up and sucking the toffee. 'No doubt I shall see too, if I'm to play for you.'

'You may find it confusing. The dance can play tricks on you.'

'If there's music, I shall manage, I expect.'

'I wish I had your faith,' said Thomas.

*

They arrived home in the middle of a shower. They didn't bother to hurry, for they were wet already from rain on the hill. The trees by the beck bent before the wind, leaves turning silver in a shaft of sun that the fleeting clouds could not cover. The beck was higher than it had been yesterday, reaching almost to the stone feet of the bridge. A rainbow spanned the valley, disappearing among the oaks, illuminating them in unaccustomed shades of blue and purple. Thomas and Naomi stopped on the bridge to look. Above their heads, the last tail of cloud was caught by the sun and dissolved, catching them with a final splatter of water. They were standing in sunlight amid golden fields, and the rainbow vanished. They looked at each other. Naomi was soaked through, her hair darkened by water to the same colour as the wallflowers. Her clothes seemed more motley than ever, patched by wet as well as mending, and her cheeks were scarlet from the rain and wind. Thomas, on the other hand, seemed quite camouflaged by the rain, his clothes turned to the colour of the wind-tossed trees behind him, his face and hands brown and roughened by weather. She smiled slowly, and took him by the hand. 'You belong all right, don't you?' she said.

They strolled back to the house without further words. The big windows flashed the afternoon sun back into their faces, so that they were left blinking, green rectangles dancing before their eyes. When Naomi looked up again, there was a woman pacing slowly in front of the house, apparently inspecting the wallflowers. She was a stranger, tall and slightly stooping, her hair almost white, and her clothes a faded brown.

'Who's that?' asked Naomi.

Thomas looked up, and instantly let go her hand. He hurried up the slope ahead of her, and when he came to the top he began to run. He had almost reached the end of the wallflower bed when the stranger saw him. She straightened up and strode towards him, almost running herself.

They met halfway along the wallflowers. Naomi watched him run straight up to her and hug her unreservedly, like a little boy. Naomi waited no longer, but turned sharply and disappeared back into the shelter of the trees. She approached the house again from further along the beck, climbing over a stile into the orchard.

When she came into the yard where the outbuildings were, she found Thomas's cousin Peter with his back to her, examining the feet of a pony which was tethered to a ring on the byre wall. Naomi stopped. She liked Peter. He had been friendly to her the first morning, and hadn't complained when someone else had lent her his clothes. He was by far the oldest of the cousins, most of whom she had hardly troubled to distinguish. She had found him quite ready to chat about safe topics like the weather, and not at all demanding. He was taller than Thomas, with straight sandy hair that was turning grey quite early. He looked up at Naomi now, and gave her a welcoming smile.

'Would you look at this?' he said. 'It doesn't look good.'

Naomi wasn't sure if the question was meant literally, but decided to take it as such, and crouched beside him. 'Lame?' she asked.

'Do you know horses? Feel that, then.'

She examined the leg gently. The tendon was considerably swollen, the joint below hot to the touch. 'It's a strain, isn't it? Not a kick, or anything like that.'

'Mm,' said Peter non-committally. 'Say more.'

She felt down the leg again. The pony shifted, and raised its hoof warningly.

'Now then!' said Peter sharply, and waited.

'It's quite fluid. It shifts about. I wouldn't say it was serious. I'd just bathe it in cold water, I suppose, and rest her,' said Naomi, considering. The she recollected herself, and said, 'But you're a farmer! You must know much more about it than I do.'

'Mm,' assented Peter. 'I was just thinking the same as you. Though I was thinking perhaps a compress first, with hot water, and then cold. Would you agree to that?'

'I'm quite sure you don't need my opinion.'

'I thought you were handy, when we spoke before. Will you stay with her a minute?'

Naomi stayed, speaking softly to the pony, who nuzzled her jacket and butted her impatiently while they waited. Presently Peter returned with a pan of hot water and a roll of cloth. 'Now, if you could hold her. She may not take to this, being young.'

She didn't take to it at all. Her eyes rolled, and she tossed her head. Naomi faced her squarely and held her firmly by the halter. 'Now then you bugger,' said Peter reassuringly, shoving the pony over. She leaned on him heavily, and he made her stand, swearing gently throughout. 'She's just young,' he remarked to Naomi. 'Means no harm. Let's try again.'

This time the mare nipped Naomi sharply on the arm. 'Stop that!' said Naomi, and grabbed the halter again in both hands.

Peter grunted, and managed to apply the bandage before the mare kicked out again. 'Bugger you,' he remarked, as soothingly as before, and began to wind the bandage tightly round, while Naomi and the mare faced one another, eye to eye, in a moment of uneasy truce.

'Done.' Peter straightened up just in time as she kicked out again. 'We'll hope that stays on until tomorrow. She's a good mare, not broken yet, hardly.'

'So I gather.'

'Did she nip you?'

'Not much. My jacket's thick.'

'We'll turn her out, shall we?'

They did so, and watched her limp off across the small paddock behind the orchard. 'That's a nice pony,' remarked Naomi. 'It's all ponies here, is it? I suppose you'd have no use for horses, with the mountains.'

'Mm,' agreed Peter. 'You'll see no carts here. We use oxen for the field work. The only ways out are over the passes, and we use pack ponies for all our goods. And the way you came in by, you'll have seen you'd get no animal through that.'

'It's the same where I come from. We just use ponies, because there's too much weather for anything else. Ours are different though, smaller, and neater about the head.'

'Yours is a good country for horses.'

'The best in the world. Only not my part of it. There's no grazing there, except for the toughest.'

'I'm feeding the sheep now,' said Peter. 'We've some in the field across the beck. Thomas doesn't think much of them; he likes flocks that make their own way on the hill, but I'm pleased enough. Do you want to come? One of the boys was meant to, but he's gone and lost himself, as usual.'

'I'll come.'

It took a while to feed the sheep. The hay had to be carried out on a handcart and then scattered. There were goats to feed after that, a couple with kids, and one with two caddy lambs trailing after her. Peter showed her the pigs after that, of which he seemed extremely proud. Naomi found she could keep her end up over the lambs, dredging up knowledge she hardly knew she had from the depths of memory, but over hogs she had to admit complete ignorance. It didn't matter. Peter was happy to enlighten her. They spent a contemplative half hour leaning over the gate, watching the pigs rooting, until the next shower sent them strolling back to the yard.

'I think a cup of tea,' said Peter, regarding the sky, 'while this clears, and then I've jobs to do. Would that suit you?'

'That would suit me.' Naomi hesitated as they reached the back door. 'Your mother — no, your aunt, it would be — I saw she'd got back. She'll want to be with Thomas, I suppose.'

'Mm. So Alice is back. Well, we'll not disturb them. They won't be in the kitchen, I don't suppose.'

They weren't. Naomi and Peter hung their wet jackets over a couple of chair backs, and ensconced themselves by the fire.

'So in your household,' began Peter, 'how many head of cattle, would you reckon?'

'I've no idea. It was fifteen years ago that I left home.'

It took him a moment to digest that. Then he said, 'You'll be lonely then, sometimes. But it stays with you, all the same.'

'How can you tell?'

'The way you speak. When you speak about farming, your speech changes. More rhythm in it,' said Peter unexpectedly. 'That's the way you spoke at home, I suppose.'

Naomi blushed scarlet. She had almost forgotten what it felt like, it was so long since anyone had disconcerted her that much. She covered her hot cheeks with her hands, and almost stammered, 'It doesn't. I speak the way I always did. Don't I?'

'No,' said Peter simply. 'It's hardly to be expected, is it? They wouldn't understand you along the road.'

'Oh,' said Naomi, and added defensively, 'Well, I've never noticed it.'

'No. You wouldn't.'

There was a silence.

'Mind you,' said Peter presently. 'It's lonely both ways, whether you stay or go, sometimes. Your home would be lonely enough, if you were to lose the ones you loved.'

'Has that happened here?'

'To some.' There was another long silence. 'Naomi?' said Peter, pronouncing her name for the first time.

'Yes?'

'You'll not be here long, I know,' said Peter. 'I wouldn't say anything, but I know Thomas, so I know what kind of friendship you must have between you, and therefore I think perhaps I'll not be speaking out of turn.'

'When you speak of what?' asked Naomi, but she already knew. She realised she was blushing again, and felt slightly breathless. It seemed extraordinary that this countryman should so disturb her, when so few people she met on the road had any power to do so. But there had been a growing tension in her during the last few days, and perhaps only Peter had spotted it.

'If you want me,' said Peter simply. 'While you stay in this valley, I'd be glad. Perhaps you want to love, in a particular kind of way, and perhaps you have no one to accept it. And perhaps I do too, things here being as they are. You can have me, if you want me.'

'Oh,' said Naomi, suddenly so hot with confusion she felt as if she couldn't even see properly. In this state she was sure to hurt him, and that was the last thing she wanted to do. She took a deep breath, and made herself be calm. 'Thank you,' she managed to say. 'I appreciate it. Only I'm too confused. I understand you, and I'm privileged that you offer. Only it confuses me too much. It's not that I don't want ... I know what kind of love you mean, of course I do, and I know too well what I want, and what I can't have.'

'Perhaps I'm not much use to you, but perhaps again, it would help you out of your confusion. It would do more than that for me.'

'I don't know.' Naomi looked at him, and met an intent gaze, so that her eyes immediately dropped. 'I can't answer you very well. It helps me, what you say, but that doesn't help you. I think I'm too much involved with you already. If I said yes, I might not be treating you right. Does that make sense?'

'The past is over,' said Peter. 'I wouldn't bother with it. I keep my memories, but they're my own.'

She had no idea what he meant, and tried to frame a question that was not inquisitive. Before she could do so there was a familiar thumping of footsteps on the stair outside, and Linnet and Jo burst into the room with characteristic speed.

'Oh,' said Linnet. 'I didn't know you were here. My mother's back. I forgot to tell her about you, but Thomas probably will.'

*

Late that evening Naomi sat on the window seat in her room, looking out over the valley. The moon had not yet risen, and above the outlines of the mountains the sky was bright with stars. Naomi watched them for a long time, her fiddle across her knees. She had been playing, but it was growing late now, and people might be disturbed. It was not their kind of music she had been playing, but the other, which she had travelled so far and sought so long to understand. It took her back into her own world again, where the music was paramount, always offering her a new horizon, a life's adventure that she might follow with all she had, and never any confusion, none at all.

It would be so easy, thought Naomi, if only that were all. It was private now, and dark. She let the grief inside her rise and spill over, until her eyes were suffused with unshed tears, so that the stars seemed to coalesce in a mass of undifferentiated sparks. Naomi wiped her nose, and stared upwards at the broad band of the Milky Way, straddling the valley from one side to the other. The tears ran down her cheeks, and she let them fall unheeded. She was alone now, and the night was her own.

She was interrupted by a gentle tapping at her door. It might have been a thunderbolt. Naomi jumped, and smeared her sleeve across her face. At least it was dark. 'Who's that?' she called out sharply.

'Me. Thomas.'

She hesitated, then called: 'Come in.'

He came in, carrying a candle, so she could see his face clearly. He, on the other hand, couldn't see her at all. 'Where are you?' asked Thomas. 'Are you in bed?'

'No. I'm here.'

'I'm sorry to disturb you,' said Thomas, peering in the direction of the window, 'but I didn't see you again. I left you rather suddenly, so I just came to say goodnight.'

'Goodnight,' said Naomi promptly.

Thomas raised the candle and looked at her anxiously. 'I wish I could see you,' he said anxiously.

Naomi obligingly got up and came into the light, but not too near. 'There's nothing new to see. It was nice of you to come. Goodnight.'

'Is something in here making you sneeze?'

'Sneeze? No.'

'You sound that way.'

'Then I expect there is.' Naomi sat down on the bed, and began to remove her boots, hoping that he would take the hint.

'Feathers?' suggested Thomas, sounding concerned.

'Oh shut up! Go away!'

'Naomi,' said Thomas, dropping to his knees beside her. 'What's the matter?'

'Go away.'

'No.'

She flared up at him instantly. 'I said go! Have you no respect? Have you no sense of anyone's privacy? How dare you invade me like this?'

'There's a limit,' said Thomas doggedly. 'We keep too much to ourselves. It's too dangerous. It will make us mad.'

Through all her choked-up grief and anger, she heard him, and felt a pang of fear, though she didn't understand. 'I'm in no danger,' whispered Naomi. 'I only want to be alone.'

'Are you quite sure?'

She swallowed. 'I know myself well enough,' she answered caustically. 'There's a half moon, and I have too many feelings. I'm a long way from any women I know, and it makes me notice it more. You should probably leave me alone.'

'I'm not much use to you, am I?' asked Thomas, humbly and infuriatingly.

'If you're useless,' snapped Naomi nastily, 'I suggest you go away.'

'You might be wrong.'

'Oh shut up!' She was perilously close to tears.

'I'm sorry,' said Thomas, and gently touched her cheek.

Naomi pushed him violently, rolled over, and burst into tears.

It was terrifying, that her private feelings should well up so forcibly into a situation that wasn't private at all. She choked into the quilt, and tried to hold her breath. She didn't have to cry. She hadn't cried unbidden for fifteen years. Naomi held herself tight, and nearly stopped herself. A hand was laid on her rigid back, not at all suppressively, but comfortingly. It was too much. She pulled the quilt round her head, her back firmly turned to Thomas, and shook with uncontrollable sobs. They began to overwhelm her. It was like breaching a wall to let in a little trickle of water, and finding the whole weight of the sea behind it. She was awake, and engulfed by the images of dream. It was terrible to be so helpless. Naomi began to shiver. Thomas pulled the rest of the quilt round her, and went on rubbing her back, up and down her spine, without saying a word.

At last the grief that was choking her began to subside, and she found herself fighting for breath, damp and shivering, smaller sobs still shaking her, and slowly dying away. She could hardly breathe, so she jerked the quilt away, and raised her head. She noticed him properly, although she had been aware of his presence all the time. He was lying beside her, the thickness of the quilt between them, his head almost touching hers. She couldn't see his face; the candle was down on the floor below them.

Naomi leaned her head on her hands, so she could see nothing but the darkness of the covers in front of her. She felt him touch her hair, but only just, as if he didn't intend her to know it. 'I have had a dream,' sad Naomi shakily, without looking up. 'The same dream, for several nights. It's an old dream. I'd almost forgotten it.'

She felt him push her hair back off her face, but she shielded her eyes with her hand, and went on disjointedly, 'I dream that I'm looking for a boat. The tide is rising. There's no time. It may even be too late. The land on the far side . . .' She paused, shuddering, '. . . it changes. The details change, from one dream to another. But I belong there, and if I am to live, I know that I must get across. But there is no boat.'

He said nothing, but went on stroking her hair. It was distracting, as though she had waited all her life for someone to touch her precisely like that, and she wanted to concentrate. But she made herself go on. 'Or sometimes there is a boat, but there is something wrong with it. Or many boats, all wrong. Or there are no oars.'

There was silence. Then Naomi reached up and took his hand, stopping him. 'Thomas?'

'Yes?'

'That's all. Please, go away now.'

He held her hand for a moment. She felt him shift his weight on the bed, then he kissed her lightly, just above her ear. 'I will,' he said. 'There is a way, you know. You have to go on with the dream. Goodnight.'

'Goodnight,' said Naomi, without looking up.

'I'll leave you the candle.' She was aware of his weight gone from the bed beside her. There was a soft movement in the room, then the quiet click of the latch behind him.

Eleventh Day

Naomi woke late the following morning. There was bright sunshine outside. She got up and dressed quickly, then cautiously opened her door. There was no one about. Specks of dust swam in the sunlight which poured in through the window above the stairs. Naomi trod quietly down the stairs in her socked feet, then along the kitchen passage. The kitchen door was open, and the room was empty. She went in swiftly, dipped a bowl in a bucket of water, and washed her face, splashing cold water ruthlessly over her eyes. Then she found her boots, which she had left to dry by the fire, and emptied the straw out of them. They were dried hard, the laces bunged up with caked mud. Naomi forced her feet inside, and pulled at the stubborn laces. One snapped in her hand. She swore, and knotted it. When she was ready she slipped back down the passage, and let herself out at the front door.

It was like stepping into summer. There was no wind at all. The sky was deep cloudless blue, and the sun was actually hot. She turned her face towards it, and drew a deep breath. Then she set off in the opposite direction from the garden, along the edge of the oakwood.

She crossed flat fields with the dew still drying on them, finding a narrow path which led her to stiles set in the stone walls. The ground at the foot of each stile was trodden bare. This must be a fairly frequented path, then, although she could see no reason why. Presumably all this land belonged to Thomas's family. There was no telling.

Presently she had her answer. There was another settlement ahead, the familiar pattern of low stone buildings surrounding a big yard. She heard dogs barking from inside the buildings, and the lowing of cows, together with movements and clatterings from the longest byre. They must be milking. The yard itself was deserted apart from an assortment of hens, who were picking over the fresh scraps on the midden. The air was hot and heavy with mingled smells of hay and dung. Big black flies swarmed over the muck heap, hatched out by the first heat of the summer.

Naomi hesitated, wondering if there was a way round the buildings. Presumably the path ended here, and she didn't want to go tramping through the farmyard. The last thing she felt like doing was talking to anybody. They would realise she was here because of the dogs, but if she went quietly round the outside she might get away with wishing them good morning.

She picked her way across the mud to the yard gate, meaning to turn off round the back of the byre. Her thoughts had already drifted off again. She was hardly aware of it, but she was thinking about Thomas. His hair was beginning to grow again, she thought irrelevantly. It was quite straight; somehow she had expected it to be curly.

There was a shout behind her. She turned, startled, her hand almost on the gate. There was a man there, running. He shouted again, but she did not hear what he said. There was another shout behind her. She turned, and saw people in the yard. A moment earlier there had been no one. It was too sudden to take in. She opened her mouth to call out, and something struck her on the shoulder, sharp and painful, so that she staggered. She turned to run, and there was another blow from behind, between her shoulder blades. She swung round, but there was nothing there, only the man, twenty feet away or more. Something flew past her head and her arms went up to protect herself. A pain shot across her forearm, like a burn. She clutched it with her one hand, and nearly fell. She looked into the yard once more, and another stone came flying. She was trapped between the man and the gate. Another stone whizzed past her, and then she saw a gap, through the mud into the field again. She fled, stumbling in the dirt, and another stone shot past her ear. Then she was round the back of the building, and running desperately across a boggy field.

There was a stone wall in front of her. She scrambled over it somehow, but her legs were shaking. She sank down in the lee of it, panting and trembling. She needed to go on, she knew. It wasn't safe here. She couldn't even see, wouldn't know even if they were right the other side of the wall. But she was exhausted. It seemed easier to give up. Her head fell back against the stones behind her, and for a moment she shut her eyes.

She thought she heard a sound behind her. Alert again, she crouched behind the wall, her heart suddenly pounding. She took her hand away from her hurt arm, and saw that it was wet with blood. No time to think about that. She ran the length of the wall, almost doubled up in the shelter of it. She reached a corner, and stopped. Cautiously she straightened, and looked back over the top. There was no one there. She could only see the roofs of the farmstead now. There was smoke rising from one chimney. The way home led straight past it.

She leaned on the wall, still trembling. To get back to Thomas's, either she'd need to get up to the oakwood, and pass by in the shelter of the trees, or make a detour right across the valley. She felt dizzy. The woods would be quicker. Slowly she climbed the next wall, and walked across the field towards the trees. The centre of the field felt very exposed; the trees were like a far-off haven. There was more blood on her hand. Suddenly it seemed to register, and she looked at it in sudden panic, then smeared the blood away on her shirt. She studied the hand, flexed her fingers, and turned her wrist one way, and then the other. There was a sharp pain in her forearm, but that was all. She drew a long breath of relief, and wiped her other arm across her forehead, leaving a smear of blood across it.

Once in the trees, she felt safe. There wasn't a path. She skirted the very edge of the wood, within the field wall, but she kept her eyes open, ready to climb back into the sheltering trees whenever necessary. The valley had taken on a new aspect. It now seemed perilous. The bare flat fields belonged to an alien people who would hurt her if they found her. She realised then how utterly remote this place was. The world was full of danger, but in most places there was a clear road, and a way out. Here, there was only Thomas. What have I done, thought Naomi, clutching her wounded arm, to give anyone so much power over me?

By the time she reached Thomas's house her arm had stopped bleeding, but she still felt slightly faint. She approached the door cautiously. If she could get some water, she needn't ask any of them to help her, but it would be surprising if she could get to the kitchen or to the pump without encountering anyone.

The last person she had expected to find in the kitchen was Thomas's mother. Indeed, she had almost forgotten about her arrival, so much else had happened. Naomi hesitated in the doorway, realising that it was too late to retreat. She had been noticed.

'Come in,' said Alice. 'I'm sorry I wasn't here to welcome you earlier.' Her tone changed. 'Are you hurt?'

'No,' said Naomi, and realised that sounded surly. 'I mean yes. I only came for some water.'

'Sit down.' The tone was sharp, and Naomi automatically obeyed. She tried to adjust to this, but her mind refused to work clearly. This was Thomas's mother. The whole household was hers. It mattered what Naomi said to her; she was quite aware of that. She had been in danger this morning, and for all she knew there was still danger. She needed to be careful what she said, and think properly. She was cold, and her head spun.

'Can you roll your sleeve back? No? Take your jacket off.'

'Oh!'

'What is it?'

'I think it's a bruise,' said Naomi, as clearly as she could. She glanced down at her arm, and noticed that her shirt sleeve was ripped to the elbow. And I only just mended it, she thought irrelevantly. And I washed it too, and now I'll have to get the blood off. If I'd known, she thought dreamily, I'd not have bothered.

'Who did this?' The question cut sharply across her wandering thoughts, and made her jump.

'It's nothing,' said Naomi warily. 'I'm all right. As long as my wrist's not hurt.'

Alice caught the note of apprehension. 'Your wrist? Oh, of course. Your trade. You realise they could have killed you?'

That's not so important. Naomi thought that if she said that aloud, Alice would think her hysterical. She pulled herself together, and watched the other busy herself about the kitchen. It took her a moment to realise that these preparations were for her, and when Alice came to dress her arm, she drew back in surprise.

'Don't be foolish!' Startled, Naomi submitted, and there was a brief silence. Then, 'Did this happen in my household?'

Again, the question was rapped out so that she jumped. 'No,' said Naomi, and waited.

'If you don't tell me, I shall find out. Don't you realise your own danger?'

'Not until today. I saw no reason why I should be in danger.' To her relief she was feeling better. Her head was clearing, and the bruises had settled to a dull ache.

'There is always danger.' The voice sounded almost weary. 'This is a wild country. Do you know where you are?'

'Of course I do,' said Naomi with some asperity. 'These are the empty lands. I have heard stories, of course, but nothing happened until now to make me beware.'

'The stories are nothing. We have suffered, that is all.'

'There is suffering everywhere, surely?' Naomi raised her eyes, and stared at Alice. She must have been a strongly built woman once, but now even her thick brown jacket couldn't hide her thinness. Her skin was deeply wrinkled, and very brown. Her eyes were sharp and lively, like Thomas's. There was something contradictory about her, as though youth and age uneasily inhabited the same body. Her hands were twisted, and swollen at the joints. Her face was that of an old woman, and her expression was that of Thomas, exactly.

'How can you understand this place?' said Alice at last. 'I can't make you understand. I suppose you think that I belong here. And that's true. I was the first child to be born here since the world changed. Do you understand what that means?'

'Thomas told me how the people came back.'

'Did he tell you what it was like to come back?'

'No.'

'No, he wouldn't. Thomas would tell you legends and dreams.' Which shows how well you know him, thought Naomi, watching her closely. There was bitterness in Alice's voice, but also affection, she thought. 'Do you know how this valley was cleared, so that we could make fields?'

'No.'

'Of course you don't. To you, every village and every field has been there since time began. Two generations ago this valley was a forest. We burnt it.'

'I suppose you would have to.' Naomi was puzzled, unable to see where this was leading.

'I'm trying to explain to you why you meet violence here, as you might do anywhere. Do you think we chose to come back to a land that was perhaps still dangerous, to carve a living out of a wilderness? We suffered. When our crops failed, we starved, and if a sickness came, we had no resources, and so we died. Did you expect that because this is a world apart, it would have no pain in it?'

'I expected nothing. Thomas told me the names of the mountains, and how they had been remembered. I can understand why anyone would wish to return to the place where they belonged.'

'Can you?' Thomas's mother got up suddenly, taking the bowl of bloodstained water, and disappeared through the back door. When she came back she began taking herbs from various jars on the dresser, and mixing them into a tea. When she spoke again, her words were curiously at variance with these homely activities. 'The people came back to the valleys, not so much because they belonged here, but because they belonged nowhere else. You know why we left?'

'Because the land was poisoned.'

'And so the people were cursed. In particular, our children were hurt, and our unborn children. So over the years, no man or woman would choose to make a child with anyone who had fled from the empty lands. That danger is past, but the taboo still remains. You know what happens to a people who cannot share their children with the rest of the world?'

'They grow apart.'

'And therefore they live in danger. How do you think the names of the mountains were remembered for so long? No one who was safe, who knew their place in the world, would need to remember such a thing as that. Do the children in your country need to learn the names of places that no human eyes have seen since the world changed? Why would you want to teach them anything like that? Do you have a dance, so that you can count the years of your exile? Of course you don't. Instead you celebrate planting times and harvests in your own fields, and you don't worry about the past. Isn't that so?'

'It used to be,' said Naomi slowly.

'You can't expect my people to love you, when you have hated us so long. Quite apart from the matter of the fiddle player. Thomas knew about that, but he never gave a thought to the real truth of the matter. He should have thought of his own people. We have struggled hard to regain our own, and we need no strangers here.'

'But I am no enemy.'

'Have you been treated as a friend?'

Naomi stared at her. 'But that wasn't my doing!'

'Do you think it's mine?'

Naomi spread her hands in a gesture of despair. 'I have tried to understand. When Thomas told me the names of the mountains, I thought that they were beautiful.'

'And so they are. I also blame Thomas. He hasn't been honest with you.'

'I think he has been as honest as he can.'

'And perhaps that's not enough. But he told me why you came and what he had offered you. I said he should show you all, and give you what he promised. Indeed, we could hardly do otherwise now. But I'm fearful of the consequences.'

'Are you talking about the music for the dance?'

'I'm talking about the gift he offered you. As to the dance, perhaps he's right, and there will be healing. And perhaps the reward to you is worth it, even though you've placed yourself in great danger. He has been honest with you about that?' Once again the question came so fast that Naomi jumped.

'I think he has been honest,' she said.

'He must tell you everything, before the dance. It would be unjust to hide it from you. As for me, you must understand that I take no part in this. The dance is nothing to do with me.'

'I thought everyone in the valley bore a part in it?'

'My part in this valley is dead, and has been for seven years.'

'I don't understand.'

'It suits me,' was the reply. 'I give my time now to the plants. In this household, you can look to Linnet. I'll stay until the dance is over, but I resigned my part long ago. You can't look to me, whatever may happen. I'm sorry, but you have to understand that.'

'So you warn me of danger, but you can't help me?'

'I once held power in this valley, and when I resigned it, I promised myself I would never take it back. I can't help you. Unless there's anything you want me to tell you now. I'm willing to do that, if I can.'

Naomi considered. This woman owed her nothing, and she was not inquisitive. On the other hand, there were gaps, and even one piece filled would make the whole a little clearer.

'Is there anything?'

'Yes,' said Naomi firmly. 'I'm not inquisitive, but there is one thing that would help.'

'Yes?'

'Will you tell me the name of your elder daughter?'

Thomas's mother shot her another look. There was pain in it, not unmixed with appreciation. 'Judith,' she said. 'Her name was Judith.'

*

Much later, Naomi found Linnet sitting on the front doorstep, mending a fishing line. 'Jo's asleep,' said Linnet, as soon as she saw Naomi. 'I wondered if it would be a good time to show you the music for the dance?'

'All right.'

'Where do you want to go then? Can we do it in your room? Jo's asleep in mine.'

They went upstairs. Naomi had forgotten how she had been feeling first thing that morning. She hurriedly made the bed, and picked up her nightshirt. 'Did you find my mother?' asked Linnet, watching her. 'She wanted to see you.'

'Yes, thank you.'

'She made me realise we should have got on with this sooner. I didn't think. There's not much to it, really.'

'Well then, it won't take you long to teach me, will it?'

Linnet stared at her. 'Teach you? I can't teach you a thing, you know that. It's just a matter of finding out if you know the tunes. There's a theme that runs through, that comes back whenever the dancers come together, and a different part for each dancer. As I said, the dance is in two parts. The tune for each dancer in the second part echoes their tune in the first, but differently. It begins with the Fool. Shall I play it through to you?'

'Play me the whole lot,' said Naomi, sitting down on the window seat cradling her arm. 'Tell me what each part is, then play it. I won't interrupt.'

She kept her word. Presently Linnet ceased to be nervous, and the tunes began to flow more freely. Naomi sat listening, watching Linnet through half shut eyes. There was no telling what she was thinking. Linnet resolutely kept her eyes away from her, and gave her mind to what she was doing. She only paused to give the name of each dancer, before she began to play the piece that belonged to them. The names were not unfamiliar to Naomi. Some of them were slightly different from what she had heard before, but she began to recognise the theme. She had never heard of it as a dance before, however, and the idea intrigued her. But the music . . . Naomi listened silently, but gradually she began to look puzzled, and then angry. Linnet was absolutely right: there was nothing unusual about any of it. Naomi said nothing, however, and Linnet never looked at her.

'That's the first half,' said Linnet at last, and lowered her fiddle. 'The dancers come back together, like they do at the beginning, only a little different. Then they make up the same circle, only going in the opposite direction, and they take new parts. The tunes do the same.' She looked at Naomi. Naomi looked remarkably forbidding, and all Linnet's nervousness came flooding back. 'Did I do all right?' asked Linnet, with a timidity that made her voice scarcely recognisable, even to herself.

'You did,' said Naomi shortly. 'Go on.'

Not at all reassured, Linnet obediently began again. This time she played with her back almost completely turned to Naomi, facing the door. The music in the second half was predictable, following exactly the pattern that Linnet had described. Naomi listened very carefully, and heard nothing at all that she might not have expected to hear. The pieces were new to her, certainly, but the form was old enough. With a little practice, she could play the people through their dance with no further thought at all.

'That's it.' said Linnet at last, with obvious relief. She turned to face Naomi. 'It would be a privilege to play it with you,' she faltered. 'I know I'm not much good. I hope you're not insulted.'

Naomi gave Linnet her attention with some difficulty. 'What? Of course not! If all you could play was "Baa baa black sheep", it would be totally unfair for me to object, and I would never be so disrespectful.' Linnet stared at her in dismay, wondering what on earth she had done. 'Anyway, I told you. You're good. I don't tell lies, and you should respect me enough to believe what I say. You haven't insulted me, or wronged me. But someone has. It's nothing to do with you. I'll practise this with you later, as I promised.'

She had left the room before Linnet was fully aware of what was happening. Linnet stared after her open-mouthed, then fled back to her own room, and the reassurance of her sleeping baby.

*

Naomi didn't slow down until she was half way across the valley. She was too angry to think of danger. She crossed the other branch of the beck by a bridge she hadn't found before, and strode on furiously, neither knowing nor caring where the path took her. After crossing the bridge she found herself back among oak trees. The path petered out in a carpet of anemones and wild garlic. She paid no attention. Presently she found the way blocked by a stone wall. She climbed over, and followed the contour of the hill. There was a break in the long slopes ahead of her. Sure enough, there was the familiar shape of the mountain between the two arms of the valley. Naomi glared at it resentfully, as if the hill itself was responsible for betraying her. Then she scrambled heedlessly along the edge of the hill.

There was a cluster of buildings just below her, the same ones as she had seen from the slopes opposite with Thomas. In front of them there was a well-defined path, winding up to the pass. Naomi stopped on the path and looked down at the farm below her. It was deserted, the yard overgrown with weeds, the windows boarded up. The roof looked sound enough, although there was an ominous mossy growth along one gable. There were nettles growing right up to the door, so evidently the place had not been opened up this year, or perhaps for many years before that. A sense of desolation pierced the red mist of anger that had driven her blindly along thus far. She gave a small shudder, and took the path that led uphill towards the hidden pass.

It soon brought her back to water, tumbling down the slope in a series of pools and waterfalls. The path climbed steeply upwards beside it, forming treacherous slides of solid rock interspersed with thin gravel. Naomi found herself using both hands to pull herself up, and was grateful for the holds provided by the skinny oaks that clung to the side of the gorge. How the ponies managed this she could not imagine, unless there was a longer way round. In her present mood it suited her very well. She felt like a fight, and gravity was as good an opponent as any other, since the one she was really after was away thinking about sheep. Naomi ground her teeth, and pushed her way upward like a thing possessed.

She stopped at last because she was too out of breath to continue. The path crossed the beck by a rough wooden bridge, where the gorge evened out. There had been ponies here, for they had left their droppings. Naomi leaned over the wooden rail, fighting for breath, and wiped the sweat from her eyes. She ran her hands through her hair until it was all standing up on end. Then she thought of Thomas, and spat furiously into the unheeding water below. She flung away from the bridge, and fought her way on uphill, pitching her fury against the indifferent slopes.

When she could keep going no longer she flopped down on the grass at the path side, panting, and looked round properly for the first time. The country had completely changed. The valley had dwindled to a small patch of green behind her, caught between the hills. She was sitting on the floor of a bleak hollowed-out corridor between two ridges. Scree-covered slopes rose up on either side of her. The weather was changing too; summits were lost in cloud, and the colours had faded with the departing sunlight. She was hot and sweating, but she realised suddenly that in fact it must be cold. She had come right out of the valley without thinking, and had no idea where she was. It was lucky she had followed the pony track, which meant that there was no doubt about the way back. Naomi shivered and stood up, mopping her face.

She took one last look up towards the pass, and nearly jumped out of her skin. There were figures moving down towards her, four-footed, silent, not far above. She felt panic clutch at her stomach, then in an instant she had placed them. Ponies. Small dun-coloured ponies, with the mist behind them. She turned hot again at her own folly, and peered past them. Sure enough, there was someone walking behind. Only two ponies. Naomi composed herself, quite unconscious of the wildness of her appearance, and waited.

The ponies stopped and looked at her curiously, then continued to pick their way down. They were heavily loaded, each with two covered panniers. Their drover followed a little way behind. It was a man, on his own. He looked at Naomi in surprise, and said courteously, 'Good evening.'

'Good evening,' she replied.

He looked like a shepherd, being dressed in a thick tweed jacket of undyed wool, and baggy trousers tucked into stout boots. Unlike most of the people she had seen here, he wore a hat of battered grey felt with a wide brim. Now that he was close enough for her to see him clearly, she noticed that his face was badly scarred down one side, the skin white and puckered. Perhaps that was the reason for the hat. 'It's been a fine day,' said Naomi.

'Clouding over now,' he said. 'Are you meaning to cross the pass tonight?'

'No. I was just out for a walk.'

He concealed his surprise, and said with elaborate politeness, 'Then I hope our hills will give you pleasure. You're a stranger here, I think?'

'That's so.'

'And a musician perhaps?' he said gently.

It was her turn to be startled, but she was not to be outdone. 'So my fame has gone before me,' she said easily. 'I'm sure I don't deserve it.'

'I'm sure you do. Your fame, and your courage, perhaps.'

'You're very civil. My name is Naomi.' There was no way he could get out of that, and still keep up this charade.

He didn't attempt to. 'And mine is Paul,' he said formally. 'It's a great pleasure to meet you, Naomi.'

They shook hands. 'We were expecting you,' said Naomi, and congratulated herself on a hit.

If the shot went home he gave no sign of it. 'I'm so glad. You knew I would come if I could, being a fiddler myself.'

'Well, you certainly don't talk like a shepherd,' she said caustically, feeling that this had gone on long enough. 'And I can't believe you came to play tunes with me, when you've kept away for seven years.'

'Are you walking back?' asked Paul gently, 'because the mist will soon be down, and dusk is falling. I brought no light, and you don't seem to have come equipped for emergencies.'

She didn't bother to respond to that one, but fell into step beside him. 'Have a toffee,' said Paul, after five minutes' silence. This time she did jump, quite visibly.

'I'm sorry. Is anything the matter?'

'I didn't expect you to be fond of toffee,' said Naomi, watching him as if he might turn into something unexpected.

'Habit,' said Paul, offering her a crumpled bag.

'It's become a habit of mine too, lately.'

'It ruins your teeth,' remarked Paul dispassionately.

'I dare say,' said Naomi, and helped herself.

They walked on. He was right: it was already twilight. A thin film of greyness was settling over the hills, dividing the little procession from the fields that were still surprisingly far below. They reached the first waterfall, and the ponies turned away from the beck. Naomi saw that a new path was already being carved out, away from the treacherous rock above the gorge.

'What do you think of my pupil?' asked Paul conversationally, as they negotiated a patch of bog.

Naomi jumped across the wet bit before she replied. 'I think she's good, though she suffers from isolation. As a musician, I think she's wasted.'

'And not as a musician?'

'I have no idea.'

'You're right, of course,' said Paul, as if pursuing an interesting point of discussion. 'But would it be worth it to her? Talent isn't everything, as you and I both know. You have to have desire.'

'No doubt.'

'And fortitude,' he went on, as though answering a point that she had made. 'Now I, for example, have desire, and no fortitude. And so I set off, oh, several times a year, perhaps, and then it rains maybe, or I am hungry. And then I go home.'

'You must make a lousy shepherd, then.'

'I go home from my sheep,' said Paul, undismayed, 'and I sit by the fire and play the fiddle. No wonder I come to nothing, while you go far. How far have you gone, incidentally?'

'I've just reached here,' answered Naomi, 'and you can tell me where I am, by the way. The ruined house down below us — what is that?'

That silenced him. She turned to see his face, but his eyes were hidden by the ridiculous hat. His mouth had dropped open, in consternation, it seemed.

'Naomi,' said Paul, and the voice might have belonged to a different man. 'Has Thomas not told you why he brought you here? Truly, has he not?'

'What? I don't know what you're talking about. But since you ask,' Naomi added bitterly, 'Thomas has lied to me, and I've just discovered it. So I suppose anything is possible.'

'You don't trust him then? You can, you know, so long as he is well. Something must have happened.'

'That much I had noticed. Paul,' said Naomi, confronting him. 'I don't know you, and you don't know me. But I know who you are, and you know who I am. I can't afford to play games with you at this stage, agreeable though it might normally be.'

'Very well,' replied Paul, watching her closely. 'Listen, we must keep walking, or we'll be benighted. I'll tell you what I want. I would like to ask you two questions, and I would like to know that I was hearing the truth. It may be more important than you think.'

'I doubt that. But I'll make a bargain with you. I'll give you two true answers, if you'll give me the same. Is that fair?'

She waited, watching his profile. From this side the scar was hidden, and he was remarkably goodlooking, with a straight nose and strong chin, and thick fair hair not entirely obscured by the hat. He turned to her with a sudden smile, that would have been delightful if it had not been cruelly crooked. 'That's fair,' said Paul. 'You start, then.'

'I already have. You heard my first question.'

The two ponies halted in front of them, and Naomi made out a closed gate through the thickening twilight. Paul went ahead to open it, and Naomi followed the ponies through, and found herself back among the fields.

Paul closed the gate carefully, and rejoined her. 'That house,' he said clearly, with no trace of emotion in his voice at all, 'was rebuilt by Thomas and his sister Judith. They made a farm there and brought up two boys, who were Judith's sons.'

'Thank you.'

'My turn. Tell me about my friend Thomas. Is he well?'

'Perfectly well. Is that all?'

'In his mind?'

'His mind is as sound as any I have known. Always.'

'Thank you,' said Paul.

'My turn. Why did you come?'

This time she had to wait even longer for her answer. It was almost dark. She could hear the rushing of the beck, loud in the stillness of the evening, flowing on regardless.

'To see my dearest friend,' said Paul, so lightly that he could have been jeering. 'My turn. Why did you come?'

She remembered her anger. Already it was beginning to seem stale. She might have come if Thomas had promised her nothing at all, if she had known then what she knew now. 'I came because Thomas promised me a music out of the past, that belonged to the time before the world changed. All that I am is bound up in that music. I couldn't have refused. It matters to me, and it's the only thing that I expected to take away from here. Nothing else.'

'So why do you say he lied?'

'That's a third question.'

'It's too important to be missed. Thomas wouldn't lie about that, if he is well.'

Naomi sighed. 'All right. He asked me to come, promising what I told you, and said that I should be asked to play the music for the dance. Linnet played it to me today, and there was nothing in it. It was delightful, yes, of its kind, and moving. But it was not the thing that I was promised.'

'Of course not.'

'What do you mean?' she asked sharply.

'I mean that I think you very clever, but perhaps too much involved to think clearly. I've done the same myself, so I don't blame you. It wasn't the music for the dance, of course not. Didn't he tell you that the dance was made in exile? He's speaking of music that has lain silent for far longer than that.'

'Explain!' she commanded, seizing him by the arm and forcing him to face her.

'It's not mine,' said Paul. 'Don't you trust him?'

'I don't know,' she admitted. 'I think I did.'

'You were right. Don't make a mistake now. Is Alice back?'

'Yesterday.'

'That's why he waited. It's hers, not his, to give away. Once he would have given it to me, but she forbade him. I think now she was right. I would have made nothing of it. But I was younger then, and still believed that one day I might be different. But enough of that. The bargain is kept, so now we can have a more comfortable conversation. Another toffee?'

'Thank you. Tell me about your music, and who you play to.'

'I brought my fiddle. I hoped we might meet; that part was true enough. I play through all the valleys, right down to the coast, if I'm asked. Not at this time of year so much, because we're busy. But after harvest, that's when my season starts. And you?'

'My season is all the year round, and has been for fifteen years.'

'You never go home?'

'No.' There was a pause. 'I didn't come this way. Does it take us back to the house?'

'It takes you back, if you turn left where the tracks meet.'

'Not you?'

'I wasn't intending to turn up unannounced after seven years. They're expecting me at the farm at the foot of the mountain. They're waiting for seed potatoes, so I've brought them.'

'I saw that farm from the hill. But you also came to see Thomas.'

'I came for reasons of my own, which are various. We played a game just now, you and I, and I kept the rules. I'm sure you'll keep the rules too.'

'I shan't say anything. But no one will ask me, anyway.'

'Tomorrow I have business of my own to deal with, of one kind and another. It may entail an early return. It may not. This is your turning. If you take that path across the fields, you'll find yourself back at the beck in a few minutes. I hope I'll see you again, and I'd like to play music with you. If not, I wish you well.'

'And I wish you the same,' said Naomi. She held out her hand, and they shook hands again. 'I hope your business prospers tomorrow.'

'Thank you.' Paul hesitated, and then said, 'I'll confess to you, I'm a little afraid. Though less so, for having met you. Farewell.'

By the time she reached the beck it was dark. Luckily the track was smooth under her feet, and the sound of the water was a sure guide home. Just as she reached the bridge, and saw the lights of the house above her, there was a sudden pattering all round her, and a shower enveloped her. The lights grew dim, as if the house itself were dissolving into water. Naomi hurried up the slope, stumbling over the still unfamiliar ground, and reached the door just as the clouds burst over her, and the shower turned to a deluge.

Twelfth Day

All that night the sound of running water permeated Naomi's dreams. She drifted, half-waking, with a restless tide. Sometimes the river was swollen with mountain snow, sometimes the current funneled between one island and another. When she woke, the light was grey and heavy, though she guessed it must be late. Rain poured down the long windows in a steady stream. Naomi pulled her quilt right over her head, and went to sleep again.

She was in a boat with Thomas, only it was not a boat. It was a flying craft that skimmed the mountain tops like a gull dipping over the crests of the waves. They flew down low over a stony summit, then touched land. The moment to get off, thought Naomi, if I am to get off. She half slid over the side, but the boat was moving again, sliding fast downhill. She could still fall out if she chose, but the motion was so enticing, she held on. Suddenly the mountain fell away below them. They drifted out over a precipice, with the ease of a gull soaring out over the cliffs.

Only it was not water below, it was a valley, vast and forested. She was afraid; there was no reason in the world why they should not fall, but they did not. She gazed downwards enraptured, because the land was untouched and beautiful. The boat hovered like a hawk, and Thomas stood in the prow watching, oblivious to their danger, watching the land below because that was the only thing that mattered to him. Naomi held her breath, as if only her care could hold them up. Slowly the boat began to dive, its nose dipping into nothingness. I must remember who I am, she realised desperately, and woke up.

It was still raining.

She stayed where she was for a while, but sleep had fled, and the clouds outside would not break. Finally she gave up staring at the water running down the window, and got up. This morning she must find Thomas. Paul's words had quenched her anger, but she wanted an explanation. Only not very much, perhaps. A little affection would be preferable, or even a good breakfast. Naomi sighed, and dressed herself with grim determination, losing another button in the process. Then she went to look for Thomas.

In the kitchen she found Peter, who instantly offered her a good breakfast.

'No thank you,' said Naomi. 'I must speak to Thomas. Do you know where he is?'

'In the hall,' said Peter promptly. 'One of the children came from across the valley with a message for him. He's talking to her now.'

Naomi thanked him, and left the room. Sure enough, there were voices from the hall at the end of the passage. She heard Thomas say something, and then Linnet's voice, loud and emphatic.

'You don't have to! Not if you don't want to! I know it's better not!'

Naomi hesitated, but it was too late. She had been seen, not by Thomas or Linnet, but by a girl of about ten who was standing near the door, on the other side of the round table, her hair and jacket dripping with rainwater. She stared at Naomi with widening eyes, then backed towards the door. 'Is that her?' she said in a frightened whisper. 'Is that the fiddle player?'

Linnet turned round, distracted. Naomi didn't look at her. She and the child stood staring at each other, Naomi in perplexity, the girl in open alarm. 'There's nothing to be afraid of,' said Naomi gently. 'Whoever told you that there was?'

The girl's mouth dropped open, but no words came out.

'Of course there isn't,' interrupted Linnet stormily. 'I can't stand much more of this! I'll go and tell them myself. Somebody must, before the dance. Wait!' she commanded, as the child was about to slip through the front door. 'This is nonsense! Come back in. Look at her!' she demanded, waving her hand at Naomi. 'There's nothing the matter with her, is there? She was never here before in her life, in any shape or form. She's as alive as you or I. You can pinch her if you like. And then go and tell your family, and let's have no more of this nonsense!'

'I think we might forego the pinching,' said Naomi mildly, and addressed the girl directly. 'If anyone told you I was a ghost' — the child winced, and drew back — 'they were quite wrong. Come here.'

She shook her head, still staring.

'Who told you to be afraid of me?'

'They all did,' interrupted Linnet bitterly. 'But if you ask them, they'll deny it. I'll go over there myself. And I'll answer the message too. I will, Thomas, not you. He should never have come!'

Thomas looked at her vaguely, as if he hadn't listened to any of this. Naomi took him in for the first time, and was shocked. He had gone quite white, but it wasn't that that frightened her. He didn't seem to have noticed she was there. He was like a sleepwalker who cannot properly wake up.

'I will go,' said Thomas to Linnet. 'I must. Now he's come, I have no choice.'

'Of course you have a choice! Don't see him, Thomas. It's not worth it!'

He looked at Linnet, trying to bring her into focus. 'Why not?' he asked her slowly. 'What are you afraid of?'

'Please,' said Linnet, almost tearful. 'Please Thomas. Let me speak to Alice. Don't go.'

'It's nothing to do with you or her. I must go.'

'I've got to go home now!' gasped the child at the door, and fled before they could stop her.

'Thomas,' said Naomi.

She was fairly sure he hadn't even noticed she was there. He jumped, then seemed about to stretch out his hand to her, in a plea for help, perhaps, but he thought better of it, and his arm dropped to his side. 'Naomi,' said Thomas, with an effort. 'I'm sorry. I've had a message. I have to go and meet somebody. It's important.'

'I know.'

'You can't know,' snapped Linnet. 'He mustn't go. That's all.'

'How do you know?' asked Thomas, regarding her steadily.

'I walked up to the pass yesterday,' replied Naomi carefully, mindful of her promise.

She heard Linnet gasp, and saw her cover her face with her hands. Thomas stared in horror as if she were indeed a ghost. 'I've done more than I meant to do,' he said hoarsely. 'I enticed you here, and now I'm afraid. But it's too late, and we can only go on.'

'I don't find that particularly reassuring,' said Naomi tartly. 'It strikes me you'll feel worse if you don't go than if you do. But it's none of my business. I came here looking for you.'

Her tone seemed to bring him to his senses a little. 'Why?' said Thomas, still dazed, but trying to concentrate.

'About the music. I'm willing to know nothing of your private lives, but I've earned the gift you promised me, and I deserve to know something of it now.'

'Yes,' said Thomas, trying to give his attention. 'Yes, Alice said the same. I meant to show you this morning, but then the message came.'

'For goodness sake!' Linnet swung round and faced Naomi. 'Can't you wait? It's hardly the moment. We've quite enough to worry about.'

'I was promised.'

Linnet's jaw dropped. She remembered how Naomi had made her feel yesterday. If the fiddle player were to demand her due at this moment, then she would have to have it. In Linnet's view a travelling musician was little more than a beggar, but Naomi was rapidly turning this idea upside down, and was frightening her a little in the process.

'It's true,' said Thomas wearily. 'You've waited long enough. I'm sorry. Only something else has happened. But you seem to know about that too.'

'The music is more important to me.'

'I see.' Thomas had an unaccountable feeling that the solid earth was shifting under him. For some reason he had expected her to understand. She had never been demanding or unsympathetic. He had thought she was his friend. But now she stood there implacably demanding her rights as though his feelings meant nothing to her at all. But that was his mistake, he realised. She had always been quite clear about it. 'Indeed, you told me so,' said Thomas, and tried to ignore the gulf of pain that seemed to open up inside him. 'It was wrong of me to suppose anything different.'

'It would be wrong if you broke your word.'

Thomas pressed his hands to his head, and tried to work out what to do. 'Linnet,' he said at last.

'What?' Linnet sounded quite subdued.

'I must go. No, don't say anything. This is only to do with me. You take her. Take her now, and show her the room. I'll come back as soon as I can, I promise. No harm will come of it. What is it?' he asked, as Linnet once again hid her face in her hands.

'Nothing. Only . . .'

'Only?'

'I wanted to spare you. You don't know what you've done! I wish you'd believe me. Thomas, I'm scared.'

'So am I,' said Thomas. 'But I know what I must do. That's enough. Take her.' He turned to Naomi. 'She'll show you. You'll find it there. I'll be back. I'm sorry,'

Before either of them could answer, he had gone. They heard his retreating footsteps running down the passage, and were left facing one another.

Linnet glanced cautiously at Naomi, and nearly said something. Then she shut her mouth and opened it again, but evidently thought better of that too. As Naomi still waited, she said nervously, 'Do you want to come with me? I can't stay, but I'll show you the room.'

'Very well.'

'I hope you're not angry?'

'No.' But I must hold on to the thing that I came for, thought Naomi, yet didn't say it. I am desperately lonely, and I wish I could turn to you as to a friend, but you seem too young, and you know nothing. I came for the music, and I will have the music. Otherwise I will forget who I am, and Thomas's world will swallow me up.

'I wish you would treat me like a friend,' said Linnet impulsively, and waited for an answer, quaking inwardly.

I wish I could. Naomi looked round the hall to steady herself, at the black and white chequered floor and the bowl of hyacinths on the round table. She still hadn't asked if it were a game. 'Very well,' she answered. 'If you were my friend, I would tell you now that I feel very much alone. I can see that I represent something in this place far other than what I am. I am a musician, and I came here because I was promised a gift of music out of the past. If I forget that, I am afraid of becoming the thing that you have made me.'

'I don't understand.'

'Why are the children being told that I come from the world of the dead?'

'I know you don't!' cried Linnet.

'That's not what I asked.'

'Please, you wanted to see the room. Let me show you.'

Naomi shrugged. 'If that's what you want, then what are we waiting for?'

Linnet stared at her helplessly. 'There was another fiddle player,' she said in a rush. 'It all happened before. I would tell you everything if I could!'

'Thank you,' said Naomi. 'Which way do we go?'

'Along here.' Linnet abandoned any further attempt at explanation, and led Naomi down another passage, through a door on the opposite side of the hall. Naomi hadn't been in this part of the house before. It was very cold, and smelt musty, as if it were kept shut up too much. They turned a corner, passing several doors. Naomi tried to keep her bearings, but she had never been in so large a house, and it oppressed her. It was like being in a maze, but without the sky overhead. Linnet stopped at a door at the end of the passage, and opened it. 'Come in.'

Naomi followed her. She stopped just inside the doorway, and took a deep breath. It was quite unlike any room she had ever seen. For a start, it was full. Full of strange things, indefinable objects lumped together, stored higgledy-piggledy up against the walls, or in heaps on the floor. Too many to take in all at once. The room was not arranged to be lived in, that was clear, or to be worked in. It was nothing, there was no meaning to it, only a store of unrelated things.

The room itself was huge. The ceiling seemed to tower above her, its edges moulded into strange patterns like carvings of wood, only it wasn't wood. There were no windows. Or perhaps those were windows, built in a great arc on the far side, but they were all boarded over with wooden shutters, so that the daylight filtered in through thin chinks. The place was dim as twilight, and smelt old. Naomi sneezed.

'What is it?' she asked, when she had recovered her breath. 'What is this?'

'Out of the past,' replied Linnet, watching her. 'It all comes out of the past.'

'But how?'

'Our land is not like other lands,' said Linnet. 'This was the empty land. The poison came, and the people fled. They knew they would come back, but they had no idea how long. They left all that they had, and even though they fled at once, many of them died. But in this house, they must have intended to come home, or for their children's children to come home. They sealed a room, so there was no light, and the air didn't change, nor anything moulder away. So when we came back, it was still here. My grandmother, she broke the seals, and opened it up again, because she said nothing was ever intended to be suspended in time. Things as well as people live their day and depart, and there is no crueller thing than to force anything out of its own time. Everything has the right to die, and must not be denied.'

'So that's what's happening here?' asked Naomi in awe.

'Slowly. What we could use, we used. But mostly it was too old. Even if things are still intact, the reason for them has gone. So here they stay. Thomas was determined you should have the freedom of this place, and my mother has agreed to it. I wasn't sure. The past is a burden, sometimes, and I said I liked you too much to want to inflict our history on you. But they said I didn't understand, and that you were already promised.'

Naomi smiled at her for the first time that day. 'That was kind of you,' she said.

Linnet blushed. 'Well, it's true. And you liked my baby. I could see that. I wanted to protect you, but I know really that nobody can protect anybody. So here you are.'

'You can't protect your brother, either.'

'No. But I'm much more afraid for him. You've done nothing to hurt anyone, and you're strong. Listen, I have to go back. Peter's got Jo, but he can't feed her. Can I leave you here?'

'To do what?'

'I thought you knew. About the music.'

Naomi looked round slowly. 'If you can't tell me, I daresay I shall find out.'

'Or you could wait for Thomas.'

'No, I won't do that.'

'Well,' Linnet still hesitated, 'come back when you're ready. If you're not around by dinner time, I'll come and find you.'

'Thank you,' said Naomi, and waited until the door closed behind her.

When she was alone, she stood quite still for a long time, looking around her. She felt overwhelmed. It was difficult to look at anything in isolation. There was so much, and it all seemed so complicated. These were not things that she understood. There was furniture, but it wasn't beds to sleep in, nor tables to eat off, nor benches to sit upon. There were small objects, but they were not plates or bowls or tools or musical instruments. It was all too much. Naomi sneezed again. Then she stepped cautiously over to the window, and unfastened a shutter.

It was still pouring with rain. The room looked out on to sodden woodland, enveloped in a haze of cloud that had sunk right down to the valley floor. Naomi turned her attention to the room. In daylight the things seemed more sharply differentiated. She began to wander about, tentatively touching, so that ancient dust clung to her fingers and made her eyes water. She pulled out a tattered handkerchief and continued her exploration, ignoring the thick air that caught at her throat, until she was reduced to helpless sneezing. She blew her nose hard, and went on, handkerchief held across her mouth.

The furniture did make some kind of sense after all. There were chairs stacked against the wall, but they were oddly shaped, wood forced into extraordinary convolutions, so fragile one would hardly expect it to bear a person's weight. The chairs had no seats; they had mouldered to dust long ago. There was an object like a dresser, with a curved front and drawers with handles. She pulled at one gently, but it was wedged hard. Then there was another strange wooden device, not like a dresser, that had a kind of shelf half way up, with a close-fitting lid. Naomi lifted the lid carefully, and nearly dropped it again. There were teeth underneath. A row of yellowed teeth, interspersed with strange black patterns, as if someone had written out a secret spell. The hand that held the handkerchief made a sign against evil. Don't be silly, said Naomi severely to herself, and made herself touch one of the teeth. It gave under the pressure of her finger with a faint thud. Meaningless. She carefully lowered the lid again.

There was another chest, with tiny drawers. She squatted in front of it and tried the handles. A drawer slid out so easily that she jumped. It was full of tools. Only they were not tools, at least, they were not hammers or chisels or knives, or anything recognisable. She picked one up. It was like a knife, with an unstained blade and a blotched yellow handle. She tried the blade against her finger. Too blunt for anything but spreading butter. She laid it down again. And this thing, this was recognisable. A spoon, just like any spoon. She was almost relieved. There were many spoons, all in a little section of their own. And the one next to it ... she picked up a curious implement like a miniature pitchfork, only it was shaped differently, more like a shredded spoon. What for? She shrugged, put it back, and shut the drawer.

Next to the chest there was a heap of square objects like boxes, but they had no lids. They were not made of wood or metal, but of queer black material. Naomi ran her finger along the surface, and sprang back with a shudder as if it were hot. It was like nothing in the world, neither hot nor cold, alive nor dead, not like anything natural nor anything made with hands. She backed away from it as if it might be harmful, and crossed to the far side of the room.

There was a table there covered with strange objects. She picked one up at random: a large wooden artifact, carefully carved. It seemed to have no purpose, but it had a round face with symbols drawn upon it that she couldn't interpret. Naomi put down her handkerchief and held the thing in both hands, and its blank face seemed to reflect her own bewilderment. They must have been uncommonly drawn to magic, these people, to make so many things that had no other function. There were twelve symbols in a circle made of lines that she couldn't decipher. How many dancers were there? Eleven, Thomas had told her, but she could think of nothing else in this valley that looked like that.

There were lines on the face: two lines, one long, one short. When she looked closer, she saw that they were not drawn, but attached at the centre of the circle. She touched one with her forefinger and it gave under her hand. She drew in her breath, and moved it again. There was a faint click from the heart of the thing. She tried the other line. It wouldn't move. She pressed a little harder. There was a crack, and the smaller line slipped off and lay detached in the palm of her hand, like a little arrow.

Naomi stared down at it in dismay. She had no right to break anything. No one would mind, probably, but it felt like sacrilege to meddle with something that had survived so many centuries. For a moment the whole room, herself included, seemed to spiral away from her into an unimaginable distance, so that she felt as though she were looking down on herself from a long way off, with the room of ancient things surrounding her. She could see herself down there quite clearly, but not as she had ever understood herself to be. A wild, outlandish thing she seemed, with rough red hair and loose thick-woven clothes dragged together at the waist by a ragged sash. A savage out of another world playing among the ruins of a forgotten age, holding a tiny arrow in the palm of her hand, that pointed directly to her heart.

Naomi shook her head slightly, and carefully laid the arrow down, next to the object to which it belonged. Then she moved slowly on. There was a big cupboard next to the table. She opened one of the doors, and instantly recoiled. There was light inside, and in the midst of it a figure like herself, only a foot or so away from her: same hair, same clothes, same fright writ large upon her face. Naomi felt her heart thump, even as she understood. There were mirrors in her world too, but not like this. This was a huge flat sheet of glass, as tall as she was, and the reflection it gave was only slightly dimmer than the world itself. There were brown spots across it, the fruits of age, but it still seemed to catch all the light in the room and hold it, with herself in the middle, staring back at her.

In spite of the strangeness of it all, Naomi found herself fascinated, not by the illusions of the past presented to her, but quite simply by her self. She had never had a chance to see her own image so clearly, and she liked what she saw. A slow smile spread across her face, and across the face of the woman in the mirror. It was an attractive smile. It made her eyes sparkle, and crinkle up a little at the edges, where faint lines of past laughter had etched themselves upon her skin. Definitely a very fetching smile. She did it again.

She moved a little closer. It was interesting to note that she had lost nearly all her freckles. As a child she had been covered in them. They had nearly all gone. She turned sideways a little. Not quite. No doubt some would come back with the summer. She liked herself without freckles, just as she had liked herself with them. Her eyes were a clear green today; sometimes they seemed to be hazel. Perhaps it was the light. Naomi turned herself round, squinting back at her own image over her shoulder. She hadn't realised that her clothes had grown so faded. She was wearing pink trousers again, still creased with washing, and a jersey that had faded from crimson to a soft russet. Her orange sash had grown tattered, and had turned to the colour of birch leaves in autumn. The effect was muted and delicate; she had had no idea that her colours had grown so subtle. She turned full face again, and considered her body. She liked her own shape. Travelling had kept her very fit, perhaps a little thin for someone as tall as she was, who had borne a child. She didn't look particularly old. She moved right up to the mirror again, and pushed her hair back. It was definitely grey at the temples. She shook her head so her hair fell forward again, and the grey hairs vanished.

This is not what you came for, she said to herself at last, and moved away reluctantly. The room seemed dead and silent in contrast to the animated figure she had found in the mirror. It was difficult to know where to turn next. There were no clues, only the silence of centuries, which seemed to offer her nothing.

She turned her attention to the conglomeration of objects in the middle of the room. There was a glass-topped table with a little cabinet inside, which seemed to be full of old plates. Quite incomprehensible. Next to it there was a high uncomfortable-looking stool. It had once been covered with some kind of velvety material, but there were only shreds left hanging forlornly. She looked closer, and saw hinges along one side. It must be a lid. She raised it very cautiously, afraid that the thing might come to pieces in her hands.

There were papers inside. Books. Only not books, as she understood them. She had seen books before, which had been carefully kept through many generations, handed down from the past. She had seen papers too, with writing, in the houses of merchants and chandlers and shipowners, people who had to keep accounts. These seemed to be neither one thing nor the other. Naomi was interested in books. She could even read a little. She touched the top page gently. It seemed solid enough. She had been afraid that it might crumble to dust in her hand. She knelt beside the stool, and very carefully lifted the whole sheaf of papers, holding her breath.

Her heart was thumping again. No clues had been given her, but she had an obscure feeling that this was important, that this was the thing that Thomas had intended her to find. It was almost as if she heard his voice encouraging her, although he was far away, entangled in another world, facing the man who had once been his lover. She felt a pang in her stomach, of fear for Thomas perhaps, or a reminder of a present danger that she had temporarily forgotten. Thomas had meant to bring her here himself, and show her this. But she could manage without him, as he must manage without her. Naomi banished him from her mind again, and began gingerly to separate the papers, spreading them out in a semi-circle round her as she squatted on the bare floor.

They seemed to be arranged in booklets, each one large and thin and dangerously floppy. The pages were torn and dogeared, rough at the edges. She tried to open one out, her tongue protruding a little in concentration. The paper tore slightly, and then she had the book spread open in front of her, two full pages of black and white.

It was quite meaningless. She knew her letters. At least, she knew all the small ones, and had some idea of the archaic capitals, but this was nothing like writing. It was more like a long picture arranged in straight lines, a sort of stylised drawing. More than anything else she could think of, it looked like a swarm of tadpoles entangled in a net. Unlikely, decided Naomi. There has to be a better translation than that.

She turned over the pages, as many of them as would turn at all. They were all the same, just sheets of parallel lines with the tadpoles moving up and down in serried ranks, sometimes two or three right on top of one another. She looked more closely. The lines came in sets. She counted them. Five together, then a space, then five together again. There were strange cabbalistic symbols at the beginning of each line, and then the tadpoles.

She tried another book, to see if that would tell her anything. The first page she opened was no different, except that the tadpoles were even thicker. The next page had letters at the top. She seized upon them, and tried to spell them out. It was a long word, and to her intense disappointment it was unpronounceable:

Preludio.

She closed the book. Unlike the first, it had a cover. It was half torn off, but there was more writing. Some of it was unreadable, stained with some unidentifiable liquid that had become hard and brittle, but there were a few words, and they seemed to be in her own language, or something not unlike it. She followed the letters with her finger, her lips moving, trying to formulate a word.

There was a word. She understood it. Her heart leapt, but she didn't understand. It meant nothing. Frustrated, she went over it again, and the answer was still the same:

Well-tempered.

She stared down at it, biting her lip. The adjective might be a mockery of her. But who could have known? What kind of magic could this be? She peered closely at the rest of the page, trying to decipher the letters through the film of brown adhering to them. There were two together. Not letters. Numbers. She knew her numbers very well, had even had cause to write them down herself.

48.

Forty-eight what? Naomi put her hands to her head, and pulled her hair hard, until it was all sticking up on end. Why she felt such urgency she couldn't think, but she was sure that this was the thing that was important. Almost in tears of frustration, she picked up a third book.

The tadpoles were not nearly so thick. Somehow encouraged, she turned the pages. The five lines were still the same, and the peculiar symbols. But not just symbols. There were also numbers. Ordinary numbers that she could read, at the beginning of every line. There was a three, quite clearly, and underneath it a four. Another 4. Only sorcerers used numbers with strange symbols, but for some reason she wasn't afraid. There was something about all this that made sense, but she couldn't quite grasp it.

Three, four. That was very familiar. Three, four. She heard her own sudden indrawn breath. She turned the page, and noticed that her hands were shaking. There again. Three, four. And the lines. Five lines. Why five?

There was a word again, at the top of a page. She forced her brain to be calm, to concentrate. It was all in capitals, and she wasn't very familiar with capitals. But it mattered. She traced the lines with her forefinger, and tried desperately to remember. And then she had it. It was a word and she knew it. Moreover, it was the right word. It fitted.

Minuet.

Naomi put her shaking hands over her face, and burst into tears.

Presently she got up and fetched her handkerchief from the table where she had dropped it. She walked over to the window and blew her nose. She looked out at the sodden trees, for as long as it took for a drop of rain to course down the whole length of glass in front of her. Then she took a deep breath and held up her hand in front of her face. It had stopped shaking.

She found the page with the minuet again, and stared at it for a long time. Slowly she began to separate details in her mind. A long curly symbol with a little box beside it, then three, four. Three tadpoles in a row, with a line piercing their hearts. A line, more tadpoles moving up, right over the top of the five lines.

Her eyes, unused to black lines on white paper, kept sliding off the page sideways, seeing not the figures but the texture of the paper, the stains, the flickering tails of a swarm of tadpoles drifting among reeds over soft mud. Wind on water, the feel of mud between her toes, feet sinking into softness, tadpoles that wriggled in her palm. No, insisted Naomi, exasperated with herself. That's the wrong way to think about it. There is a way to approach this. There must be a way in which I can use my mind which will make sense of this. Only I have never been taught it. I know how I have to think, but I don't know how to set about it.

She counted up to ten very slowly, and tried again.

The pattern of a tune.

She pressed her hands to her head, and thought furiously. It was those straight lines. Music did not happen in straight lines. If it were truly music, it couldn't be drawn that way. Music is different, it makes patterns, like weaving colours. It goes in curves and circles, it plays with themes and returns to them. It is all up and down, backwards and forwards, interwoven and intricate. To draw music, there would have to be a proper pattern. The music is an image of this world, and no part of the world could be drawn in such a way. To live is to be born, to follow the circle, and to die. It would have to be drawn like that. Unless the circle were too big, then you could make it like this on a page, with bits of curves. In segments. The line would be like the horizon between the sea and sky: the greater it is, the more there is a curve.

Unless it were seen as a journey.

If music happens in time, which it does, then perhaps you could begin to draw it at the beginning, and make a line, which is the time, until you reach the end. Only time is not a line. No one ever lived along a straight line. No tune was ever played along a line.

She studied the page again. She tried to look at the tadpoles individually, but it seemed very difficult. Then she looked at them as a pattern. That was not so difficult. It was possible, probable even, that the pattern on the page fitted the pattern of the tune. If the tadpoles were the notes . . .

The tadpoles are the notes.

She looked at them again very carefully, and thought about the tune. Three notes the same, and a fourth. Then up, line, space, line. But why? I suppose that doesn't matter. If that place there is the first note, is it the same again when it comes somewhere else? Is it possible to assume that? Perhaps I can try it out if I follow the tune.

It was torture, trying to do it. The tune kept carrying her onwards, and it was almost impossible to look at where the tadpoles came on the lines. They were far too small for what they seemed to convey, and she kept losing her place. She tried following with her finger, and singing each note as she went, as it came in relation to the last. It was more fiddly than writing, far more difficult, because the symbols didn't have different shapes, just different places on a line.

'Are you there?'

Naomi almost cried out, the sound of a human voice gave her such a shock.

'Are you all right?' asked Linnet. 'I didn't mean to startle you, but I kept knocking on the door, and you never answered. Did you find what you wanted? Will you come and have some dinner?'

'Yes,' said Naomi, slowly standing up. 'Yes, I think I did, and thank you, I think I will.'

Thirteenth Day

The next day, Naomi began by going through the whole pile of music systematically, studying each book. There was writing at the beginning of most of them and, where she could read it, it confirmed her conclusions of yesterday. About halfway down the pile, she opened the next book and spelt out the words on the title page. They were not even written in her own language. Disappointed, she was about to pass on, when one word leapt out at her. *Violino.*

An archaic word, which very few people could put a meaning to nowadays. But she could.

Naomi picked up the book with shaking hands, and stared at the writing until it began to take some shape around that word.

Fur Violino Solo.

No, she didn't know that. She tried the words just above. *Drei Sonaten und drei Partiten.* Naomi tried saying them out loud, and recognised them. It was the language she had learned to speak a little when her travels had taken her across the sea to the country where she had learned the other music. So there was a connection. Her thoughts whirled ahead, flung into a vortex of possibilities.

A name. If there were a name . . . She re-read the first page carefully. It was torn, and on the following page there did not seem to be a name. But perhaps that wasn't important.

'Violin,' read Naomi aloud, and turned to the first page of the music.

*

Just after midday, Thomas knocked at the door, and receiving no answer, he opened it and went in. Naomi was sitting crosslegged in the middle of a circle of papers, her fiddle across her knees, studying the book in front of her. Thomas felt that he had never before encountered such intense concentration, and he might not have dared to interrupt, but before he could move again she looked up and saw him. She smiled at him vaguely, as if he were some acquaintance from long ago whom she couldn't quite place or name.

'You found what you expected?' asked Thomas

'I found your gift,' she replied. 'At least, I think I'm finding it.'

'Are you happy with it?'

'It's tearing me apart. I suppose some might call that happiness. But I thank you, all the same.'

'If it's worth something to you, then the journey was worth making.'

She caught the note of bitterness in his voice, and looked at him more sharply. 'Thomas?'

'I won't interrupt you. I just wanted to make sure you'd found your way.'

Naomi stood up, and realised how cramped her legs were. 'You don't interrupt me. I have to keep stopping because I can't think straight. Do you want to talk to me?'

'Our journey,' said Thomas. 'It was important. It seems now like the only real thing in this world.'

Naomi banished the last trace of swimming tadpoles from her sight, and looked at him clearly. He was white and distraught, his jacket streaked with rain. He wouldn't ask for anything, she realised, unless she gave it of her own accord.

'I want to talk to you,' she said, 'but not in here. Can we go somewhere else?'

'Come up to my room.'

She had never been in Thomas's room before. It told her very little. She had expected that it might still hold the clutter of his past life, or at least that some trace of his presence would be evident. But it was as bare as the room they had given her, containing only a low bed, a couple of woven rugs and a carved chest. Only the magician's bag with the pentacle embroidered on it indicated that the room had an occupant at all. It lay upon the chest, in which he must have placed his other baggage. As for the past — Naomi remembered the boarded-up house at the foot of the pass, and what Paul had told her. Thomas had spent his childhood here, but that was long ago.

Thomas sat down on the bed and indicated that she do the same. He seemed to have shrunk into himself, though he could hardly have lost weight in twenty-four hours. The lines on his face seemed more harshly etched than before, and she remembered her first impression of him in the mill above the island. He was appallingly unhappy. She had forgotten that.

'I owe you an explanation, I know,' said Thomas. 'I should have told you everything at the beginning. But I wasn't able to.'

'I don't need an explanation.'

'Then what?'

'You've given me all I want. All I have for you are two questions.'

He looked at her with hopeless eyes. 'I'll try to answer, if it helps you.'

'Not me. I came for purposes of my own, which are fulfilled. But I've been thinking about you as well, because I regard you as my friend.'

'Thank you. That may not alter my fate, but it alters the way I face it.'

'I don't know if I have any power over your fate. But as I say, I have two questions.'

'Then ask.'

There was a silence. 'What hurts you, Thomas?' asked Naomi at last.

It was a long time before he answered. 'The past,' he said at last. 'What was done to us, and what I have done. Are we cursed? I don't know, Naomi. I never meant to commit a crime. Is that what they all say? Does anyone ever accept the consequences of what they do?' He looked at her in despair. 'You should have nothing to do with me!' he cried out, and hid his face from her. 'I should be untouchable. I destroyed the ones I loved, and I struck down my only friend who would still have given up his life for me. I should have died, Naomi. I'm not fit to live. A curse was laid on this land in the past, and I perpetuated it. There has been suffering here, and I caused it. The world is full of evil, and I have added to it!'

She almost denied it, but realised that there was no point speaking. His head was buried in his hands, and she could see he was shaking, unreachable behind a barrier of guilt, or fear. Naomi laid her hand on his shoulder and said, 'I care about you, Thomas.'

She could feel his whole body shaking under her touch. She came closer and put her arm round him, and laid her other hand on his. He was so cold it was like touching someone dead; he seemed to be hardly breathing. She put her arms right round him, and felt him rigid and shaking, but he was aware of her. He shifted just a little, adapting himself to the curve of her body. She hugged him tightly, as she might offer comfort to a child, and laid her cheek against his downbent head. She could smell the sweat of fear on his body, cold and slightly sweet. She held him hard, as if only the warmth of her own body could recall him to life.

'I have another question, Thomas.'

'Yes?' His voice was breathless and shaken, but it was still his. She kissed the top of his head in sheer relief, and presently asked, choosing her words carefully, 'What purpose does this serve, Thomas?'

'I wish I knew!' He sat up and faced her, gripping her hands in his own. 'Why is there such pain in the world, Naomi? What have I done to inherit this? I would never willingly have harmed a hair of their heads. I loved them, Naomi, and I destroyed them. There is no purpose in that, unless the world is evil.'

'No,' she said, and held his hands between her own.

'This world is not evil!' cried Thomas passionately. 'Look at this land. It is so beautiful, like a piece of heaven fallen upon earth. I don't understand why these things have to be, but I won't believe my world is evil. If it were evil, there would be no hope for us. There must be hope, because we are alive. I don't want to be cast out of life!'

'You are not,' she said, and held him with all the strength she had.

Much later on, Naomi went in search of Linnet, and finally tracked her down in her room. She found her lying on her bed, curled in a half circle round her baby, who was lying on her back half naked, kicking her legs in the air.

'Hello,' said Linnet. 'I wondered where you were. I kept some food hot for you. It's in the bottom oven.'

'I was with Thomas.'

'There's enough for both of you, if he's hungry.'

'He's asleep.'

There was no mistaking the alarm in Linnet's eyes. 'Is he all right?' she asked quickly.

'Yes. Why shouldn't he be?'

Linnet seemed at a loss for an answer. She looked hopefully at Jo, as if seeking inspiration. Apparently she found it, for she went on to say, 'Come and sit down if you like. I was worried about Thomas, you see. He left because of a message from Paul. You met Paul.'

'Yes.' Naomi sat down on the edge of the bed. The baby heard her, and turned to look at her. Naomi absently touched Jo's cheek with one finger, and said to Linnet, 'I did gather that you were worried. It was fairly obvious.'

'Oh dear. I suppose it must have been.' Linnet sat up, and did up her shirt. She had evidently been feeding her baby. 'I know Paul,' she said. 'When I was quite young he taught me to play the fiddle. You get to know a man in that situation. You get to trust him.'

'Yes, I know.'

'Do you?' asked Linnet, mildly surprised. Then she doggedly pursued her own line of thought. It was hard enough being left with all the explanations, without being distracted. 'Oh Jo,' she interrupted herself. 'Now she's peed. Wait while I find another nappy.'

Naomi obediently waited, and gave the baby one of her fingers to hold. It was clutched in a firm grip, and the other small hand came up to meet it. Jo tried hard to guide Naomi's finger into her mouth, but they were interrupted by the return of Linnet, armed with a clean nappy.

'I wanted to explain it to you,' announced Linnet, folding the nappy with one hand. 'I think you deserve it. It's not easy. It's not my story, and I have to respect Thomas's silence, if that's what he chooses.'

'I never asked you to do otherwise.'

'I just want to make it clear that it wasn't Paul's fault. I was horrified that he came, because I was afraid for Thomas. But I don't blame Paul. He acted out of love, just as he did before. It was brave of him, when you think what happened then.'

'I don't know what happened then, so I can't think.'

'But you saw his face!' said Linnet, startled. 'You met him. You said so.'

'Oh yes. I saw his face.'

Linnet wrapped the nappy deftly round her baby, and tucked in the ends. Then she picked Jo up, and held her against her chest, as if to protect herself. 'Thomas did that!' she burst out suddenly. 'Hadn't you understood? He didn't know. He didn't see him again. He didn't know until now what he did.'

Fourteenth Day

When Thomas came to find Naomi the following day, he saw that she had removed herself and her papers to the window seat, and had spread out the music on an ancient carved table. The window was slightly open, and sunshine streamed in, lighting up the heavy dust that stirred in the unaccustomed breeze. Naomi didn't notice him. She was playing the fiddle in a most unusual manner, one note at a time, with long hesitations between each one. Her eyes were fixed on the paper in front of her, as if it were the source of the music itself.

A draught eddied between the open door and the window. The pages were ruffled, and the thread of music broke. Naomi looked up.

'I'm sorry,' said Thomas. 'I'm disturbing you again. How's it going?'

'These tadpoles,' she said, smoothing out the page without seeming to see him. 'They change. Some have frills on their tails, and some have none. Most of them are joined together, and a few are hollow inside their heads. It has to make sense.'

'How unpleasant,' observed Thomas, confused but polite. 'Some sort of parasite, I suppose.'

'I think it's to do with the time. I'm trying to see if it fits. But it's so difficult, like trying to draw a map of someone's soul. It makes my head ache.'

'Hunger,' said Thomas soothingly. 'I came to ask if you wanted a meal.'

'Is it time?' she asked, surprised.

'Long past. I was out, and they said they hadn't seen you either. Would you like to come and eat with me?'

She rubbed her eyes vigorously. Her hair was standing up on end again. 'Yes. Thank you. I'll come. I'd better shut the window. I hope it didn't matter, opening it, but the dust was making my eyes water, and the tadpoles are very small.'

'Tadpoles,' repeated Thomas, looking at her with slight concern. 'Are tadpoles connected with the music?'

'Haven't you ever looked at this?' she gestured towards the papers.

'No. My mother did, long ago. She showed them to the man who was my father, and he worked out what they must be. Only Paul has looked at them since.'

'And what did Paul make of them?'

'Nothing. He said he might look at them again when he was old, but while he was young he would rather spend his time living.'

'I see,' said Naomi, following Thomas down the passage. 'How did your father work it out? Was he a musician?'

'No. He was some sort of magician, I think. He was making a map of the stars.'

They came into the kitchen and Thomas set out two wooden plates, two mugs, two spoons and a loaf of bread. 'Rabbit stew,' he said. 'With onions. And in here we have potatoes. Help yourself.'

Naomi sat down opposite him. 'How could anyone make a map of the stars? They're always moving.'

'I told you he was a magician. This is elderflower wine. Would you like some?'

'It won't help the tadpoles, I don't suppose. But yes, please.'

Thomas gave her a strange look. 'My mother told us what my father had said about the music. But tadpoles were definitely not mentioned.'

'Don't worry about it. Tell me what was mentioned.'

'That was all. He wasn't here for long. He was a traveller. He was looking for the ancient star maps which were written in the past upon the stones.'

'Oh that. Now I understand you.'

'No, you don't. He wasn't a maker of circles. All he made was charts on paper, with numbers.'

'You can do sailing directions like that,' offered Naomi. 'Only hardly anyone does, because who could read it?'

'I've no idea. I only know what my mother told me, and she had no idea either. He was here less than a month, and she showed him the room, and he told her what it held. He said that if ever she were to find a musician who was truly wise about this world, she must bring them here, to find for themselves a gift beyond price.'

Naomi resheathed her knife, and began to wipe the gravy off her plate with a piece of bread. She was frowning a little, evidently lost in thought.

'Have some more wine,' said Thomas.

'Thank you.' Naomi bit off a piece of bread, and said as soon as she could speak again, 'What made you think I was truly wise?'

'I didn't think. The moment presented itself to me. But I was right. Wasn't I?'

She gave him the same smile she had bestowed upon the mirror. 'Is there anything more to eat?'

'There's more stew. Help yourself.'

They ate in silence, while the fire roared in the chimney, and the sunlight came and went outside the window.

'Naomi,' said Thomas suddenly. 'I must apologise to you for yesterday. I was not myself.'

She gave him a quick unguarded look, full of compassion. He didn't see it, because his eyes were fixed on his hands, which were tearing bread into little pieces, kneading it back to dough. It was a moment before she said anything, then she answered lightly, 'Does that mean I have to apologise to you for the other night?'

'What night?' He looked up, distracted. 'Oh, that. Of course not. It was all I could do. I'm sorry, I seem to bring unhappiness wherever I go,' said Thomas bitterly. 'A dangerous friend for anyone.'

'That's not what I meant,' she said impatiently. 'Of course it isn't. I mean that pain isn't something we have to apologise for, either of us. Sometimes it's too much to bear alone. It's still private. I know, and you know, but that doesn't mean we have to talk about it now.'

'You're saying you can forget it?'

'Of course I can't. I wouldn't wish to. I mean that it's not what I'm thinking about when I have my dinner with you. If I couldn't keep such things in their right places, I couldn't live comfortably with anyone, at least, not anyone that I was moderately intimate with.'

'Oh,' said Thomas. Then he said. 'I think I know what you mean. I saw an old friend of mine yesterday. There was too much to say, too much suffering from the past. It was terrible, until we began to talk about sheep, then life began to fit back together again. Can you understand that?'

'But you still suffered.'

'Yes, but I landed it on you, not him.'

'How sensible,' said Naomi lightly. 'This is very good wine. Who made it?'

Later that afternoon Naomi had another interruption, this time from Linnet.

'Sorry to disturb you,' said Linnet, in the tone of one getting through the formalities as quickly as possible, 'but we've got to think about the music again sometime. If you don't mind, that is.' She gave Naomi a wary look, as though prepared for any kind of reaction.

'I wasn't thinking about anything else.'

'I meant the music for the dance. It's only two days now. I know you didn't like it,' went on Linnet hastily, before Naomi could say anything, 'perhaps you won't do it now. But if you will, we need to practise. Or perhaps you know it, now you've heard it.'

'I don't know what kind of memory you think I've got. It must be all of two hours long. To tell you the truth, I'd forgotten all about it. And I did like it.'

'Really? It didn't seem so.'

'That was a mistake. I'm sorry if I upset you. Of course I shall play. I promised Thomas, and I know I owe it to you. You'll have to teach me. Two days isn't very long.' Naomi looked down at the papers in front of her, and sighed. 'When do you want to start?'

'As soon as you like. You seem to be very busy,' remarked Linnet, giving the papers a cursory glance.

'I'll come now,' decided Naomi suddenly. 'I can't stand this any longer. I want to play music the way I understand it. This is like trying to turn my brain inside out. It doesn't fit me. I'm never busy.'

'You must be,' contradicted Linnet, 'or you'd never have got anything done. And you've done a lot, haven't you?'

'I don't know. Have I done a lot, or am I truly wise?' asked Naomi ruefully, picking up her fiddle.

'I don't know what you mean,' said Linnet, but not as if it bothered her. 'Come up to my room. I haven't got Jo this afternoon, so it's a good time.'

Practising with Linnet was exactly what Naomi had needed. It cleared her mind. It was so easy to pick up music from someone else, to listen to another player and echo the same tune back again. The patterns were perfectly clear when she could hear them, and the variations came as naturally as breathing. It was good music. Her anger had stopped her appreciating it before. It was very clearly intended for dancing, and that made her whole body feel more alive while she played it. Gradually her head stopped aching. Her eyes grew less tired now that she could rest them on real things: on Linnet's concentrated expression as she played, on the way she played her fiddle, on the sun and clouds and hills outside the window. Paul was right, thought Naomi. Life is happening now. But perhaps I can bring something new into the present, and give it life again. Then that too will be alive, and happening now. Am I doing right? I don't even know. Naomi listened while Linnet played the next piece. It was a set of three jigs, that slipped easily into one another, each one seeming even livelier than the last. Naomi abandoned her train of thought, and let the music take her.

They were interrupted by a sudden pinging noise, and Linnet stopped abruptly. 'String broken. I don't even know if I've got another.'

'I have. In my room.'

They went through to Naomi's room. Linnet sat down on the bed and watched Naomi rummage in her pack. Naomi brought out a small leather bag from the very bottom, and tipped it up. Linnet caught a glimpse of what looked like a couple of pebbles, and something that looked like an amulet, and a little box. She tried to get a closer look without appearing to be interested, but Naomi extracted a coil of strings, and swiftly replaced everything else. 'Here. Which one is it?'

Linnet returned her attention to her fiddle with an effort, and began to restring it. She felt clumsy and inefficient under Naomi's eyes, so was relieved when Naomi left her to it, and stood at the window looking out over the valley instead.

'You're a good teacher,' said Naomi, without looking round. 'That's a gift.'

'I'm hardly teaching you,' protested Linnet, 'just showing you the tunes.'

'That's teaching. Did you ever show anyone else?'

Linnet hesitated, her fingers on the string, 'Yes,' she answered reluctantly. 'Once. I began to teach my nephew Julius.'

'From the beginning?' There was no overt curiosity in Naomi's tone, only a professional interest. Encouraged, Linnet went on.

'More or less. He started with Paul, when he was seven, but Paul wasn't patient enough with him, so I took over. I liked it.'

'But Paul was patient enough with you?'

'Julius was not at all like me,' observed Linnet. She took a deep breath. It would be a relief to talk about it. Silence oppressed her, and surely there could be no disloyalty in telling her about this? 'He wasn't at all easy to teach,' said Linnet almost chattily. 'He asked so many questions. It made Paul furious. I just ignored them mostly. He wouldn't concentrate. Always asking irrelevant things like, Where did this fiddle come from? Who made it? Why don't we make our own? How do you know that tune? Who taught it to you? Where does it come from? Who made it up? Why doesn't anyone make up any new ones? On and on and on. And never listening to a word I was saying.'

'I'm not sure those questions are irrelevant.'

'Well, he never practised. He preferred taking things to pieces. He unstrung my entire fiddle once, said he wanted to see how the strings went. Always making a mess of things, and never clearing up afterwards. But you couldn't really stay angry with him,' said Linnet, almost in the tone she kept for Jo. 'He could talk his way out of anything, and make you laugh in the end.'

'You probably taught him more music than you thought.'

'Why, are you used to teaching children?'

'Here and there, all the time. But not continuously. I miss that sometimes, not being able to stay with anyone's music, and watch it change.'

'Well, you can't have everything, can you?' said Linnet prosaically. 'Let me just tune this. Can you give me the note?'

*

By the time Naomi found time to go out that day it was almost sunset. She walked slowly along by the beck without crossing the bridge. Presently she came to a big bend. There was a pool below her, deep enough to swim in, if only it were summer. Naomi stopped and watched the current eddying in a myriad circles as it swept across the deceptively smooth surface of the pool. She scrambled down the bank, and stood on the strip of shingle between the river and the floodwater mark. She squatted down and dipped her cupped hands in the water. It was cold as snow. She splashed it into her face. Her eyes felt bruised with exhaustion, retaining images of endless black and white squiggles, caught in static shapes upon a page that had been suspended out of life for generations. The cold stung her eyes, and she blinked. It was good to gaze down into moving water, and watch the shifting images of pebbles caught up in the current as if they too were flowing seawards. The stones here were very pale, gleaming white through water, shades of grey and pearl on land. She picked up a small pebble from the beach beside her and dipped it in the stream. Under water it was white and translucent, like a jewel. She lifted it out and watched it slowly fade to the soft colour of the rocks around her. She stood up and dropped it in her pocket.

It was almost dark. There was a faint breeze coming off the mountains, bringing the smell of wet soil and growing grass. The hills were losing their rounded contours, and turning to shadowed outlines whose edges were blurring with the sky. The moon had not yet appeared above the mountains, but she turned her face to where it must be, and registered it in her mind. Not quite full, the same shape as the little oval rock she had just taken from the shore, same pattern of grey and pearl etched upon its surface. A curious thought struck her. The person who had collected that music and played it from those books so long ago, had that one lived in this valley? Had that person stood upon this shore? At what phase of the moon had they stood here, and had they taken note of it, as she was now? She would never know, but if so, the shape of the hills would still have been the same, and the music of the water rushing at her feet, that would have been the same then as it was now. If I could stretch out my hand across time, thought Naomi, if I could put out my hand now, and touch the hand of that person, I think I would touch the hand of a friend.

Fifteenth Day

There was no avoiding the growing tension in the house. Naomi tried to go on with the music the next morning, but even in the room apart she was aware of an undercurrent of apprehension that seemed to run right through the place. Breakfast had been dealt with hastily; the family were silent and strained, and seemed to have lost their usually excellent appetites. She was feeling slightly queasy herself, and her stomach was upset. She ignored it. She was too old a hand for stage fright, and the midden was not the most attractive place to spend the morning.

No one had spoken to her about the dance except Linnet. That in itself was extraordinary. It must be one of the most important events in their calendar, and only occurred once every seven years. Presumably it would once have entailed feasting and celebration. After all, a dance was a dance. And if every adult in the valley was either a dancer or a musician, and every child came to watch, then all of them were involved in it. A curse seemed to be hanging over them, which had the power to turn their feast to mourning. She realised that more than one of them looked to her to release them from their spell. That frightened her a little. She had no idea what she was supposed to do. There was too much mystery attached to it, and she was not sure that she had asked the right questions. Perhaps a wiser person would have understood by now, and known what to do. Naomi thought back to all the other events she had played for: other people's feasts, other people's days of remembrance or festival, so many celebrations in other people's lives. But they were of no help to her now. None of those occasions belonged to the empty lands. Nor did she, which was presumably why they looked to her to save them, when they could not save themselves.

But she didn't know enough. 'I'm not wise enough,' said Naomi out loud, and pushed the papers away from her. She couldn't concentrate on them now. They had waited so many years; they would wait a little longer. The matter of the dance was growing urgent.

She put away her fiddle and went out into the garden. She should have come out sooner. There was a blustery wind blowing round the house, stirring up last year's leaves from the edge of the forest, and sending them sailing up into the rain-rinsed air. Everything was soaking wet. The plants were slowly shedding their night's burden of water and standing upright again. New rows of vegetables looked frail and gleaming under the open sky, the bare earth damp and vulnerable. Naomi walked round slowly, and went through the gate at the end into the orchard. The grass was all bowed down, shimmering with water, which soaked through her boots as quickly as if she were wading through the beck.

The blossom had all gone from the pear tree. It stood naked, pale leaves just unfurling, amidst a carpet of petals that clung to the wet grass like heavy flakes of snow. Naomi wandered away from it again, into the yard behind the outhouses.

She found Peter there, just as she had done before. He was loading dirty straw into a wheelbarrow, and a strong smell of dung permeated the air about him. He waved to Naomi, and called out to her, 'I thought you were working, or I'd have waited to feed the pigs until you came.'

'I was working.' She stepped over the runnel in the middle of the yard, and came over to him. 'Only I stopped. I felt unsettled, and the sun is out again. So I came out.'

'You too?' said Peter. 'You can help me for a bit, if you like. It'll settle the stomach better than music, anyway.'

'If I'll be any use, I will.'

'Can you get clean straw then? From the barn, behind you.'

Presently she began to feel better. It was tough, working against the wind, but it seemed to clean the dust out of her lungs, and made her head feel clearer. She spread clean straw where Peter had mucked out, then sluiced down the cobbles with buckets of water from the pump. She waited while he scrubbed himself under the pump, then he took her off to the dairy. She hadn't been in there before. There were two buckets of milk standing on the stone shelf, and milk churns soaking in a sink full of water.

'Can you make butter?'

'I wasn't born yesterday,' said Naomi.

'There's a churn over there.' Peter took down a cheese in a muslin cloth, which had been dripping into a wooden bucket. 'I'll just take the whey to the kitchen. They want it for bread. We won't be able to make cheese today. Too many young beasts.'

'Which milk do I use?'

'This. It's stood a couple of days. It'll be right.'

The milk was already thickening, and slightly sour. Naomi tipped it into the churn and put back the plunger. It was a long time since she'd done this. It took a while to get back into the rhythm of it, and at first she sent splashes of milk across the stone floor, which spread into circles like pennies. She grimaced and carried on. Presently the motion began to come right: lift and twist. It was easy, so long as thought remained suspended. Yesterday's dance tunes began to filter through her mind, falling into time with the motion of the plunger. She started to hum, fixing them in her head. They would need to come naturally tomorrow. There might be far too many other things that required thinking about. Lift and twist, plunge down and twist. She was aware of Peter returning, filling churns at the stone sink, taking buckets out into the yard, the sound of water splashing from the pump outside.

Presently the butter began to come. Yellow blobs began to float to the top. The churning was getting harder. Lift and twist, plunge down and twist. Three jigs, sliding into one another. One of them was already familiar. At least this music wasn't altogether new. That would have made the task impossible, given the time. The butter was gathering fast, a thick layer across the top of the churn. The plunger began to move sluggishly. She could feel her cheeks glowing. And then when the dancers come back together, sixteen steps to the right, sixteen steps to the left. Four, four. And so back to the beginning again. The butter was solid now. Naomi stopped and looked round. There was a big earthenware basin on the shelf. She lifted the butter carefully out, and searched for a clean bucket.

Before she found what she wanted Peter came back, both buckets brimming with water. He glanced at her work, and nodded. 'I'll wash it if you like. You maybe want to get back.'

'I'd rather finish, now I've started.'

He nodded again. 'There's salt in that jar. Don't use much. We'll not be storing any, not at this time of year.'

Naomi rolled up her sleeves, and tipped in the cold water. The second part of the dance was easy to memorise, now that she had grasped the first. The tune for each dancer echoed the part they played in the first part. Not the same, but a development of the same theme. But the music becomes more interesting, thought Naomi; it goes deeper. The first is merely a dance tune, a celebration of the world in which we find ourselves. Whereas the second — Naomi sang softly under her breath, and began to slap the butter on the slab — the second is almost the same tune, but turned inwards, the world that we hold inside ourselves. Anticipation stirred inside her, overriding her fears. I want to see this dance, thought Naomi. I want to take part in it, after all.

When Peter came back, she had worked her way through to the end of the dance, and eleven small squares of butter lay on the slab before her.

'That's an interesting way of doing it,' remarked Peter.

'It'll taste the same.'

'You've done a good job. Thank you.'

'It was just what I needed. Thank you.'

'Since we're so polite,' he replied, 'shall we have a cup of tea together? I brought some out.'

There was a bench in the corner of the yard, a plank set on two upturned logs, carefully placed to catch the morning sun and not the wind. They sat down, and Peter offered her a brimming mug of tea, spilling some on to the cobbles as he did so.

'Feeling any better?'

'Much better,' said Naomi. 'And you?'

It took him a while to answer that one. He shifted a loose stone clumsily with one heavily booted foot, and then said, 'Fair enough, considering. It's not an easy time for us.'

'I'd gathered that.'

He glanced at her. 'I'm sorry you've been dragged into it,' he said simply, 'but for our sakes I'm glad you came.'

'It would help if I knew what I was supposed to do.'

'I think you've done most of it already.'

'Then I wish I'd noticed,' said Naomi dryly. 'I could have awarded myself some credit.'

'You deserve it. It was brave to take such a part upon you at all.'

'That's just it. I seem to have come in on cue, and perhaps speak my lines right. But it would help if I knew who I was supposed to be.'

'I never saw a play,' said Peter inconsequentially. 'You have, then?'

'One does, on the road. I travelled with players once. They needed a fiddler, at a time when I was lonely. But then I left them. I had work of my own to do, which became clearer to me.'

'I suppose the dance is a kind of play.'

'I suppose it is. I wish I knew the plot.'

'I thought Linnet explained it to you? That's what we decided.'

'Oh, she did. That wasn't quite what I meant.'

There was a silence. 'My cousin Thomas . . .' began Peter, and stopped.

'Your cousin Thomas . . .?' prompted Naomi, when she had waited a little.

'It's not so much that he won't explain,' Peter seemed to find the words hard to formulate, as though the thoughts behind them were too difficult. 'I imagine that he can't.'

'I think you're right.'

'He never has,' said Peter.

'Never has what?'

'Put it into words. Said what happened. I think it would be better if he could.'

'It would certainly help me.'

'You need help?' asked Peter, turning to face her, as if she had presented him with quite a new proposition. 'I would help you in any way I could. I hope you know that. Is there anything I could do to help you now?'

Naomi struggled with herself. She wasn't inquisitive. Thomas knew that. It was not idle curiosity that was driving her to this. If she were expected to play a part, then she had to know a little more. Peter was right: Thomas had wanted to tell her, right from the very beginning. She would be taking no advantage; she would be acting out of respect.

Naomi made a decision. 'It would help me to know what happened to Judith, and to her sons,' she said.

There was a long silence. 'You're right to ask me,' replied Peter at last. 'No one can tell you more, but perhaps no one would find it harder to tell. That doesn't matter. I said I would help you, and I will.'

Having promised so much, he relapsed into silence. Naomi waited patiently, and drank her tea. It was warm out in the sun. She had been indoors far too much in the last couple of days. She was beginning to feel sleepy.

'When Judith and I grew up,' began Peter, with his face averted, so that she had to lean forward to hear him, 'we became lovers. That in itself would not have been forbidden, being cousins, only we belonged to one household, and that is not acceptable, as you know.'

'Yes.'

'There was only one thing to do, which we did. Judith left, and started a new household. She chose a ruin on the other side of the valley, at the foot of the pass.'

'I've seen it.'

'You have? I didn't know. It wasn't easy. There are few women in this family, and she was wanted here. But that seemed less important to us, at the time.'

'I can understand that.'

'She decided to go, but obviously she couldn't go alone. One woman couldn't be expected to make a household, particularly if she intended to have children, which Judith did. To bring up children alone would be far too much to ask of anybody. It wouldn't be right. So Thomas said he would go with her.'

'I see,' said Naomi, as Peter paused, evidently waiting for her to respond.

'They made a household there. They rebuilt the house, and made a garden. The soil wasn't good, so they worked mainly with the sheep, and bartered wool and meat for grain, with us. We were very interdependent, for obviously their holding was small. But all that they did was done excellently. They knew the land, those two, and they loved it. They treated it as well as anybody could.'

'I've seen how much he loves his land.'

'Judith was the same. She had two sons, Jonathan and Julius. Jonathan was the one I spent most time with. He was like his mother. He was big for his age, and very handy with the sheep. He cared about this valley, and I think he would have stayed here. Julius was quite different. But they got on pretty well together.'

'For how long?'

'They lived there fourteen years. Julius was just turned twelve. It was this time of year, seven years ago.' He gave Naomi a quick glance, to check that she was listening, then bent his head, so she couldn't see his face. 'The way it used to be, the dance was a festival. Everyone waited for it, and the feasting and the celebrations went on for days. Every one of us has a part in it. I expect Linnet told you that. That year, Jonathan also had a part. If anyone becomes too old to dance, or dies within the seven years, the next child in age must take their place. For Jonathan it was the Moon. Each dancer keeps the same part all their life, until it is passed on again.'

'Is the Moon not a woman?'

'Can a man not dance as a woman, or a woman as a man? Some of the dancers are one, some the other. There are masks. What do our bodies have to do with it?'

'I see,' said Naomi. 'Go on.'

'Jonathan should have danced. Julius was to watch. He wanted to be a musician. He made himself an instrument out of old pans. But he never practised. That was Julius.'

'I like Julius,' said Naomi.

'Everyone liked Julius.' Peter paused again. 'Naomi, I'm sorry. This part is hard to tell. I'm doing my best.'

'I appreciate it. I don't want to ask too much.'

'You don't. You needn't fear for me. I'm not Thomas, and hearts don't break, whatever they may feel, so I can tell you.

'Thomas was more interested in the dance than any of us. It was he that thought most about what must be done, and the organisation was all left to him. He enjoyed it; he's a bit of an actor, our Thomas. Maybe you've noticed that?'

'Yes.'

'Perhaps the whole thing was too important to him. There's a ritual to these things which catches up on you. Do you know what I mean?'

'I know that any performance has a magic of its own, and all magic can be dangerous, if a person isn't strong.'

'Of course you know. I was forgetting who you are. Anyway, there is a tradition about our dance, which is, that if a musician can be brought in from the world outside and made to play for us, it will bring us good fortune through the seven years which are to follow.'

'Yes. I've met that belief elsewhere.'

'Thomas had gone away for a night, over the pass to the next valley. That was customary: he had a lover there.'

'I know.'

'Ah, you know that too. He was on his way home. It was nearly sunset, and the mist was coming down over the pass. He came over the hill in a hurry, and overtook a man on the road. A travelling fiddle player.'

'I see.'

'It wasn't such a coincidence as you might think. Our dances are well known, and any musician who was brave enough, and was seeking a few days' living, might choose to come to this land at the right moment. But Thomas wasn't thinking that way, not then. He stopped and spoke to the man.

'I realise now that I'll never know what they said. It doesn't matter. The fact is that the fiddle player was dying. Whether he knew it or not, we can't know; what he told Thomas, we can't know; whether he told Thomas that a sickness lay upon him, and Thomas made light of it, because the tradition was fulfilled, we can't know that either. The fact is the same. Thomas brought the man home as his guest, and took him into his own house.'

Naomi put her hands to her cheeks. 'I begin to understand,' she said.

'The fiddle player died the next day. It was Judith who knew what must be done. She put the signs on the doors and across the boundaries, and she barred the gates. She and Thomas buried the man, and waited.

'So later that day, when I came up to the house, I found my way barred, and the warning against pestilence marked on the boundary. I almost ignored it, but I didn't. I stood at the gate and called her.

'She heard me at last, and came out. We stood about a dozen yards apart, and she told me what had happened. She wouldn't let me go near her. She told me Julius was sick, and that she was afraid for him. She asked me to bring supplies and leave them at the gate each day.

'I wanted to go to her, but she was always stronger than I, and she wouldn't have it. She made me promise that I would never pass the gate until the signs were taken down, or the time of danger was past. I promised. I don't know what I said. I think I said how I wished I could get her out. That was the nearest she came to telling me her thoughts. She laid her head down on the gatepost just for a moment, and she said, "I'd give up my life tomorrow, Peter, if I could get my children out of here". Then she made me go away.'

Naomi's hands were cold against her cheeks. She said nothing, but he went on without encouragement this time. 'The next day I spoke to her again. She told me Julius was worse. The next day I called at the gate, and Jonathan came. He looked very small, more like a child than a lad of fourteen. He told me she was sick, and that Julius was dead. The next day I called, and no one came.'

'Thomas?' asked Naomi, but the word only came out as a whisper, and perhaps he didn't hear.

'When I came back the food had been taken, and it was taken the day after that. On the third day it was not taken.'

'I would have gone in then. I didn't care. But I'd promised Judith, the last promise I'd made to her. And there was all the rest of the valley to think of. They were waiting too, and we were all afraid. So I didn't go in.'

'So what happened?'

'Paul came. Paul came over the pass to see Thomas, and he too found the signs upon the boundaries. He knew what we did not, that a deadly sickness had broken out along the coast, and had reached the valley beyond his own. So when he saw the signs he guessed that someone must have come from there, bypassing his own valley. He saw the signs, and he did what I had not done. He threw caution to the winds, and jumped the gate, and went in to find them. It was done for love, you understand. He acted out of love.'

'So did you.'

'Is that true?' asked Peter cynically. 'I've had seven years to wonder. Paul saved Thomas's life.'

'So Thomas was sick too?'

'Yes. I don't know what order things happened in. I'll never know. But when Paul came, there were graves made. For the others, and for Thomas as well. When he found the sickness on himself, he dug his own grave. To protect the rest of us, I suppose. He wouldn't have the whole valley on his conscience, and whoever touched his body would be at risk. I suppose that was what he thought. So he made his own grave, and when he grew weak, he laid himself in it, so that no other would have to do it.'

'But Paul came.'

'Paul came, and Paul brought him back to life. Why Paul was unscathed, I don't know. There is a pattern in these things, some say, and the time of infection passes, though the patient's own life may still be in danger. Perhaps it was that. I don't know. Paul stayed at the house with Thomas. No one came, because no one knew he was there. We were waiting for enough time to pass, and by now we knew what we must find.'

'It must have been the worst time.'

He didn't answer that. 'And of course, there was no dance. The moon passed. We decided we would do it a month late, because the dance must be done. It was a vow made by our people, which we must keep, whatever we suffer.'

She couldn't let that pass unchallenged. 'Must vows always be kept?' she demanded passionately. 'Things change, and no one knows what is right for the future!'

'We have to remember who we are.'

'We are people! All of us! That's more important than any ritual, or any tradition. Isn't that what Thomas forgot?'

'Is it? Explain to me.'

'People suffer through famine and pestilence, and through what they do to one another. No one would die if there were no dance. No one would even suffer. I can see why you care. I have a past which I care about too. But has it made Thomas any happier, or any wiser, to know the names of the mountains? Would he be a lesser man if he'd never taken part in the dance? What good have your memories done you?'

He sat up and faced her. Either she had hurt him to the quick, or he was furious. She wasn't sure which; she had never seen him moved before. 'Who are you to say that?' He seized her wrist. 'You belie yourself! Look at your hand!' He turned it palm upwards. In contrast to his own it was fair and smooth, unmarked by work. 'What do you do in this world? Do you offer anyone food or sustenance or medicine? You don't! You give them dreams. Dreams out of the past that tell them they are different from the beasts. No happier, perhaps, but of a different nature. What did you come here for? Because you needed food or shelter, or even love? No! You turned your back on such security years ago. You came because of a dream. Dreams out of the past, for which you'll suffer anything. I taught those children the names of the mountains, and I'm glad I did. If you had a child, wouldn't you give him your music, if you loved him? You belie yourself, and us!'

'I'm sorry,' said Naomi at once. 'You're right. Sometimes it would be easier to have no dreams, but I know it would be intolerable.'

He let go her wrist and held her hand between his own. 'I didn't mean to be angry with you,' he said more calmly. 'Only you echoed my own thoughts, and my own thoughts have made me angry enough. Thomas made two dances before these things happened. The way he made them was magical, an enchantment. He transformed an outworn routine into something new and beautiful. It became to him what I think your music is to you. He wanted to make it perfect. He forgot that we are only people, and must think first of our own survival.'

'And so he found a fiddle player,' said Naomi, and sighed. 'He told me once that he wanted to lay a ghost. He's not cured then, is he? He wants to complete the circle, and appease the spirit of the play. But we're not living in a play.'

'I think he wronged you.'

'Me?' she said, confused. 'What have I to do with it?'

'What you said. You're not the ghost of a fiddle player. You're not the solution to our pain. You're on a path of your own, and he failed to think of that. He's done the same thing all over again.'

She gave a wry smile. 'I think I'm tougher than that. I'll remember who I am, even if Thomas doesn't.'

'Well, you can remember me too. I deal with things my own way, and I don't need anyone to enact the past again for me. I told you before, my feelings about the past are my own, and if you want anything from me in the present, as man to woman, I would gladly give it.'

She let her hand lie in his, but shook her head. 'I'm too confused. It's not only your past I'm finding here, but my own. Thank you for explaining to me. I asked more of you than I knew.'

'I should tell you the rest,' said Peter.

'There's more?'

'I told you that Paul brought Thomas back to life. Thomas is very strong, and he lived. But he was not himself. Not in his mind.'

'I know his fear.'

'You do? But not all the reasons for it, perhaps. When Thomas came to himself, and faced what he had done, and that because of Paul he still lived, he couldn't bear it. Hearts don't break, but minds can do so. He would have destroyed himself, and when Paul prevented him, he turned his despair upon Paul, and would have destroyed him too.'

'So that is it,' whispered Naomi, and twisted her hands together so that her knuckles turned white.

'He was weak, of course, from sickness. But a man outside his mind has a strength of his own. And he had a knife, and Paul had none.'

She realised she was shivering, and remembered how cold Thomas had been when she held him in her arms. 'To be afraid of oneself,' she said to Peter. 'Does anyone deserve to live with that?'

He put his hand over hers again. 'Paul got out,' he said. 'How, I don't know, but we found him within the gate. We went in then, Alice and I, and we saw all that had happened. We brought Thomas home.'

'Peter,' Naomi said shakily. 'Peter, I am sorry.' Words had never seemed less adequate. She turned and hugged him, and was received in a warm embrace. She held him, still shivering, and realised that it was she that wanted comfort, not he. He had come to terms with the past, and for him it was a memory. So much stronger than Thomas, she thought, and suppressed her tears. She had no right to inflict them upon Peter. They were not for him, but for her friend.

Sixteenth Day

Naomi slept soundly that night in spite of the dance being imminent. Now that things were clearer she could afford to let them go until the morning. She woke in the middle of a pleasant erotic dream, which featured Peter, and struggled against returning consciousness. But daylight pressed against her eyelids. Reluctantly she acknowledged it, and rolled over. She lay on her back, frowning at the patterns of light and shade that flickered across the ceiling. She felt frustrated, and a little disconcerted. My body seems to have different ideas from my mind, thought Naomi, but at least no one else need know about it.

Presently someone tapped on the door. 'Come in,' called Naomi.

'Sorry to wake you,' said Linnet briskly, before she had even shut the door, 'but the other musicians will be here pretty soon. It's our last practice. You haven't forgotten?'

'No, I hadn't forgotten.'

'There's breakfast. I don't know if you want any. It doesn't seem to be a habit of yours.'

'Only when it's brought to me,' murmured Naomi.

'What?'

'Nothing. I'll be down in a minute.'

The practice took place in a large room overlooking the wallflowers and the bridge, next to the chequered hall. Naomi hadn't been in here before. The room was high and bare, with a floor of mellowed pine, and whitewashed walls. There was nothing in it except a few rugs and cushions piled in a corner. The ceiling was carved into patterns like those in the room where the music was, concentric circles moving out from the centre, and a border round the walls like a scroll. Naomi stood in the middle of the room while Linnet busied herself with opening windows, and looked about her. She felt like a child in a forest, awed by this extraordinary combination of size and space. It seemed an enchantment, to bring the proportions of the living world inside a house. She clutched her fiddle to her chest, feeling naive and foolish, for nothing she had ever seen had prepared her for such a place as this. She found herself wondering if this house had a shape to it that could be encompassed by the minds of those who knew it, or whether it were something more intangible, offering only an illusion of separate rooms and spaces, being in itself as insubstantial as the colours in the air. It was strange living inside a house she couldn't visualise as a whole, like being a pawn in someone else's game. Naomi shuddered, and went to look out of the opened window.

'They're coming up the track,' said Linnet. 'We can start in a minute.'

Naomi had forgotten until that moment that there was anything to be afraid of. But the sight of the little group of people carrying instruments, moving in a body towards the house, sent a prickle down her spine. She had been called upon to lay a ghost, and people were afraid of ghosts. Her arm still ached, when she thought about it. They could have stopped her playing forever. The only child she had met in this valley had run away at the sight of her. The actions of children mirror the thoughts of adults. Thomas had dealt out the parts in this play, but Thomas was not master even of himself. Naomi laid a light hand on Linnet's sleeve, and Linnet started.

'Is this going to be difficult, do you think?'

Linnet thought it over. 'If it were anyone but you, I think it would be,' she said judicially.

Naomi was still trying to work out if that were comforting or not when there were voices at the door, and the musicians came in.

As soon as they saw her, there was dead silence. There were five of them: five pairs of eyes instantly riveted upon her. Their fear hit her like a wave. Instinctively she turned to where Linnet had stood beside her, but Linnet had moved away to greet them.

'This is Naomi,' said Linnet, loudly and firmly. 'She's a fiddle player from the lands to the west, and she has never been in our country before.' She fixed the newcomers with an accusing gaze, and their eyes dropped. Two of them spoke at once, too quickly, then each fell silent in deference to the other. There was a moment's uncertainty, then one of the women stepped forward and held out her hand. 'You are welcome to our country.'

'Thank you,' said Naomi, and shook hands.

The others followed suit, more or less reluctantly.

'Well,' said Linnet, as soon as they had done. 'Hadn't we better begin?'

There was a guitar, a mandolin, a flute, pipes and a drum. The woman with the guitar who had greeted Naomi first was evidently the leader. The players assembled themselves after a little muttered discussion. Linnet remained glued to Naomi's side like a terrier defending a bone, glaring at any of them who dared to glance at Naomi.

'Can you move across, Linnet?' asked the woman with the guitar. 'That's better.'

It was better, thought Naomi. Bodyguards oppressed her. She stood back a little, silent and alert, following every move.

Considering what a tiny community they sprung from, they were not at all bad. They were quite professional about their music, though not exactly cheerful, considering the lightness of some of the music they were playing. Obviously they came together a good deal more often than every seven years. Naomi was relieved about that. If they were used to playing for parties, they might mitigate the fateful element that seemed to be attached to any production of Thomas's. Certainly she herself felt better for every minute that she played with them. This was her world again. The rehearsal was about music. They might have arrived with their minds full of past spectres, but now they were ready to work, and she had done this so many times that it was the simplest matter in the world to work with them. Nobody said much, but when they did speak, it was about the music, and they were soon able to address her almost normally. The musicians will be no problem, thought Naomi, when they were about half way through the first part. I hope the same will be true of the dancers.

By dinner time she felt quite confident about what they had to do. It would have been a help to see the dance rehearsed as well, but no one had suggested such a thing. Presumably they had worked through it with the dancers before, and it never occurred to them that her picture of the whole was necessarily vague. It doesn't matter, she decided. I know my own part, and the rest doesn't sound too complicated.

It was hard to know what to do with the afternoon. There was a restlessness about the place. Everyone dispersed quickly when they had eaten. Thomas never appeared at all. Someone said he had gone up to the dance place. Some of them were to follow with firewood and torches. There was talk of carrying up boxes. Containing the masks, presumably, thought Naomi, or the costumes. She wondered what it was like for Thomas. Presumably she wouldn't see him again until the dance took place.

It was a golden afternoon. The wind had dropped, and the sun shone enticingly. She could go for a walk, or she could return to her own work. Both, she decided, in that order.

She went further than she had planned, carefully avoiding the scattered settlements, following the left-hand beck almost to its source, right round the west face of Thomas's mountain. The valley grew steeper and stonier, and slowly the peaks ahead drew nearer. She was tempted to climb right up to the ridge, a thought which might not have occurred to her if Thomas hadn't come into her life. But the day was passing, and the shadows were already lengthening on the western slopes. If she wanted to walk in sunshine she ought to go back. She turned unwillingly, halting several times to look at the fells lying blue and untrodden behind her, shimmering a little in the heat of the afternoon.

As soon as she entered the house she sensed anticipation. Only a few hours to go. A thrill of apprehension ran through her. There had been so many performances before this, but she had never become quite indifferent. And tonight there was too much invested.

She still had about two hours' daylight. The most sensible thing to do would be to return to the papers. It seemed an immense effort. When she actually had the music spread in front of her, however, the old excitement took over. It didn't matter how difficult it was, or how long it took her. She was beginning to work out patterns in the unknown music, and they were unprecedented. It was like climbing up the familiar slopes to the ridge she saw from the valley, and seeing the infinite ranges of peaks beyond. They might appear unreachable, but they belonged to the same earth, and all that was required was the patience to walk to them, one step after another. It wasn't the sudden flash of genius that was needed for this job, it was application. That was nothing new to her, though it wasn't an aspect of her calling she tended to emphasise. But being alone, with no audience, she was able to sit down and get on with it.

The rewards were already beyond anything she had imagined, even though she was only just beginning to glimpse them. She decided to concentrate entirely on the *Violino* book. The others seemed to be more complicated, being inscribed with strange lines and symbols that she could find no meaning for, and when she tried to play the notes consecutively, the pattern was obscure. Often the tadpoles were all heaped up together in a way that no single instrument could play. But in *Violino* there were only single lines of notes, and if she worked out carefully what the relation of one to another was, by counting the lines and spaces, a pattern began to emerge. It was a desperately laborious way of creating music, but there was definitely a tune, and such a tune as she had never heard in waking life before. She sensed perfection, and it tantalised her, driving her on to decipher this dead code that revolted all her instincts, in order to abstract the life that lay within.

She tried one tune and then another, testing her theory. It seemed to work, more or less. There was no way of knowing which note was supposed to be which, or even if they indicated anything more fixed than the relationship between them. And the length of each note could only be guessed at, as far as she could see. It was going to be a long job. Naomi sighed, and turned over a few more pages at random. There were words written here and there. *Corrente. Sarabanda. Giga.* She read them out loud. *Giga?* Jig? If that were so ... Naomi picked up her fiddle, and began to try out the notes, one by one. If it was really a jig, it would be like coming out into daylight, after groping through the dark.

She kept trying it, and presently the notes seemed to flow into a pattern far more easily. When she looked at them on the page, she was slowly beginning to get a sense of how the tune might sound. Once she had grasped what the notes said, it was no effort at all to play it on the fiddle. The hard part was to go on looking at the paper while she played. The tune was exquisite: no one could stare at squiggles on a page while they played music like that. And there were so many more. It would be weeks, months maybe, before she had them all safely in her head, but there was no hurry. They had waited for generations, and they were not about to vanish now. She began to approach the notes methodically, going over the same ones again and again until she was sure she had them right. She worked on the jig for a long time, and when at last she was satisfied she looked up, and noticed that the sky was darkening outside, and there were dim shadows surrounding her in the crowded room.

Her immediate thought was to fetch a candle. Then she remembered that the coming of dark signified the time for the dance. She felt a sudden sinking in her stomach, and her mouth was dry. She was conscious of disappointment too. Having got so far with the work, it was a shame to leave it while it was coming so easily. There's always tomorrow, she told herself, but wasn't satisfied. She allowed herself to play through the bit she had by heart once more, to fix it in her memory. Then she put away the papers, and left the room.

It was quite dark in the passage, but she knew her way by now, and didn't hesitate. At the corner she crashed into someone coming the other way, who had made the same assumption.

'Oh, there you are,' said Linnet breathlessly. 'I was just coming for you. Are you ready?'

'Just let me get my jacket.'

'They've gone on,' said Linnet. 'I waited to feed Jo. I wanted her to be asleep. My cousin's carrying her. I think it'll be all right. He's a sensible boy, and I shan't be far away.'

'I'm sure it'll be all right.'

'Peter went up with them. I gave them some carrot sticks, in case she wakes up.'

'I'm sure it'll be all right,' repeated Naomi. 'I won't be a minute.'

When she came back Linnet had lit a lantern, and was blowing out the lamp in the hall. 'We'll only need this under the trees,' she said. 'The moon's bright as daylight.'

They stepped out into a world transmuted by light. It was very quiet. Only the rushing of the beck was the same by moonlight or daylight, flowing on undiminished. It implied to Naomi a hint of a way out; water finding its way from this valley, undaunted by the circle of fells, out into the lake and the river beyond the lake, to the sea where all things ended. It reassured her. She turned her back on it and faced the moon, which had already risen free of the encircling mountains. It stared down at her unshadowed, filling the valley with liquid light that seemed to run over the ridges like a cup overflowing. The hills seemed nearer than they had ever done before, washed in light above the shadowed precipices, bare and open as the faint contours of the moon above.

'Sometimes the moon is like the valley,' said Linnet entirely unexpectedly. 'When it's full. It's the same shape, and it has the shadows of the same rocks. Almost as if it fell out of here a long time ago. When I was little I used to be scared it might want to come back.'

'The moon came from the sea,' said Naomi.

'Is that what they say in your country? I suppose the truth is different, depending on where you are.' Linnet led the way across the grass towards the oak trees. 'I hope you don't think I'm stupid?' she asked, just before they stepped into the shadows.

'Absolutely not. How could I?'

'I know I'm not particularly clever. My cousins tease me, but you're very polite.'

It was pitch dark under the trees. Naomi tried to feel her way forward, at the same time as responding to this extraordinary statement. 'Wait. I can't do two things at once. Have you still got that lantern?'

'Oh, sorry. I forgot. Is that better? Can you see the path?'

'Your cousins have a lot to answer for,' said Naomi, and walked into a tree. 'Ouch!'

'Where are you? Oh, sorry. How about you taking the lantern?'

'Give me your hand a minute,' said Naomi, and transferred her fiddle to her other arm. 'Thank you. I've not been this way before.'

Linnet's hand in hers felt uneasy, conveying a diffidence which Naomi found perplexing. It made progress much easier, however, especially now that they were both within the small circle of lamplight. The trees rustled overhead, showing a glimmer of white sky beyond. 'Your cousins are quite wrong,' said Naomi. 'You are an intelligent woman, and you are a musician. You must never forget it.'

Dead silence. Linnet's hand in hers was small and cold; it felt like holding a bird that had given up attempting to escape. Now what have I done? thought Naomi, and waited.

'There's a beck here,' said Linnet. 'Can you see the stepping stones?'

The water was very shallow, spreading out over the path, and they negotiated it without difficulty. A moment later they were out of the trees again, standing on a white hillside among half uncoiled bracken stems. Linnet let go Naomi's hand and led the way straight up, along a ribbon of white path which followed the line of the beck. At first the water seemed so loud and the moon so bright that Naomi felt all her senses dazzled. She had hardly adjusted to it when Linnet spoke again. 'Peter told me what he said to you,' she said, and waited expectantly.

Not all of it, I bet, thought Naomi, and made no comment.

'I realised when he told me,' went on Linnet hurriedly, 'that it should have been me.'

'Why?'

Linnet scrambled over a steep bit, and waited for Naomi to catch up. 'I'm not used to being with women,' she said almost apologetically. 'My mother doesn't talk to me, not since Judith died. I don't see many strangers. You remind me of my sister.'

'I see,' said Naomi. 'And now you have a daughter.'

'I don't see what that's got to do with it,' said Linnet, puzzled. 'I'm only saying, I haven't quite known what to say. I hope you didn't mind.'

'What on earth could I mind? You've treated me very well.'

'You said you felt very much alone,' said Linnet. 'I couldn't see how. After all, you had Thomas.'

'I had Thomas?' repeated Naomi. 'What do you mean?'

'I don't know. I thought he was your friend. He's the same age as you, anyway. But I feel as though there's something I haven't done.'

'That last thing you should do is feel guilty. There's no reason.'

'You're staying on after the dance, aren't you?'

'If you'll have me. I want to go on with the music.'

'Then that's all right,' said Linnet, and hurried on ahead, as if the subject might now be safely postponed.

The path was taking them right into the hills. When Naomi looked back, the valley lay like a silver bowl below them, already remote beyond its encircling trees. It was like stepping out of a magic circle into a dimension that had nothing to do with the world she knew. The floor of the valley looked quite smooth from here, like a spinning top. It had spun her out of one world into another, and there was no telling where she was. She looked at the mountains opposite, trying to remember their names. That reorientated her; there were still signposts, and they only seemed to have changed. She turned to the path again, and saw that Linnet was some way ahead. As she hastened after her, a new country began to open up around her. It was no longer mountainous, but seemed to level out into a rough plateau. Round hills rose to left and right of her. The path was plain to see, heading directly towards the moon. It led her in a gentle curve, so that when she looked back again the valley had vanished.

There was a faint touch of a breeze on her cheeks. The beck had dwindled to nothing; the fells were silent. The small figure of Linnet on the track ahead of her was edged with silver, colourless. The only sound in all that space was the slight crunch of her own footsteps on shining gravel. The sky was wide open, as if the veil of dark had been drawn back to reveal the unseen expanses of the night. There was nothing above but emptiness, the stars dimmed out by moonlight. The sky seemed to expand right down to her feet, encompassing her, as though space had overflowed its limits and reached down to touch the earth.

She sensed a change. In the world behind, the earth was solid and full of colour; people were full-bodied, separate. In that world she was someone particular, a musician whose stock in trade was the tunes of the waking world and the colours of daylight and fire. In this place, there was another music that had no audible voice. It was still hers, just as the moonlit air she breathed was hers. In this place she had no colour, only the reflected whiteness of the moon, like the rocks around her. She was not different from them; merely, they were silent and eternal, while she was quick and transient, a tune played for a moment, voicing the substance of them all.

The land under her feet no longer seemed static. It was alive. She could feel it as clearly as her own breathing. It was like standing on a ship, feeling movement under her, staring out to a limitless horizon. She had made many voyages, but never through country as strange to her as this, or so familiar. She had not thought of Thomas's country as home, but now it seemed as if it were all home. The earth was alive, and it was the same earth, wherever she might be. There was a music to it beyond the range of human ears, but within the compass of her body. She couldn't hear it, but she recognised it, a vibration too vast for any instrument, spinning out into space, the beginning and end of every human tune, the sound of home.

The road ahead was empty. She didn't wonder about Linnet. She had stepped outside the circle, and from here it would all be the matter of a dream. Naomi accepted the road as she found it, and followed.

The path dipped, curling among rocks, and then the moon was below her, shining up from the depths of a tarn that lay flat as glass in the lap of a corrie scooped out between the hills. She followed it down, and the path revealed itself again, winding to the water's edge.

It was not empty any longer. There were people moving slowly down to the water, and at the tail of the procession she recognised Linnet by the fiddle tucked under her arm. As Naomi drew nearer she saw more people, like moving stones at the water's edge, passing to and fro across a flattened area just beyond the tarn. There was a red flicker right by the water, then another. Even as she watched, the light spread into a circle of flame surrounding the dancing place.

When she reached the shore the musicians were waiting for her. They no longer had the faces of strangers. They were her own people, and their ranks opened to receive her without question. Their place was between the water and the fire, on the dry shingle above the shore. They spent a little time tuning their instruments, then turned to face the circle.

When the music began she was part of it. Perhaps she had learned better than she knew in so short a time, but it seemed to flow effortlessly, as though it were already present, and all she had to do was let it in, and give it substance. It was a strange place to play. The sound they made did not echo back to them, but seemed to wheel away into space, as though it might continue through the night for ever. She had a weird sense of not hearing herself properly, as though even her own music had passed beyond the range of human ears. She could feel it, however, if she couldn't hear it, almost as though it were not different from her at all.

She never saw the dancers come into the circle. She looked up once, and the place was empty; she looked again, and there were figures within the circle of torches, masked and motionless. She realised afterwards that she never at any point tried to identify the dancers. Even Thomas was forgotten. They were all outside themselves that night, or perhaps they had merely shed the part that was not themselves. She was no longer with the people she had met in the valley. She was among the dancers of the empty lands.

The dancers raised their arms, stepped forward, their hands touched. The circle joined, and moved. Masked faces caught the firelight, so that they seemed mobile: alive, but alien. They were human faces, but larger than anything mortal, vivid with emotion, but at the same time blank. Painted eyes gleamed, apparently lit by anger, tears or laughter, but when they moved again they were flat and static. Naomi recognised them. They were faces she knew, mirroring the faces of the world where she belonged, and yet not any of them. She saw her own face, and faces she had not known were hers, and acknowledged them, both like and opposite.

The dancers stepped back. The circle broke, and the music altered with it.

The Fool stepped into the centre of the circle.

He was dressed in leaves, young and green as springtime, the innocent at the beginning of the journey. His painted face was round and vacant, unmarked by any trace of feeling. He bowed to the moon above him, and began his dance. Naomi watched him as she played his music, and was stirred with compassion. His naivety was pitiful; there seemed to be no strength in it, certainly not enough to face the world into which the journey must lead him. But perhaps she was wrong: the music was changing, and the Fool with it. He exacted no pity now. His dance grew vibrant, and savage. He was not in danger, he was dangerous. The music accelerated into a frenzied swirling melody, underscored by the raw beat of the drum.

There was a crash like thunder, and the Fool was gone. In his place stood the Magician, in the dead centre of the circle. The journey had begun.

It was a strange and complicated journey, moving not in a straight line, but by a progression of opposites. It was like standing in a room full of mirrors, turning first one way and then another, and seeing a different reflection every time. Some dances were of an unearthly beauty that brought the tears to her eyes even as she played their melody; others were chaotic and frightening, and she would have drawn back like a scared child, were she not contracted to play their music too. Eleven images were held up in the circle before her, and in each of them she saw the face of her own world.

At last the circle closed again, and began to spin, both moonwise and sunwise. Its shape altered: it became two circles, spinning together, one flowing endlessly into the other, merging with it, until again there was only one. Finally it broke. The dancers stepped back into the dark beyond the flickering torches.

There was no real dark, only moonlight, but she seemed to be mesmerised by the empty circle within the firelight, and could not turn her eyes away from it. The music was low and soothing. She could hardly have looked down for a moment, but when she looked again they had materialised within the ring of fire, motionless as statues. The faces they bore were not the images of any daylight world. She recognised them, however. They belonged to her own dreams.

The first dancer was like an image of herself, as she knew herself in certain dreams; a woman whose dance was all controlled power, her mask fierce and resolute. She is who I am, thought Naomi, in those moments when I know who I am. She watched, fascinated, until the dancer withdrew, leaving the circle seemingly more empty than before. Naomi felt a stab of loss as she vanished beyond the flames. Then the circle re-formed, and the moment passed.

The Hanged One stepped into the centre of the circle.

He was dressed in motley, like a Fool, and his face was the face of innocence. It was not the innocence of the Fool, but of one who has completed their turn in the world and returned unscathed. He carried his noose around his neck, but there was no fear in him. His mask looked two ways at once, as one who stands upon a threshold. He faced the moon, so that his other face was hidden in his shadow. They were serene faces, but there was nothing quiescent about his dance. It was tumultuous as the spring itself, overflowing with life and joyousness. It was a dance of renewal, the beginning of another journey.

His dance merged into a larger theme, like running water into a lake. There was a moment's brightness, then the drum began, measuring out the time with a beat like a human pulse. The torches seemed to flicker, and when Naomi looked again, there was Death at the centre of the circle.

It was a journey into the heart of a dream. The living world was left behind and they seemed to be traversing a vast desert in which images rose up before her, untempered by any warmth of daylight. None were entirely inimical, none entirely reassuring. There was neither good nor evil, neither alien nor known, neither self nor other. They were simply another series of mirrors, but many-faceted this time, so that instead of seeing a form she recognised, she saw an infinite pattern of possibilities. Every dancer was herself, and her whole world was faithfully reflected in all of them.

There was danger in it. She felt she might sink down into this realm entirely, and so be lost to waking life for ever. Only the music guided her, like a thread leading her through a featureless desert. If it were not for the music, she could not have stayed, and yet it was only the music that bound her to remain. She played like one in a dream, her eyes fixed upon the circle, spellbound.

The dance wound on. The Stars, the Moon and the Sun danced before her, and faded out in turn before the Last Day. The music swelled and altered, returning to the very beginning. The last dancer was at the centre. She was the World, in the image of a woman.

She stretched out her hands, palms upwards to the moon above her.

A scream of anguish tore the music apart. The circle broke, disintegrated. The Hanged One pitched forward, falling on the trampled grass. He screamed again. The music shattered into fragments. His third scream filled the whole air with pain. Then he lay silent, unconscious at the feet of the World.

Seventeenth Day

Nobody moved.

The World turned away from the moon, and looked down at the man lying at her feet. As though it were a signal, a ripple of movement spread among the dancers in the circle. The painted faces were horrifying in their non-reaction; it seemed as if the bodies supporting them were incapable of any human response. As if Thomas did not exist, thought Naomi, still stunned by such an abrupt awakening. She slowly lowered her bow, still held suspended across her fiddle, like music frozen on one note.

It was like struggling out of an enchantment, which was the more dangerous because it was uncompleted. When she was a child she had hated to wake up too soon, and find the world still dark about her. Silly to think of such a thing now. Naomi shook her head, and lowered her fiddle.

They were not doing anything about him.

She realised then that they were more shocked than she was. They were standing petrified in their places. She glanced at the musicians, and saw their faces, white and aghast. The dancers were worse, because they had no faces, not for any human crisis.

Naomi thrust her fiddle into Linnet's hands, jumped over the circle of torches, and knelt beside Thomas. She shoved her hand under his tunic, and after a moment found his heart, beating as regularly as the drum that had heralded Death. She undid his top button and loosened his collar. She took hold of the mask, one hand on each side of his head, and after a moment's struggle managed to slide it off quite easily. Then she rolled him on to his side. She looked up, and saw a circle of expressionless faces staring over her head. 'We should get him off the ground,' she said, addressing the slits of eyeholes. 'It's wet.'

They didn't move. She felt a flicker of sheer panic. This was the stuff of nightmare. There was a rustle behind her, then Linnet's voice in her ear, high and shaky. 'Tell me what to do,' she quavered.

'Take his legs,' Naomi told her promptly. 'That's it.'

It could only have taken them a moment to get him outside the ring of fire, but it felt like eternity. Illogical fear made Naomi clumsy. She had a foolish feeling that one of them might spring to life and grab at her, or Thomas, or Linnet, and destroy them all. Thomas's body was heavy and inert, and crumpled up as soon as they lifted him. There was a coldness between her shoulder blades that made her shudder, the terror of being watched. Somehow they negotiated the fire. Naomi laid Thomas down, keeping her arm under his head. Something soft was shoved at her. 'Take my jacket,' said Linnet.

There was a touch on her shoulder. She turned and found herself looking up at the Horned God, his face not a foot from hers. She screamed.

'Sorry,' said Peter's voice, rather shaken, 'I forgot. Is he all right?'

'No,' snapped Naomi. 'He's off his head, just like the rest of you. But he's not dead, if that's what you mean.'

'Wait,' said Linnet. 'He moved.'

The Horned God leaned over Naomi and took Thomas's wrists between his thumb and fingers. 'He'll do,' he said after a moment. He straightened up, and faced the circle. 'The dance can go on!' It was a command from the lord of the underworld, not like Peter at all.

'Bloody hell!' swore Naomi, under her breath.

'What?' said Linnet anxiously, crouched on the other side of Thomas. 'I think he's coming round.'

Naomi took Thomas's cold hand between her own, and chafed it gently, watching his face as she did so. He looked as white as death, but that was the moonlight. So must they all. She glanced up, and yet another shock hit her like a blow in the stomach. There was another circle round them, white frightened faces staring down at them. She heard herself gasp, and at the same moment the music began again at her back, ushering in the World for the second time.

Then she recognised them, and was ashamed of her foolishness. They were the children. Their gaze drifted away from Thomas for a moment when the music began, then they were looking down again with frightened eyes. The biggest one stepped forward so he was standing right over her. He was holding something carefully to his chest, a bundle that was strapped firmly round by an enveloping shawl. Jo, Naomi realised. The world was becoming more normal every minute.

'He's not dead, is he?' asked Thomas's youngest cousin, his voice breaking into a squeak as he spoke.

'Certainly not,' said Naomi firmly. 'He's fainted. The important thing is to keep him warm, and make sure he doesn't choke. That's why I rolled him over. There's nothing to cover him up with, is there?'

The little circle parted, then a moment later a couple of thick jackets materialised, and a cloak. Naomi wrapped them round Thomas as best she could, and Thomas gave a faint groan.

'I told you so,' said Naomi. She might have been speaking to herself. 'He'll soon be all right.'

Thomas moaned again, and rolled over further, curling up in a tight huddle, his face almost touching her knees. The music washed over them, thin without the two fiddles, like an echo through space from a distant world.

'Why did he faint?'

'Because it was too much for him,' said Naomi absently, her eyes on Thomas.

'Why?'

'Oh, do shut up!' snapped Linnet. 'Can't you see this is serious!'

'It must have reminded him of something that was too hard to bear,' replied Naomi.

'Judith's part, you mean?'

'She means Julius and Jonathan,' said another voice.

'I think that was probably it,' said Naomi. 'Thomas?'

'They were my cousins.'

'And mine.'

'And mine.'

'We're all cousins here.'

'Except me,' said Naomi. 'Thomas?'

The music changed. The dance of the World had ended, and the circle reformed. Thomas gave a small choking sound, and hid his head in his arms. Naomi laid her hands over his. His arms were rigid, his hands knotted together. So he was conscious, then. 'Thomas?'

'I don't think he wants to hear.' The children seemed to have instituted themselves as chorus.

'Perhaps he wanted to be dead.'

'He tried to kill himself before, because of Julius and Jonathan.'

'Well anyway, he didn't, did he?'

'Oh, stop!' broke in Linnet. 'Go and watch the dance, can't you?'

'We want to stay here.'

'Then shut up.'

'She doesn't mind,' said a voice behind Naomi, which she recognised. 'Do you?'

'No,' said Naomi, without looking round to the child who had run away from her. 'I'd rather be spoken to than not spoken to.'

The music was drawing to its close. The dance must be nearly over. 'I didn't know who you were,' said the voice behind her, not apologetically, merely stating a fact.

'Thomas?' said Naomi again, and shook him gently. It was like trying to move a rock. 'Thomas?'

The music stopped. The silence was complete. They might have been on a dead planet, where only rock and water reflected back the moonlight, unseen and voiceless. Time seemed suspended, as though they had shifted from the woken world into the unnumbered years of silence that surrounded it. Not one of them moved. The dancers stood like a ring of stones. Naomi held her breath, knowing that she had no choice, because no one else was breathing either.

A sound broke the spell, a long wail from the shawled bundle just by Naomi's ear. A pause for breath, then another cry, more substantial than the first, followed by heartbroken sobbing.

'Jo!' said Linnet, instantly recalled to her sense. 'It's because the music stopped. I'll take her.'

Naomi was dimly aware of the movement and bustle which followed. She and Thomas were suddenly in the middle of a crowd. A babble of talk broke out, even laughter. There seemed to be people everywhere and a confusion of clothes and masks and instruments. People stood over them; some of them squatted down beside her and peered anxiously at Thomas in the moonlight. They were speaking about him now. She wasn't listening, but she could hear his name tossed around on the sea of talk, repeated back to her again and again. She nodded without taking in what they said, and still held Thomas's clutching hands under her own.

'Thomas?' she said to him again. 'Thomas?'

Someone touched her sleeve. It was Peter, dressed only in shirt and trousers, his hair all rumpled from the mask. 'We're talking about carrying him down,' he said, 'if he doesn't come round.'

'I don't think so,' said Naomi.

'Why not? He can't stay up here. We'll have to get him home.'

'I think it might hurt him more.'

'Then what's to be done?'

'Thomas!' commanded Naomi. 'Wake up! The dance is over.'

A tremor ran through the hands she held, but that was all.

'I don't think we have a choice,' said Peter.

'Very well.' Naomi stood back, and let them take him.

As soon as she let go of Thomas, she was aware of them all. Everyone in the valley was here. She remembered then that to some of them she was an enemy, but she didn't know to whom. They were crowded all around her, but they ignored her. She seemed to be standing in a space of her own which none of them would enter. Even the children had drawn back. In the moonlight it was hard to recognise anyone, for in the shadows their faces were hidden, and when they turned to the light their features were drained of colour, ghostlike. As long as Thomas had been there she had been linked to them by his presence. He cared about her, and he was one of them. No one else knew her, not even Linnet. Naomi remembered the stones, and shuddered. During the dance she had been unaware of herself. Now she knew herself alone, and in danger.

No one accosted her, or even spoke. She drew back, and stood at the edge of the tarn. They began to drift away down the path, laden with their burdens. She couldn't see Thomas, only the knot of people who had taken him moving slowly along the path above her, like a strange creature of the mountains returning to its lair under the moonlight. The last people were leaving. One of the children detached itself from the group and came towards her uncertainly, carrying something. She thrust the objects into Naomi's hands, and fled. It was her fiddle and her bow. As if woken from a spell by the slight attention, Naomi started, and stepped forward.

She couldn't stay here. Even less could she join them. They were not her people. She was afraid of them. Enchanted as they were by a spell of their own making, there was no knowing what they would do to her if their attention were turned towards her. She waited until the tail of the procession reached the foot of the path, and slowly began to follow.

I should never have come. The thought struck her unawares. She began to climb without noticing, thinking it over. No, that's not true. If I hadn't come, I wouldn't have found the music. But I am an enemy in this land where every stranger is the cause of their suffering. Perhaps I shouldn't have seen what happened tonight. A new fear struck her, that she wouldn't be allowed to take such a tale away with her: perhaps had never been intended to. But what of Thomas now? Unthinkingly she quickened her pace, only to fall back again when she came upon the last people only a few paces ahead, around the next outcrop of rock.

She had never felt more isolated. Thomas had been taken away from under her hands, when she had been sure she might have helped him. Had he not known his own peril? But he did, thought Naomi, stopping short. He has been desperately afraid from the beginning. It's I who didn't see it. I should have understood. There is always violence, not so very far from the surface. He couldn't tell me what I should have known. There's no safety in this world, and I should have expected none. They would have stoned me, but it's Thomas who has fallen. What have I been thinking of, not to have understood?

I was thinking about the music. Naomi realised she was falling behind again, and hurried onwards. They were out on the open moorland now, and the moon was behind her. I haven't been foolish, and I have done nothing wrong. There is still the music. I'm in danger here, but isn't the whole world dangerous? I told him I trusted nobody, and I was right. But I would still have come through all of this for the music I have found. And I will still stay, because of it. And because of Thomas, perhaps.

The last thought was so radical that she stopped again. Because of Thomas? He's among his own people now. He hardly needs me. But I care about him, thought Naomi. I think I'd still stay, if Thomas needed me, even if it weren't for the music. I don't think they know what to do.

It was too confusing to go on thinking about it. Naomi turned her attention to the path. It was still white in the moonlight, but the magic had drained away. It was merely a stony path winding across a bare moorland. She realised she was tired out, and her arm hurt. It couldn't be so long now before the dawn, and it was very cold. She was relieved when the way dropped down again towards the trees, so that she could see the valley beyond, encircled by the blackness of the trees.

Presently she reached the first oaks. The path grew dark, and disappeared beneath them, but a short way ahead she could see a glimmer of light. So the people had brought lanterns after all. At least they showed her which way she should be heading, although she had to feel carefully for each foothold over the invisible ground. She held the fiddle to her, tucked under one arm, and with the other she felt her way.

She came to the stepping stones, but there was no way of picking them out in the dark, so she splashed across the beck, still following the lanterns. I wonder if Linnet remembered me at all? she thought briefly. But Linnet had been part of the group that carried Thomas. Naomi sighed, and followed the lanterns out into the moonlight again, up the steps of the house.

There she paused. She could hear voices just inside. Naomi waited for a moment, then slipped back into the shadow of the house, and walked round to the back door. She went up by the back stairs, and reached the passage outside Thomas's room. The door was shut, and she paused outside it, listening. Then it was opened from the inside, and Linnet stood there. She jumped back when she saw Naomi.

'Is Thomas there?'

'He's not well,' said Linnet. She sounded defensive, though it hardly seemed appropriate.

'Can I come in?'

'I suppose so,' said Linnet ungraciously, and stood aside.

Thomas was curled in a heap on the top of the bedcovers, as though he had just been dumped there. His face was hidden, turned away from the single lantern that had been placed on the chest. Naomi took a step towards him, and became aware that the room was not empty. She looked away from the light, but only darkness met her dazzled eyes. No one spoke. She felt a moment's fear, then ignored it, and went to Thomas.

'Thomas?'

'It's no good.' She recognised Peter's voice, sounding desperately weary. 'It happened before. There's nothing to be done. I'll stay with him until morning.'

Naomi found Thomas's hand. He was so cold that she was afraid for one moment that he might be dead. She thrust her fingers up his sleeve, and held his wrist. His arm under the cloth was warm, so she didn't bother to find his pulse, which had been her first thought. But his hand was quite unresponsive to hers, and he never moved.

'I'll stay, if you like.'

There was a pause. 'No need,' said Peter roughly. 'You must need to sleep.'

'Why not you?'

It was Linnet who answered. 'We're his family. This isn't for any stranger to see.'

'And what if the stranger is his friend?'

Silence.

'What if I am his friend?' repeated Naomi.

'You're not one of his people,' said Peter at last. 'He is my cousin, and I can't let you see him shamed.'

'There is no shame,' said Naomi firmly. 'Not in my eyes.'

'Then you're a fool,' said Peter curtly.

Naomi swung round, her hand still holding Thomas's, and her mouth opened to contradict him.

'You know nothing about it!' burst out Peter, before she could speak. 'If it wasn't for me, you'd have been left even more ignorant than you are. He shouldn't have brought you here. We've tried to treat you as a guest, Linnet and I, and all the time we knew your peril, and never troubled you with it. He knew. He was out of his mind to bring you. Out of his mind! Can you understand that? Can you begin to understand?'

'And what if I am his friend?' said Naomi for the third time.

'You can't be,' said Linnet. Unlike Peter, there was no anger in her voice, only sadness which made Naomi look round at her, trying to see her expression through the gloom. 'My people are not friends with your people.'

Naomi held Thomas's cold hand, and found no answer. There seemed no point telling them that her experience was different from theirs. As soon as she formulated the words in her mind, she dismissed them as foolish and arrogant. It wouldn't help them to know that she didn't feel any such despair, any more than they needed to know that where she came from there was no need for any dance, for there were already ceremonies for planting time and harvest, and the stone walls around the fields had marked the same boundaries for a thousand years. In this land, thought Naomi, I am further from my own than I have been in my life. But I still choose to treat him as my friend.

'Very well,' she said wearily. 'It is for you as you say it is. But for me, Thomas has done nothing to be ashamed of, and I would like to stay with him.'

There was a pause, then she heard Linnet whisper, 'Let her.'

'No,' said Peter flatly. 'Not a stranger.'

Silence, then Linnet's voice again, this time full and steady. 'This woman is a guest in my household,' said Linnet firmly, 'and I say that we shall give her what she asks.'

Naomi held her breath, and opened her eyes wide, trying to see their faces. She hadn't realised what else was happening here. Then there were footsteps crossing to the door, and the door opening, then shutting again with a sharp click. Which one? She sat still, her breath still caught. Which one?

'I'll leave you the lantern then,' said Linnet. 'Goodnight.'

Before Naomi could find words to reply, she too had gone.

It was very cold in here. The moonlight outside had faded to the pale grey of dawn, which was beginning to filter through into the room, dissipating the sharp lines between moonlight and darkness. Naomi removed her fiddle from the bed and laid it on the chest beside the lantern. Then she tugged the quilt from underneath Thomas and laid it over him. He didn't stir. She looked down at him and remembered waking in the back of a cart with a blanket over her which hadn't been there before. Her heart stirred with pity, remembering the man he was.

She found his hand again under the quilt, and laid her own over it. Then she leaned back against the bedhead, her feet tucked up under her. Her eyes were drawn to the uncurtained window. It was growing rapidly lighter, and the silence was broken now by birdsong. It seemed that she had no sooner registered the first notes than the single song swelled to a chorus. There must be a blackbird just below the window, thought Naomi sleepily, and that's a finch. There was no possibility of sleep. The square of sky visible from where she sat was changing from grey to white. She could see the shapes of clouds, slowly drifting inland with the dawn. The light was brighter now, more full-bodied, and the blackbird was excelling itself in response. The cloud shifted to reveal a streak of pale gold. I can't sleep now, thought Naomi, it's morning. It was hard to keep her eyes open. Thomas seemed to be sleeping normally now. When she looked down she could see the quilt rise and fall a little with his breathing. His hand had grown warmer than hers. She realised she was getting too cold, but it seemed too much effort to do anything about it. The shape of the window was etched in a bright green square against her closed eyelids. She watched it slowly swim from her, along with the birdsong and the day.

*

She awoke some hours later, feeling prickly and uncomfortable, and sat up. Her clothes felt too tight, and she tugged at her collar, trying to loosen her shirt. When she moved she found she was freezing, and her feet had gone to sleep. She wriggled her toes, and felt pins and needles right up the soles of her feet. Then she remembered Thomas.

He hadn't stirred. She slid her hand cautiously from under his. He took no notice. I probably needn't have bothered, thought Naomi drearily. He's dead to the world. No doubt he'll wake up and everything will be normal again, and I could have got a proper night's sleep. Even as she wished that were true, a weight that already seemed familiar settled itself again on her shoulders. It had taken so small a thing, only a moment, to bring him to this. It seemed impossible that it could not be undone, and that Thomas should not be Thomas, as he was yesterday afternoon. While he slept there seemed to be no difference. It need not have happened; it could so easily not have happened. The step from that to deciding it had not happened seemed very small, when, sleeping, he seemed to be so much himself. I wish I could make myself believe it, thought Naomi bitterly, and stood up.

She picked up her boots and her fiddle, and limped to the door.

There was no one about. In her own room the sun was bright, making rectangular patterns across the floorboards. She dropped her things on the bed and wandered over to the window. The warmth of the sun was very pleasant. Naomi yawned, and stared out over the empty garden. It was another bright day, but the wind had got up. The wallflowers bent before it, their colours changing with the motion. She felt strangely at a loss. It was tempting to seek the comfort of her own bed, and sleep again. But too much had happened, and the day was brisk and sunny, demanding action. But what? Last night she had felt so sure that Thomas needed her. Then all he had done was sleep, so perhaps she had merely been ridiculous. She thought of Peter and Linnet. Perhaps all that had been unnecessary. She had no idea.

'Oh, you're awake,' said Linnet's voice behind her. 'I came to see.'

'I left Thomas asleep.'

'I saw.' Linnet looked at her anxiously, and Naomi noticed deep shadows under her eyes. 'Was he all right? I mean, he slept, didn't he?'

'Yes. He slept.'

'Well, perhaps it will be all right,' said Linnet vaguely, but not as if she believed it. 'What about you? Do you want anything?'

Naomi sighed, and tried to think. 'I don't know. Perhaps some hot water.'

*

When her next visitor knocked on the door, about half an hour later, she was crouched over a bowl of steaming water, trying to rinse the soap off herself with a damp flannel.

'Oh,' said Naomi. 'Who's that?'

'It's me. Peter.'

She opened the door to him, draped in a large towel.

'Oh,' said Peter. 'Shall I come back?'

'It's all right. What is it?'

'He's awake,' said Peter, without preamble. He glanced at Naomi, then politely turned to look out of the window instead. 'I think it was as well you stayed with him,' he said stiffly. 'We can only be grateful.'

That seemed to be unanswerable, so she said nothing, but searched in her pack for a clean shirt.

'But I don't think you know . . .' began Peter, and stopped.

Naomi found a shirt and put it on. It was soft and clean against her skin. 'Know what?'

'She should never have told him to come back,' exclaimed Peter, walking up and down her room. 'In fact, she should have laid it upon him not to do so! She refused. She said she couldn't exile him for ever.'

It took Naomi a moment to follow him, then she countered swiftly, 'Of course she could not! She's his mother!'

'What of it? She was responsible for the well-being of the valley. If she couldn't be detached about him, then she should have refused to make the judgement.'

'And then what would have happened?'

'And what must she do,' went on Peter, ignoring this, 'but receive his promise that he come back in seven years, to take his part in the dance again, and heal what he had done. Madness! She knew what state he was in! Of course, it's healed nothing. She only said such a thing because she wanted to see him again.'

Naomi watched him thoughtfully, doing up her trousers as she did so. 'And you didn't?' she enquired casually.

'He's my cousin,' said Peter stiffly. 'Of course I was glad to see him. But I guessed what would come of it. In fact I said so, seven years ago, but by then it was too late. Thomas had made his promise, and gone.'

'So what was the point of saying so?' asked Naomi, apparently intent on selecting two socks.

'You may well ask,' rejoined Peter bitterly. 'I never suggested that Alice leave, I swear it! It was the worst thing she could have done. Judith was gone. Thomas was gone. There was no woman to hold this household except Linnet. And Linnet — well, some women of nineteen could have dealt with it, but you can imagine how it was with Linnet. Alice left, and said that she wanted nothing more to do with the affairs of our people, and I had to do the best I could. She comes and goes, but you can imagine it hasn't been easy.'

'Easy for you, do you mean?' asked Naomi politely.

'We can't deal with it again,' announced Peter.

'With Thomas, do you mean?'

'He was like this before. For a long time I thought it would be better if he were dead. But he lived, and as soon as he was fit, he left us. But I don't think I can stand it happening again.'

'What happened before?' asked Naomi, standing up straight and confronting him directly.

Peter seemed to take in the question, and searched for an answer. 'It was months,' he said at last. 'He was like a man not living in this world. As if it were all a dream, or, more often, a nightmare. He didn't know what was real and what wasn't. He was so fearful, not like a man at all. All his mind turned upon pain, and he thought he was responsible for it all.'

'He tried to kill himself?'

'He did himself no violence, not after we brought him home. If to deny one's own mind is not a violence,' added Peter with another flash of bitterness. 'But I suppose he couldn't change it, any more than we can change our dreams.'

'You think it may be like that again?'

'I appals me. I'm not a patient man. I couldn't do it. Not again.'

'I see,' said Naomi, sitting on the bed and picking up her boots.

'She wants to see you,' said Peter suddenly. 'I came to tell you that.'

'She? Alice?'

'Who else? Oh no, not Linnet. Linnet says no, we ask too much of you. After all, you're not one of us. To Alice, it seems to make no difference. She seems to think of nothing but her own son. I suppose you'd say that was natural.' It sounded like an accusation.

Naomi slowly laced her boot. 'Thomas lost you everything, didn't he?' she said, as casually as before.

'I never said he should be punished! Nor ever thought it, either!'

'Of course not. He's your cousin, after all.'

Peter stopped pacing, and frowned at her downbent head. She seemed intent on her bootlaces. 'My aunt will be waiting for you,' he said at last in a different tone. 'Can I take you to her now?'

*

Alice's room was at the other end of the house, along a passage similar to the one downstairs leading to the room with the music. Peter took Naomi to the door, knocked, and when a voice called, 'Come in!' he nodded to her to go ahead.

Naomi found Alice sitting at the window. She could see the tops of oak trees from where she stood, and the mountains rising beyond.

'Sit down, won't you?'

There was only a bed, or the other end of the window seat. Naomi chose the window, and saw that this part of the house overlooked the garden. She could see rows of vegetables inside the walled garden, and the tops of the trees in the orchard beyond.

'I'm sorry,' began Alice formally, 'that I have spent so little time with you.'

'That's all right. Don't worry about it.'

'They told me about the dance.' Alice stopped, and looked at Naomi. There seemed to be nothing to say, so Naomi remained silent. 'You've been a good friend to my son.'

'As he to me.'

'They were angry that he should bring a stranger here,' went on Alice, watching her. 'It was a dangerous thing to do, for a man who is already known to be unlucky.'

'I begin to understand that.'

'You're not angry with him yourself?'

'He has given me more than I ever hoped to have. How could I be?'

'For using you, perhaps.'

'We made a contract, Thomas and I,' said Naomi. She sounded cold rather than angry, but her flush betrayed her. 'It concerns no one else.'

'But it does. He bargained with matters that were not his own.' Alice sighed, and paused. Naomi watched her. Although she maintained a calm that Naomi suspected was habitual, her eyes were restless, looking now out of the window, and now around her own room, almost as if it were strange to her. Then she looked directly at Naomi, and Naomi registered the same shock she had felt before. Those were Thomas's eyes, and the expression in them was all Thomas, a curious mixture of shrewdness and emotion. 'You have your own people,' said Alice at last, 'and you must know that any contract you make affects them, even if they are far away. You can't cut yourself off from them entirely.'

'Haven't you?' The question seemed brutal, put like that.

Alice gave her another sharp glance. 'It's not possible,' she said. 'However much one suffers. Do you believe that it is? Perhaps you never had a child, but you still have memories, and dreams, no doubt. You can't tell me that you have no people.'

'Thomas didn't want to come back,' said Naomi, avoiding an answer. 'He was happy where he was. He wanted none of this.'

She waited, wondering if she had allowed her anger to show too much.

'I had to judge him before,' said Alice, looking out of the window. 'It was hard, being his mother, but I was the one to decide. I made him dance the following month, because I knew that would bring him back to this world. I sent him away, because I knew he couldn't live with himself here. But then I laid it on him that he must come back. That wasn't justice.' She looked directly at Naomi, and spoke to her without reserve for the first and last time. 'It was a mother's selfishness that asked that of him. Not justice. Tell him from me, when you can, that he is released, and need never come back here again.'

Naomi watched the fruit trees bending before a gust of wind, wasted blossom swirling into the air unpollinated. 'Won't you tell him yourself?'

'If he can hear me. I fear he may not.'

'Why not?'

'Because he can't hear me at the moment. He can't hear what I say, and he can't think clearly. He can't trust his own mind, and he's afraid. It's happened before.'

'I know.'

'It's not because I have no respect for him, or for you, that I take it on myself to speak for him.'

'Do you know what he would say?'

'I can't know. But I know what happened in the past. I think you've been told, haven't you?'

'Yes.'

'It mustn't happen to him again.' She was suddenly vehement. She faced Naomi and put out her hand, almost as if she would touch her. She didn't, but went on speaking instead. 'He must go. It's dangerous for him here. He must go and not come back. He must get back to this island where he has found out how to be happy again. And he must not come back.'

Naomi stared out of the window, biting her lip. 'You're right,' she said at last, because she couldn't lie about it.

'It won't be easy for him, to belong no more among his own people.'

'What is it that you want of me?' asked Naomi. The words seemed to be dragged out of her. Anyway, she thought dully, she already knew. She felt numb. The implications were too great to consider. She would have to come to terms with it later, on her own.

'I can't help him. I'm his mother. Take him away from here, if you love him.'

The sky was suddenly lowering, dark grey and heavy. There was a flurry of rain, almost horizontal, glancing across the glass like needles. Outside the garden was submerged in a whirl of petals and waterdrops. So it had come to this. *Drei Sonaten und drei Partiten.* She thought of a gift, lying still almost untouched, tattered sheets of paper mouldering back to dust through all the unheeding generations. Perfection, glimpsed through a welter of ancient signs, amidst the outworn debris of another time. Music too exquisite for the waking world, except that she, and she alone, had power to give it life. She thought of Thomas, who had bestowed this upon her, and had never lied to her. He had proved himself trustworthy. 'All right,' said Naomi, in a lifeless voice quite unlike her own. 'I'll take him.'

*

It was not until some time after she left Alice that Naomi felt able to face Thomas. She found him in his room, not in bed, but kneeling at the hearth. The fire had only recently been lit; the carefully laid kindling was just beginning to crackle, and it was still cold inside the room. It was raining again outside. Thomas crouched on the hearthrug, his hands held over the thin flames, like a creature starved of warmth or comfort.

He didn't look up until she squatted down on the rug beside him. His face shocked her. It looked pinched and yellowish, with heavy lines like a caricature, a painted mask of suffering. His eyes were huge and hollow, and seemed to be all pupils. She had an uncomfortable feeling that he wasn't seeing her. That unfocused gaze had no acknowledgement in it. His body seemed to have shrunk into itself, stripped of any vestige of youth or health. Yet the uncanny thing was that he was not unbeautiful. There was a transparent quality about him, as if a layer had been peeled away to reveal a Thomas she had already sometimes guessed at. He looked old, as if he had suffered the experience of all the waking world, and had fixed his eyes on something different, which she could not see. It wasn't her, or the world she perceived about her. He could slip through the fingers of this world very easily, thought Naomi, and we should lose him. She was surprised by her own thought. The danger that had been spoken of was that reality should be lost to Thomas, not Thomas to reality.

They sat in silence for a few minutes. He didn't seem at all discomposed that she should be there. She had come thinking that she must try to speak to him, but now she wasn't sure. There was more happening here than she had realised. The whole idea of rescuing him was perhaps an intrusion. She tried to face her own confusion. Thomas as he was at the moment was something new to her; she realised that everything she had been told was merely other people's thoughts, and they had probably understood as little as she had. She thought about speaking to him several times before she actually broke the silence. When she finally did so, it was more out of her need for something to happen than because she had anything intelligent to say.

'Thomas?'

He frowned at her a little. 'Your music,' he said.

'What about it?'

'There was a promise in it, and it was not kept.'

'I don't understand.'

'I have been here before,' said Thomas. She looked round the room, as though it would tell her what 'here' meant. 'It is not where your music told me we would be.'

'I'm sorry. Music has a power of its own. It can tell you things that the player knows nothing about.'

'Through the mountain,' said Thomas.

She looked at him helplessly. 'I'm sorry. I don't understand.'

He made a small impatient movement. 'If you go through the mountain, you come out in the country that was promised. It isn't the way we choose to go, because we accept our limitations.'

She floundered after him, trying to catch his meaning. 'Is there a way through the mountain?'

'You know that. The music was yours that promised it.'

'Thomas,' said Naomi. 'The dance is over. Your obligation is fulfilled, and we can go home.'

'Home,' repeated Thomas. 'What is home?'

'We can go back to the island now.'

'With blood on our hands?' demanded Thomas, as though she had suggested something monstrous.

'There's no blood on our hands,' said Naomi, and quelled an impulse to look down at her spread palms. She was here to bring him round, not follow him.

'Have you seen the book?'

'What book?' Naomi was beginning to feel a complete fool. If he were out of his mind, then she was a fool to try to make sense of him; if he were not, then she ought to be able to understand.

'There is a book,' said Thomas, emphasising the words, as though trying to convey important information to a slightly deaf child, 'which holds pictures of the dancers. It's hidden in the valley, and I have seen it.'

There could be a meaning in that, on the other hand, there might not be. Naomi waited.

'The Hanged One,' went on Thomas, 'in the book, he hangs by the foot, and he gazes from one world into another.'

'Ah,' said Naomi, with a surge of relief. 'I understand now. I know that book.'

He frowned. 'You've seen our book?'

'Not yours, no. But pictures like it.'

He dismissed that with a gesture. 'In our dance he carries his noose around his neck. Do you know why?'

'No,' said Naomi, completely at sea.

'If a man has blood on his hands, there is only one thing to do with him.'

She thought about that, and suddenly an image flashed into her mind that made her hands fly up to cover her cheeks. It was revolting. It was the most revolting thing that could ever have been thought of. He must be sick indeed, to entertain such an idea for a moment. The fate of his family must have turned his mind to nightmares more morbid than anything anyone conceived. 'No!' said Naomi. 'Don't think of it! No one can ever have done that!'

'They did. In every village, every valley, every settlement in this land, that was precisely what they did.'

'No! I won't believe it! Think about real things, Thomas, for your own sake!'

'It is real.'

She stared at him, and swallowed. 'No, Thomas, it is not. If a person were hanged by other people in the way you imagine, they would suffer too much, and they would die.'

'And therefore you don't believe it?'

'Oh!' cried out Naomi. 'I don't understand! Why do you want me to believe it?'

'I'm sad for you,' said Thomas, 'because I love you. You're living in a dream, because the pain abiding in this world has hurt you too much, and you think you cannot bear it. But you can't put a part of yourself to sleep. The world is more beautiful than any dream, and I want you to see it.'

'By telling me of torture and cruelty?'

'There's no other way.'

'Are you sure it's not you who's living in a dream?' As soon as the words were out she wished them unsaid. It was cruel to put his condition to him like that.

'We all live in our dreams,' said Thomas, 'or we would die. But my nephews died because I killed them.'

'No. They died of sickness.'

'A hanged man dies because the noose pulls tight. He chokes. He can't breathe. If a man chokes, he coughs out his own tongue. His blood…'

'Stop it! Thomas, you must not think such thoughts as this!'

'Have you ever tried to dig a grave on the side of a mountain?' asked Thomas. 'There's not enough earth. There's not enough earth in the world to absorb the blood that we have shed.'

'I've shed no blood! And nor have you!'

'Look at your hands.'

She stared at him, not knowing what to do. If she looked down, it would be admitting his dream. If she did not, he would take it as guilt. 'There is no blood,' said Naomi clearly, holding out her hands. 'Look.'

'A boy of twelve,' said Thomas, 'is half grown, something between a child and a man. He can't trust his own voice, being neither one thing nor the other. A boy of twelve grows very quickly. He might reach to about here.' He drew a line across his chest with his forefinger. Naomi watched him apprehensively, sensing she was being led to some conclusion she did not want.

'A boy of fourteen,' went on Thomas, 'is a man, or so it seems, until he is hurt, and shows you the face of a child too frightened to think, who still believes that you can save him. A boy of fourteen might be as tall as I am, and walk as far across the mountains, but when he is in doubt, he still watches his mother to see what she is thinking.'

'Thomas . . .'

'A man who requires no help,' said Thomas, 'would never be afraid of his own dreams. The whole world would be his, and the one who brought him up would be satisfied, knowing that he would never do any creature harm, because he would never be afraid. There never was such a man in our world, but there was never a boy born who couldn't have become himself.'

'Thomas, why do you torture yourself?'

'For the same reason as you do, I suppose.' His voice was suddenly hopeless, and he turned away from her, covering his eyes with his hand.

'Do I torture myself?'

'Not knowing,' said Thomas. 'There are so many fates that might befall a child, or a man, or a woman. You dare not look at them. You dare not know what pain can be inflicted in this world. Why don't you dare? Who are you afraid for?'

'I don't know what you mean!' She was almost shouting at him.

'I killed my nephews. No danger threatens the dead. So I should be safe from suffering, shouldn't I?'

'Please,' said Naomi. She felt as exhausted as if she'd been wrestling with him. 'Please, Thomas. Your mind goes round too fast. Don't think about it. Come with me. Come back to the island, and it will be all right.'

'I dare not think of the island.'

'Why not?'

'It lies in ruins,' said Thomas. 'You think you can go back to the past? I destroyed it, didn't I?'

'You never hurt the island,' said Naomi urgently. She cast about for anything that would bring him to himself. 'There is a man there who loves you. You remember that?'

Thomas turned away from her, and gazed vacantly at the little fire. 'To dig his grave would not be so difficult. The place is all sand, but then the sea would wash over it. Have I destroyed him too?'

She seized his hands. 'Thomas! You don't know what you're saying!'

'You don't know what I'm saying,' he repeated, like an obedient child.

*

It seemed like the longest day she had ever lived through. After she left Thomas she found Peter waiting for her in the kitchen. It was almost impossible to respond to him sensibly. He was determinedly unemotional. His chief concern in life seemed to be that she should eat something, while he talked to her about the practical details of getting Thomas out of the valley. After being with Thomas it was difficult to remember she wasn't dealing in riddles any more.

'If we start at daybreak, you could even get back to the road by nightfall,' said Peter.

What makes you think there's still a road? she nearly said. 'Yes,' she replied meekly.

'I'll come a day's journey with you, then I'll have to get back.'

There's no going back, Peter. 'Thank you,' said Naomi absently, trying to rearrange her thoughts again.

And all the time there was a weight of loss that seemed to crush her heart, even while her mind responded to him. She hadn't even been to look at the music. Today it was all people, all enquiring something of her, all demanding that she be what she was not. I am none of these things, she wanted to scream at every one of them. I am a musician, and you are breaking my heart.

When at last they left her alone, it was late afternoon, grey and overcast like twilight on a winter's day. If she fetched a candle she could still have one last evening. Time was slipping away from her, but there was a little still to run, if she could take it.

She could not. She was too weary, and the house was too cold and barren. Already she seemed separated from the music by endless stairs and passages and doors that seemed to lengthen into infinity even as she contemplated them.

She was so tired. Naomi retreated to her own bed and lay face down, shivering with cold. It was all too much. She shed a few tears into an unresponsive pillow, but she was too weary even to sob, although it hurt not to. So this is the truth about being alone, she thought bitterly. Not one of them knows who I am, or what I want to do. I want to go back to the island, but I go empty-handed. And perhaps the island's an illusion too. No one there will ever know what I have seen, and if they did it wouldn't matter to them. There is no comfort to be had anywhere, when I have had to abandon my own dreams.

Eighteenth Day

When Linnet came looking for Naomi at daybreak next morning, she found her already up, with her few possessions piled around her, stowing things into her pack. She was holding the little leather bag Linnet had seen before, and something round and white gleamed in the palm of her other hand, like a little moon. As soon as she saw Linnet, she dropped it quickly into the bag.

'Oh, sorry,' said Linnet automatically. 'I came to say goodbye.'

'I thought you'd be downstairs.'

'I will be. I thought I'd say goodbye first. On my own,' said Linnet awkwardly. She stood half in, half out of the room, hanging on to the door, so that a draught whistled between the door and the window, catching Naomi in the middle of it.

'Come in then,' said Naomi, trying not to sound reluctant. She had nothing to say to any of them. Only pride forced her to remain scrupulously polite until she was a guest no longer. She was aware of Linnet shutting the door and moving tentatively towards her, but she didn't look up again. She went on stuffing clothes into her pack, while Linnet cleared her throat nervously.

'I'm sorry you're going.'

'Thank you.'

'I'm glad you came,' Linnet struggled on, 'not because of Thomas. Not just because of Thomas. I was glad because I liked you being here.'

'Thank you,' said Naomi distantly.

'Are you angry with us?'

'I have no right to be angry.'

'I shall remember the music,' said Linnet, determined to persist. 'I think it may have changed a lot of things for me.'

'I'm so glad.'

'I wish you'd been able to stay longer.'

'That's very good of you.'

'But as you can't. . .' Linnet paused.

'That's life,' said Naomi with finality, firmly strapping her fiddle on to the top of the pack.

'I wanted you to know that it made a difference. What you were doing here. It mattered.'

'I'm so glad you think so.'

'I don't know how to repay you,' said Linnet. 'I don't think there is a way. But I wanted to thank you, anyway . . .'

'You really needn't bother,' said Naomi, standing up and testing the weight of her pack. 'We'd better go down.'

Linnet ignored her. 'And to give you this. I wish it were more, but I don't think you could carry more, not all that way.'

She thrust a flat linen bag under Naomi's nose, so Naomi had to look. 'What. . .?'

'You'd left it on the top,' rushed on Linnet, 'so I thought it was probably the most important. And it's quite fat, so it should last you a good long while. At least, I hoped it might.'

Naomi felt the blood rush to her face, and found herself fumbling with the string.

'Don't pull the loops,' said Linnet kindly. 'It's a bow. It's just a sliver of wood at the back to keep it flat. I'm afraid it'll be awkward to pack.'

Naomi took it very carefully out of the bag, and stared at it unbelievingly. Her face was burning, and there were hot tears in her eyes. She blinked, so she could see the familiar writing plainly: *Drei Sonaten und drei Partiten.*

'I hope it's the right one,' said Linnet, shifting from one foot to the other.

'Oh.'

'I mean, I hope you feel all right about it. It's not paying you, you know, or anything like that.'

'Oh.'

'Only I like you. I mean, I don't pretend to understand why it's so important, but I could see that it was, to you. So I know it must be,' ended Linnet in a tangle of words.

'Oh,' said Naomi again, and laid her gift very gently down on her pack. She looked up at Linnet. Her face was as red as her hair, and she stared at Linnet as if she were seeing her for the first time in her life, and was overcome by what she saw. Linnet wriggled uncomfortably, and opened her mouth to start talking again. Before she could get a word out she found herself caught up in a passionate embrace, and hugged as she had never been hugged in her life before. 'Oh,' said Linnet in her turn, only it came out as a squeak. She was rigid with shock, as though someone had suddenly pushed her off the bridge into the beck. She was too polite to struggle, in fact she was dimly aware that she didn't want to. In a sudden access of courage she hugged Naomi briefly back, then to her relief Naomi let her go.

'Thank you,' said Naomi, holding her tightly by the shoulders. 'It was all I wanted, your gift.' She looked at Linnet and felt a stab of doubt. 'As long as you feel that it should be parted from this household.'

'This household is mine,' said Linnet with unexpected dignity.

'Then I must thank you.'

'The gifts of this house are mine to give.' Linnet paused, then said, 'I don't know how long it will take you, to do whatever you're doing with it. But when you need more . . . My house is open to you, I want you to know that. I know you came from far away, and people don't often travel to the empty lands. But if you ever want to come again, it will be as my guest, I hope, and nothing further would be asked of you. What I'm saying is,' added Linnet, with a touch of her usual manner, 'you could stay until you'd finished, and I wouldn't mind. I'd like it. We could play music. And if Jo was bigger then,' she said as another thought struck here, 'you could teach her some of your music. Only if you wanted to, I mean.'

Naomi had knelt down and was untying her pack again, but at the end of this speech she looked up and smiled affectionately at Linnet. 'Only if she wanted to, you mean. But thank you, I'll take you up on that, when the time comes.' She unloaded her belongings, until she could slide the linen bag containing the music down the back of her pack, then she carefully repacked round it.

'Do you feel all right,' asked Linnet a moment later, 'about taking Thomas, I mean? I don't think it'll be all that easy, and he's no kin of yours, to mean you should.'

'I feel all right about everything.' Naomi stood up and swung her pack on to her back. 'Now.'

'Oh, good. Well, maybe we'd better go down. Peter was fussing about starting at dawn.'

'I'm ready.'

Their journey that day was dull and featureless. The cloud had settled right down in the valley, so there were no mountains to bid farewell to, nor any landmarks to look back on. It was not actually raining, but the moisture in the air slowly penetrated their clothes and soaked their hair. There was nothing else that changed: no vista or event made one end of the day different from the other. If Naomi hadn't already seen the country through which they travelled, it might as well have not existed. In a way it was a relief. There was nothing familiar to say farewell to, nothing new to react to. The mist was like a blanket, under which she could forget the world, and retreat into her own thoughts.

It was probably the best way it could have been for Thomas too, she thought. The sight of his mountains might have aroused him to wakefulness, and the threading of the path out of the valley would have been agony to him, knowing as he must that it was for the last time. As it was, he passed through the whole of that unlightened day like a sleepwalker, following Peter almost step for step, registering nothing. The sound of the beck had no power to move him, and when they left it behind to skirt the shores of the lake hidden in the mist below, he showed no sign of emotion, nor glanced back once. It frightened her. You can't put part of yourself to sleep. Who had said that? wondered Naomi, trying to recollect. She did so with a start. He knew what he was doing to himself. This apathy might be a relief to Peter, and it might get them through a substantial chunk of the miles ahead, but it would have to be paid for, in full.

Peter seemed to have no qualms about it. He led the way at a steady pace, very seldom stopping. He was clearly determined to get them as far as he possibly could, and if there was a price to be paid for Thomas's acquiescence, then it was worth it to him. Especially as he won't have to be there, thought Naomi with a touch of resentment. But she didn't challenge him, because she shared his motive. Every step was something gained. The mist would lift sooner or later, and it would be better if they were out of sight. Naomi remembered her first view of the mountains of the empty lands, from far to the north of here. For a moment the vastness of this undertaking almost overwhelmed her. There was no telling how Thomas would be when this lethargy left him, and there was a whole country to traverse before they were among his friends. Apprehension made her quicken her own pace, until she was almost treading on Thomas's heels.

It was better not to start worrying about him now. There would be time enough when it was all up to her. Today there was Peter, and she would make the most of it. Naomi was quite content to bring up the rear, grateful for the chance to contemplate her own affairs.

She was happy. She was just beginning to perceive how happy. Yesterday had been so wretched, and today the weather was so miserable, that it was hard to grasp that she had been given her dearest wish by a friend from whom she was completely happy to take it. It would take a while to absorb what it meant. She began to work it out. It would mean staying on the island again, having work to do that would fulfil her entirely, among friends who would acknowledge its importance. She allowed herself to drift into fantasy. It would be summer. She would find herself a place to work within sight and sound of the sea, and she would follow wherever the music took her, until her quest was completed.

She was longing to get back. Now they were out of the valley, she was suddenly on fire with impatience. It was as well they had Peter keeping them to the right pace, or she would have wanted to run, as though she could make those endless miles disappear in no time by the strength of her own body. Since she had no such magic, patience would be necessary. Thomas must not be upset. But she was happy. She realised with surprise that the faint shadow which had hung over her memories of the island had dissolved. There would be Francis. It didn't matter now. Francis and Thomas could weave whatever web of emotion they pleased, but she had work to do. Naomi jumped a puddle in a sudden burst of energy, and the pack thumped against her back, as if warning her against too much exuberance.

They crossed the open valley at the head of the lake, and were back on moorland, but the mountains were still obliterated in fog. They might have wandered into a desert far beyond the living world, where there was neither day nor night, nor hills nor valleys. Only sometimes the trickle of running water told them that life had not ceased to flow. Naomi wasn't particularly conscious of weariness, though as the hours passed her legs began to ache. But it didn't matter. They were nearer the island with every mile.

At last they descended again, following a straight path through lower country. It made no difference, except that the damp air was warmer on their faces. The mist seemed to be thickening, but then she realised it was not mist, but twilight. The beginning of this day seemed a world away. Her mind was blank. There seemed to be nothing left but mist and wet grass. If it wasn't for Peter we'd be lost, she thought suddenly. It hadn't occurred to her all day. The way had seemed inevitable, and now that she thought about it, only an inhabitant of this country would have known where to go at all. Take it as a holiday, Naomi told herself. Tomorrow you'll have to start thinking.

As if in answer to the thought, a string of soft lights illuminated the road ahead of her, as they rounded the last bend in the path. A village, and a proper road. There was an inn about halfway along the street. She recognised it, and for a moment the notes of the carter's whistle were as clear in her memory as if they were still sounding in her ears.

'I know where I am now,' remarked Naomi to no one in particular, and followed them into the inn.

Nineteenth Day

Naomi had hoped that they might get a lift along the road north, as they had done coming south, but luck seemed to be against them. The mist was not thick down here as it had been on the hills, but it was persistent, drifting in from the sea with a mizzling rain that tasted of salt. If Peter had not been so determined to see them on their way she would have opted for a day by the fire in the inn, so that Thomas could rest and she could work. It didn't happen, and perhaps it was just as well. She wanted to get on, and there was only one way to do it. But the road was cheerless and empty, and she felt as though she had been wet through for ever.

Thomas was pale and silent. He had eaten nothing since their journey began, and she suspected he hadn't slept either. He was unreachable. When she tried to talk to him he merely looked at her with eyes full of pain, and said nothing. The road was no place for him. She felt as though she were torturing an animal, leading him on like this. She had no comfort to offer in this weather. The rain made each person retreat inside themselves, their only warmth coming from within. She couldn't touch him, and as long as he remained untouched, frozen into his private nightmare, he would keep going. Her instinct told her it was dangerous, and that however great their urgency, he must be given time first. But Peter had been so sure, and a large part of her agreed with Peter.

When they reached the ferry there was nobody there. The hut at the water's edge was shut up, and no smoke issued from the chimney. Thomas stood passively on the river bank, staring down into the water. Naomi found the oars of the rowing boat tucked under the bench in front of the hut, and carried them down to the shore. When she saw where Thomas was, she felt a stab of fear, and knew that her nerves were all on edge about him. He might be no trouble, which was what Peter had said to her when they parted that morning, but this was agony, to her as well as to Thomas. His pain was palpable, and yet they were both ignoring it. It's not human, thought Naomi, hating herself, struggling with the boat. 'Thomas?'

He looked up, and came slowly over to her. Luckily she needed no help; boats were second nature to her. She got him to sit in the stern, stowed the baggage in the bows, and pushed off into the current. The river was high: it must have been raining hard in whatever mountains gave it birth. She had to pull hard upstream to keep them on course at all. By the time they touched the farther shore she was quite out of breath. She beached the boat and made Thomas sit down on the rocks by the jetty. She was worried about leaving him, even for a few minutes, but there was no choice. 'Will you be all right, Thomas? I won't be long.'

He turned his gaze on her, as though from a long way off. 'I'll be all right,' he said vaguely. She wasn't reassured.

She hurried down to the shore again. It was a real struggle to launch both boats on her own. She had the second boat firmly tied behind, but the current caught it even while she was trying to get the oars in the rowlocks, so that by the time she was making any headway, she had already been swept nearly thirty yards downstream. Every time she pulled she could feel the drag of the second boat pulling her seawards. It took several minutes to come level with the jetty again. By the time she had beached both boats, and pulled one far enough up the shore, she could feel the sweat running down inside her shirt. She put one pair of oars back under the bench, and sat down for a moment to get her breath. Then she looked anxiously across the river to Thomas. He was sitting exactly where she had left him, his head bowed on his hands. Naomi got up again, and set out across the river for the third time.

At last all was in order, with one boat and one pair of oars safely beached on either bank, ready for the next traveller. It was raining steadily. He must be chilled through, but he hadn't moved.

'We're going on now, Thomas,' she said gently.

They trudged on, sodden trees lining their route, through ruts full of puddles into which the rain fell with a soft splashing like a distant river. She couldn't recall coming down this stretch of road, then remembered she had slept most of the way in the back of the wagon. Just now the thought of a wagon was like a seductive mirage, and about as useful, though Naomi bitterly. She couldn't remember when she had ever been so wet. She had a cloak, but it was wrapped round her precious baggage, so she couldn't use it. Thomas had one, but it was soaked right through, flapping dismally, and dripping as he walked. He never said anything. Physically he was indomitable, but she was frightened all the same that this would make him ill. There seemed to be no resistance in him, and she felt sure he needed to be warm, though she couldn't have explained why.

She was trying to think how long she had slept on the southward journey, and whether they had stopped anywhere. She couldn't remember. This forest was beginning to seem inimical. There was no end to it. Perhaps they had not progressed at all; perhaps all this struggle was a mere trick of the mind. One thing she was sure of: if they reached a house, they would stop, and they would stay until it stopped raining, even if a hundred Peters were standing over them.

Having decided that, she quickened her pace a little, and studied the trees around her. She had walked this road before, though not at this time of year, nor in this weather. The rain came down in sheets, making it hard to raise her head to see clearly where she was. The city wasn't far from here. She tried to remember, but all that came to mind was a dull sense of foreboding. If only it would stop raining, and she could see. She glanced dubiously at Thomas, but he never looked up. He had been awake when they came south in the wagon. She wondered what was in his mind now. It had been hot when she had walked this way before. She recalled a place which was not exactly a clearing, but where the trees had not grown thick, jagged edges of unfamiliar stone, nettles as tall as she was, air thick with midges. She had passed as quickly as she could.

It was growing lighter. She shielded her eyes with her hand, and tried to peer through the rain and see if there were a break in the clouds. There was none, but the trees had fallen away from the verge, and they were passing through a kind of low plain. It was not completely flat, but interspersed with unnatural hummocks and strange shapes, sheets of crumbled white rock protruding from the undergrowth like decaying teeth. A film of green lay over everything, a tangle of nettles and ivy, willow herb and twisted saplings which had seized unlikely footholds in the hidden rubble. Her heart jumped with unexpected terror. She had forgotten it was so big.

Impulsively she seized Thomas by the hand. 'Thomas, we must hurry! We need to get through this as fast as possible.'

He looked up. Instantly she realised what she had done, and cursed her thoughtlessness. Thomas looked round slowly, and saw the ruins of the city surrounding him. He stood still, while the rain swept over him.

'Thomas, come on. We can't stop here.'

He ignored her completely. Now they had stopped walking she could hear how loud the rain was. It sounded like a river, water pouring down on trees, splashing down on the road until the mud was drowned in puddles, battering the sea of nettles which surrounded them, running over ground which concealed a past that no living person would dare even to imagine. Naomi listened to the rain, and realised how cold she was, soaked through. Her vigilance relaxed, just for a moment.

'Thomas!' She flung off her pack and was after him in a moment. She almost grabbed his jacket, and lost her balance. 'Thomas! Come back!' She registered the terror in her own voice, almost as if it belonged to somebody else. Then she was after him, before she had time to think.

The road was higher than ground level, but the nettles were deceptive. She dropped further than she expected, and floundered among wet leaves which stung her viciously as she forced her way after him. The ground was uneven; things kept tripping her, but she couldn't see where to put her feet because of the nettles. Then her foot struck a solid lump, and she crashed down on something hard.

It was a platform of rock, hidden under a layer of bright green mosses that were slimy to touch. She was right under one of the pieces of wall she had seen from the road. Naomi stood up very carefully, for the moss was treacherously slippery, and put out her hand to balance herself.

It wasn't rock. She withdrew her hand suddenly as if the stuff had stung her, and nearly slipped. There was movement behind her, on the other side of the wall: a scraping sound, and the slither of stones. Thomas. She was round the wall and after him in a moment.

There was a hollow there, so thick with scrub it was invisible, until she found herself falling into it. She was up against something thin and hard, inside the nettles. Her hand touched it, and closed on the coldness of metal. She looked down, and saw stuff like twisted iron, its shape hidden by the green. She backed off. There was something terrifyingly wrong about it, something she couldn't place. She tried to scramble up towards the next piece of wall, where she had heard Thomas. If it was Thomas.

At the top she saw him. The walls formed a right angle, though they were tilted crazily. There was rubble heaped up in the angle. The walls were blackened by fire, rising from a mass of willow herb. Thomas had got himself into the corner and stopped, turning as if he were trapped. She forced a path through high red stems, and reached him. Then she grabbed him by the jacket, and held him tight.

'Thomas, stop! We can't go in here!'

He stared at her blankly. 'You have no choice, in the end,' he said at last.

At least she could see him properly. It wasn't raining here, or rather, they were sheltered from the downpour by the two walls. The rain was still loud all round them. 'Thomas, come back to the road. This is no place to be.'

'There's no road out.'

For a moment panic seized her. The idea of it came close to nightmare. It wasn't canny. Like the iron. She suddenly knew what was wrong. The stuff hadn't rusted. She had touched metal forged in an unimaginable past, and there was no fleck of rust upon it. And the road was invisible from here. The tilted walls rose up above their heads, blocking out the forest. If they were rock, it was rock so thin and dead she could not recognise it. Naomi stared in desperation at the sky, and saw only grey mist, pierced by a broken edge of wall.

'Thomas, don't! I can't stand it! It's not true!'

He looked at her, as though he had just noticed that she was with him. 'You know what happened,' said Thomas.

'No one knows. It's nothing to do with us. Thomas, come back to the road. Let me take you back.'

She was still holding him by the jacket, but he twisted round. She thought he was going to break away, but before she could grab him again, he gripped her by the arm. 'If this is nothing to do with us, we don't exist. We're not different.'

She was shaken right out of any notion that she should take care of him. Before she could think, Naomi had flung him off her. 'Of course I am! Kill yourself with it if you like! It's nothing to do with me, and I won't have it!'

He rounded on her, so she stepped back, and found herself up against the wall, which leaned inwards on her, forcing her away from it. 'Naomi,' said Thomas, suddenly quiet again. She watched him warily, aware for the first time that he had her trapped. But that was foolish, to bring that into the nightmare. She was not afraid of Thomas.

'Naomi,' said Thomas again. 'I'm sorry.'

Standing in the darkness, and the howling wild dogs. The memory was so vivid that she almost thought the sound was real. The touch of his hand, warm and reassuring. Not now. Naomi waited, between Thomas and the corner of the wall, and never took her eyes off him.

'These people.' Thomas gestured round him at the empty ruins, investing them with a possibility that made her shudder. 'If they are not our people, then we have none. We are only what is left.'

'No.'

'It's part of your world. You can't afford to be afraid of it.'

'Anyone in their right mind would be afraid in this place.'

'I'm not afraid.'

Naomi was silent. Droplets of rain drifted down between them, forced by the downpour into the shelter of the wall.

'At first I was afraid. But I made myself stay, until I understood.' He seemed less agitated now, almost relaxed. That was worse. Naomi waited, tense and ready to jump if he should try to grab her again. 'We have to go much further, and then you'll see.'

'What do you mean?'

'Further in, where the walls still stand, and you can walk between the buildings, over the stones that fill the streets. The place isn't dead, you know. You can hear the people, when you listen.'

She thought of the smooth metal under her hand. 'Thomas, we are going back to the road.'

'So many voices. Would you wish the dead to be silent? How can you wish that, when you too must die?'

'Thomas, we are going back to the road.'

'They are your people, Naomi. Did they not teach you to respect your dead?'

'They taught me to keep away from the ruins of the past.'

'And therefore you don't know who you are.'

'Thomas, I am going back to the road.'

'No.'

She was afraid of him then. It had never crossed her mind before, but she realised now he could actually prevent her. Being a man, he was probably stronger than she was. She had a knife. So had he. She might still get out, if she surprised him. He was watching her intently. Naomi moved along the wall a little, away from the corner. Thomas took a step towards her.

'Keep off me!'

'Why?' He seemed surprised.

Naomi tried to pull herself together. 'Thomas, this place is evil. My thoughts aren't my own. I want to get out.'

'By denying your thoughts?'

'You frighten me.'

'Then come further, and I will take you to the beginning of fear, and beyond it.' He held out his hand.

'No.'

'Why not, Naomi?' He was gentle again, reasoning with her.

'I never meant to come into this place. No one enters the ruins of the cities. There is a border that should not be crossed, and you've dragged me over it. I'm not coming into this, Thomas. I won't be forced to fear you. I'm getting out.'

'You left the road yourself.'

'To follow you.'

He shrugged.

Naomi hit him.

It was the last thing she had meant to do. They faced each other, rigid with shock, as if the blow had unleashed a far greater violence than a moment's spurt of anger.

'I'm sorry,' whispered Naomi, shaken. 'I didn't mean to do that.'

He seized her by the shoulders before she could dodge him, and gripped her so hard she cried out. 'Don't you hear?' said Thomas hoarsely. 'Don't you hear it now?'

'Hear what? I don't hear anything!'

'Come out!' He pulled her round so sharply that she nearly fell, and, grabbing her hand, pushed his way down through the willow herb. Running, she felt his panic as though it were her own, and needed no further telling. The undergrowth seemed to rise up and cling to her, dragging her back, trying to hold on to her. There were brambles clutching at her just under the first wall as she forced her way through. She let them rip her clothes, and scrambled round the wall. There was a sharp edge to it; she felt something cut at her. Then she was back among the nettles, which slashed at her, stinging. The sense of something following was growing behind her, the touch on her back almost tangible, so that she almost succumbed, and let herself sink beneath it. Her breath was almost gone, but then there was a ditch in front of her, and she slid into thick mud, the rain beating it into chaos. Then a bank, so slippery with mud it was almost impossible to get up. She rolled over on to the top of it, and stood up, gasping for breath, and shaking uncontrollably.

She was on the road, and so was Thomas.

*

As soon as she stepped into the inn Naomi realised that she had been there before. There was a wide corridor with the counter to one side, and barrels on shelves behind it. She could see the inn parlour through an open door, and on the partition between a collection of antique knives was arranged in a circular pattern. She remembered them, and also the big brass bell on the counter, which she now rang to attract someone's attention.

A woman came in answer to the bell. It occurred to Naomi that she and Thomas must look considerably the worse for wear. She glanced at him, but perhaps he looked no more wet and muddy than a day on the roads in this weather might account for. There had been rain enough since to wash off any traces of the ruins. Naomi pushed her soaked hair out of her eyes, and spoke to the woman. 'We've just come up from the south. We need a meal, and a lodging.'

The woman looked her over, suspiciously at first, then her face suddenly cleared. 'I know you!' she exclaimed. 'Even in that state. You played at one of our midsummer festivals — when was it? Five years ago? Six? What brings you out on the road in this weather?'

'More than that, I think. But I remember now. I'm glad to be here again.'

'You're welcome to this house. And your friend.' She looked enquiringly at Thomas. He looked terrible, Naomi realised, on the verge of collapse. She had grown used to it, and had forgotten how he would seem to a stranger.

'My friend needs to rest,' she said. 'If it's possible. Is there room for us?'

The woman didn't take her eyes off Thomas, but she said slowly, 'There's room.' She seemed to decide something, and turned back to Naomi. 'There's always room for the midsummer fiddle player. I'll show you the room. You'll need to get your wet clothes off.'

It felt extraordinary to be warm again, and dry, in a place that was already familiar to her from what seemed another life. She even recalled the woman's name now, Kay, and with that feat of memory the world seemed more normal and her own. Thomas wouldn't eat, but he seemed glad to lie down. Naomi left him with some apprehension, but she had needs of her own, and he seemed quiet enough. It was not until she had eaten a large meal that she felt able to relax at all. She sat by the fire, and slowly the comforting atmosphere of the place seeped through to her. The settlement had seemed very frail and isolated, when at last they had come upon it, standing as it did within a clearing in this forest that hid more fear within it than anything she had ever dreamed of. But inside the inn, fear seemed as effectively shut out as the rain itself, which she could still hear beating on the roofs and cobbles outside. It was even pleasant to hear it now, from this place where it could no longer reach her. Naomi stretched out her feet to the fire, and sipped punch reflectively.

They had found shelter, but that was temporary. Her fiddle had survived the day without even getting damp, and so had the music. Her clothes were drying, and so were Thomas's. She had felt uncomfortable about opening his pack, but she could hardly leave everything soaked. She hadn't looked inside the bag with the pentacle, and the rest was mostly clothes, so she hadn't invaded his privacy.

It would be easy if she only had small things to think about. Her mind shied away from the events of the day, busying itself with the things that had to be dealt with. There was also the matter of money, or rather, the lack of it. On her own she could pay her way with music, but she was not on her own. She should have asked Peter for some more substantial currency, but she hadn't thought of it, and living as remotely as he did, the necessity had clearly never occurred to him. Maybe Thomas had money, but there was no way of finding out, short of searching, which she didn't propose to do.

Thomas. Naomi drank more punch, and gazed into the fire.

There was no way she could get him across the mountains like this. For a start, she didn't know the way, at least, not well enough to trust herself. More importantly, it was wrong to allow him to remain in this state, and keep travelling. I'm not leaving here, decided Naomi, until Thomas is recalled to this world, even if it takes weeks. The thought filled her with dismay. It won't take weeks, she admonished herself, not if I apply myself to it. I shall start as soon as he wakes up.

The door opened, and Kay appeared with a plate in her hand. 'I was just making pancakes,' she said. 'I wondered if you'd like one.'

'Very much, if I've still got anywhere to put it.' Naomi accepted the plate, and said, 'Do you want to stay a minute? I've been thinking.'

'Well, I was hoping I might have a word with you. It struck me that your friend might be sick, and I did wonder.'

'Oh,' said Naomi. 'I never thought of that. I should have said — I'm surprised you let us in at all.'

'I recognised you,' said Kay simply. 'And I remembered that you were trustworthy.'

'It's more than I deserved, to be so thoughtless. No, he's not sick. There's nothing your village need worry about. He's suffered too much, that's all, and his mind is filled with pain. What I wanted to say to you was, I'd like to stay here until he's ready for the journey that we have to make.'

Kay looked her over shrewdly. 'Can you give me your word that it implies no danger to me or mine?'

Naomi thought fleetingly of Paul, and decided that wasn't relevant. Thomas had loved Paul. If anyone needed to take care now, it was only herself. 'I give you my word,' said Naomi.

Twentieth Day

The days that followed were strange and disjointed. It was like a journey through unknown territory, catching snatches of conversations or events, but seeing no connection. She was trying to follow Thomas, and had no idea where it would take her. If it were not for the music she might have lost her bearings altogether. Every evening she left him and played for the customers at the inn. She was pleased to see that she must have more than earned their keep: the inn parlour was packed each time. But even that seemed remote and unreal, as if her whole waking life were turning into a dream.

The first day he never slept. Lack of sleep was torturing him, and he was afraid of being alone. She didn't suggest to him that he got up. Instead, she lit the fire in their room and kept him company. It seemed important not to disturb him, so she settled herself on the hearthrug, with her music spread out in front of her. His presence did not distract her, but she was aware of him, and sometimes when she looked up, she found that he was staring at her with dark-shadowed eyes.

She wasn't conscious of him making any demands on her, but as the hours passed she realised that she was growing exhausted. There seemed no reason: Thomas was silent, and the work she had to do, though difficult, usually left her tired but also exhilarated. Today she merely felt drained. He might say nothing, but she never ceased to be aware of his presence, and it was an effort to keep her attention from being dragged back to him. About midday she could stand it no longer. She stood up abruptly. 'I'm going out for a while, Thomas.' No response. Naomi regarded him uneasily for a moment, then left the room.

She stood at the back door of the inn, watching the thick drizzle that had succeeded yesterday's rain. There was nothing to tempt her out, but she could breathe more freely here, where the air was cool and damp, and the world outside was ordinary, untouched by anyone's nightmares. Naomi gazed at the dirty inn yard, and the wet trees beyond, as if they could anchor her in something recognisable, a world uninfluenced by Thomas, where things were as she had always known them to be.

Someone splashed through the mud towards the door, head downbent against the rain. Naomi stood aside, and Kay pushed past her, weighed down by a big basket of wood.

'Sorry, I didn't see you there. Did you want me?'

'No, I just came down for a breath of air.'

'I wouldn't go out in that if you don't have to. You can sit in the kitchen if you like. I haven't lit the other fire yet.'

Naomi hesitated, then followed her. It was fairly obvious Kay didn't want guests under her feet, but for once Naomi chose to ignore the fact that she was not actively wanted. Even as she did so she realised that she was growing a little desperate, and was shocked by her own neediness. She sat in a corner near the fire, and watched Kay bring in a selection of vegetables, and start to scrub them and chop them.

'I can help you, if you like.' Naomi tried not to sound too diffident. She wasn't used to begging for company, and she didn't like it.

'Oh, thanks.' Kay pushed over a knife and chopping board, and Naomi pulled up a stool, and meekly set to work.

'You gave me your word,' said Kay suddenly, so that Naomi's hand slipped, and half a carrot flew into the fireplace. 'As I said before, I trust you, and remembering who you are, I wouldn't turn you away. I've turned others away, sometimes.'

'And I'm grateful to you,' said Naomi cautiously, wondering what would come next.

'You came from the south. You must have passed the ruins.'

'We did.'

'Living so near,' said Kay, watching Naomi's face, 'we can't help being aware of these things. I've learned to be cautious over the years.'

In spite of herself, Naomi felt a small stab of apprehension. 'Cautious of what?'

'Most travellers pass by and never mention them. And rightly so. I ignore it too, as far as I can.'

She's going to start telling me ghost stories, thought Naomi. I'd be a fool to take it seriously. She chopped another carrot with a firm hand, and remarked, 'So do I. Who wouldn't?'

'Oh, quite a few. That's why I might have turned away your friend, if I hadn't recognised you.'

'Thomas?' She almost protested that Thomas's sufferings had nothing to do with any ruins, but then she knew that would be a lie.

'It seems to draw them. They come here, and want to start poking about down there, stirring things up. They don't know the danger, and they don't think about what brings them.'

An absurd image came to Naomi's mind of earnest people with sticks and spoons, poking and stirring among the nettles. She suppressed a giggle, not entirely successfully.

'You may laugh. But would you have stopped there yourself?'

'Not in yesterday's weather,' said Naomi flippantly. Then she realised that she had lied, and froze.

Kay didn't seem to notice. 'You may not take it seriously, and I don't blame you. I'm not about to start telling you silly stories, if that's what you think. I'm telling you that people come here, and their idea is to go inside those places, and see what they can find. Some of them hope for wealth, and some for knowledge. Some of them just can't leave ill alone, call it curiosity if you like. But all they come away with is dreams, dreams that anyone would be better without. I've seen it happen, and I could tell them, but they won't hear. But I'll have nothing to do with it now. No one who enters those places is welcome here.'

Naomi was silent for a while. 'What do they say they've seen?' she asked at last.

'Nothing good,' came the sharp answer. 'Nothing that I'd choose to mention in this house. We live too near. I can't afford to let that in.'

'What happened to Thomas,' said Naomi slowly, picking her words, 'happened many miles from here, in another country. It was nothing out of the past; it was something that he did, and suffered. I don't know what you think lies in the city, but, whatever is in your mind, Thomas hasn't brought it here.'

She was aware of Kay's eyes on her. 'Can you give me your word that your friend has not searched among the ruins of that city?'

'No,' said Naomi. 'How can I? I am not him.'

'But you speak for him, when you say that he brings no danger under this roof, to me or mine.'

'To you or yours, no, I can vouch for that. But to tell you what he has or has not done, how can I say?'

'I know you,' returned the other. 'I know you wouldn't go into that place. And so I'll take your word for him. I think if you'd seen what I've seen happen here, you'd understand the danger. But I trust you.'

Naomi felt her cheeks burning, and bent her head, chopping vegetables furiously. So she had given up her honesty for him too, and deceived this woman who had been generous to them both. For a moment she hated him, for daring to demand so much. She realised it was too much, and impulsively she looked up. 'I went. . .'

The innkeeper had her back to her, reaching down a big pot from a hook in the ceiling, and never noticed. 'After all, the world is full of danger,' she was saying. 'We each have our own, and we each have to protect ourselves. It's not a safe world for any of us.'

'No,' said Naomi, too confused to protest further. 'No, it's not.'

*

She only once left Thomas again, to play in the inn in the evening. When she returned she was exhausted, although nothing seemed to have happened that day at all. There was only one big bed in the room, in which Thomas lay with his back to her. The alternative was a thin mattress rolled up in one corner, where she had slept last night. Naomi hesitated, then got into the bed beside him, and instantly fell asleep.

Being woken up was like being dragged up from fathoms deep. She groaned and tried to shield her eyes from the insistent light. This was unbearable, to be denied her own dreams.

'Naomi?' said Thomas.

At first it seemed quite normal, and she tried to roll away and fall asleep again. Then the implication slowly filtered down to her. He had said her name. 'What?' she muttered, and forced herself to sit up.

'Naomi,' said Thomas again, urgently.

She blinked, and gradually her sight cleared, so she could take him in. He was sitting crosslegged, bolt upright, taut and restless. 'Naomi, I want you to tell me. You're the only one here who can tell me.'

'I'm the only one here at all,' she said thickly. 'Tell you what?'

'Why do we have to live?'

Why do you have to pick the middle of the night, thought Naomi resentfully, struggling to think. I sat there all day, and you never said a word. 'You want me to answer that now?'

'It has to be now. It was time to light the candle.'

'It was what?' Sure enough, the candle was lit. It must be a dream, if things proved themselves backwards.

'Why do we have to live?' insisted Thomas, 'when death is all round us? Why should we be tortured so?'

'It was you that woke me up,' she said a little tartly. 'I don't know, Thomas. Because the Ones who give birth to this world love life, I suppose. Can we go to sleep now?'

'Then what is life, that they should love it?'

'It's the middle of the bloody night. If this isn't a dream, I'd better put some more wood on the fire. I'm cold, and so must you be.'

'I already said there should be fire. What is life, Naomi?'

'Hold on a minute.' She swung her legs out of bed, and poked the fire back to life. Luckily there was plenty of wood in the basket. 'What is life, did you say?'

'I know that you know. You played me through the mountain.'

'Well, I'm glad you think so, but I'd do this much better in the daytime. I can't answer that, Thomas. Only with stories, which you'll have heard already.'

'Tell me,' commanded Thomas.

'There is a story they tell on the island,' said Naomi, as the mists of sleep gradually cleared from her mind. 'They say that waking life is like the flight of a sparrow through a lighted hall. It flies in from the dark, stays for a moment in the brightness and the heat, then it returns to the dark from which it came. Will that do?'

'Tell me more.'

She searched her mind. 'They say that whenever a tune is played, it travels on through the air forever, until it reaches out to the stars. Music once played is gone, but it never ceases to exist. Will that do?'

'Tell more.'

She thought again. 'There is a story told in my country. They say that life came from the sea, and everything that lives on earth goes back to the sea. In the depths of the ocean there is always the slow drift down of all that lived, returning to its beginning. Can I go to sleep now?'

Thomas stirred restlessly. 'Why is it all stories? Why can you only tell me stories you have been told? I want to know the truth.'

'The truth is in the stories. There's no other way to tell it that ever I heard of.'

'I want you to tell me in words, not images.'

'What are words, if they're not images?' She was cold and tired, and her mind was spinning.

'Is there nothing else?'

Naomi pressed her hands to her head. It was the same as the pages of tadpoles, realising that there must be a different way to think, if only she had been taught it. It eluded her. 'I can't give you your words, Thomas. I don't think they exist. I'm not a philosopher. I can play you the fiddle, but that's all.'

'The fiddle, yes,' demanded Thomas, suddenly fired with excitement. 'Play me the fiddle.'

'I didn't mean now. Someone might wake up.'

'That's right. Play me the fiddle,' agreed Thomas.

Twenty-first Day

When at last she was able to sleep Naomi was overtaken by dreams that tugged her down into a chaotic realm of jostling images, then tossed her back, exhausted, into semi-consciousness. Part of her was uncomfortably aware of the unaccustomed presence of another body, which seemed to expand and take over all the space there was, leaving her hanging over the edge of the bed while creeping fingers of icy air found their way inside her shirt. Sometimes she woke up enough to shove Thomas along a bit, then sleep would overpower her again, troubling her with more fantastic dreams. She found herself back on her familiar shore, only this time the night was dark and moonless, with a gale rising from the sea. She was hurrying along the beach, stumbling among rocks and seaweed, burdened by the toddler whom she carried on her hip, a little boy of about fifteen months or so, who clung to her jacket, too scared even to cry out. She couldn't stop to comfort him. The boat was just along the shore, and in a moment it would leave them. The child was so heavy; her arm holding him steady felt close to breaking. With her other hand she groped her way forward, slipping over piles of banked up seaweed dumped by many tides. If it wasn't for the boy she could still make it, but she dared not leave him here, even to run ahead with a message, lest he be lost for ever. She could see the outline of the boat, a black shape faintly etched against the water. It was pulling out. There was still a whole stretch of beach to go. She tried to cry out, but couldn't find her voice; tried to run, with the weight of the boy pulling her off balance, knowing that it was too late . . . There was a sheet all knotted round her, and she was right over the edge of the bed, with only the sheet still holding her.

Naomi rolled back into the middle, and fetched up against Thomas's back, which was at least warm. She was tired out after being up half the night, but the world outside seemed more restful than sleep at the moment, so presently she sighed deeply, and got up.

When she was dressed she bent over Thomas and listened to his even breathing. Even if there were complaints today about the times she chose to practise, it was worth it, if she could so easily bestow the gift of unconsciousness. She wished she had thought of it three days sooner, but it was no use regretting that now. She crept quietly out of the room, and went out while she had the chance.

The rain had cleared completely. It was a cold, clear morning, with traces of a late frost along the roadside verges. Carts had already passed this morning. It was a busy village, right on the highway from north to south. Yesterday she had counted more than a dozen carts or hoofbeats passing under their window. The inn did a good trade with travellers, which was lucky, as it guaranteed a fresh audience every night. Naomi wandered along the road, avoiding the mud, until she was some way from the settlement, back among the ranks of trees. Then she retraced her steps, letting her fantasies drift in the direction of food.

When she returned to Thomas she found him awake, sitting up in bed, with the quilt huddled round him. His face was still drawn, and his eyes deeply shadowed, but there was a trace of colour in his cheeks, and when she spoke to him, he responded, though not very coherently. He refused any food, but watched her closely as she cleaned the hearth and relaid the fire. When she came back with more wood he was still sitting up, apparently waiting for her. Over to you, Thomas, decided Naomi, sitting down in her chosen place on the hearthrug, and opening her music.

This time she made no attempt to be silent, but took out her fiddle, playing note by note through the next piece as she deciphered it. Thomas said nothing, but appeared to listen attentively, never taking his eyes off her. Soon she was deeply absorbed, so that when at last he spoke to her she jumped, as though she had forgotten his existence.

'Naomi?'

'Thomas,' she replied, and laid down her fiddle.

'Where are we?'

'On the road to the island. About five miles north of the ruins of the city, on the edge of the plain between the mountains.'

'The ruins of the city,' repeated Thomas. It was so long before he said anything else that she had returned to her work, assuming that their conversation was over. 'Before the cities lay in ruins,' said Thomas suddenly, 'did you see them then, Naomi?'

'How could I possibly have?' she expostulated. 'I haven't lived forty years, let alone four hundred, or whatever it must be.'

'Cities crowded with people,' went on Thomas, ignoring this. 'Grey streets thronged with people. They never dream of hunger or disease or violence. They never dare to dream because their end is so close it seems impossible. They know what they have done, but they don't dream of it. Only so many of them are children.'

'Thomas,' she said sharply. 'You didn't see it like that either.'

'I see it all the time.'

'It's nothing to do with you!'

'Who buried them, Naomi? Who had the strength to dig so many graves?'

'I suppose the answer to that lies in the forest. That's why no one goes into it.'

'Do you ever think about your own death?' asked Thomas.

'No,' said Naomi firmly. 'Yes,' she corrected herself. 'Of course I do sometimes. Who doesn't?'

'Aren't you afraid?'

'No.'

'Is there nothing you would regret?'

'How do you mean?'

'If you were facing death, as you are, as I am, is there nothing you would want of life?'

'I love life, so I'd be sorry. But I have to die sometime.'

'So you wouldn't be afraid if it were now?'

'I'd be furious. I've got a lot of work to do. Besides . . .'

'What?' he said quickly, pouncing on her uncertainty.

She hesitated. But only the truth would do in this game. 'There is someone I still have to seek. Not that he is lost, but I would like to find him again one day in the waking world, if that is possible.'

'I have searched among the crowds,' said Thomas, 'so many years, in the streets of so many cities.'

'Thomas,' she said, suddenly afraid again. 'There are no cities.'

'I have searched the cities of the dead, but there are so many of them.'

Naomi jumped up, and sat down on the bed beside him, seizing his hands. 'Thomas, this is too difficult for me. Please explain to me. What are you thinking?'

'Difficult,' repeated Thomas dully. 'What is difficult?'

'It's like a dream. I can't follow. I don't know what you think is real.'

He was silent for some time, and she thought he hadn't heard her. 'In which world?' he asked then. 'In which world do you speak of "real"?'

'In this one. You are awake, Thomas. The rest is dreams.'

'Do you know that? You're sure of that? Can you show me that it's real?'

'Oh Thomas, I wish I knew what to do! This is all words. The world is beautiful, you said so yourself. You have to keep yourself anchored in it, although the tides may pull you. Do you understand me? This waking world is what you are, Thomas. Your body is made of it. I don't know how to make you know it.'

He gestured impatiently. 'All words, you say. Are we made of words, then? There are no words among the dead.'

'No!' she was almost shouting at him. 'I don't know what you're doing! You make everything I say unreal. I can't follow that. Can't you see what I'm saying?'

'How can I see words? They're not real. You said so.'

'Then, Thomas, I shall give you something real.' She got up quickly and went to her pack, lying half empty at the end of the bed. She searched about for a moment, then came back to him. 'This is my gift to you, Thomas. It belongs to the same world as you do, made of the same stuff as yourself. I can't help you by anything I say, but I can give you something that you may recognise. It's a strong gift, because it matters to me, but you matter more. Do you understand me?'

She took his hand, and turned it palm upward, and placed her own palm over it. When she took her hand away, there was a round stone lying in his.

Thomas looked at it closely. It was curiously mottled, grey and red, with little flecks of brightness in it. It was worn perfectly smooth, refined by water until it was almost spherical, though slightly flatter at top and bottom. Thomas held it between his finger and thumb and contemplated it, apparently deep in thought.

'Where does it come from?'

'From the same place as I do. From the beach, lying between high and low water. I took it from there, and I've kept it for fifteen years.'

'And now you're giving it to me?'

'Yes. To keep, to remind you what you are, and to which world you belong.'

Thomas turned his gaze from her gift at last, and gave her a straight look, vivid and compassionate, as focused as she had ever seen him. 'It must be hard to give it away,' he said.

'Yes. But I want you to have it more.'

'Thank you,' said Thomas.

Twenty-second Day

That night Naomi found herself in the house at the top of the beach, the last house in the village. It was many years since she had been inside it, even in her dreams. She knew the kitchen perfectly. If there had been time she could have traced every detail, down to the cracks in the table top, and the lines of flagstones on the floor. Only there was no time. The place was bright and crowded. Her sisters were there, but there was no time to look into their faces, and they remained vaguely blurred. She longed to stay and rest at last among the old familiar things, but time was distracting her, tugging her away, reminding her of the boat that waited outside, but would not wait for long.

There was a little boy to be dressed. It was so fiddly; he wriggled and squirmed, and all his buttonholes seemed too tight for the buttons. She had to pack his things, but they were everywhere, and it was impossible to hurry. She knew the jersey he was wearing very well. It was yellow, the wool had matted together, and the little buttons on his shoulder were round and slippery. She thought she had packed, but when she looked round, she hadn't after all. There were his toys strewn across the floor, and small garments everywhere.

She knew then that they were going to miss the boat.

Naomi woke up, and realised where she was. With recollection came a sense of loss so acute that it was a physical pain. He had been so substantial. She seemed to still feel the imprint of his body against hers, as though he had just been torn from her arms. She turned face down, and hid her face in the pillow. She couldn't feel all those feelings again. She couldn't live through all that again, when she had borne it once in silence. It hurt far too much, never to allow herself to speak of it.

Years ago, she would wake up and find herself crying inconsolably through the dead hours of the night, but always without a sound. She wasn't always alone, but her grief she had kept to herself. She didn't cry now. There were too many years between, but the pain had not changed, after all.

She wasn't alone now. There was Thomas. She had played him to sleep again, as she had done the night before, and it was imperative not to wake him. He needed sleep like a drowning man needs air. She tried to lie still, and banish the thoughts that would not be suppressed. It was a cruel dream, because it had awoken memory as if time did not exist, and left her with an impression so strong that it could have been the present. She could recall exactly how he felt, the shape of his small hands, the sweet smell of him when she buried her face in his neck. And yet there was no such child, not in this world. Perhaps there was a man, whom she didn't know. Perhaps there was not. All she had, apart from a figment of her own mind, were a few strands of soft red hair, coiled in a little box, hair that might just as easily have been her own.

*

Thomas seemed more himself when he woke up than he had been for days. He even managed to eat a little, and when she suggested that they go out for a while he was quite willing. It was another frosty morning. They found a path that wound beside the river among banks of faded daffodils. The hawthorn hedge that divided them from the fields was dense and green. Naomi helped herself to a few young leaves as they passed, and chewed them absently. They were bittersweet in her mouth, a welcome change from winter stores.

Thomas seemed glad to be out. He said very little, but she could see the change in his face. In the sunshine he was pale and haggard, like a man just emerged from a long illness, but his eyes were bright, and when she spoke to him he answered her quite easily. She wasn't sure of him though. He wasn't quite the old Thomas. There was something missing, some part of him which was not present. She was no longer frightened for him, but she was wary.

When they got back he seemed tired, so she left him to lie on the bed, and returned to her music. She was making progress. The symbols in the book were becoming less daunting. Now that she was beginning to get some sense of how some of the tunes sounded, she was able to fill in the gaps which the tadpoles did not explain. The hardest part was to work out the time. Usually it was given at the beginning, but that did not tell her how many notes belonged to each beat. She could only play it until it sounded right. It was possible that there was a direction being given which she had missed. The notes were attached to each other in various ways, or not at all. When she tried to think about it they turned back into tadpoles and swam about mockingly in front of her eyes. Then there was the curious symbol at the beginning of every line, like a magician's mark. Because it was like nothing she knew, her eye had drifted over it, but it was possible that it deserved greater attention. She tried not to think too hard about it, but contemplated the mark, while deliberately banishing irrelevant thoughts from her mind. If there were a message being given, the only thing to do was to listen. She stared at the curly symbol until it no longer seemed extraordinary, but quite sensible. It was like a maze. She traced it thoughtfully with her finger.

She was deep in reflection when Thomas suddenly got up and came to sit opposite her on the rug. She studied the symbol for a few moments longer, then she put the book aside and turned to him.

'Did I give you that book?' asked Thomas.

'No.'

'I was trying to remember how we left,' he said, almost apologetically. 'I saw you had the music, but I couldn't recollect how. I did give you what you came for, then?'

'You did. Then we left, and Linnet gave me this.'

'And that was all right?' he asked her anxiously.

'It was more than all right. You've given me a gift worth any journey, Thomas. Thank you.'

'You have nothing to thank me for. Are we going back to the island?'

'Of course. Isn't that what you want?'

'I don't think I have any right to go back.'

'Why not?'

'I failed,' said Thomas bitterly. 'It happened, exactly what I was afraid of. I couldn't do what was asked of me.'

'But you did. You did it all. Everything that was required was done. Surely you know that?'

'I can't remember,' he said unhappily, and looked at her almost pleadingly. 'At least your quest is fulfilled. Perhaps that was all that fate intended. But it's a bitter thing to me to be of no more use than a broken instrument that you have to carry away out of pity.'

'I don't pity you, Thomas. You don't need it.'

'I've been outside my mind, I know that much. I don't know what it meant, and as you pity me, you won't even tell me what I have done. It's like drifting in and out of nightmare, Naomi, and not knowing whether I sleep or wake. I can't trust myself, and I dread to think what has happened, but I need to know. Even if you tell me it may not seem real. I don't know any more. I'd be safer dead than not trusting my own mind.'

'But you're a magician, Thomas. Surely a magician is one who has the courage to look beyond the confines of his waking mind?'

'But such a one must control it, and so I've failed.'

'It isn't that, Thomas.'

'Then what?' he asked listlessly.

'I don't know. But in these last few days I've thought about it more than I ever did before. I understood, which I hadn't before, that I can't run away from my own dreams. I can only turn and face them. Your dreams are no worse than mine, but yours have followed you into the daylight, and I've never dared to let mine do that.'

'I face them all the time. What else can I do?'

She picked up her fiddle, as if that would help her to think, and absentmindedly tested the strings, making small plucking sounds like the ghost of a departed tune. 'I think you have to speak them,' she said at last.

'The dreams? But there are no words. There would be no sense.'

'No, not that. You have to speak about what happened. Listen, Thomas, it's hard for me to find words, because the thoughts are new to me. You made me think them. For fifteen years I have kept silent, and I thought that was courage. Then we set out upon this journey, and very soon I found that a puzzle had been set me. I was able to work it out, as far as facts went, but that wasn't the key. The point I missed is that you never told me yourself.'

'I would have,' he interrupted. 'I knew it wasn't fair. I would have, if I could.'

'But you could. I didn't need to know. That was immaterial. It was you that needed to speak.'

'I don't follow.'

'Then listen to this instead. You think you committed a crime, don't you?'

He covered his face with his hands, and nodded.

'Then I offer you expiation. Do you want to know what it is?'

'You have no power to do that.'

'Oh, but I have, more than you know. Do you want to know what it is?'

'Tell me, then.' He sounded resigned.

'You must tell me what you did.'

He started. 'But you know! Peter told you. I didn't dream that. He told me that he had told you.'

'Peter told me nothing that changed anything. But you can.'

'I can't,' said Thomas desperately. 'I suffered it. Isn't that enough?'

'No,' said Naomi, although her heart went out to him. 'You have to speak it.'

There was a silence. 'I'm scared,' he said in a low voice, not looking at her. 'I'm scared of my own mind.'

'I know. But when you speak, you will bind that fear into the past for ever.'

'You don't know. You're safe. Your dreams stay where they belong, and they don't pursue you into the waking world.'

'I'm not so sure. But this isn't a dream. I want you to tell me what happened.'

'I can't.'

'I can wait.'

She wasn't as sure of herself as she sounded. Perhaps he was right, and it was different for him, but she was almost certain he was wrong. He wasn't different; she was in a better position to know that, because she knew what she was hiding, and he could not. She might be wrong, but she had nothing else to offer. This might fail: doing nothing certainly would.

'There are words, Thomas. You know that.'

It was so long before he said anything that she was on the point of giving up. Just as she opened her mouth to say something else, he spoke first.

'I was on my way home,' said Thomas. 'I came over the pass just as the sun was leaving it. The path was in shadow, and the mountains were still in sunlight. I came to one of the outcrops, just at the place where the beck flows into a little tarn. There was a man sitting on a rock by the road. He seemed to be resting from his journey. I stopped and spoke to him, as anybody would. He was a fiddle player, so he told me. I could see that was the truth, because he carried a green baize bag, the sort that travelling musicians use. I thought at once of the dance. Or rather, I had never ceased to think of it. It was imminent, and it had become very close to my heart. I had been thinking about the dance, and then I met a fiddle player. It felt as if I had conjured him there by the power of my own dreams. To find him like that seemed absolutely right.'

Thomas put his hand across his eyes, as though he couldn't bear her to see him, but he went on talking. 'I told him my thoughts, and I invited him home with me. He hesitated. He told me he had a touch of marsh fever, which afflicted him now and then, and he feared a bad attack, which would make him useless to me. I swept aside his protests. It would be a cruel thing anyway, I told him, to leave a man out on the hill if he had the ague, and maybe he'd be better in time for the dance, in which case he could repay my hospitality. That's how I put it to him. He thought for a little, then he agreed to come.

'By the time I got him home I realised he was pretty sick. I told my sister what had happened. We got him to bed, and she examined him herself. When she came out. . .' Thomas's voice trailed away, and he buried his head in his arms. 'I can't! Naomi, I have tried to forget this for seven years! Why must I recall it now?'

'With every word you speak you bind it. Go on! You bind it into the past, Thomas, and then you can be free.'

His voice was anguished. 'But I still did it! I don't deserve to be free!'

'You punish yourself. No one else wants to, either the living or the dead. Go on, Thomas!'

He pulled himself together with a great effort, then continued, the words coming with difficulty, as though under duress. 'Judith came to me, and she was anxious. "Tom," she said, "are you sure this man has the marsh fever? I'm not familiar with it, but there are signs on him which frighten me." She didn't seem over-agitated about it. Judith never would. But she was afraid. I wasn't used to that.

'I didn't want to hear her, though. Maybe her fear communicated itself to me, but I wouldn't have it. The thing was perfect, and I was thinking about the dance. What she was thinking of… Well, I didn't dare let my mind turn to that.' He stopped again, then cried out suddenly, 'I can't remember, Naomi! I can't remember what I said!'

'Yes you can, Thomas.'

'No!'

'Speak it,' she commanded him. 'Then you can be free.'

'I think then I took her by the shoulders.' He spoke so quietly she could hardly hear him. 'I took her by the shoulders, and I think I said to her, "Oh, come on, Judith, I've seen marsh fever before. Surely you can trust me?" '

Thomas seemed to crumple up then. Naomi caught him and held him. He was colder than she ever thought a living body could be. His hands were held rigidly against his face, and he was shaking violently. She was scared. This might cure or break him, and she wasn't at all sure what it meant. Naomi took her courage in both hands, and said to him, even as she held him tightly to her, 'Go on, Thomas! Go on. You have to speak it all.'

*

When Naomi came down to play in the inn that night, she found Kay looking out for her.

'You never had any supper,' Kay said. 'I was worried. I came up to ask, but you never noticed me. Is your friend all right? You look worn out.'

'I am worn out. But I'm ready to play now.'

'Come into the kitchen and eat first. I saved some for you. They can wait a little while.'

'That's very kind of you.'

Naomi hadn't realised how hungry she was. Kay apologised for producing bread and beans yet again, explaining that there was still almost nothing in the garden. 'You know how it is at the hungry time of year. But we had a good harvest so at least there's plenty of what there is.'

'It's very good,' said Naomi automatically. She was far too weary to think clearly, and even the most elementary conversation seemed an effort.

'I came in,' said Kay again. 'I wouldn't have, but I didn't know. That man is suffering, isn't he? Is he running away from something? Do you mind me asking?'

'No, I don't mind, and he's not. Not now.'

'That's your doing, is it?'

'I don't know,' said Naomi, with sudden complete weariness. 'I don't know. I knew what he was doing, when I saw that I was doing it too. So perhaps I knew what to do. When it was done I played to him until he was able to sleep. I can do that much, anyway.'

To her astonishment the other woman leaned across the table and touched her hand. 'I think you do more,' she said gently.

Naomi realised she was more tired than she knew. She could feel her own tears rising, and she couldn't stop them. 'I don't know,' she said again, and took her hand away to hide her face with it. 'I don't know. Nothing hurts more than what we do to ourselves. I'm sorry.'

'You need not be.'

If Kay had evinced more signs of sympathy, or of curiosity, Naomi knew she would never have broken her reserve. But she remained quietly sitting on the far side of the table, and merely looked at Naomi as if she recognised her.

'The mistakes we make are so small,' said Naomi. 'We punish ourselves out of all proportion. As though love has to hurt. That can't be true, can it?'

'Well, they do say you hurt those you love most. I suppose you have to take the pain along with the rest. You can't pretend part of you doesn't exist.'

Naomi looked up at her, no longer attempting to hide her tears. 'Thomas said that,' she said. 'I didn't want to hear. How can a man who is unfailingly kind punish himself to the point of destruction? All he sees is the pain. He forgets what he must have given them.'

'Every gift in this world is two-edged. You have to accept the whole of it, I suppose.'

'You think so?' Naomi pondered this. 'Can I ask a question?'

'Of course.'

'Not out of curiosity, but because what you say is important, and I want to know why you say it. Do you have any children?'

'I have a son, Jamie. You've probably seen him round the place.'

'The little boy with the freckles? Yes, I talked to him yesterday. I didn't know. To give life is a two-edged gift, I suppose, from which everything else follows. You can't be sorry you have given it.'

'What anybody does with a gift is their own responsibility.'

'I don't know. I know what I've done to myself. I may still have hurt someone else, though I never intended it, and I may not know it.'

'You can't know. You may think you know what you've done. What you never know is if it made any difference at all. It might all have happened anyway. There's no point holding yourself responsible.'

Naomi looked at her, frowning though her tears. 'The fiddle player might have come to the foot of the pass anyway,' she said. 'It's logical.'

'What fiddle player?'

'It doesn't matter.' Naomi held her knife between her hands, apparently examining the blade. 'I have a son too,' she said. 'I left him to grow up in the midst of a family whom I trusted more than anybody in the world. It was a household where any child would be happy. I was happy there myself.'

'Now that's interesting,' said Kay chattily, moving to put the kettle on. 'My sister did the same, had a daughter and left her here, because she went in for the metal trade. It was all the merchants passing gave her the idea. Do you want anything more to eat? Or a cup of tea?'

'I'd like some tea. Then I must go and earn my keep before they all leave again.'

'Oh, they won't do that. They've heard about you.'

Twenty-third Day

It was impossible to concentrate. The pattern behind the lengths of the notes obstinately refused to reveal itself. The sun was bright outside, and Thomas was restless, pacing up and down the inn parlour studying the hangings on the walls, and fiddling with the objects on the cluttered shelves. Naomi pushed the music away impatiently, and watched him with increasing irritation.

Perhaps they could soon go on, she thought. Most of the time he seemed quite himself, but then he would lose himself again in a fit of abstraction. One moment he couldn't settle to anything, and the next, exhaustion would take hold of him, and he would turn white and pinched, and have to rest again. He had slept for hours this morning. Presumably he had a lot to catch up on. She couldn't help feeling that if he tried to pull himself together his will was no less strong than hers, yet she had seen how much he had suffered, and knew that he was recovering himself as fast as anyone reasonably could.

Caught between two frustrations, and stuck at this inn when she wanted to be on her way, she wasn't finding it easy to keep her temper. She'd gone for three walks today already. It was a beautiful day, just right for tackling the mountains. She could see the foothills from the road looking deceptively close. Thomas didn't want to go out; he said it made him tired. I'd make a rotten nurse, thought Naomi, my thoughts are too violent, and it would probably show. I could leave you behind, Thomas, and go straight back home and seduce Francis before you got there. I could pick up that large blue and white dish hanging over the mantelpiece and hurl it at your head. I could tear the music right in two and never forgive myself. Perhaps I shall go for a fourth walk.

'Do you play chess?' asked Thomas suddenly.

'Not if I can help it.'

'There's a set here. Would you like a game?'

'I'm not in a very good temper.'

'All the better. Are you any good?'

'I'm quite wonderful.'

'Oh, good,' said Thomas, without a trace of sarcasm. 'So am I.'

Naomi sighed. 'I'll play a game with you if I must, but only if we can sit outside.'

There was a little courtyard between the south and west walls of the inn, with benches and tables set out as if it were already summer. Naomi felt much better out here. It was May, after all, and she had the whole season before her to do whatever she wanted. There was no hurry. She turned her face to the sun and shut her eyes. There were bees buzzing in a clump of lavender and the air was full of the scent of herbs. She stripped off her jersey, and unbuttoned the top buttons of her shirt.

'Are you ready?'

'Yes.' She opened her eyes and found he had set out the board on the low table between them. A doubt struck her. 'Do you suppose this is wise, Thomas?'

'You think my mind may go up in smoke if I use it?' He sounded amused, not insulted.

'I'm sorry,' said Naomi, realising that she wasn't being civil. 'I'm sure you know yourself best.'

'It never was my mind anyway, it was my heart. But neither is broken. You want to be on your way, don't you? I won't keep us here long, I promise you.'

Naomi felt shamed, and the blood rose to her cheeks. She'd been angry with him, as if he were irresponsible or stupid. He was thinking just as clearly as she was, and she had given him no credit. 'I'm sorry, Thomas. That wasn't fair. It's the weather. I'm finding it hard to stay still, that's all. Black or white?'

Thomas picked up two pawns. 'Which hand?'

She really wasn't feeling very interested. She made her first three moves almost at random.

'Checkmate,' said Thomas.

'What?' Naomi sat up straight, startled into attention. She studied the board. 'Your game, Thomas.'

'Perhaps you've had enough?' enquired Thomas.

'Certainly not! Shall I take white this time?'

She hadn't thought so hard about a game for years. She had once been quite good, and when she concentrated she found she hadn't entirely forgotten how to think about it. Her blood was up. She didn't say another word, but gave complete attention to the board in front of her. It was a curious process; the answers seemed to come before the reasoning for them, but she had to think very hard about the reasoning to be sure of getting it right. And she must get it exactly right if she was going to beat him.

She did want to beat him. All thoughts of looking after him had fled entirely. He didn't need it. She realised within five minutes that she was up against far greater skill than her own. He would win, but she'd make him fight for it, every step. She took a long time to think before she made a move, and Thomas made his moves the instant she was done. She refused to let that disconcert her. This was his idea, so he would have to be patient.

He didn't seem to find patience difficult. Naomi never looked at him, and might have been furious if she had. He wasn't looking at the board most of the time. He was watching her, and his face was alight with amusement for the first time in many days.

He only once hesitated over a move, but then he made it anyway. 'Checkmate,' said Thomas regretfully.

Naomi studied the board thoughtfully for some time. 'Thomas!'

'Yes.'

'Do you know anything at all about music?'

'I thought you'd never ask. Would you like me to sing you a ballad?'

'Can you?'

'Indeed I can. Shall I sing you Thomas the Rhymer? That's my favourite.'

'I'd like that very much, but I want to ask you something else first.'

'Yes?'

'Wait.' She hurried back into the house, and came back two minutes later with her book of music. 'Will you look at this, Thomas?'

'If you want me to.' He seemed quite startled that she should ask him, but moved along the bench readily enough, so that she could sit right beside him.

'I don't think it matters whether you're a musician. Just look at this.'

Thomas glanced at her, as if to ascertain that she really intended to share her work so openly, then he obediently looked down, following her pointing finger.

'These are notes. I know which is which now, from the lines. But the lengths are different. Look, it tells you how many beats at the beginning. Three, four. I can make it fit, if I keep trying until it sounds right, but I don't know when to start counting again. Some are short and some are long, which is why all their tails are different. And sometimes it doesn't even tell you that, and there are no numbers at the beginning. What I need to know is how many of each sort of note makes a beat. Do you follow me, Thomas?'

'I certainly don't,' said Thomas.

'You don't? Then let me try and make it clearer. If you count up to four . . .'

'Naomi, not so fast. Start again.'

'I have started again. Well, you know four, four. Of course you do. Imagine if it were in four, four.'

'Do I know four, four?' interrupted Thomas. 'It doesn't feel like it.'

'Oh, come on, Thomas. Your own dance. Four, four.'

'Is that so?'

'Thomas,' said Naomi, turning slightly red. 'You danced it. I saw you. The time. It goes in fours.'

'Oh that. Now I see what you mean.'

'I should hope so. So listen. This one is in three. For each beat, there are so many of these notes. Sometimes just one. I need to work out the length of the notes by looking at their tails. There must be halves and quarters, and so on, adding up to one. But the way they're drawn is confusing.'

'Why must there be?'

She looked at him helplessly. 'Because it's music, Thomas. What else could they be?'

'I see. Can I ask some more questions?' asked Thomas diffidently.

*

It was difficult to make it clear to him, but once he had grasped what she was after, he gave the matter complete attention. That in itself helped. She realised she hadn't been sure she was talking sense, even to herself. Thomas seemed to think it was perfectly sensible. That was reassuring, but nothing else was. It was bad enough trying to apply her own mind, but waiting for someone else to apply theirs was unendurable. Naomi held on to her patience as long as she could bear it, because it mattered so much. Thomas wasn't deceived, however. He looked up at her at last, and suggested, 'Why don't you go for a walk? Now that I know what you want, I could think better on my own.'

She hesitated. 'You'll look after my book?'

'I'll guard it with my life,' said Thomas patiently.

She was gone some time. Her head ached, and she felt more frustrated than she had ever felt before. It was the only thing that mattered, and it was going completely wrong. There was music there, and some idiot had tied it all up in knots that could never be undone, not in her world. It was all useless. Naomi stood by the river, hating herself for having reduced her life to this. Then she trailed back again, and found Thomas still in the yard, head bent over her book. He had moved into the far corner to catch the last of the sun.

'Naomi?'

She wandered over to him dispiritedly.

'I've thought of something.' She nodded without much enthusiasm. 'Have you got your fiddle?'

'Yes.' She looked down at the page in front of him. 'What are you thinking?'

'These lines. Didn't you notice them? Across the five lines, look, there and there. I think you'll find the notes between each one add up to three. And I found four as well. You said some had no numbers. Well, that's not true. When there are four beats between the lines, you get a C at the beginning. Which makes it quite possible to put a value on each tadpole.'

'Does it? What value? Explain to me,' demanded Naomi, squeezing herself into the space on the bench beside him.

*

When Naomi woke up that night she knew she hadn't slept for long enough, but it seemed imperative she should wake herself up. It had happened so many times, being woken by crying in the night, and having to force herself awake yet again, even though it seemed impossible. She had to respond to him even if she couldn't wake up. She struggled out of her dreams, but perhaps she had not. She couldn't remember. Naomi rolled over, and made herself open her eyes.

It was quite dark. Even as she put her hand out she remembered where she was. The child was not there, but only part of the dream. In the dream she had made herself wake up, and now that was real. Desolation flooded over her; she lay face down, stupidly trying to retain the image that had fled. She knew where she was and fought against it, but she was not awake enough to resist properly. Or not asleep enough. Caught between one state and another, she was hit by a wave of loss, as sharp as it had been on the day she left, so that all the fabrications of fifteen years crumbled to nothing. Naomi pressed her hands against her face and felt hot tears. In the dream she sobbed aloud, as though grief were tearing her apart, forcing itself out into the waking world, where it must not make a sound.

'Naomi?'

'No!' That wasn't in the dream. And she must not be awake, because she was crying aloud. She remembered Thomas, and fought him off, still sobbing. If she could get rid of him she need not be awake.

'Wake up! You don't have to hit me.'

That woke her. 'Go away,' wept Naomi furiously.

Instead, he put his arm around her. Naomi stopped sobbing, and went rigid. She had given him much comfort, but she had always kept her distance. He had seen her cry before, but he hadn't come as close as this. She was still confused by dreams, and too aware of what she could not have. She would not accept tenderness from him; she dared not. Naomi put her hands against his chest and held him away from her.

'Naomi,' said Thomas. 'Why are you crying?'

'It's all right,' she said thickly. 'I can manage on my own.'

'I know that. You don't have to.'

'Of course I have to. I'm not a child.'

'That doesn't mean you have to hide everything.'

'I'm not hiding anything.'

'Don't lie to me,' said Thomas sharply.

It was so unexpected that she was shaken right out of her defences. She was about to refute him, for no one had ever called her a liar, then she realised that she couldn't. Naomi turned out of his arms, and faced the pillow, her head in her hands, bereft of words.

'I've been truthful with you,' said Thomas presently. 'You told me to find words, and I found them.'

There was a long silence. 'What do you expect me to say?' asked Naomi, and realised that her voice was shaking.

'I asked you why you were crying.'

'I had a dream.'

'Not for the first time.'

'You can't know my dreams.'

'I know one of them. You told me.'

'Then you know.'

'Listen,' said Thomas, and touched her arm in the darkness. 'You do yourself no justice. You won't disclose yourself, to the point that even a friend must remain deceived. It's dishonest. I don't like being treated dishonestly.'

If there had been any accusation in his tone, she would have flown at him. No one had ever questioned her honesty, least of all herself. She would have defended herself against such a charge with all her strength, except that he was not attacking her. She felt tears rising again, and choked them back. 'You think I lie to you?' she said at last.

'I think you fail to tell the truth.'

It was dark, so he couldn't know she was crying, so long as she made no sound. Naomi let her tears fall unchecked, and said nothing. Thomas touched her face, drawing his fingers across her cheek. She didn't resist; he wouldn't be deceived, not now.

'Why are you crying, Naomi?'

He waited a long time before she answered him. His eyes were wide open, as though he could see her through the dark. He didn't take his hand away, and this time she didn't push him off.

'For what I have lost,' said Naomi at last.

'Go on.'

'For my son. You know about him.'

'It wasn't you who told me.'

'I dream about him so much on this journey. More than I have for years. It reminds me, somehow. When I'm awake I don't think about it, but in my dreams it all comes back, and I can't stop it.'

She spoke very quietly, and he had to move closer to hear what she said. Her face was turned away from him, looking down.

'What reminds you?'

He felt her shrug. 'Loving somebody, I suppose,' she said presently, with a casualness that completely failed to deceive him.

'And so do I love you. Tell me about him.'

'Tell you what? His name is Colin, and he has red hair. When I last saw him he could stand, holding on to things, but he couldn't quite walk.'

'Go on.'

'He was born with blue eyes, but they turned greener, depending on the light. I don't know what to say. I've never said this to anyone before.'

'I can't think why not. Go on.'

'His birth was not pleasant. Sometimes women talk about birth as if it were the ultimate experience in life,' said Naomi, with a touch of her habitual manner, 'and I feel like giving them a piece of my mind. It was hell. They say it's worse for women with red hair.'

'Do they? I never heard that before. Why don't you tell them?'

Another shrug. 'What's the point?'

'Because you know. It happened to you. Why deny it?'

'Because it hurts to recall it, I suppose.'

'Like now?'

Silence again. 'No,' she said eventually. 'Not like now. It's only remembering. I can tell you.'

'Then go on.'

Twenty-fourth Day

Sonata I. Adagio. Violino. Four notes heaped together, incomprehensibly.

'Oh, I give up!' Naomi shut the book, and marched over to the window. She grabbed her fiddle and played furiously through three reels, then stormed out of the house.

She returned hot and flushed, feeling a great deal better. If all went well, she decided, they could go tomorrow. Thomas still looked ill, and was noticeably thinner, but he had said himself that he wanted to get on, and then he had gone out by himself, which was an excellent sign. They seemed to have been staying at this inn for ever, and yet the odd thing was that she hardly knew the place, apart from the building itself, and the stretches of road where she had walked in both directions. But she hadn't been exploring, even then, merely finding enough space in which to think clearly. She had stayed in so many places, and none had made so little impression on her as this. In a sense she had still been travelling, but the journey had taken place within the confines of the inn.

She wanted to get out into open country again. She felt a flicker of apprehension as well as anticipation: there were still the mountains to cross, for which she would have to rely mostly upon Thomas. He seemed to think he could do it now, so she could only trust that he was right.

When she came into the back yard, she found Kay struggling across to the scullery door with a large sack. Naomi lifted the other end for her, and they carried it together over the puddles.

'More turnips?' said Naomi. 'I thought you said it was all beans now?'

'This isn't turnips.' Kay paused for breath, and hoisted the sack up again. 'Sugar beets. Not a job I'd planned on, this week, but your friend's used up all the sugar we had left. Not to worry. It has to be done sooner or later.'

'I'm sorry,' said Naomi, surprised. 'What's he doing?'

'I dread to think. Go in and see.'

Naomi found Thomas at the stove, stirring something in a huge black cauldron, from which steam rose alarmingly. A little boy stood on a chair beside him, holding an earthenware bowl. The room reeked of sweetness.

'Now,' Thomas was saying. 'You've got the cold water?'

Jamie nodded, open-mouthed.

'Right. Do you want to stir for a minute?'

They pushed the chair closer, with its back to the stove. Jamie took an enormous wooden spoon, and Thomas held him by the back of his shirt.

'You don't have to hold on to me!'

'I will, all the same. Make sure you scrape the bottom of the pot.'

'Hello,' said Naomi.

Thomas looked up and nodded to her. Jamie didn't look up at all.

'That's right,' said Thomas. 'Right round the edges. Does it feel any thicker?'

'No,' said Jamie doubtfully.

Naomi sat down at the table. There were greased trays spread out at the far end, and a couple of bowls with a pestle beside them. The first contained crushed herbs. She sniffed them cautiously. Lemon balm. The other was full of broken nuts. She helped herself to a pinch.

'Hey, stop that!' said Thomas from the stove. 'We need those.'

'Sorry,' said Naomi, crunching.

'Now,' said Thomas. 'Hold the bowl. Good, Take a spoonful. That's right. Now drop it in the cold water. If it goes solid, then it's done.'

'How can it go solid? It's all runny.'

'Alchemy. Try it.'

There was a pause. Naomi glanced at their backs and took another piece of nut.

'That's it. Perfect. We can pour it out now.'

'Can I pour?'

'No, it's too heavy. You can cut it into squares, though, soon.'

No one said anything until all the trays were filled. Jamie heaved a sigh of satisfaction, then cried sharply, 'Hey, she's eaten half our nuts!'

'Sorry. I'll do some more if you like.'

'You'd better be quick then.'

*

When Naomi came back from playing that evening, she found Thomas already asleep. She undressed quickly and got into bed. She was tired, and they had a long way to go tomorrow. She didn't feel ready to sleep, however, but lay on her back, her hands behind her head, staring out of the window. She could see the stars from here, still subdued by a faint moonlight, but growing brighter. Two nights from now she would be out under them, and there would be no shelter. The warmth of the bed suddenly seemed luxurious, and she wriggled her toes in appreciation. It was possible now to envisage the end of their journey. She was relieved and excited, and perhaps a little sorry. It would seem strange to be without him now, although she was beginning to long for her accustomed solitude. A two-edged gift. She glanced across at him. He was curled up in a heap under the quilt with his back to her, and all she could see in the half dark was a blur of black hair between the white of sheet and pillow. Without quite intending to, she put out her hand and touched him. His hair was soft and straight, noticeably longer than when she had first seen him. She felt her whole body quicken, and snatched her hand away as though she'd burnt herself. Thomas stirred and half turned over. Naomi watched him wide-eyed, willing him not to wake up. She could feel her heart thumping, and she longed to touch him. He didn't open his eyes, but he put out his hand, as if expecting to find her there, or somebody else.

Naomi looked down at his open hand. You can't put a part of yourself to sleep. I have to accept this, she thought, the whole of it. She slowly stretched out her own hand and took his. He was warm, and at her touch his fingers closed on hers in a strong grip.

She turned on her side and fitted herself around their clasped hands until she was comfortable. She stayed like that for a long time, her eyes wide open against the dark. The diminishing moon rose higher, and the shadow of the window slowly shifted across the floor. Naomi shut her eyes, and eventually she too fell asleep.

Twenty-fifth Day

She seemed to have been asleep for no time at all when she was dragged awake again. 'Naomi?'

Oh no, not again. 'What is it now?' she muttered crossly.

'Morning,' said Thomas, with a hint of laughter in his voice. 'That's what it is.'

Naomi sat up with a jerk. 'Oh no!'

'What?' said Thomas, in surprise. He was already fully dressed, sitting on the edge of the bed watching her.

'We've got a lift! As long as we haven't missed it. She said be ready soon after dawn. I meant to wake up.'

'There's no need to panic about it,' said Thomas mildly. 'It's not very late, and if she's gone we can always walk. Do you want me to go and see?'

'Please. She's a pedlar, selling cloth and dye and stuff. She's got blue and orange hands. You can't miss her.'

When Thomas came back, he found Naomi stuffing her belongings into her pack. She looked up anxiously. 'Did you find her?'

'Having breakfast. She says we've plenty of time, so you can stop worrying.'

'I wasn't worrying,' said Naomi, rather peevishly. 'I just don't like missing things.'

It was a lift well worth catching, as it turned out. The pedlar had a high cart, the back part of which held all her wares, battened down under a heavy canvas cover. There was a high bench for the driver in front. The pedlar herself was a hefty woman who took up more than half of it. Naomi sat beside her, and Thomas perched on the back, his arm linked round the back of the driver's bench to keep himself from sliding off.

The weather was glorious. The road was still deep in mud, and in low places it had become impossibly wide, where a succession of travellers had tried to skirt the expanding puddles. The horse plodded on regardless, its hooves rising out of the wet places with soft sucking noises. Overhead the sky was deep blue, and the forest around them was loud with morning birdsong. A thin film of mist was rising and melting over the river, while the sun grew steadily hotter at their backs.

Naomi contemplated her dry boots with pleasure, and talked to the pedlar about the linen trade. Thomas said nothing at all, but whistled under his breath, and supplied them with toffee at infrequent intervals. He seemed uncannily cheerful today. Naomi didn't quite know what to make of it; perhaps it was a natural enough reaction, and it was only her suspicious nature that made her question its stability.

They had been travelling for about an hour when they rounded another bend in the river, and came into full view of a large settlement on the opposite bank. There was a humped bridge across to it, and an empty field between the water and the houses.

'I'd no idea we were so near,' exclaimed Naomi. 'We're back where the fair was, Thomas.'

'So I see,' he replied. 'Didn't you know?'

'I was asleep that day in the wagon. I hadn't connected it.'

'So you were at the spring wool fair?' asked her companion. 'So was I. I never saw you.'

'I wasn't at the trading part. Just playing music at night.'

'So you would have been. I must have just missed you. I heard something about it, though. There was a fire-eater, they said. Something like that.'

'At your service,' said Thomas from just behind her.

'Goodness me, was it you? Whatever persuaded you to take up a trade like that? There's no understanding some folk.'

'Too true,' said Naomi. 'Was it a good year for cloth?'

They followed the road north into the wide valley that led them back into the heart of the hills. Every yard of this road awoke memories of their walk south. Naomi mentally retraced their steps, while keeping up a casual flow of talk about dyes. This woman was clearly an expert, but after a certain point she had no intention of parting with any secrets. However, once she had ascertained that Naomi had no ulterior motive of setting up in the trade herself, but was merely intrigued by unusual colours, she became quite chatty, and said that when they stopped again that afternoon, she would show Naomi some of her choicer wares.

'I'd like to look at some of your linen,' said Naomi. 'I was thinking of making myself a new shirt.' She suddenly remembered something. 'Only I've nothing to trade, but I'd like to look anyway.'

'I have money,' said Thomas from the back, and went on whistling.

'Shirts aren't part of the contract,' said Naomi.

'I think the contract's changed,' replied Thomas, and returned to his tune.

The pedlar drew up in a small settlement about half way up the valley. She was evidently well known here. It was not long before a small crowd had gathered round the cart. A trestle table was brought out from somewhere, and they helped her to spread out her goods. There were not only rolls of cloth, both wool and linen, but skeins of wool, and even garments readymade, dyed by the pedlar in a variety of shades, some of them quite unlike any Naomi had seen before. She was fascinated, but there was no point in asking more. Colours were not like music: there was money in them. She contented herself with examining everything with great care, while a brisk trade flourished round her.

Presently Thomas touched her on the shoulder. 'Aren't you hungry? We could eat before we go on, and save our supplies.'

'I'll join you. I won't be long.'

'Very well,' said Thomas. 'Here.' He handed her a coin.

'I didn't agree to that,' she retorted indignantly. 'You said the contract had changed. I don't see how. I wasn't going to talk about it in front of anyone.'

Thomas took her hand, and closed her fist over the coin. 'Listen. I owe you something.'

'What?' she growled at him, looking quite ready for a fight.

'You paid the inn,' said Thomas. 'Didn't you?'

Naomi opened her mouth and shut it again. Someone jostled her, struggling to get close to the stall. When she looked round again Thomas had gone.

After a while she selected a roll of linen in a shade that was not exactly maroon, and bought two yards of it.

They walked the last few miles up the valley. Naomi had forgotten how long this road was, but at last the hills were drawing nearer, closing in on either side. The sun was low behind them, so that their shadows stretched ahead, pointing to the hills.

It was surprisingly restful to be like this again. Thomas said little, but there was a calm about him that she didn't think she had ever experienced in him before. It was like the first journey they had made, except that everything had changed, and they knew each other as they had not done then. Naomi looked up at the hills, which had turned faintly pink in the light of the setting sun, and felt the first touch of the night breeze against her face. There was a little huddle of grey buildings ahead of them, dwarfed by the slopes above, which she recognised as the place where they had stayed before.

She stopped for a moment, and Thomas stopped too. She was acutely aware of the moment. It was like touching the thread of her own life, and feeling the current that pulsed through it. Time slipped by, like the river at her back, but the present was a gift that would live undiminished in her memory. The journey would never be over. There was a pain of parting, not very far ahead of her now, but that would not obliterate herself, or Thomas.

'It's like standing on the edge of the world,' said Naomi, 'looking down into a country where we don't belong. It makes me feel humble.'

'It makes me feel safe.'

She turned her eyes from the valley where the red deer grazed, and looked at him. He was leaning back against a rock, still looking down on the slopes far below them, inside the valley where neither of them would ever tread. 'Why safe, Thomas?'

'Knowing that what we are, or what we do, isn't really so important. It's not my world. It relieves me of a responsibility, knowing that.'

'I should think it would! Delusions of grandeur, I should say.'

'What are they?'

'I don't exactly know. It comes out of an old story. But it sounds good.'

The hills today seemed like old friends. Naomi reckoned there had been far too many people in her life lately. Not that she wasn't used to people on the road, but it was very different to encounter a stranger for a day or an evening, and part as easily as one had met. The last three weeks had been more intense than anything she would wittingly have chosen. In retrospect she wouldn't have missed it, but she was glad to be up here again, with no more demanding company than Thomas.

That was an extraordinary thought. Naomi had been lying on her front, staring lazily down into the valley, but now she sat up and looked at him in amazement, as if she'd expected him suddenly to have changed shape. He hadn't. He was still leaning against his rock, delicately picking his teeth. 'What is it?' he enquired, without moving.

'I was thinking about you.'

'Really? What?'

'I thought how peaceful it is getting away from everyone and being alone again. And then I thought, that doesn't make sense. He is everyone.'

'Not quite,' murmured Thomas. 'But thank you.'

'I mean,' she said with some asperity, 'that I've had less peace with you than with anyone I ever met. And now more. It's what I said before, about the chameleon.'

'I remember. You said that there were dragons in the empty lands.'

'Dragons would have been nothing. Thomas?'

'Yes.'

'How does one swallow fire?'

'You don't,' he answered, 'unless you're a magician. Then you use magic.'

'I thought you wouldn't tell me. But it was worth asking.'

'You'd be very bad at it,' said Thomas firmly. 'Shall we go on?'

The road over the mountains had changed. The hills were the same, long rolling slopes stretching away into the east, with the forest lapping at their northern shores. The sky was different. It was hot and blue, and as the day wore on the sun beat down on them, so they tied first their jackets and then their jerseys on to their packs, then unbuttoned their shirts and rolled up the sleeves. The land lay blue and shimmering on the far horizon. Curlews called across the moor, and sporadic bursts of song accompanied them from larks invisible in the haze above. There were flowers strewn across their path where before there had been none, as though their arrival had been heralded and the way prepared in triumph. The grass was green under their feet and smelt of summer, studded with shepherd's purse and tormentil, sometimes scented with thyme and bog myrtle. Once a little band of deer crossed the ridge only a few yards ahead of them, then vanished down the northern slope with soft thudding hoofbeats. Winter was over. The hills were open again. Even the peat hags were rimmed with thick green mosses, and adorned with ragged robin and cotton grass.

It was no drier underfoot than it had been a month earlier. Presently Naomi took off her boots and hung them round her neck. Her feet were soft and tender after the winter, so that even the grass tickled her, and the peat water was icy on her unaccustomed skin. Soft brown mud oozed between her toes, leaving her feet stained with peat.

'That's no way to walk through mountains,' remarked Thomas severely. She laughed at him.

May was the best month in the year for travelling. Wherever one went, life was picking up again after the chill of winter and the hunger of spring. It was a time of festivals and plenty, when even the meanest settlement would welcome a musician and find something to celebrate. And if there were no settlement, the nights were no longer dangerous: sometimes they were balmy and luxurious, holding the heat of the day with hardly a breath of wind so one could lie out under the stars and listen to the sounds of a nocturnal world. Nothing seemed to matter then; there was a whole summer ahead, with no need for providence for many months to come.

Yet this journey was nearly over. Naomi was experiencing a disconcerting reversal of all her conceptions. For days the mountains had felt like a barrier ominously looming ahead: an arduous and dangerous adventure that lay between them and their destination. She had had her sights set upon the island for so long. Every time she had thought of Thomas's road that must still be tackled, her spirits had sunk a little, and the longed-for end had appeared to recede behind a host of difficulties.

As it turned out, the road was revealing itself in quite a different guise. It offered her all the forgotten delights of summer, and restored her to a harmony that had eluded her during the days of strain and suffering. Upon Thomas it appeared to have worked a greater miracle. He was still thinner, and his face seemed finer drawn than when she had first seen him, though it was hard to remember, but he was at peace for the first time since she had known him. His journey had marked him, but it had also released him. I don't think he's unhappy any more, thought Naomi, watching him as he carefully circumnavigated another bog. He just looks older. And why not? He is, and so am I.

They reached the pass between the hills where the ruins of the ancient road lay, and stopped to eat on the slope above it, on the opposite side from where they had once rested in a hollow. They weren't very hungry because they were too thirsty, and their water had to last until they reached their night's resting place. They lay down for a while in a sheltered hollow, letting the sun beat down on their backs.

'I'd forgotten what this felt like,' remarked Naomi. There was no answer. She drifted into a doze, and dreamed she was picking poppies in a ripe hayfield, only every time she broke one off, all the petals fell off, and floated away into a magenta sky.

'You'd better wake up. Your back's going bright red.'

That was not part of the dream. Reluctantly she admitted it, and sneezed. 'Oh, no,' muttered Naomi, and sat up.

'So has your face,' said Thomas. 'You've got more freckles, too.'

Naomi sneezed again, and glared at him through half shut eyes.

By the time they reached their resting place the sun had tired them out. They were too thirsty to talk much, so that the sound of the little stream running through the hollow among the ancient earthworks seemed to promise the fulfilment of all desire. They scrambled down the last slope, and dumped their packs on the grassy shelf where they had slept before. They both knelt down at the water's edge and drank without stopping, then splashed their faces with icy water from their cupped hands. After that they were able to tackle their bread and beans, which they ate with their feet dangling over the stream, so that they could paddle in the water as much as was bearable. The sky was turning to dark blue above them, and the evening star was already bright.

'It's going to be cold again,' remarked Thomas. 'Maybe frosty.'

'I'm hot.'

He leaned over and touched her cheek. 'You've caught the sun, that's why. You're burning.'

'It's not fair,' said Naomi, without resentment. 'Well, if it's going to be cold, I'd better get dressed.'

She put on a couple more jerseys, her second pair of trousers, and several socks, then buttoned her jacket over the top, and pulled the hood over her head. 'Right. I'm ready for whatever the night has to offer.'

'It would be warmer if we put the blankets together.'

They put one blanket under them, and tucked the other round them squeezing themselves in to make it fit.

'This won't work,' said Naomi. 'We're like two clothes pegs. I'll get cramp.'

'Well, how do you normally sleep then?' asked Thomas, a little put out, while he tried to batten down the other end of the blanket.

How do I normally sleep? She lay on her back, looking up at the Seven Sisters who were just making their appearance overhead, and thought about it. 'It depends on whether I'm alone, or with a friend,' she said to them cautiously.

'Thanks.'

Images of Thomas obtruded between her and the stars. Thomas naked in the sauna, Thomas on the summit of his own mountain, Thomas whistling in the back of a cart, Thomas sleeping, and the feel of straight silky hair under her fingers. A friend is one thing, thought Naomi, and a few private feelings are quite another. 'With a friend,' she said aloud, 'like this.' She turned and faced him, and put her arm round him.

He received her very willingly, and put his arm under hers, so her head was resting on his shoulder. Naomi curled up around him, to the relief of her aching back, so that they were twined together. Presently, even through eight layers of clothing, she began to feel the warmth of him. She wriggled a bit, making herself more comfortable, and Thomas shifted himself in response.

'It makes more sense,' he remarked presently, so close that it tickled her ear. 'People die of cold very easily in the mountains. These spring days are very treacherous.'

'You didn't tell me that, coming.'

'I didn't know you could cope with anything, then.'

'Goodnight,' she said sternly.

He laughed in her ear. 'Goodnight.'

Twenty-seventh Day

They woke to a morning that might have belonged to a different world. There was dampness all around them, that had crept under the blanket and inside their clothes. Mist hung a little way above them, blocking out even the low horizon of the valley. Naomi sat up and rubbed her eyes. It made nothing any clearer. The long grass that bordered the stream was weighed down with heavy beads of water, and the stream itself sounded subdued and mournful.

'Oh,' said Naomi, still dazed. 'Now what?'

'Now we find out how much I know. Are you all right now?'

'When wasn't I?'

'I thought you were having a nightmare again. You were talking in your sleep.'

'What did I say?'

'I couldn't hear exactly. Something about "the wrong boat", and then you half strangled me, which is what woke me up.'

'I'm sorry,' said Naomi stiffly, and stood up.

'Not at all. I was flattered. Do you want some breakfast?'

'Beans, you mean? Purely out of necessity, yes.'

It was too wet to delay. They ate standing by the stream, then they packed up their damp things, and set off into the mist. Before they had gone a hundred yards uphill the cloud enveloped them. There was nothing to be seen except a few yards of soaking grass, and fog swirling past them. Sometimes it lifted a little, so they could see up to a hundred yards ahead, then it descended again like a thick white blanket, clammy against their skin.

After the open warmth the hills had shown yesterday, it felt to Naomi like a trick which would have been merciless if she had been alone. The way had seemed so easy that she had wondered at her own apprehension. Now it appeared impossible. The slopes were all the same; there was no sign of the sun. She realised that she was completely helpless, and that made her a little frightened, but more angry. She hadn't been caught out, because she had Thomas, but she had let herself be deceived. She didn't like meekly following in Thomas's footsteps, all unknowing. It wasn't that she didn't trust him, it was that she didn't want to rely on him.

Thomas said nothing at all. He walked a little in front of her, peering into the fog as if the power of sight could disperse it. Sometimes he stopped and thought for a moment, his gaze fixed upon what little slope could be seen, and then he set off steadily again. Twice he began to lead them downhill and then stopped, and carefully retraced his steps. Naomi didn't interrupt, but watched him while he considered, then followed him without a word when he started again.

'Ah,' said Thomas presently, and the relief in his voice betrayed his own doubts.

Naomi looked ahead, and saw a cairn looming out of the mist ahead of them, seeming only a little more substantial than the cloud scudding past it. They walked up to it and stood on the summit. Naomi waited while Thomas cast about for a direction, rather like a dog sniffing after an elusive scent. Then he set off again, and she followed. As soon as they stopped, even for a moment, she realised how cold it had become. Her hands were red and numb, and she clenched her fists inside her sleeves to warm them.

Thomas seemed sure of himself now they were back on the ridge. The only thing that seemed different to Naomi was the wind. Its direction varied: sometimes it came from the right or the left, until the exposed side of her face was red and tingling; more often it drove straight at them from in front, so whenever she looked up her eyes filled with water. She wasn't cold any more. They were moving fast, and she was sweating inside her tightly buttoned jacket. It was not comforting up here, but it was exhilarating.

When at last they reached the summit with the jagged rocks, Thomas stopped on the sheltered side to wait for her. He was sure of the way now, and was ready to turn his attention elsewhere.

'Which boat?' he asked her.

'Boat?' For a moment she almost panicked, thinking that his mind had begun to wander. For her this place was like the sea; she hadn't expected him to see it like that.

'You had another dream. I told you but there wasn't time to stop this morning. You were talking about a boat again.'

'Was I? It's possible. It doesn't matter now.'

He stopped and faced her, so that she couldn't keep walking. 'No,' said Thomas. 'You said once that private things should be respected, even between those who shared them. But the other night — you talked about your dreams to me. You can't go back on it now.'

'I can't share all my dreams with you! I told you what I dream about. It helped, I know. But the boat's not important.' She looked at him, puzzled. 'I don't know what you expect me to say.'

'I don't share your dreams. No one can. But you can still tell them. What are you afraid of losing?'

Naomi looked down at her feet uncertainly, tracing a pattern through the wet grass with her toe. 'Just any boat,' she said at last. 'The kind my people use for the sea-fishing. It's not even that I left by boat, because I didn't. I walked. Just took my fiddle and a few things, and walked away one day. It wasn't at all a dramatic way to leave, and no one saw me off. I wouldn't let them. But in the dream it has always been a boat.'

She paused, but he said nothing.

'To walk away,' said Naomi. 'It was so easy, and so difficult. It was the hardest thing I ever did. But walking — there's no means by which you can measure it. No point at which you can say the thing is done. Or not done. There was always the possibility of turning back, but I didn't. There must have been a point at which the balance shifted, when it was no longer possible to return. It's not recorded in my mind. Do you follow me?'

'More than that. I know.'

'Since then, I've made many voyages. There is a moment when the boat pulls away from the quay, or the beach, when the thing is done. There is a stretch of water that widens slowly, between the boat and the shore. Whether I take the boat, or whether I miss it, there is still the same stretch of water, whichever side of it I'm on. Even when the gap is very small, it opens up the possibility of regret. Do you understand that?'

'I think so.'

'I never grieved,' she told him. 'I never even spoke of it again. But in the dream, I didn't walk away. It turned into a boat. I may be on the boat, or I may be left behind, but the thing is done. The way I made my life, Thomas, I had to lose something. There was a moment when I made it that way, but I don't know when it was. Do you still understand me?'

'It must have been much harder to walk.'

'I think it was.' Inexplicably she was near to tears again. Naomi wiped her nose on the back of her hand. 'I think it was. When you walk, you think. You know what I mean?'

'I know. What did you think?'

'Only memories. Trying to learn it by heart. It works in a way, but not altogether. You don't lose it, it just grows fainter.'

'What does?'

'When I left him,' said Naomi clearly, 'I gave him to my sister. She carried him down to the beach to look at the boats. That was what he liked best. To distract him, you see. It worked. He didn't look back. When they'd gone, I picked up my fiddle and left. I didn't say goodbye to him.' She looked Thomas in the face. 'I think now that was wrong. I owed him that. However small he was, he would have understood it in some way. But I didn't even give him that.'

Apparently he did understand, for he made no attempt to comfort her, but took her by the shoulders and held her. 'I'm sorry,' said Thomas.

*

When they went on again, it was near dusk. They were out on a spur of the ridge, and the forest had infiltrated the narrow valleys on either side of them. Steep slopes fell down to it on their right, and under the rising mist they could see winding space between the trees that must be the stream, growing gradually more distinct as it moved north.

In spite of the twilight it had grown much clearer. Naomi felt as if her vision had been blurred until the point when they moved on again. She followed Thomas with lighter steps, although the day had been long. Curiously enough, she didn't feel embarrassed in his presence, although he had witnessed more of her private feelings than anyone had done before. It didn't seem particularly important. She saw that he was waiting again, and caught him up.

'It's getting late,' said Thomas. 'Maybe we should drop down to the treeline at the next beck. We could camp down there. Make a fire if we wanted.'

Naomi looked down at the valley, half shrouded in twilight. 'We can do. I don't particularly want to end up where the dogs were again, in any case. It can't be so very far ahead.'

'They probably range all over here.'

'In that case, it's all the same to me.'

*

By the time it was fully dark they had made themselves surprisingly comfortable. It wasn't easy to get the fire to light, because it had been wet here too, but once it was hot there was plenty of old wood to keep it going. They hung their blankets behind them like a screen, to keep out the draught and to get the damp out of them. The smell of wet wool hung in the air, and Naomi sneezed desultorily. They dined on hot beans and toast, which made a welcome change, then Thomas cleaned out the pan in the beck and set about making tea. Naomi watched him, and chuckled.

'What's so funny?'

'The way you make tea. As if it were a spell, or a ceremony.'

'Well, so it is.'

The air was quite dry now. There was a gentle dripping from the surrounding trees, but the sky seemed to be clearing. There were even one or two stars. Naomi got up and fetched her fiddle.

Thomas settled himself comfortably by the fire, using his pack as a backrest, and closed his eyes. She played to him for a long time, nothing new or complicated, just tunes from her own country which she had known all her life. She stopped when Thomas produced tea and toffee, but when she'd drunk her tea he shut his eyes again, and said, 'Go on!', so she complied. When she stopped again the fire had burned down to a glowing heap, and the wind had blown all the stars clear above their heads.

Thomas sat up and piled more wood on the fire. He didn't say anything for a while, but when she had packed away her fiddle and sat down opposite him again, he spoke. 'Naomi.'

'Yes.'

He took a stick, and poked the fire into fresh flames. 'I don't know what you'll think of this,' he said a little hesitantly. 'But in my country we have a ceremony, a ritual. A way of making a contract, between friends. Do you follow me?'

'I've been following you all day,' she said flippantly, because she felt suddenly shy. Then she looked straight at him and said quite seriously, 'Yes, I do. In my country we have something similar, I think.'

They talked about it for a little while. Then Thomas knelt by the fire, and brushed a clear space on the turf. He unsheathed his knife and cut a circle out of the turf. He raised it carefully, so as not to break it, then laid it upside down beside the round hole that he had made. Naomi knelt opposite him on the other side, unsheathed her own knife, and gave it to Thomas. He hesitated for a moment, then drew her knife across his wrist, making a shallow cut. He gave her back her knife. Naomi bared her own wrist. It was much whiter than Thomas's, blue-veined and vulnerable. She caught her breath, then drew the knife across, so that her own blood flowed. She held out her hand to him. He laid his cut wrist against hers, so that their blood ran together and dripped down into the exposed earth. His blood seemed to sting her a little, so that her eyes watered, and she blinked. In the firelight their blood seemed to be the same colour as the earth, so that when it touched the soil it was at once absorbed, invisible.

When they parted hands, Naomi took the turf and pressed it carefully back into the hole. Then she took his hands again, and they swore a bond to one another, according to the ritual, of friendship that might not be broken. When they let go of one another at last, both their hands were wet with mingled blood.

Twenty-eighth Day

Just as dusk was falling on the following day, Thomas and Naomi came over the crest of a hill on the road through the forest, and saw the island.

It lay like a jewel on a deserted beach, golden in the last rays of the sun. To the north low sand dunes merged with a haze between sea and sky; to the south a vast stretch of sand was surmounted by dim shapes of buildings, with one rock rising like a fortress behind them. It seemed less than several miles away, but it was vanishing fast into the twilight, even as they watched.

Naomi pulled a damp handkerchief from her pocket, and blew her nose hard. Thomas glanced at her. She'd been doing that all day. They were out of the pollen-laden air of the inland forest now, and there was a fresh breeze coming in off the sea, but presumably it would take a little while to have any effect. Anyway, whatever was going on with her, he was fairly sure she didn't require sympathy. He looked back to the island.

'Tide's right out,' he remarked. 'I'm trying to remember. When would it turn? How long have we been away?'

'A month.'

'You're quite sure?' Thomas frowned and began to check on his fingers.

'Positive. It'll be low tide just after dark. We can cross just after sunrise. It'll be lighter earlier now.'

'Oh. Well, it beats me how you can know exactly, just by looking.'

'Don't be silly. I've been working it out all month.'

'You never said so.'

'No. Shall we go on? We'll be benighted if we wait any longer. There's no moon.'

By the time they reached the mill it was pitch dark. Luckily the last part of the road was fairly open. They negotiated it hand in hand, finding their way as best they could by the feel of the ground under their feet. The lights of the mill came into sight suddenly round a bend in the track, bright and welcoming.

*

No one at the mill seemed very surprised by their return; the same people were always departing and returning to the island. They were given fresh fish for supper, which they ate in appreciative silence, as though they had forgotten what it was like to taste anything. Afterwards they arranged their bed on the mattress, which they laid in front of the fire so that they could both keep warm.

They curled up back to back, Naomi lay with her eyes open, watching the shadow of the flames flicker on the wall. His back was warm against hers. She savoured the feel of it: things would never be quite like this again. She was confused by too many feelings. The island was there at last, not a dream, but real, and tomorrow she would be back. It was safe to acknowledge her longing for it. She had brought back something much greater than she had reckoned. Her gift from Linnet had survived the journey safe and dry, and tomorrow she would be home, with a whole voyage of discovery in front of her.

But she would miss him. He'd still be there, certainly, and she was glad about that. No complications troubled her now. Merely, it would be different, because the journey would be over. She was happy about that, but at the same time she could feel tears inside her, not so very far down. One surfaced, and trickled silently down her cheek, and dripped off her nose.

He couldn't possibly have known, but at the same moment Thomas reached out with his hand and felt for hers. She promptly gave it to him.

'It was a good journey,' said Thomas.

'It was indeed.'

'Thank you.'

'Thank you, Thomas,' she responded politely, and closed her eyes, his hand still held in hers.

Twenty-ninth Day

'I told you we'd be early,' said Thomas.

Naomi hitched her pack higher up her back, and followed his gaze out over the sea. The island was a dark outline against a flame-coloured sky. The sun had not quite risen, but its approach was heralded by a burst of colours like a fanfare. Between Thomas and Naomi and the island the sea was calm, flat as a pond, black in the shadow of the island, and ablaze with unaccustomed colour where the light caught it. It looked deep and alien, and there were no boats on this shore. It was quite impassable.

'Better early than late,' said Naomi. 'We can wait at the end of the causeway.'

Thomas followed her obediently along a sandy path that wound along the shore between the salt flats and the fringes of the forest. The grass was no longer yellowed, but newly green, and between them and the sea the land was carpeted in thrift. Pink tussocks were soft under their feet, and the dunes were bright with patches of pink as far as they could see. The scent of thrift reached them, mingled with the tang of salt, like a touch of honey. They came to the place where a track extended out over the salt marsh, and vanished into that silent sea.

'We'll wait here,' said Naomi.

Thomas lowered his pack. 'We could have had another hour's sleep,' he said a little irritably. 'You said yourself it would be after sunrise, then you insist we get up in the middle of the night. Oh well.'

'I'm not taking any chances this time,' said Naomi, dumping her own pack, and sitting down with her back against it.

'Well, I'm going to get my sleep.'

He was as good as his word. His head fell back against his pack, and his mouth dropped open. Presently he began to snore softly.

Naomi sat with her eyes fixed upon the water. The sea wasn't often like this. There was no hint of a wave, only little ripples that spread across the surface, breaking the light into a million pieces, then lapping at the shore at her feet. Gradually, as she watched, the water retreated a little, each ripple coming lower up the sand than the last, leaving a delicate pattern behind it, like the ghost of the vanished sea.

The smell of the sea was sharp in her nostrils, reminding her of so many things that she couldn't begin to give form to them. There was no need of any form. It was like a thread leading her along the entire path she had followed, taking her back to the very beginning, but without pain, as subtly as the path of light that dappled the water in front of her, in a direct line from where she sat to the heart of the rising sun.

There was a bank of soft cloud behind the island, tinged with red, so she couldn't see the horizon. The sun was rising out of it: she could see the place where the red intensified to crimson, banded with a ring of gold. The sky above it was lightening from dark blue to a pale brightness, against which she had to squint to see. There was a sliver of light above the cloud, a red streak that shot across the whole horizon, then the curve of the sun itself, brighter than she had expected, freeing itself from the clinging cloud that gave it birth.

It rose remarkably quickly. The cloud seemed to dissolve, and the sun hung free, still tinged with redness, illuminating the sea, touching the island so that it leaped into sudden daylight, no longer a silhouette, but substantial as the earth on which she sat.

Naomi looked down at the shore at her feet. It had stretched much further. An expanse of rippled sand shone in the sunlight, and out of the sand, directly ahead of her, the road was rising, appearing out of the sea itself. It was wet, shining with a string of puddles, strewn with seaweed, but solid, extending into the water as though the earth were reaching out a long finger to the island, reclaiming it as her own. Naomi stood up.

The sea slipped slowly back. In the middle of the causeway the road was built up with breakwaters on each side, like a long bridge.

There were posts marking the way, gradually resurfacing as the sea swirled away from them, making long eddying patterns around each one. There was only a little stretch uncovered now.

The sun rose higher. She could see the houses on the island quite plainly, slate roofs reflecting back the light. The sea was pouring off the road, pulled away on either side by an irresistible force. There was only a thin channel of fast-flowing water left over it. By the time they reached it, that too would have disappeared.

Naomi held out her hands to the sun for a moment, in a gesture that might have been gratitude, or recognition. Then she turned to the sleeping man at her feet, and shook him gently by the shoulder.

'Thomas! Thomas, my dear friend, wake up. The tide's out. We can cross over now.'

Lightning Source UK Ltd.
Milton Keynes UK
UKHW01f0647221018
330961UK00001B/373/P